75 Classical Myths

Condensed from Their Primary Sources

by David Mulroy

University of Wisconsin, Milwaukee

cognella
San Diego, CA

Bassim Hamadeh, Publisher
Michael Simpson, Vice President of Acquisitions
Christopher Foster, Vice President of Marketing
Jessica Knott, Managing Editor
Stephen Milano, Creative Director
Kevin Fahey, Cognella Marketing Program Manager
Al Grisanti, Acquisitions Editor
Jamie Giganti, Project Editor

First published in the United States of America in 2012 by University Readers, Inc.

Trademark Notice: Product or corporate names may be trademarks or registered trademarks, and are used only for identification and explanation without intent to infringe.

15 14 13 12 11   1 2 3 4 5

Printed in the United States of America

ISBN: 978-1-60927-034-6

www.cognella.com 800.200.3908

Contents

Appendix 1: Some Myths of Other Nations   143

Appendix 2: Three of Plato's Philosophical Myths   157

Appendix 3: Pronouncing Glossary   163

Acknowledgments

The interest and encouragement of my friend and colleague, Bruce Precourt, a great teacher of both classical and Egyptian myth, persuaded me to enlarge and publish this work, which was originally just a set of xeroxed handouts for my own mythology students. Bruce pointed out some important omissions in my original list of myths and contributed several synopses of his own, e.g., *Philoctetes, Helen, Iphigenia among the Taurians, Isis and Osiris*, and a mercifully succinct *Enuma Elish*.

The condensed myths found in the body of this work are based on the original Greek or Latin—with the occasional help of the Loeb Library translations. Portions quoted directly from the Greek and Latin sources, e.g., the choral song at the beginning of Aeschylus's *Agamemnon*, are my own original translations. The sources of the nonclassical myths in Appendix 1 are cited in head notes. The pronunciations given for names and places represent my best judgment, based on consulting the Tenth Edition of *Merriam Webster's Collegiate Dictionary*; the glossary in Morford and Lenardon, *Classical Mythology*, Oxford 2003; the glossary in Powell, *Classical Myth*, Prentice Hall 2007; and my own experience. Geographical information in the glossary of places, e.g., mountain heights and the square mileage of various islands, comes from Wikipedia.

Needless to say, readers whose interests are stirred by these condensed stories should go on to read them in their entirety. Numerous, fine English translations of the works involved are readily available for that purpose.

Given the time to read them, the original works are far more rewarding than any condensed versions. On the other hand, there are many good reasons that a person might want a shorter version of the stories told in one, several—or all—of the works that constitute the world of classical myth. In fact, a plurality of the questions directed to me as a classicist over the years boil down to asking for a quick summary of one or another of these great tales. With the publication of *75 Classical Myths*, I feel as though I will be able to go on answering such questions indefinitely.

By way of dedication: It is my special hope that my granddaughters, Cassandra and Isabel, will have occasion to dip into this book at some time in the future when they're a little older.

Introduction

The Historical Context of the Classical Myths

The earliest human cultures are classified by archeologists as representing either the Paleolithic Era (Old Stone Age) or the more advanced Mesolithic Era (Middle Stone Age). In the former, people survived by hunting and gathering; in the latter, they made the gradual transition to producing food. The Mesolithic Era lasted in the Near East until somewhere between 8000 and 6000 B.C. It was followed by the Neolithic Era (New Stone Age), when people settled in permanent communities, practicing agriculture, domesticating animals, and using finely carved stone implements.

The next stage of civilization was the Bronze Age, which began around 3500 B.C. in the Near East. The Bronze Age is marked by the development of cities with monumental walls and buildings, armies, wealthy kings, and the use of tools and weapons made of metal. The earliest Bronze Age civilizations to affect the Mediterranean area were those in Egypt and the Near East, in the valleys of the Tigris and Euphrates rivers. Under the influence of these two areas, the eastern Mediterranean basin became the site of many powerful Bronze Age kingdoms by 2000 B.C., including one on the island of Crete. At this point, however, there was no trace of the ancestors of the Greeks.

Archeological remains show that the Greeks established a Bronze Age culture on the mainland of Greece at some time between 2000 and 1600 B.C. Fortified citadels with wealthy royal tombs, dated to about 1600, have been found in several sites. The most famous are those at Pylos on the southwestern coast of the Peloponnesus (southern Greece) and Mycenae in its northeastern corner. The period of Greek history that began with these palaces is known as the Mycenaean era, which lasted from 1600 to about 1200 B.C. It represented the first blossoming of Greek civilization. Mycenaean tombs have yielded precious gold and silver objects and other fine works of art. Archaeology also shows that the Mycenaeans engaged in foreign trade and had a form of writing, the "Linear B" script. At the height of their power, around 1400 B.C., the Mycenaeans apparently conquered the island of Crete.

Myths are stories that take shape in an oral tradition and are passed along by word of mouth for a significant period of time before being written down. Their special appeal depends on the fact that their origins are undocumented. The relevance of the

Mycenaean period to the study of the classical myths is that it is the period in which the Greek myths originated. They are stories that were transmitted in the Greeks' oral tradition from the Bronze Age until they were finally written down, a process that did not begin until the eighth century B.C.

Around 1200 B.C., Mycenaean civilization suddenly collapsed. The citadels were destroyed and abandoned. The underlying causes of this collapse are not known. There is evidence of widespread warfare. The city of Troy lay on the outskirts of the Greek world, at the entrance to the Black Sea. Archaeology shows that it too was destroyed at this time. Hence, it seems that the famous Trojan War of legend was really part of a general pattern of violent upheavals that overtook the Greek world about 1200 B.C.

Between 1200 and 800 B.C., Greek civilization experienced a Dark Age. There is little evidence from this period of foreign trade, urban life, or works of art, and no evidence of writing. A person observing Mediterranean cultures in the ninth century B.C. would have predicted that Greek civilization was dying. To judge by later developments, the only bright spot was a rich oral tradition. The Greeks evidently kept memories of their ancestors alive by telling each other stories of the great days of Mycenae, when they were the kings of the earth—not subsistence farmers.

Starting around 800 B.C., Greek civilization made an amazing recovery. At the heart of the recovery was the *polis*, the Greek city-state (plural *poleis*). Flourishing poleis cropped up everywhere, not just in Greece but on the islands of the Aegean and the coasts of Turkey, the Black Sea, northern Africa, Sicily, southern Italy, and even southern France. Although historians give many different explanations for this rebirth of Greek civilization, this writer thinks the basic cause must have been the invention of the Greek alphabet, which also occurred around 800 B.C.

People in several areas of the globe knew how to write before the Greeks. The Greek alphabet, however, was a system of revolutionary simplicity in writing. Whereas Egyptian hieroglyphics and the cuneiform scripts of the Near East used hundreds of different signs, the alphabet provided the Greeks with a system of 24 signs that accurately represented their speech. It was so simple that children could, and did, master it easily. In fact, the Greek alphabet has never been radically improved upon. Our own alphabet is a version of it with minor variations.

This period of rebirth is called the Archaic Age. Trade, art, and philosophy flourished in the independent Greek city-states. They were also sites of constant political ferment. Some were governed by warlords, some by kings or aristocratic clans, others by constitutional systems of government. Toward the end of the period, a revised constitution was adopted in Athens. It is now thought of as representing the world's first constitutional democracy. Besides allocating the greatest power to the assembly of all citizens, its most revolutionary feature was that citizens were rearranged into voting groups—defined not by family ties, but place of residence. This apparently reduced the influence of the patriarchal tribal groups into which the Athenians and other Greeks were traditionally divided.

The relevance of the Archaic Period to the study of mythology is that at this time, poetic accounts of the Greek myths were first committed to writing. Homer's epics, the *Iliad* and the *Odyssey*, the poetry of Hesiod, and the anonymous *Homeric Hymns* represent archaic Greek literature.

Near the end of the Archaic Period, the Persians emerged as a dominant power in the Near East. Under the leadership of Cyrus, they overthrew their former masters, the Medes, and subjugated all the kingdoms between the Persian Gulf and the Greek world. By 500 B.C., the entire Near East, including Egypt, was part of the Persian empire.

Among the Persians' many subjects were Greek city-states on the coast of Turkey. These city-states attempted to revolt against Persian domination in 499 B.C.—and were quickly reconquered. Before they fell, however, they received some assistance from the mainland city of Athens. In 490, the Persians, under the emperor Darius, launched a punitive invasion of Athens. Though outnumbered, the Athenians defeated the Persians at the battle of Marathon. In 480, Darius's successor, Xerxes, launched a massive invasion by land and sea, hoping to subjugate all of Greece. This offensive also came to grief in a series of battles, of which the most famous was the naval battle of Salamis off the coast of Athens.

This victory over Persia marks the beginning of the Greek Classical Period. The Greeks were now a dominant military force in the Mediterranean, as well as a cultural one. Athens emerged as the leading city-state of the Greek world. At first, she was the leader of the Greeks, both militarily and culturally. After a long war with Sparta, she lost her military dominance but retained her cultural leadership. Greek philosophy and historical writing flourished. The relevance of the period to mythology is that the tragic dramatists—Aeschylus, Sophocles, and Euripides—were all Athenians who wrote during the Classical Period. With the exception of one play by Aeschylus on the Persian Wars, all the surviving tragedies dramatize ancient myths.

Late in the Classical Period, a powerful dynasty emerged in Macedonia, the northern frontier of the Greek world. In the past, it had been a culturally backward region, crippled by internal dissension and border wars with barbarians. King Philip II changed all that through military and diplomatic skill. He secured his kingdom by molding his army into a superior force. He then put an end to the constant struggles for dominance among the Greek city-states in the south by entering their wars and defeating their most powerful armies himself. His victory over Thebes and Athens at the Battle of Chaeronea in 338 B.C. marked the end of ancient Greek independence.

Philip's son and successor, Alexander the Great, invaded and conquered the Persian Empire. Alexander died in 323 B.C. in Babylon at age 32, at the conclusion of his campaign. As a result of his efforts, Egypt and the Near East were absorbed into the Greek world. Alexander's conquests and death mark the beginning of what is called the Hellenistic Age because of the expansion of Greek or "Hellenic" culture over a vast area.

Alexander's heirs divided his conquests into four kingdoms. Of these, the wealthiest and longest-lasting was that of the Macedonian general, Ptolemy, in Egypt. His capital was the newly constructed city of Alexandria. His successors ruled there until the last of them, Cleopatra, was defeated by the Romans in the Battle of Actium, in 31 B.C.

The Hellenistic Age was characterized by professional scholarship. Hellenistic kings built libraries and employed learned individuals to preserve, study, and build upon the artistic and intellectual achievements of the archaic and classical Greeks. One product of the age is a book known as *The Library*. It was originally attributed to Apollodorus, an Athenian polymath of the 2nd century B.C., but a reference in it to an author who flourished later, in the first century, has cast serious doubt on that attribution. *The Library* is now said to be the work of "pseudo-Apollodorus." It is the earliest surviving prose summary of myths, a forerunner of *75 Classical Myths*.

Less typical is the *Argonautica*, by Apollonius of Rhodes, a scholar who lived in Alexandria around 200 B.C. An ironic epic poem on the subject of Jason and the golden fleece, the *Argonautica* is an ambitious attempt to outdo Homer,in a period when short personal poems were more fashionable than epics.

During the Hellenistic Age, Rome gradually grew powerful. Its victory over Carthage in the Second Punic War (218–201 B.C.) made it one of the dominant powers in the Mediterranean. Greece became a Roman province in 146. The Romans absorbed most of what remained of Alexander's kingdoms in the ensuing decades. As mentioned above, the last kingdom to fall was Cleopatra's Egypt in 31 B.C., as a result of the Battle of Actium. The winner at Actium was Julius Caesar's heir and nephew, Octavian, later known as Augustus. At Actium, Augustus not only conquered the forces of Cleopatra but also those of his only Roman rival, Antony. Rome had previously been a constitutional republic, governed by a senate and consuls elected annually. Romans of the republic were proud of their independence and freedom of speech. By his victory, Augustus gained absolute power over the Roman state, thus becoming the first Roman emperor. Rome was more prosperous than ever—but for the ruling class, at least, personal freedom became a thing of the past.

Though the Romans conquered Greece militarily, they did not impose their culture on the Greeks. To the contrary, the Romans became as thoroughly Hellenized as any of the nations conquered by Alexander. Roman poets flourished during the reign of Augustus. Two of the most famous works from this period are versions of Greek myths told in Latin and provided with links to Roman history. They are Vergil's *Aeneid*, an epic poem identifying the Trojan hero Aeneas (a character in Homer's *Iliad*) as the founder the Roman race and Ovid's *Metamorphoses*, a lighthearted, poetic handbook of myths, unified by the motif of magical transformations. The historian Livy is another Roman author from the Augustan period who played a critical role in shaping classical myths. He is responsible for transmitting the most famous legends of early Rome—e.g., the birth of Romulus and Remus, and the rape of the Sabine women.

The Romans worshipped their own gods. When they assimilated Greek culture, they identified their gods with those of the Greeks. The major Greek gods with their Roman equivalents are:

Greek	Roman
Cronus	*Saturn*
Zeus	*Jupiter or Jove*
Hera	*Juno*
Hestia	*Vesta*
Hades or Pluto	*Orcus or Dis*
Persephone	*Proserpina*
Poseidon	*Neptune*
Demeter	*Ceres*
Hephaestus	*Vulcan*
Ares	*Mars*
Dionysus or Bacchus	*Liber*
Athena	*Minerva*
Apollo	*(no Roman equivalent)*
Artemis	*Diana*
Aphrodite	*Venus*
Hermes	*Mercury*

The Romans knew the great hero, Heracles, as "Hercules"; the wily warrior, Odysseus, as "Ulysses"; and Achilles' son, Neoptolemus, as "Pyrrhus."

With the works of the Augustan authors, classical mythology achieved its definitive shape. Later writers attempted to embellish the tradition, but their contributions are generally viewed as being less authentic than those of their predecessors since they have such long roots in written traditions.

The first Christian emperor, Constantine, transferred the capital of the Roman Empire to Byzantium in 323 A.D., renaming the city Constantinople. The western portion of the Roman Empire was overthrown by Germanic tribes in 476 A.D. Constantinople, however, was ruled by successors of the emperors Augustus and Constantine, and the city preserved Greek literature and intellectual traditions until its conquest by the Ottoman Turks in 1453, when it became known as Istanbul.

Chronological Table: Some Watershed Dates in the Early History of Western Civilization

B.C.

3100	The unification of Egypt under the first pharaoh
1600s	Greeks in Greece
1400s	Height of Mycenaean power, Greek control of Crete
1100s	Trojan War and the approximate era of Moses
753	Romulus founds Rome
700s	Homer and Hesiod perform
510	Establishment of Athenian democracy and the Roman republic
480	Battle of Salamis
399	Trial of Socrates
323	Death of Alexander the Great
201	End of the Second Punic War
146	Greece becomes a Roman province
31	Battle of Actium
8/4	Birth of Christ

A.D.

14	Death of Augustus
323	Division of the Roman Empire
476	Fall of the Roman Empire in the west
632	Death of Mohammed
800	Coronation of Charlemagne
1334	The plague decimates Europe
1453	Fall of Constantinople
1492	Columbus's First Voyage

The Stories

The following are the most important classical myths and legends, condensed from their primary sources. Apart from occasional, brief head notes and footnotes, nothing has been added. The stories are allowed to speak for themselves. They are arranged in the order in which the mythical events supposedly occurred, rather than the order in which stories were written. For example, the stories of Homer come near the end, even though they were written first, because they concern the last two generations of heroes.

1. The Castration of Uranus

Source: Hesiod, *Theogony*, 116–210 (Archaic Greek)

Chaos existed first. Then came Gaea (earth), Tartarus (the underworld), and Eros (love, desire). Erebus (darkness) and Night came from Chaos. Aether (heavenly light) and Day came from Night when she had intercourse with Erebus.

Gaea produced Uranus (heaven) without intercourse to cover her entirely, also the mountains, and Pontus (sea). Sleeping with Uranus, she bore six sons and six daughters, later known as the "Titans." The youngest was wily Cronus, who hated his father.

Gaea then bore the three Cyclopes, who later manufactured thunder and lightning for Zeus. They were strong and skillful, and were called Cyclopes (round-eyes), because they each had one eye in the middle of the forehead. Three other mighty, abominable children were Cottos, Briareus, and Gyges, who had a hundred hands and 50 heads each.

These were the worst of the children of Gaea and Uranus. Uranus hated them, hid them away in the depths of Gaea, and took pleasure in the evil deed. Gaea, however, was distressed and devised a wicked plan. Hesiod (*Theogony 159–206*) tells the rest of the story thus:

… Heaving and groaning, ready to burst,
Gaea the great conceived of a villainous scheme.
Quickly producing the gray, unbreakable substance,
she fashioned a powerful sickle, then spoke to her children.
Her words were courageous—for all her awful grief.
"Children of mine and an arrogant fool of a father,
if you listen to me we can punish his dastardly crime.
Remember who started the trouble: he was the one."
This speech alarmed her children, and nothing was said
'til Cronus the devious, Cronus the great, recovered
his courage and spoke in reply to the mother he loved:
"Entrust the deed to me, and I will accomplish it,
Mother. I hate the very thought of my father,
and he was the one, I know, that started the trouble."
The words delighted Gaea's giant heart.
Finding a spot to hide and handing to him
the jagged tool, she told him what to do.
Mighty Uranus descended, attended by Night.
Longing for love, he covered his mate entirely.
Cronus extended his weaker hand from his ambush.
Seizing the target, he took in his right the long
and jagged sickle, and eagerly cropped his dear
father's genitals, tossing them over his back.
 All the bloody drops that fell were a welcome
rain to Gaea. The cycle of seasons rolled on.
She bore the mighty Erinyes, the awful giants,
and nymphs around the world, the ash-tree sprites.
When he cut the genitals off with his adamant tool,
he threw them from land to the ever-surging sea.
They drifted on waves of the sea for years and years,
immortal flesh enveloped in foam. Behold!
A maiden takes shape within! She nears Cythera,
but then she floats away to the isle of Cyprus,
emerging there as the goddess of beauty. The grass
turned green beneath her delicate feet. The gods
and mortals named her "Aphrodite," which means
conceived in foam, "the queen divine of Cythera,"
"the goddess born in Cyprus," and the "genial deity,"
because of her genital origins.

Uranus named his children Titans (stretchers or extenders), because by extending themselves in recklessness they had accomplished a great deed, which they would pay for later.

2. The Birth of Zeus

Source: Hesiod, *Theogony*, 453–500 (Archaic Greek)

Cronus, king of the Titans, sired six children by his sister, Rhea. There were three daughters, Hestia, Demeter, and Hera, and three sons, Hades, Poseidon, and Zeus. Cronus swallowed each child as it was born since he had learned from Gaea and Uranus that he was fated to be conquered by a son.

Rhea was sorely distressed. She asked her parents, Gaea and Uranus, to devise a plan to keep the birth of her next baby secret and avenge her father's honor. When she was about to give birth, they sent her to Crete. There Rhea hid the baby Zeus in a cave on a mountain. To Cronus, Rhea gave a great stone wrapped in swaddling clothes. He took it and shoved it into his belly without realizing that it was just a stone and that his newborn son was safe and sound. Later, deceived by Gaea, Cronus vomited up his other offspring. In fact, the stone that he had swallowed last came up first. Later, Zeus fixed the stone in the center of the earth at the sacred shrine of Pytho on Mount Parnassus.

3. Zeus's Victory over the Titans

Source: Hesiod, *Theogony*, 617–725 (Archaic Greek)

Uranus had imprisoned Briareus, Cottus, and Gyges in the underworld. They lingered there in misery until Zeus brought them back into the daylight at the advice of Gaea. For ten years, Zeus and his siblings, stationed on Mount Olympus, had been locked in a desperate struggle against the Titans on Mount Orthys. After reviving their spirits with nectar and ambrosia, Zeus asked the giants for help in his battle with the Titans. They enthusiastically agreed. Heaven, Earth, and Tartarus were shaken by the noise of the ensuing battle.

Zeus charged into the fray, hurling thunder and lightning. Earth, sea, and sky blazed. It sounded as though heaven had fallen upon the earth. Cottus, Briareus, and Gyges led the charge for the Olympians, throwing volleys of three hundred stones each. They buried the Titans and imprisoned them under the earth, as far beneath its surface as heaven is above it. A bronze anvil falling out of heaven would drop for nine days and finally strike the earth on the tenth.

4. The Children of Zeus.

Source: Hesiod, *Theogony*, 881–962 (Archaic Greek)

When the gods finished their labors, they made Zeus their king on the advice of Gaea, and he distributed their honors. He first made Metis (Counsel) his wife, by far the wisest of gods and mortals. When she was about to give birth to Athena, however, he tricked her and put her into his belly. He did so on the advice of Gaea and Uranus lest any other god gain kingly honor. For Metis was destined to have exceedingly wise children: first Athena, equal to her father in might and wisdom; and then a son, who would be king of gods and men. So Zeus deposited Metis in his belly to advise him on good and evil.

Next he married Themis (Good Order). She bore the Horae (Seasons), Eunomia (Lawfulness), Dike (Justice), Eirene (Peace), and the Moirae (Fates): Clotho, Lachesis, and Atropos, who give people good and evil.

Eurynome, Oceanus's lovely daughter, bore the Charites (Graces) to him.

Demeter joined him in bed and bore Persephone, whom Hades took away from her mother with Zeus's permission.

Zeus fell in love with Mnemosyne (Memory). She bore the nine Muses, whom music delights.

Making love to Zeus, Leto gave birth to Apollo and Artemis.

Finally, Zeus married Hera and she bore Hebe (Youthfulness), Ares, and Eileithyia.

Zeus himself gave birth from his head to bright-eyed Athena, a terrible goddess of war. Hera was angry. Without making love, she gave birth to Hephaestus, the most skillful of all the heavenly gods.

Amphitrite bore a son to Poseidon the earth-shaker: Triton. He dwells with his parents in a golden mansion at the bottom of the sea.

Aphrodite bore Fear and Dread to Ares and also bore Harmonia, whom Cadmus married.

Atlas's daughter, Maia, slept with Zeus and bore Hermes, herald of the gods.

Semele, Cadmus's daughter, a mortal woman, made love to Zeus and bore him Dionysus. A mortal woman, she gave birth to an immortal son, but now both of them are gods.

Alcmene made love to Zeus and bore Heracles.

Hephaestus married the youngest Grace, Aglaea.

Dionysus married Ariadne, Minos's daughter, and Zeus made her immortal.

After he completed his labors, Heracles married Hebe on snowy Olympus. He lives among the immortals, ageless for all time.

Perseis, the daughter of Oceanus, bore Circe and King Aeetes to Helius (the Sun). Aeetes married a daughter of Oceanus, Iduia. Overcome by Aphrodite, she made love to him and bore him the beautiful Medea.

5. The Theft of Fire

Source: Hesiod, *Theogony*, 535–616 (Archaic Greek)

At a place called Mecone, Zeus and mortal men were having a dispute about the division of oxen at sacrifices. Wanting to trick Zeus, Prometheus, the son of the Titan Iapetus, volunteered to divide the ox. He offered the edible meat hidden inside the ox's stomach and under its hide to Zeus. For men, he neatly arranged bones under a layer of glistening fat.

Seeing this, Zeus said, "Son of Iapetus, how unfairly you have divided the portions!"

Wily Prometheus replied with a smile, "Most glorious Zeus, take whichever portion you want."

Zeus knew that he was being tricked and was already contemplating the revenge that he would exact from men. He took the glistening fat in his hands and seethed with anger when he uncovered the bones beneath it. (Since then, people have burned white thigh bones of oxen on the gods' altars.)

To get his revenge, Zeus withheld fire from men, but Prometheus fooled him again. He stole fire in a hollow reed. And Zeus was angry all over again when he saw fire burning among men. This time, to get revenge, he had his lame son, Hephaestus, mold the image of an awesome maiden from earth. Athena dressed her in glistening clothes and placed a wonderful crown and floral garlands on her head. When Zeus was finished creating this fair evil, she rejoiced in the finery that Athena had given her, and Zeus brought her to where the other gods and men were assembled. They were dumbfounded when they saw this trick, for which men have no cure; for she was the beginning of women—female women—a great disaster for mortal males.

They are like the drones that honeybees support with constant labor. In fact, Zeus made the situation even worse. A man may decide not to get married and to avoid the difficulties brought about by women. If so, he arrives at old age with no one to care for him. He does not live in poverty, but his estate is divided up when he dies. As for a man who marries, if he has a good wife, good and evil are balanced throughout his life, but if he has worthless offspring, he lives in a state of constant, inner pain.

There is no way to outsmart or avoid the will of Zeus.

6. Pandora

Source: Hesiod, *Works and Days*, 42–105 (Archaic Greek)

It could have been easy to get by with a single day of work a year, but Zeus made things difficult for men because he was angry at Prometheus. When Zeus took fire away from men, Prometheus stole it from him in a reed and gave it back to men.

At that time, Zeus said to Prometheus, "Son of Iapetus, you are happy that you tricked me and stole fire, but you will regret it—as will men of the future. I will give them an evil to balance fire, one that they will love and embrace."

Zeus then ordered Hephaestus to moisten some earth, put a human voice and strength in it, and to give it the beautiful form of a virgin goddess. He had Athena teach it skills—namely weaving—and had golden Aphrodite pour charm, painful desire, and limb-loosening cares on its head. He ordered Hermes to give it the mind of a dog and a thievish character.

So he spoke, and they all obeyed. When their tasks were completed, Hermes named the woman Pandora ("all-gifts"), because all the Olympian gods gave her a gift. Zeus had Hermes deliver her to Prometheus's brother, Epimetheus.[1] It did not occur to Epimetheus that Prometheus told him never to accept a gift from Zeus. He remembered when it was too late.

Before this, men lived without any evils, toil, or disease. But the woman removed the great lid from her jar, and thus brought about evils for men. Only Hope remained in the jar, under its lip, while tens of thousands of evils set forth among men. Now the earth and sea are full of them. Diseases attack us by day and night in silence. There is no way to escape the designs of Zeus.

7. The Ages of Man

Source: Hesiod, *Theogony*, 106–212 (Archaic Greek)

At first, the Olympian gods created a golden race of men. They existed while Cronus ruled in heaven. They lived like gods with carefree hearts, free of labor and grief. Old age did not exist. They spent their time feasting and died as though falling asleep. The earth produced abundant fruit by itself.

After the earth hid them away, they became holy spirits, good ones who ward off evils, protect mortal men, and give wealth. Such is their royal privilege.

The Olympian gods created a far inferior race next, one of silver. A child would be raised by his good mother for a hundred years, spending his time playing, utterly childish. When they finally reached their prime, they lived for only a short while amidst troubles caused by their own stupidity. They were not able to refrain from acts of violence against each other, nor were they willing to honor the gods or offer sacrifice. This angered Zeus, and he hid them beneath the earth. They are called blessed ones under the ground. They are second in rank but are not without honor.

Zeus created a third race of mortal men made of bronze, a terrible race born from ash-tree spears. Violence and the deeds of Ares belonged to them. They ate no grain.

---

1   Epimetheus's name signifies "afterthought"; Prometheus's, "forethought."

Their weapons and houses were made of bronze since iron did not exist. They destroyed each other and went down into the house of Hades without names.

Zeus created a fourth race, which was more just and better, a godlike race of heroes known as demigods. Warfare destroyed them, some at seven-gated Thebes, where they fought over the herds of Oedipus; others beyond the sea at Troy because of Helen. Zeus transported them to the ends of the earth, where they live the lives of happy heroes with carefree spirits on the isles of the blessed on the shores of Oceanus. The earth delivers its sweet harvest to them three times a year.

I wish I were not in the fifth generation of men, for now is the race of iron. Neither by night nor by day do men of this generation ever rest from grief and toil. The gods will continue to give us worries, but some good things will be mixed in with the evils. Zeus will destroy this race when children are born with gray hair on their temples. Father will have nothing in common with child, nor children with father, guest with host, comrade with comrade. Your brother will not be a friend. Men with no regard for the gods will be quick to dishonor their parents. No one will love the honest, just, or good man. They will honor men of evil deeds and violence. Justice will consist of force. Shame will not exist. The evil man will attack his superior with crooked words and oaths. Malicious jealousy will be everywhere. Finally, Shame and Nemesis (Vengeance) will return to heaven abandoning mortals, and there will be no defense against evil.

And now here is a fable for rulers. This is what the hawk said to the nightingale. He was carrying her through the clouds in his talons. She was weeping piteously, but he addressed her harshly: "Why all this clamor? A mightier one holds you, singer though you are. I will eat you for dinner if I want to, or I will let you go. Only a fool struggles against superior forces. He will lose and suffer pain and disgrace."

8. Prometheus's Punishment

Source: Aeschylus, *Prometheus Bound* (Classical Greek tragedy)

Hephaestus and Might are chaining Prometheus to a cliff in the wilds of Scythia. He is being punished for giving fire to men against the will of Zeus, the new ruler of the gods. Hephaestus has the job of attaching the chains because he is the blacksmith of the gods and is especially associated with fire. He regrets that he has to do this. He feels sorry for Prometheus. Might is scandalized by Hephaestus's attitude. According to him, Prometheus deserves his punishment. Besides, it is foolish to defy Zeus. Goaded by Might, Hephaestus finishes his job.

Alone, Prometheus slips into song as he calls on the wind and air to witness the suffering that he endures for being man's benefactor. He is startled by the sound of wings flapping in the air.

A chorus of "Oceanids," daughters of the Titan Oceanus, enters. They have flown to Prometheus's side to offer their sympathy. They attribute Zeus's cruelty to his being a new ruler. Prometheus says that Zeus will need his help in the future to retain his power. His defiant attitude frightens the chorus.

Prometheus describes his quarrel with Zeus to the chorus. When the war between the Titans and the Olympians began, Prometheus was told by his mother, Themis (also known as Gaea), that his wisdom could secure victory for either side. When the Titans ignored him and chose to rely on force, he helped Zeus win his victory. Afterward, Zeus had no concern for men, and planned to annihilate them. Prometheus opposed the plan. To help men, he gave them blind hopes so that they would no longer foresee their doom and the gift of fire, from which they will learn many skills.

Oceanus himself appears. He volunteers to intercede with Zeus on Prometheus's behalf and asks him to stop being so defiant. Prometheus says that it would be a waste of time to ask Zeus to be merciful. He mentions other gods being punished by Zeus: Prometheus's brother, Atlas, "supporting the pillar of earth and sky on his shoulders," and the fire-breathing giant, Typhoeus, who is buried beneath Mount Aetna in Sicily and will some day vomit fire over that land.[2] Prometheus tells Oceanus that he had better leave before Zeus gets angry at *him*. Oceanus takes his advice.

After a choral song in which the whole world is said to feel sorry for Prometheus, he lists the benefits that he conferred on mankind: building houses of brick and wood, understanding the sequence of the seasons, the use of numbers and letters, the domestication of animals, medicine, prophecy, religious rituals, and mining. "All human arts are from Prometheus."

The chorus says that Prometheus should use his wisdom to end his own suffering. Prometheus replies that he is fated to be liberated after a very long time. He refuses to go into details.

Io enters. She is a young woman with cow's horns, who is being driven through the wilderness by a stinging gadfly. Recognizing her, Prometheus addresses her by name and says that her sufferings are caused by Zeus's lust and Hera's jealousy. Io begs him to tell her what he knows about her fate. He reluctantly agrees, but first the chorus insists that Io tell her story.

Io says that she is the daughter of Inachus, the god of a river in Argos. Still a virgin, she began to have dreams in which a voice told her that Zeus desired her and that she should go to a certain meadow to meet him. She revealed the dreams to her father, who consulted the Delphic oracle. At the oracle's insistence, she was forced out of her house into a meadow. There, she grew horns and was guarded for a while by a giant herdsman, who died suddenly. She was then attacked by a stinging gadfly. She has been wandering since.

Prometheus foretells Io's further wanderings through the exotic people in the equivalent of southern Russia. After a long time, she will finally cross the mouth of the Black Sea into Asia Minor. The place where she crosses will be named the Bosporus,

---

2   This may be an allusion to an eruption of Mount Aetna, which is dated by other sources to 479/478 B.C.

or Cow's Crossing. Prometheus says that the Bosporus marks the halfway point of Io's wanderings. Her groaning at this news prompts Prometheus to say that he is doomed to an even longer term of suffering that will not end until Zeus is overthrown. This will come about through his marriage to a woman whose son is destined to be greater than his father.[3] His fall is inevitable unless Prometheus is released in his sufferings by a distant descendant of Io's.

After some resistance, Prometheus agrees to tell Io about the rest of her sufferings and to say more about his own liberator. Io will travel through Asia Minor encountering various creatures, like the Gorgons, until she arrives at last in Egypt. There she will be restored to her old self and bear Zeus's son. Five generations later, his descendants will return to Greece. Later a great hero will be born in their line and become Prometheus's liberator, Heracles. Io cries out in pain and is driven off stage by her gadfly.

Hermes enters. He demands that Prometheus reveal what he knows about the marriage that poses a threat to Zeus. Otherwise, Zeus will split the earth with lightning and cast Prometheus into a deep, sunless abyss. Years later, he will be returned to the surface, where Zeus's eagle will attack him daily, tearing his flesh and plucking at his liver. This torment will never end until some god volunteers to die for Prometheus.

Prometheus refuses to tell what he knows and trades insults with Hermes. The final choral ode is integrated into the episode. Hermes tells the chorus to leave lest they be involved in the disaster that is about to befall Prometheus. They refuse to do so.

Prometheus sees a great storm approach. Just before he is swallowed by a chasm in the earth, he calls on the earth and sky to witness his unjust suffering.

9. Another Version of Io's Story

Source: Ovid, *Metamorphoses*, 1,583–747 (Roman)

Io was the daughter of the river god, Inachus. One day Jove saw her returning from a visit to her father's stream and attempted to strike up a friendly conversation. When she fled, he covered the woods with dark clouds, chased her down, and raped her. Juno happened to notice the strange clouds and flew down to earth to investigate. Sensing Juno's approach, Jove changed Io into a white heifer. He told Juno that the beautiful creature had just sprung from the earth. Juno was suspicious and demanded that Jove give her the wondrous heifer. Jove saw no way to refuse.

Juno appointed a certain Argus to guard the heifer. Argus had a hundred eyes. Even when he slept, he closed only two at a time. Io was wretched, leading the life of a cow in the fields under Argus's watch. Once, she approached her father and scratched her name in the sand with her hoof. In this way, Inachus finally found out what had happened to

---

3   The reference is to the sea goddess, Thetis. Zeus found out in time that her son would be greater than his father and arranged that she marry a mortal king, Peleus. Their son was Achilles.

his missing daughter. He was distraught, exclaiming that he would now have a bull for a son-in-law and calves for grandchildren. Argus soon drove Io away to other pastures.

Jove sent Mercury to rescue Io. Mercury passed by Argus, disguised as a shepherd and playing music on hollow reeds. Charmed by the music, Argus invited him to sit down and asked about the origin of his musical instrument. Mercury started to tell the story of a beautiful nymph named Syrinx (Reed). She was chased by an amorous Pan but was saved by sister nymphs, who transformed her into a clump of reeds. Pan fashioned the shepherd's pipes, or "Pan's pipes," from these very reeds to commemorate his love. Before Mercury finished this story, however, Argus fell asleep—with all hundred eyes. Mercury then cut off his head with a sword. To commemorate Argus's service, Juno plucked out his eyes and placed them in the tail of the peacock.

Juno now drove Io mad so that she wandered in a frenzied state all around the world. When she finally came to the banks of the Nile, she dropped to her knees and begged for mercy in plaintive moos. In heaven, Jove begged Juno to end Io's sufferings and promised that she would never again cause Juno grief. Juno finally agreed. Io was restored to human form and bore Jove's child. Egyptians worshiped her ever after.[4]

10. The Great Flood

Source: Ovid, *Metamorphoses*, 1.177--415 (Roman)

Hearing reports of human sinfulness, Jove toured the earth disguised as a mortal and was very angry at what he saw. The worst sinner was King Lycaon in Arcadia, the rustic area in the central Peloponnesus. When Jove came to his kingdom, the peasants sensed his identity from certain signs that he gave and began to worship him, but King Lycaon scoffed. He planned to kill his supposedly divine guest in his sleep, but first he murdered a hostage that he held in his palace and offered Zeus his roasted flesh for dinner. Outraged, Zeus flattened the palace with thunder and lightning. Lycaon fled into the countryside, where he was transformed into a wolf. Jove returned to heaven, determined to blot out the entire human race.

Jove's initial plan was to use fire, but he was afraid that the conflagration would get out of control. So he started a great flood. The rainy south wind, the rivers, and Neptune all collaborated. Soon dolphins were swimming among the treetops, and farmers were rowing boats over their houses.

Eventually, only two people were left alive: a blameless man named Deucalion, son of Prometheus; and his equally virtuous wife, Pyrrha, Epimetheus's daughter. They were in a rowboat that struck land on the top Mount Parnassus. Noting the innocence of

---

4 Io was identified with the Egyptian goddess, Isis, who wore a crown shaped like a pair of cow's horns.

these two survivors, Jove ordered the rains to stop. Neptune had his son, Triton, sound retreat on his conch shell trumpet, and the waters receded.

Deucalion and Pyrrha realized that they were all that was left of the human race and did not know what to do. They cleaned themselves in a stream and went to the oracular shrine on Parnassus, which was then sacred to the goddess Themis. (It was later taken over by Apollo.) The goddess's voice told them to loosen their gowns, veil their heads, and throw their mother's bones behind their backs.

Deucalion and Pyrrha were dumbfounded by the oracle. Pyrrha told Deucalion that she could not obey it since it would be a sacrilege to disturb her mother's bones. After much thought, Deucalion suggested that the oracle might involve a figure of speech. Perhaps, "mother" meant Mother Earth. In that case, her bones would be stones. Veiling their heads and loosening their robes, they tried throwing stones behind their backs. To their astonishment, the stones that Deucalion threw changed into men, and Pyrrha's stones changed into women.

And to this day we are a hard race.

11. Zeus Vanquishes the Giants

Source: Apollodorus, *The Library*, 1.6.1–3 (Hellenistic)

Upset over the fate of the Titans, Gaea brought forth giants sired by Uranus. Born in Pallene, a peninsula on the coast of Macedonia, they were huge and invincible, and their lower bodies were serpents. They hurled rocks and burning trees at the sky. Their leaders were Porphyrion and Alcyoneus, who was immortal—so long as he remained in the land of his birth.

The gods had an oracle that the giants could only be defeated with the help of a mortal. Zeus dispatched Athena to enlist Heracles' help. Heracles shot Alcyoneus with an arrow, and then dragged him out of Pallene where he died.

Porphyrion attacked Hera. Zeus inspired him with lust for Hera. When he tore her robes and was about to violate her, she called for help, and Zeus struck him down with a thunderbolt. The giant Ephialtes was shot by Apollo with an arrow in his left eye, and by Heracles in his right. Dionysus killed a giant with a thyrsus,[5] Hephaestus killed one with missiles of molten metal, and Athena threw the island of Sicily on one as he fled. She also skinned a giant named Pallas and used his hide a shield.

Gaea was even angrier at the fall of the giants. She lay with Tartarus and gave birth to Typhoeus in Cilicia in Asia Minor. He was the largest and strongest of all of Gaea's children. From the waist up, he resembled a man, but he towered above mountains. His head often brushed the stars. The heads of a hundred serpents grew from his arms.

---

5   A *thyrsus* is a wand symbolic of Dionysus and his followers. It has a pine cone on the end and is decorated with vines and ribbons.

From the waist down, his body was a vipers' tangle. When it uncoiled, it reached his head. His entire body was covered with wings. Fire flashed from his eyes.

When the gods saw him attacking heaven, they fled to Egypt and changed their forms into those of animals. Zeus pelted Typhoeus with thunderbolts and wounded him with an adamantine sickle. He then grappled with him. Typhoeus gripped Zeus in his coils, wrenched the sickle from his hands, and cut the muscles out of Zeus's arms and legs. Then he carried Zeus on his shoulders back to Cilicia and deposited him in a cave. He also hid his muscles in a cave and had them guarded by Delphyne, who was half girl and half snake.

Hermes stole the muscles from Delphyne,and returned them to Zeus. Recovering his strength, Zeus charged Typhoeus in a chariot drawn by winged horses. In the ensuing battle, Typhoeus threw Mount Haemus at Zeus, but he blasted it with a thunderbolt, which caused a stream of blood (*haema* in Greek) to gush from the mountain. This is how the mountain got its name. Zeus then cast Mount Aetna in Sicily down upon Typhoeus. To this day, gusts of fire still issue from the thunderbolts that were thrown in this battle.

12. The Crash of Phaethon

Source: Ovid, *Metamorphoses*, 1.750–2.400 (Roman)

Phaethon is a youth who lives in Egypt with his mother, Clymene. She has told him that his father is Phoebus, the god of the sun. When he boasts about this fact to his playmates, they mock him. Enraged, Phaethon asks his mother how he can prove his father's identity. She suggests that he visit him in his house, which is not very far away. He eagerly obeys, making his way across Ethiopia to India and his father's home.

When Phaethon arrives, Phoebus is on his emerald throne, attended by the four Seasons. Phaethon can barely endure his father's radiance, but Phoebus removes his glittering crown, embraces the boy, and swears by the waters of the Styx that he will grant any request the boy makes. Phaethon asks to drive his father's chariot across the sky.

Phoebus immediately regrets his vow and begs Phaethon to ask for something else. Driving the sun chariot, he says, is beyond the strength even of other gods. Its course involves dizzying heights and passes the horns of the Bull, the Archer's bow, the jaws of the raging Lion, and the claws of the Scorpion and the Crab. The horses are powerful, and nearly impossible to control. If Phaethon could see into his heart, he says, he would know that he, Phoebus, really is his loving father. He can have anything he wants, but won't he choose more wisely?

Phaethon insists on driving the chariot. Soon the fire-breathing horses are yoked to the golden chariot, and Phaethon gets into the car. His father places his crown on

Phaethon's head, anoints his face with ambrosia for protection against the heat and gives him detailed instructions on what route to follow.

The horses take off and are soon running out of control because the chariot is light and there is no strength in the reins. Phaethon is panic-stricken and helpless. He drops the reins. The horses leave their accustomed route entirely and run aimlessly around the sky. Mountains and great cities burst into flames. The men of Ethiopia become black-skinned. Libya is transformed into a desert. Rivers boil. The Nile hides its head, which has not been found to this day.

In agony, Earth cries out to Jove for mercy. She does not understand what she has done to deserve this terrible punishment. Jove responds by blasting Phaethon out of the sky with a thunderbolt. The chariot explodes. The horses fly away. Phaethon falls to the earth in flames, like a comet. He lands by the Eridanus River,[6] where nymphs bury his remains in a tomb. The inscription reads:

> *Here lies Phaethon, who tried his father's chariot.*
> *He did not succeed, but he fell with great audacity.*

Clymene wanders the world looking for her son's body. When she finds his tomb, she and her daughters mourn night and day, flinging themselves on it. This lasts for four months. Finally, when one of the girls tries to fall on the tomb, she finds that she cannot move her feet. Her sister tries to help her, but she is also rooted to her spot. Another, in tearing her hair, finds that she is pulling leaves from her head. Then all the girls discover that bark is rapidly enveloping their bodies. Clymene runs from one to the other trying to help, but when she breaks off twigs, they bleed. Soon the girls are trees, but their tears continue to flow. These are hardened by the Sun into amber that is recovered from the river and is still worn by Roman girls on their wedding day.

King Cycnus of Liguria in northern Italy is also very fond of Phaethon. He comes to the banks of the Eridanus, weeping and wailing. His voice becomes shrill, white feathers cover his body, a membrane grows between his fingers, wings sprout from his side. He becomes a strange, white bird—a swan, or *Cycnus* in Greek. Because of Phaethon's example, he avoids flying high.

---

6   Hesiod mentions an Eridanus River where amber was found. It was later identified with the Po in northern Italy.

13. Endymion

Source: Apollodorus, *Library*, I.7.2–6 (Hellenistic)

The children of Deucalion and Pyrrha included a daughter named Protogenia and a son named Hellen. Protogenia had a son named Aethlius by Zeus. Hellen fathered Dorus, Xuthus, and Aeolus on a nymph. The sons of Xuthus were Achaeus and Ion.[7]

Aeolus ruled over Thessaly and named its inhabitants Aeolians. His children included a daughter named Calyce, who married Aethlius. They had a son named Endymion, who led a band of Aeolians out of Thessaly to the Peloponnesus, where he founded the city of Elis. Some say that Endymion was really a son of Zeus. He was a man of exceptional beauty, and Selene (the Moon) fell in love with him. Zeus granted him any wish. He chose to sleep through all time while remaining deathless and ageless.

14. The Love of Aphrodite and Anchises

Source: Anonymous, *Homeric Hymn to Aphrodite* (Archaic Greek)

Aphrodite can overpower any god or mortal—with three exceptions: the warrior goddess, Athena; the huntress, Artemis; and Zeus's sister, Hestia, who was granted the privilege of perpetual virginity when Poseidon and Apollo wanted to marry her. Otherwise, Aphrodite is all-powerful and even tricks Zeus into mating with mortal women (in secret from his wife Hera, the loveliest of goddesses).

One day, to prevent Aphrodite from boasting about this, Zeus makes her fall in love with a mortal man, Anchises, who is tending cattle on Mount Ida outside of his native Troy. Overcome by desire, Aphrodite is bathed and anointed by the Graces, dons beautiful clothes and golden jewelry, and hurries toward Troy. Lions, bears, and panthers fawn on her as she arrives. She arouses desire in them. They disappear into the bushes two by two.

Aphrodite finds handsome Anchises alone, outside his shelter, playing his lyre. To avoid frightening him, she puts on the appearance of a mortal maiden. Seeing her, Anchises is seized with love. He addresses her as a goddess, asking for her blessing.

Aphrodite says that she is no goddess, but the daughter of a Phrygian king. She speaks Trojan, she says, because she was raised by a Trojan nurse. She was dancing with her friends when Hermes suddenly swooped down out of the sky and grabbed her. He flew her high over farmlands and wilderness, telling her that she was destined to marry him, Anchises. So, she asks, would Anchises be so kind as to take her—inexperienced

---

7   The heroes catalogued in this story are supposedly responsible for the names of the Greek race, i.e., "Hellenes" from Hellen, and their principal tribal divisions: Dorians from Dorus, Aeolians from Aeolus; Achaeans from Achaeus; and Ionians from Ion.

virgin that she is—to meet his parents and the rest of his family, and also to send a messenger to her parents, to tell them what has happened to her?

Anchises replies that if they are truly destined to be married, no force on heaven or earth will prevent him from lying with her immediately—not even Apollo with arrows flying. He takes her by the hand toward the entrance to his shelter. Aphrodite follows with downcast eyes. Inside, a bed is laid with soft bear and lion skins. Anchises removes Aphrodite's jewelry and magnificent clothes, which he places on a chair, and then goes to bed with a goddess—without being fully conscious of the fact.

Later, Aphrodite puts Anchises to sleep, rises, dresses herself, and assumes her divine appearance. Then she wakes up Anchises, and asks if he notices a difference. Anchises is fearful. He says that he *thought* she was a goddess, but she deceived him. He says he knows that men who sleep with goddesses do not remain hale and hearty and asks for mercy.

Aphrodite says that he has nothing to fear. They will have a son named Aeneas, because she feels dreadful (*aenon*) regret at having slept with a mortal. She adds that Trojan men are always beautiful. For example, Zeus carried off the Trojan boy, Ganymede, to pour wine for the gods. His father, King Tros, was grief-stricken. All he knew was that a whirlwind had taken his son. So Zeus took pity on him, giving him divine horses as a gift to compensate for his son. He also had Hermes tell Tros that his son would be ageless and immortal.

Eos (Dawn) abducted the Trojan Tithonus. She asked Zeus to make him immortal, and he agreed. Unfortunately, it did not occur to her to ask Zeus to make Tithonus ageless too. She and Tithonus were very happy for a while, but as soon as his hair turned gray, she stayed away from his bed. Eventually, he was so overcome by age that he could not lift his limbs. Eos locked him in a room, where he babbles endlessly.

Aphrodite does not want a similar fate to befall Anchises. If he could retain his looks, she would be happy to have him as a husband, but unfortunately he will soon be old. She says that she bitterly regrets the madness that overcame her. Now the other gods and goddesses will not have to fear her comments.

She reveals that their son will be raised by buxom mountain nymphs, who are midway between mortals and immortals. Trees spring up when they are born, and they live for as long as their trees do. Such nymphs will raise their son and deliver him to Anchises when he is five. He will be a delightful child. Under no circumstances, however, should Anchises reveal that Aphrodite is the child's mother. If he does, Zeus will blast him with a thunderbolt. With that warning, Aphrodite soars off into the sky.

Source: Anonymous, *Homeric Hymn to Hermes* (Archaic Greek)

Maia is a shy goddess with luxuriant braids who lives in a cave on Mount Cyllene in the rural heart of the Peloponnesus. Zeus lies with her in the dead of night while Hera is sound asleep. After nine months, she gives birth to Hermes.

On the day of his birth, Hermes leaps from his cradle and sets out to find Apollo's cattle. Passing the threshold of the cave, he sees a tortoise and laughs. "Hello, my lovely lady dinner companion," he says. "Where did you get such a beautiful ornament, living in the hills? You could be quite a musician—if you die."

Hermes takes the tortoise inside the cave, cuts off her limbs and scoops her flesh out of her shell. He stretches oxhide over it, attaches horns and a crosspiece, stretches seven sheep-gut cords into position, and tries them with his hand. They make a beautiful sound. He improvises a song about how Zeus and Maia used to talk, when they were lovers. Then he stows the lyre in his cradle and leaves the cave.

At dusk, he has reached Greece's far north. He is in the region of Pieria, in a meadow where the cattle of the gods are grazing. He drives 50 of them away, inducing them to walk backward. To cover his own tracks, he weaves sandals from myrtle twigs and tamarisk.

Hermes is spotted by an old man tending his vines in Onchestus, a town in Boeotia, back in central Greece. He tells him that his vines will flourish if he keeps quiet about what he has seen.

Through the night, Hermes drives the cattle. Dawn finds him on the banks of the Alpheus River in southern Greece. He feeds the cattle and drives them into a high-roofed chamber. Outside, he makes a fire by rapidly rotating a sharp stick on a block, thus inventing the fire stick. He brings out two cattle, throws them on their backs, butchers them, roasts the meat, and divides it into 12 portions. Though hungry, he refrains from eating any of the flesh himself. He stretches the hides of the two slaughtered cattle out on the rocks. They are still there.

The next day at dawn, Hermes returns to Cyllene, entering his mother's cave through the keyhole like a mist. He snuggles in his cradle, holding his lyre with his left hand. Maia has seen him come in and scolds him. She says that he is in danger of being flogged by Apollo. Hermes replies that he is not afraid and that he and Maia are going to enjoy wealth and honors equal to Apollo and the other gods rather than living in an obscure cave. If Apollo causes trouble, Hermes will plunder his temple at Pytho.

Meanwhile, Apollo is looking for his cattle. He notices the old man of Onchestus, and asks him if he has seen his cows. The old man says that it is difficult to remember everything that passes by. Yet he thinks he saw an infant traveling behind a herd of cattle, which were walking backward.

From observing the flight of a bird, Apollo infers that the thief is a son of Zeus.

Apollo makes his way to Pylos. He finds the tracks of the cattle leading into an empty meadow and other mysterious tracks like none that he has ever seen.

Apollo rushes to Maia's cave. Seeing him, Hermes curls up like a newborn baby seeking sleep, although he is really awake. Apollo searches the cave, finding closets full of nectar and ambrosia, gold and silver, and Maia's beautiful clothes. Then he turns on Hermes and threatens to throw him into Tartarus if he does not tell him about the missing cattle.

Hermes claims to know nothing. With his eyes darting from side to side, he says that he was born yesterday and is concerned with nothing except sleep, mother's milk, and warm baths. He swears that he does not know who stole Apollo's cows—whatever cows are.

Apollo lifts Hermes out of the cradle. As he does so, Hermes emits an omen, one of his belly's bold employees—a rude messenger. And then he sneezes. Apollo drops him to the ground. Their quarrel continues. They finally go to Olympus, where the other gods are gathered for their father Zeus to give judgment. Apollo accuses Hermes of stealing the cattle and using amazing contrivances to conceal their tracks and his. Hermes claims that he is innocent. Zeus knows Hermes is lying but finds him very amusing. Laughing, he orders Hermes to help Apollo find the cattle.

Soon they are back in Pylos. Hermes drives the cattle out of the cave. Apollo sees the two hides and marvels at Hermes' strength as an infant.

Apollo picks willow twigs, intending to tie Hermes up, but Hermes causes them to start growing out of control until they entangle the entire herd.

Now Hermes starts to play his lyre. Apollo is enchanted by the sound. Hermes sings about the gods, starting with Mnemosyne (Memory), the mother of the Muses.

Apollo lavishes praise on Hermes' music. He says that it brings a choice of pleasures—laughter, love, or sleep. He adds that he never enjoyed the music of flutes so much.

Hermes presents the lyre to Apollo to use at feasts, dances, and revels. Hermes says that he will be content to watch over the herds. Apollo accepts the lyre, gives Hermes his bright whip, and places him in charge of cattle. When the two gods return to Olympus, Zeus is glad to see that they are friends.

Later, Apollo asks Hermes to set his mind at ease by swearing that he will never steal Apollo's lyre or his bow. Hermes promises never to take anything that belongs to Apollo.

Apollo gives Hermes a golden, three-leafed staff of riches, an implement that will keep Hermes safe and enable him to accomplish all words and deeds. As for understanding Zeus's plans, Apollo says that he alone enjoys that privilege. He adds, however, that three virgin sisters live on Mount Parnassus and practice divination. They fly from spot to spot, grazing on honeycombs. When they eat honey, they speak the truth. Otherwise, they lie. Apollo says that Hermes may consult these sisters, and teach mortals to do so.

Zeus confirms their agreements and adds that Hermes will be his official messenger to Hades.

Source: Ovid, *Metamorphoses*, 4.285–388 (Roman)

There is a fountain named Salmacis. That it weakens those who swim in it is well known, but not the reason *why*.

Once, a boy—the child of Mercury and Venus—was raised by woodland nymphs in the hollows of Mount Ida. His features reflected his parents' good looks, and he was named after them: Hermaphroditus.

At age 15, he left his native hills to explore unknown lands. He came at length to Lycia and Caria. There, he found a pool as clear as glass surrounded by a green lawn. It was inhabited by the nymph Salmacis, from whom the waters took their name. She was one who did not care for hunting. She never joined Diana or her sisters in their strenuous activities but just liked to bathe in her pool, comb her hair, try on lovely dresses, and take naps on the grass. The day that Hermaphroditus happened by, she was picking flowers. When she saw him, she was instantly overcome by desire and called out to him. "Are you a god? If so, you must be Cupid! If not, your parents are lucky to have such a son, but the luckiest one of all is the girl that you've decided to marry. If there is such a girl, then pleasure me in secret! If there isn't, let me be the one!"

The boy knew nothing of love. He blushed. His face turned the color of apples in sunshine, or tinted ivory. Salmacis begged him for a kiss and tried to hug him. "Stop," he cried, "or I will leave." That frightened her. "No," she said, "I leave the area to you," and pretended to go away but actually hid in the bushes to spy on him.

The boy entered the water. Finding its temperature agreeable, he took off his clothes. At once, Salmacis burned with desire for his naked beauty. She could hardly contain herself. Then the boy slapped his body and dove under the water, looking like a lily under glass.

Throwing off her clothes, the nymph exclaimed, "He's mine!" and dove in after him. She grabbed him, snatching kisses and stroking his chest as he struggled to get away. She encircled him like a serpent in an eagle's talons or ivy around a tree. Although he denied her the pleasure that she hoped to have, she held him tight. "Fight, you wicked boy," she said, "but you won't escape! O gods, may nothing ever separate us!"

Prayers are answered. Their bodies were joined together; their faces became as one. They were no longer two individuals, but one who could not be called a boy or a woman but seemed to be both and neither.

When Hermaphroditus saw that he had been made into a semi-male, he prayed to his parents. "O father and mother," he said, "let whoever enters these waters emerge as half a man." His parents heard his prayer and saw that it was fulfilled.

17. Apollo's Birth on Delos

Source: Anonymous, *Homeric Hymn to Apollo*, 1–139 (Archaic Greek)

In labor with Apollo, Leto wanders from Crete to Thrace to Cos, looking for a land willing to be her new son's home, but none dares to volunteer until she comes to the tiny island of Delos. She tells Delos that it will be a prosperous island if it makes a home for Apollo and his temple. Delos, however, fears that Apollo will despise it, since it is so small and rocky, and will sink it to the bottom of sea, and build his temple elsewhere. Delos will cooperate only if Leto swears that Apollo will build his first temple there.

Leto swears a great oath. She is then racked by extraordinary labor pains for nine days. Other goddesses, including Rhea, Themis, and Poseidon's wife, Amphitrite, gather round, but Hera stays in Zeus's palace. For some time, Hera also prevents the goddess of difficult child birth, Eileithyia,[8] from hearing of Leto's plight. The goddesses helping Leto, however, send Iris to fetch Eileithyia, offering her a great golden necklace as a bribe. When Eileithyia arrives, Leto puts her arms around a palm tree and kneels on the earth, and the child leaps out. The goddesses bathe the baby, wrap him in a white garment, and tie a golden band around him. Leto does not nurse him. He gets nectar and ambrosia from Themis instead. The moment he eats, he bursts out of his swaddling clothes and says, "Let the lyre and bow be mine, and I will proclaim the infallible will of Zeus to mortals."

18. Apollo Establishes His Temple at Delphi

Source: Anonymous, *Homeric Hymn to Apollo*, 277–546 (Archaic Greek)

Apollo travels far and wide looking for a site for a temple and finally settles on Crisa, an outcropping of Mount Parnassus at the foot of a sheer cliff. He decides to establish an oracular temple in this place that will draw men from north and south. Countless men work on the temple, following the plans of the sons of Erginus, Trophonius, and Agamedes. There is a spring nearby, where Apollo kills a great, deadly serpent, the bane of local sheep—and shepherds. This serpent was also famous for having raised the terrible Typhaon. He was a monster, whom Hera bore all by herself when she was angry at Zeus over the birth of Athena from his forehead.

Apollo pierces the serpent with an arrow. It gasps, writhes, hisses, and bleeds away its life. Apollo vaunts over its corpse, saying, "Rot (*pytheu*), right there on the fertile earth!" The serpent does. Ever after the spot is called "Pytho," and Apollo is named the Pythian.

---

8   Eileithyia means "she who has arrived" in Greek. She was the goddess that women in labor prayed to, and is celebrated for "having arrived" in answer to such prayers.

While Apollo is wondering whom to recruit to serve as priests in his temple, he sees a Cretan ship sailing from Cnossos toward Pylos on the southern tip of Greece. He transforms himself into a dolphin (*delphis*) and leaps onto the ship. When the crew tries to throw Apollo overboard, he shakes so violently that the ship nearly falls apart. The sailors shrink back in fear. A south wind pushes them up the west coast of the Peloponnesus. As they near Ithaca, a west wind blows them into the gulf of Corinth until they make land beneath Crisa.

Apollo flies from the ship in the form of a star with sparks cascading around him. Entering his shrine, he ignites such a bright fire that it illuminates all of Crisa, panicking the residents. He then emerges from his temple in the form of a handsome young man and asks the Cretans who they are and what they are doing. The Cretans tell their story, concluding that some god has delivered them to Crisa against their will. Apollo then reveals his true identity, and tells them that they shall never return to their homes and wives, but will stay in Crisa to be his highly honored priests, sharing knowledge of the gods' counsels. Since he appeared to them as a dolphin, they are to invoke him as Apollo Delphinius. The Cretans offer sacrifice to Apollo on the beach, then march in procession to his temple. There, they ask him how they will support themselves. Apollo says that they are foolish to worry. If they do their job honestly, showing mortal men his will, they will always be rich from the gifts brought to the temple. If they ever grow reckless or irresponsible, however, they will be enslaved by others.

19. Apollo and Daphne

Source: Ovid, *Metamorphoses*, 1.452–657 (Roman)

Still gloating over his conquest of the serpent, Apollo sees Cupid bending his bow and asks him what a boy like him is doing with such a brave weapon. To teach Apollo a lesson, Cupid flies to Parnassus, and takes two arrows from his quiver. The sharp, golden one causes love; the other is leaden and dull. Cupid hits Apollo with the golden one; the daughter of the Peneus river, Daphne, with the leaden arrow. Instantly, Apollo burns with love, while Daphne detests the very word. She spends her time hunting in the woods, avoiding her many suitors. When her father asks about the chances of his having a son-in-law or grandchildren, she clings to his neck and asks for permission to be a virgin forever, like Diana.

Apollo, however, burns with desire for Daphne. When he approaches, she flees. He chases her, urging her to slow down, lest she fall. He is, he says, no shepherd. Jove is his father. He reveals the future, past, and present and is master of the lyre and bow. He discovered medicine—although, alas!—he has no cure for his love.

Despite his words, Daphne just runs. Apollo chases her like a hound after a rabbit. Eventually, her strength fades. "Father, help!" she cries, "Destroy through change this beauty that makes me too appealing!" The words have hardly left her mouth when bark encloses her sides, her hair turns into leaves, her arms to branches, and her feet cling to the ground with roots.

Apollo still loves her. He feels her heart beating beneath the bark and hugs and kisses her trunk. The wood itself shrinks from his lips.

"Since you are not able to be my wife," he says, "you will definitely be my tree! My hair will always carry you, and you will be present at the triumphs of Roman generals."

The laurel tree (*daphne* in Greek) seemed to nod her head.

20. Orpheus and Eurydice, Orpheus's Songs, and His Death

Source: Ovid, *Metamorphoses*, 10.1–11.83 (Roman)

In Thrace, a master musician and son of Apollo, Orpheus, marries his love, Eurydice, but the omens are bad and the actual event is worse. As the bride crosses the grassy lawn, she is bitten by a serpent and dies. Orpheus is so grief stricken that he himself descends into the darkness of the underworld. When he comes before the king of the dead and his wife, Persephone, he strokes his lyre and sings, "I have come for my wife. She was taken by a serpent. I cannot bear her loss, although I have tried. Love is too strong. If the story is true, Love's power is recognized even down here. I beg you to restore Eurydice's life. She and I, and all people, will belong to you eventually. What I ask is a loan. If I cannot have it, I will not return to the world above."

His words make the ghosts weep. Tantalus stops reaching for water; Sisyphus sits down on top of his rock. Even the Furies cry. The king and queen call Eurydice. She comes limping forward and is given to Orpheus with one condition: He is not to turn his gaze back on her until they cross the river Acheron.

They climb in silence through the darkness. They are near the edge, the upper land. Orpheus is afraid the she might faint. He is eager to see her and full of love. He looks back, and she is gone. He barely hears her calling, "Farewell!" in the distance.

Orpheus tries to return to the land of the dead a second time, but Charon, the boatman, turns him away. After he sits, fasting on the banks for seven days, he returns to the wilds of Thrace. For three years, he lives without a woman, either because of the pain his first marriage caused, or because he had promised Eurydice. He turns his attention to young boys instead. He sits on top of a sunny hill. He sings so beautifully that trees gather around, thus providing shade. Oaks, poplars, lindens, beech, laurel, sycamore, willows, lotus, tamarisks, myrtle, verbena, rowan-trees, pines, arbutus, and palms all come to listen. He sings of boys who were loved by gods and about girls who were driven to sin through passion.

"Once Jupiter," he chants, "loved a Trojan boy named Ganymede. He changed himself into an eagle and carried off the youngster. Now Ganymede serves Jupiter his wine, though Juno strongly disapproves.

"My father, Apollo, loved Hyacinthus dearly, and left Delphi in order to be with him in Sparta. He forgot his dignity, carrying hunting nets and holding dogs on leashes as they roamed the mountain trails. At noon one day, they stripped, rubbed themselves with oil, and tried their skill at discus throwing. Apollo threw a discus into the clouds. Hyacinthus ran after it. Striking the earth, it bounced back and struck him in the face. He grew deadly pale. Apollo caught up with him and tried to stop his bleeding, but the wound was incurable. As Hyacinthus died, Apollo cried out, 'I cannot die for you, but you will be with me forever. You will be reborn as a new flower, whose markings will spell out my cries of grief.' So he spoke. On the ground, the blood was no longer blood. A flower grew instead, and Apollo kept his promise, inscribing the flowers with his own grieving words, 'AI AI!'

"On Venus's island of Cyprus once, the daughters of a man named Propoetus denied that Venus was divine. Venus punished them by having them become the first prostitutes. As their sense of shame shrank, they became harder and harder, slowly changing into stone.

"Seeing this, Pygmalion was disgusted by women and avoided marriage. Instead, he carved a beautiful figure out of ivory and fell in love with it. He talked to it, kissed it, brought it gifts, clothed it, and laid it in his bed.

"The feast day of Venus arrived. Pygmalion offered sacrifice and prayed to the gods to let him marry … a woman like his ivory maiden. He did not dare to state his real wish, but Venus understood. Pygmalion returned home and kissed his statue, fondling its breasts. The ivory grew soft beneath his fingers, blood pulsed in its veins. The statue was a living maiden. She blushed, lifted her timid eyes, and saw the sky and her lover at the same time.

"Nine months later, they had daughter named Paphos.

"Paphos had a son named Cinyras, and he had a daughter, Myrrha. Their story is horrible. In fact, fathers and daughters should stop listening. If they do not, at least they should not believe the story—for though it is a sin to hate one's father, Myrrha's love was a greater sin than any hatred.

"Myrrha realized how sinful her desires were, but could not forget them. She thought of nations where incest was permitted and that it was common in the animal world. She had many suitors. When Cinyras asked what sort of husband she desired, she blushed and wept. Attributing this to maidenly fear, he dried her cheeks and kissed her on the lips—which she enjoyed far too much.

"One midnight, maddened by desire and shame, Myrrha decided to kill herself. She tied the sash from her dress to a beam on the ceiling. Outside her door, her old nursemaid heard something happening, burst in, and saved her. She frantically begged Myrrha to tell her what the trouble was. Myrrha resisted, but eventually the truth slipped out, when Myrrha sobbed, "Ah, my husband-happy mother!" The nurse was horrified. When it became clear, however, that Myrrha was determined to die if she did not have her wish, the nurse promised to help her.

"A festival of Ceres was being celebrated. At this time, married women remained apart from their husbands for nine days. The nurse came across Cinyras, who was drunk. She told him that a young lady had fallen in love with him. He asked how old she was. The nurse replied that she was just Myrrha's age. Cinyras told the nurse to bring her to him.

"That night Myrrha made her way towards her father's dark bedroom, accompanied by bad omens. She stumbled and heard a screech-owl cry. The closer she got, the more she just wanted to leave, but the nurse took her by the hand and brought her to the edge of Cinyras's bed, saying, 'Take her, Cinyras. She is yours.'

"Myrrha left with her father's seed in her womb. She returned the next night, and many nights thereafter. Eager to see his lover, Cinyras finally brought a light into his bedroom. Recognizing his own daughter, he was speechless and reached for his sword. Myrrha escaped in the darkness.

"After nine months of wandering, she arrived among the Sabaeans of Arabia, heavy with child. In view of her sin, she prayed to the gods for some punishment that was midway between life and death, so that she would not offend either realm. Some god heard her prayer. Roots burst from her toes; her blood turned to sap. She was transformed into the tree that bears her name—the myrrh tree.

"A sinfully begotten child developed inside the tree. The trunk swelled, the bark cracked open, a wailing baby boy fell out—Adonis, as lovely as a little cupid. He swiftly grew into an even more beautiful young man. In fact, he excited Venus's love; for when Cupid was kissing her one day, she accidentally scratched her breast with one of his arrows. As a result, Venus lost interest in everything else to become Adonis's constant companion, spending her time hunting with him.

"Venus was happy when they hunted rabbits and deer, but she urged Adonis to stay away from boars, wolves, bears, and lions, beasts that she hated. He asked her why. Lying on the grass with her head on his chest, she told him the story, punctuating it with kisses.

"She said that there was once a maiden named Atalanta, who was a faster runner than any man, and just as beautiful as she was fast. 'When she consulted an oracle about marriage, she was told that her husband would be her ruin and that she should flee marriage. She announced that she would marry only a man who beat her in a race, but that death was the penalty for losing to her. Even on these terms, a throng of suitors announced that they wanted to try their luck.

"'A youth named Hippomenes came to watch the race. He thought that the suitors were foolish to risk their lives merely for a wife. Then he saw Atalanta, stripped for action at the starting line, and instantly changed his mind. She flashed past him with hair flying, her body flushed, and ribbons fluttering around her knees and was crowned the winner. The groaning losers were led away to die.

"'Hippomenes then challenged Atalanta to take on a real runner—him. She was moved by his good looks and especially his youth. She did not know whether she wanted to win or to lose, whether to despise him for his foolishness or pity him. She was confused because it was the first time she had been touched by desire.

"'As preparations were laid for the race, Hippomenes prayed to Venus, who took pity on him. She appeared to him with three golden apples that she had just picked from her sacred grove and told him how to use them.

"'In the race, Atalanta delayed taking the lead, running beside Hippomenes, and then regretfully pulling ahead of him. He was getting weak and short of breath. He threw out the first apple. Atalanta deviated from the course, retrieved it, and soon recaptured the lead. Hippomenes threw out the second apple with the same results. As the finish line neared, he threw the third apple very far off course. Atalanta hesitated and then chased it. As she returned to the race, Venus added extra weight to the apples—thus, Hippomenes won.

"'Neither Hippomenes nor Atalanta bothered to thank Venus for her kindness, however. This enraged the goddess. They were passing a temple in the woods sacred to Cybele. By Venus's action, Hippomenes was overcome by lust. He and Atalanta entered a sacred cave full of holy statues, and made love there, defiling the cave. Cybele was enraged. She was just going to cast the sinners into the underworld, but that seemed too lenient. Instead, Hippomenes and Atalanta found their chests swelling and their fingers curving into claws. When they spoke, they emitted rough growls. Now, they range the woods as fierce lions.

"'Such beasts,' Venus concluded, 'do not flee. They are dangerous, and should be avoided.' She mounted her swan-drawn chariot, and flew away to Cyprus.

"Adonis ignored her advice. He flushed a boar and wounded it with a javelin. The boar shook the spear loose, charged Adonis, and sank his tusks into the boy's groin. Venus heard his groans from afar, returned, and found him lifeless. She decreed annual mourning in commemoration of her grief. She also sprinkled nectar on Adonis's blood. It bubbled and soon produced a beautiful, but short-lived, blood-red flower, which takes its name from the breezes (Greek *anemoi*) that shake its petals loose—the anemone."

Trees, beasts, and stones follow Orpheus as he sings such songs, but the wild women of Thrace, maenads,[9] catch sight of him from a distance. One of them cries out, "Look, there is the man who despises us!" and she throws a spear. Another throws a stone. Overcome by the music, these weapons fall harmlessly at Orpheus's feet. Any number of them would be conquered by the singer's music, but the women have shrill flutes, loud trumpets, and drums. They beat their breasts and howl. The lyre's beautiful music is drowned out. The women's stones draw blood. They swarm over him like hounds around a doomed stag.

Birds, beasts, rocks, and trees all mourn for Orpheus. His limbs lie scattered every-where. His head and lyre end up floating down the Hebrus River, and out to sea. They

---

9 Maenads are the women followers of Dionysus. They are called "maenads," or "mad women," because of their wild revels.

finally wash up onto the shore of the island of Lesbos. There, a serpent is about to strike Orpheus's head, but Apollo turns it to stone, gaping jaws and all.

Orpheus's spirit descends into the land of the dead a final time. In the fields of the blessed, he finds Eurydice, taking her in his arms. Now they wander side by side, but sometimes Orpheus walks ahead and happily looks back at his beautiful Eurydice.

21. The Misadventures of King Midas

Source: Ovid, *Metamorphoses,* 11.89–193 (Roman)

Silenus, an elderly satyr and companion of Bacchus, is captured by Phrygian peasants after a revel. They lead him to King Midas. Midas has been initiated into the rites of Bacchus and recognizes Silenus. He entertains him with a festival that lasts for ten days and nights, then escorts him back to Bacchus.

Bacchus is grateful and grants Midas any wish. "Grant," says the king, "that whatever I touch with my body turns to yellow gold." Bacchus nods.

Midas is delighted. He turns a twig to gold, a rock, a clod of earth, stalks of grain, an apple. If he touches a pillar with his finger, it gleams. He washes his hands in a shower of gold.

Then he tries to eat. Bread turns to gold between his teeth, wine as it flows over his lips. Soon, he is dying of hunger and thirst. He prays to Bacchus for mercy. Bacchus directs him to the source of the Pactolus River above Sardis, the capital of Lydia. If he immerses himself in that water, he will wash his sin away. Midas does so, and to this day its waters deposit gold in the surrounding fields.

Midas now despises wealth. He lingers in the woods of Mount Tmolus.

Pan happens to be playing his pipes for the nymphs in this same region and makes a disparaging remark about Apollo's tunes. This gets him involved in an uneven contest. Mount Tmolus is the judge. First, he orders Pan to play his rustic pipes. Midas, who happens to be passing, is charmed by the primitive tune. Then Tmolus turns to Apollo. He wears a laurel wreath and a purple gown. His lyre is encrusted with gems. After a few chords, Tmolus orders Pan to admit defeat. Everyone agrees with Tmolus's judgment, except Midas, who says that the verdict is unfair. Apollo cannot put up with such stupid ears as his having human form. He makes them longer, shaggier, floppy: Midas has ass's ears.

To hide his shame, Midas wears a purple turban. The servant who cuts his hair knows the secret, however. He is afraid to reveal the king's shame, but unable to keep quiet. He withdraws to a secluded spot, digs a hole in the ground, whispers his testimony, and covers it with dirt. In time, a thick clump of reeds grows there. When it is stirred by a gentle breeze, it tells its secret: "Midas has ass's ears!"

22. Silenus's Advice to Midas

Source: Aristotle, *Eudemus, or On the Soul*, a work, now lost, quoted by Plutarch, *Moralia*, 115b–e (Classical Greek)

"This, they say, is what happened to King Midas, when he caught Silenus and asked him to name the best and most desirable thing of all for mortal men. At first, Silenus fell silent, refusing to answer. Finally, after Midas tried every kind of compulsion, Silenus spoke reluctantly. 'O wretched, short-lived spirit, why force me to tell you what it is better for you not to know? The least painful life is one lived in ignorance of one's own ills. It is impossible for mortals to obtain the best thing: not to be born. The next best thing, and the very best that can be achieved, is to die as soon as possible after having been born.' By this, he obviously meant that the time spent in death is better than that spent in life."

23. Actaeon

Source: Ovid, *Metamorphoses*, 3.131–255 (Roman)

Actaeon, the young grandson of Cadmus, founder of Thebes, has enjoyed a successful morning of hunting on a mountain. At noon, he dismisses his comrades and servants, saying that their nets and spears are dripping with enough blood. He sets off to find water for bathing.

There is a beautiful valley named Gargaphie nearby. In it are a grotto, a natural stone arch, and a stream, widening to a clear pool. Diana and her nymphs use it for bathing. They are doing so, when Actaeon finds his way there by chance. The nymphs scream, beat their breasts, and throng around Diana so that she cannot be seen, but she is taller than the nymphs and remains visible. Blushing, annoyed that her arrows are not handy, she splashes water in Actaeon's face and says, "Now, tell the story of how you saw me naked—if you can!" At once, she makes antlers appear on his head, lengthens his neck, changes his hands to feet, clothes his body in dappled fur, and makes him timid. He runs away, amazed by his own speed. Then he sees his face in a clear pool. He wants to say, "Oh, no!" but he can't speak.

As he stands there confused, he sees his dogs, the Spartan Blackie, the Cretan Tracker, the three Arcadians, the whole pack in the distance. Catching his scent, they are racing toward him over crags, cliffs, and pathless rocks. He flees. He wants to shout, "I am Actaeon! Recognize your master!" But he does not have the power of speech. Dark-Mane draws blood from his back, then Beast-Master. Mountain-Boy clamps down on his shoulder. Soon, there is no room for another wound. Actaeon's sobs are not human, but no deer could make them either. He sinks to his knees under his dogs' attack. His comrades arrive, urging the dogs on with their shouts and calling for Actaeon, as if he were not there. He turns his head when he hears his name. They are complaining about his absence.

He *wishes* he were absent.

Afterward, people disagree on whether Diana's punishment was just. Some say that she was too violent; others praise her for preserving her dignity.

24. Niobe

Source: Ovid, *Metamorphoses*, 6.146–312 (Roman)

At the advice of the daughter of the prophet Tiresias, all Thebes is praying and offering sacrifice to Latona, the mother of Apollo and Diana. This angers the beautiful queen, Niobe. What sort of madness is this, she demands, to prefer celestial beings that one has only heard about to those who are actually present? Why should Latona be worshipped, she asks, while she, Niobe, is ignored—she who is a descendant of Tantalus and the queen of Thebes, who is wealthy and has a face worthy of a goddess? Niobe adds that whereas Latona has only two children, she has seven daughters and seven sons. This makes her happiness completely safe. She could lose a good number of her children, even half of them, and still be better off than Latona, who is virtually childless.

Latona is outraged by this speech and describes it to her children. Before she can even ask them to exact revenge, they are flying toward Thebes.

Niobe's seven sons are exercising in a field outside the city. The first to fall is riding a horse when Apollo's arrow lands in his chest. A brother, also on horseback, flees. He is struck in the back of the neck. The arrow's tip emerges from the front. Two others are fatally pierced by one arrow as they wrestle on the ground. The fifth victim lives long enough to pull the barb out of his diaphragm, together with part of his lung. Apollo uses two arrows to kill the sixth boy: one in the groin, one in the neck. When the seventh brother prays to the gods for mercy, Apollo nearly relents. The arrow just touches his heart.

Niobe and her daughters grieve over the boys' bodies. "Enjoy your victory, Latona!" Niobe cries. "And yet," she adds, "what victory? Sad as I am, I still have more than you. Even after so many deaths, I am still the winner!"

As she finishes speaking, a bowstring twangs, and one of Niobe's daughters collapses on her brother's corpse. Soon, six girls lie dead on the ground. Niobe tries to shelter her youngest daughter with her robe and prays that she at least be spared, but she too falls and dies. Niobe sits down on the ground and becomes perfectly still. Her hair no longer stirs in the breeze; her eyes are fixed. She has turned to stone. And yet she continues to weep. A whirlwind takes her away to the top of a mountain in her native land of Phrygia. To this day, her tears trickle down the marble.

Source: Ovid, *Metamorphoses*, 6.1–145 (Roman)

Arachne is a young woman from a poor family in Asia Minor. Her mother is dead; her father ekes out a living, dying wool in the little town at the foot of Mount Tmolus. Despite her humble circumstances, Arachne becomes famous as a seamstress. The patterns that she weaves are so beautiful that the nymphs of Mount Tmolus come to admire them. Her manual dexterity makes it obvious that she received her skill as a special gift from the goddess Pallas.[10] But Arachne proudly denies her debt. She declares that she is willing even to compete against the goddess in weaving and will accept any penalty if she loses.

Pallas disguises herself as a gray-haired woman and visits Arachne. She urges Arachne to apologize to the goddess for her rash words. Arachne rejects the suggestion scornfully, saying that old age has destroyed her visitor's mind. "My feeling," she adds, "is not going to change. Why is Pallas avoiding a contest? Why doesn't *she* come to me?"

Pallas throws off her disguise, saying "She *has* come!" The onlookers bow reverently, but not Arachne. Only a slight blush betrays her fear.

They set to work without delay on separate looms. They interweave threads of different hues so skillfully that the colors blend like a rainbow. It is hard to say where one ends and another begins.

Pallas's tapestry depicts the ancient contest over naming Athens.[11] Jove sits in the middle of the 12 gods. Pallas and the god of the sea confront each other. Striking the ground, he produces a well of salty brine, while she brings forth an olive tree. Victory hovers over her work. Pallas adds smaller pictures of mortals, whom the gods punished with transformation, and frames her tapestry with olive branches.

Arachne depicts the gods' love affairs. She shows Jove in the form of a bull with Europa, as an eagle with Leda, as a satyr with Antiope, as a golden shower with Danae, and as a serpent with Proserpina. She adds many more scenes, including ones in which Neptune seduces women as a bull, a ram, a horse, a bird, and a dolphin, and similar pictures of Phoebus, Bacchus, and Saturn.

The tapestries are finished, and Pallas finds nothing to criticize in Arachne's. Envy herself could not. Infuriated, Pallas tears up Arachne's work. Then she starts hitting Arachne in the face with her spindle. Arachne cannot endure that. She ties a noose around her neck. Pallas sees her dangling, feels pity, and makes her light. "Live," she says, "live and hang, bold girl, you and all your descendants!"

---

10   Pallas is an alternative Greek name for Athena. Here, Ovid uses it instead of her proper Roman name, Minerva.

11   Athena/Minvera and Poseidon/Neptune each wished to be the patron of the city of Athens when it was founded. Poseidon staked his claim by producing saltwater on the acropolis. Athena countered with an olive tree, and was declared the winner.

Saying that, Pallas sprinkles magical potions. Arachne's hair falls off. So do her nose and ears. Her head and body become tiny. Fingers growing from her sides replace her legs. Only her belly remains, and threads shoot out of it. As a spider, she pursues her former occupation.

26. The Abduction of Persephone

Source: Anonymous, *Homeric Hymn to Demeter* (Archaic Greek)

Persephone, daughter of Demeter and Zeus, is gathering flowers in a meadow with the buxom daughters of Oceanus. She sees an incredibly beautiful narcissus, which Gaea produced at Zeus's decree, as a snare for the blossoming girl. When she reaches for it, the earth gapes, and Hades rushes toward her in his chariot. He snatches her up as she weeps and calls on her father for help.

Demeter hears her cries, and searches frantically for her daughter. She wanders the earth with flaming torches in her hands for nine days, during which time she neither eats nor drinks. On the tenth day, the goddess Hecate joins her search. She too heard Persephone screaming but knows nothing further.

The goddesses ask Helius (the Sun), the watchman of gods and men, if he knows what happened to Persephone. He replies that Zeus gave her to Hades to be his wife. Hades seized her and took her to his dark kingdom. He says that Demeter should not be angry because Hades is a worthy husband for her daughter. Demeter, however, *is* angry, and stops associating with the gods.

Disguised as an old lady, Demeter goes to the kingdom of Eleusis. She meets the daughters of the King Celeus, drawing water at the Maiden Well. Demeter claims to be a woman of Crete named Doso.[12] She says that she was captured by pirates to be sold into slavery, but escaped. She would now like to be employed in caring for young children or doing housework. The girls say that she would be welcome in any of the leading households, especially their own, since their parents have just had a late-born son, who came as the answer to many prayers. Demeter agrees to work in their palace and follows them there. Upon arriving, she is silent and sad until the jokes of the one of the daughters, Iambe, make her laugh and smile. She refuses wine but drinks a mixture of barley, mint, and water.[13]

Queen Metanira asks Demeter to nurse and care for her baby son, Demophon. Demeter agrees. Demophon grows like a young god due to Demeter's special care. She anoints him with ambrosia during the day. At night, she secretly places him in the fire like a log. This treatment will eventually make him ageless and immortal. Unfortunately, Metanira spies on Demeter and cries out when she sees her putting her baby in the

---

12   *doso* used as a verb means *I will give.*

13   In historical times, worshippers of Demeter at Eleusis consumed a drink fitting this description.

fire. This angers Demeter, who snatches the child out of the fire and flings him on the ground. She declares that Metanira's foolishness has made it necessary for Demophon to grow old and die, although he will always be honored. She reveals her identity and demands that the Eleusinians build a temple in honor of her visit. If so, she will teach them her rites. Having spoken, she casts off the appearance of an old woman and leaves as a beautiful goddess. In the morning, Celeus is informed of the events and decrees the building of a temple, which is quickly completed.

Still avoiding the other gods, Demeter takes up residence in her new temple. She causes a worldwide famine. No seeds sprout anywhere. Afraid that the human race will be wiped out and that the gods will no longer receive any gifts, Zeus sends Iris to summon Demeter, but she refuses to budge. Then all the other gods and goddesses go to Demeter, offering beautiful gifts, but to no avail. Finally, Zeus send Hermes to Hades to bring Persephone back to her mother. Hermes finds Hades sitting in bed with his wife, who is bashful and uncooperative because she misses her mother. He explains the situation, and Hades gives permission to Persephone to rejoin her mother. As she leaves, however, he surreptitiously gives her the sweet seed of a pomegranate to eat.

Borrowing Hades' chariot, Hermes drives Persephone back to her mother in the temple at Eleusis. She rushes out to meet her like a maenad. Mother and daughter embrace joyfully, but as they do so, Demeter has a premonition. She asks if Persephone ate anything while with Hades. If she has, she will have to spend a third of the year in the darkness beneath the earth. Persephone admits that as she was leaving, Hades slipped a pomegranate seed into her mouth and forced her to taste it.

Zeus sends Rhea to invite Demeter to come back to Olympus, where she can have any honors that she likes. Demeter agrees to come. Flowers bloom all over the earth. Before she leaves Eleusis, Demeter teaches Celeus and the other leaders of Eleusis her mysterious rites. The man who witnesses them is happy. He who does not has no share of blessings after death.

27. The Birth of Dionysus

Source: Apollodorus, *The Library*, 3.4.2–3 (Hellenistic)

The daughters of Cadmus, king of Thebes, are Autonoe, Ino, Semele, and Agaue. Zeus loves Semele, lies with her in secret, and agrees to do anything she asks. Tricked by Hera, Semele asks Zeus to come to her in the same way that he visited Hera when he was courting her. Unable to refuse, Zeus arrives in Semele's bedroom in a chariot accompanied by lightning and releases a thunderbolt. Semele dies of fright. Zeus seizes a six-month-old fetus from her funeral pyre and stitches it into his thigh.

With Semele dead, her sisters spread the story that she slept with some mortal and falsely accused Zeus. That is the reason, they say, that she was killed by a thunderbolt.

In due course, Zeus removes his stitches and delivers Dionysus. Taking the baby, Hermes gives him to his aunt Ino and her husband, Athamas, persuading them to raise him as a girl. Jealous Hera drives them mad. Athamas hunts down his older son, Learchus, like a deer, and kills him. Ino throws her other son, Melicertes, into a boiling cauldron, and then jumps with it into the sea. (She and her son are now called Leucothea and Palaemon, respectively. They help sailors in distress.) Zeus saves Dionysus from Hera by changing him into a kid. Hermes takes him to the nymphs on Mount Nysa in Asia Minor. There, he discovers the vine.

28. Dionysus and the Pirates

Source: Anonymous, *Homeric Hymn to Dionysus* (Archaic Greek)

And now I will speak of Semele's son, Dionysus. For once he stood on the shore of the barren sea, looking like a young man. His beautiful dark hair waved in the wind, and he wore a purple cloak. Suddenly, men came speeding over the sea, Etruscan pirates led there by an evil fate. Seeing Dionysus, they nodded to each other, rushed forward, seized him, and gleefully hustled him into their boat. They assumed that he was the son of a king.

The pirates tried to bind Dionysus, but chains would not hold him. They slipped off his arms and legs, while he sat smiling darkly. Noticing this, the pirates' steersman cried out, "You fools! Who is this god you're trying to bind? He's Zeus! He's Apollo! He's Poseidon! He's not a mortal man, but an Olympian god! Let him go at once, or else he'll cause a hurricane!"

The pirates' captain answered him angrily. "You're the fool! Take care of the mast and sails, and let the real men handle this fellow. Sooner or later, he'll tell us where his kinsmen live, and where their treasures are hidden."

At this, fair winds filled their sails, but soon thereafter strange things started to happen. First, sweet fragrant wine bubbled up throughout the ship, and the air was filled with an ambrosial odor. Then a grape vine full of ripe clusters and dark, blossoming ivy with pretty berries covered the sails and coiled around the mast, and all the oars had floral garlands.

The pirates ordered their helmsman to head for land, but then Dionysus turned into a terrible lion right there in the ship and let out an awful roar. Then he made a shaggy bear appear, and they stood glaring at each other.

The pirates huddled around the good helmsman. Seeing this, the lion leapt forward and seized the captain. The other pirates panicked and dove into the sea. There they were transformed into dolphins. The god held the helmsman back, saying, "Cheer up, good man. You please my soul. I am Dionysus. Semele, daughter of Cadmus, bore me after joining in love with Zeus."

Farewell, child of lovely Semele! It's impossible for anyone who pays no heed to you to make sweet music!

29. How Tiresias Became a Prophet

Ovid, *Metamorphoses*, 3.316–338 (Roman)

Once baby Dionysus is safe, Jove relaxes with Juno, drinking nectar and joking. "Honestly," he says, "your pleasure in sex is much greater than what the male gets, isn't it?" Juno denies it. They decide to get the opinion of Tiresias, who had experienced both types of pleasure. For one day in a green forest, Tiresias had struck two huge mating serpents with his walking stick and—presto!—he was changed from a man to a woman for seven years. In the eighth year, he saw the same serpents mating again and said, "If the effect of striking you is to transform the striker, take that!" His prior shape returned.

Tiresias is chosen to judge the lighthearted quarrel between Juno and Jove. He agrees with Jove that women's pleasure is greater than men's. Juno is more upset at this than she should be and afflicts Tiresias's eyes with eternal night. It isn't permitted for gods to undo each other's actions, but to compensate Tiresias for being blind, Jove gives him knowledge of the future, and the honor that comes with it.

30. Dionysus in Thebes

Euripides, *Bacchae* (Classical Greek tragedy)

Dionysus appears before the palace of Cadmus, disguised as a stranger from Lydia.He notices his mother's grave and her shattered house, tributes to Hera's jealousy. Having taught his mysteries to people in Asia Minor, Persia, India, and many Greek cities, Dionysus has come to Thebes to refute the story that his mother lied when she said she had slept with Zeus. The women of Thebes have been driven mad. They are wandering in the hills in Dionysian costume, crazed. Cadmus has yielded the royal power to his grandson Pentheus, who opposes the worship of Dionysus. Dionysus says that he will prove his divinity to Pentheus. He summons a chorus of maenads who have followed him from Asia Minor and leaves the scene. The chorus enters singing of the blessings of Dionysus.

The blind prophet Tiresias calls on Cadmus at the palace. Both are dressed like maenads, and plan to join the Theban women dancing in the hills in honor of the new god. They are delighted to forget old age. As they prepare to leave, Pentheus arrives. Before he notices them, he denounces the new evils that have erupted in Thebes. He thinks that the women are only pretending to worship a new god. According to him, they have mixing bowls full of wine in their midst and sneak off one by one to deserted places to service men's desires. Pentheus has arrested some already, and will soon apprehend the rest. He has also heard about a stranger from Lydia who has come to Thebes to recruit women for these "mysteries." He intends to arrest him and have his head cut off.

Pentheus sees Cadmus and Tiresias. He is shocked that his grandfather is dressed like a maenad and blames Tiresias. He accuses Tiresias of wanting to have a new god just to make more money as a priest.

Tiresias defends the worship of Dionysus. He says that Dionysus and Demeter represent mankind's two greatest blessings. The story about Dionysus being sewed into Zeus's thigh (Greek *meros*) arose by a misunderstanding. When Hera wanted to cast Dionysus out of heaven, Zeus molded aether into his likeness and gave it to Hera as a hostage (Greek *homeros*). Dionysus confers prophetic powers, can panic enemy armies, and will be honored some day at Delphi. He does not compel women to be chaste, but he cannot corrupt a virtuous woman, either. He enjoys praise just as much as Pentheus himself does. It is mad to dishonor him.

Cadmus adds that even if Dionysus is not a god, it is in their family's interest to pretend that he is, since he is said to be Semele's son. Besides, Pentheus should learn humility from Actaeon, who was torn apart by his own hounds because he claimed to be a better hunter than Artemis.

Pentheus tells the old men to leave him alone. He orders his soldiers to arrest the stranger who is seducing the women of Thebes. When he is caught, he will be stoned to death.

After a choral song, an attendant brings "the stranger" bound to Pentheus. The attendant says that he did not resist arrest. The women who were under arrest have escaped, however. Their chains broke, and the prison doors swung open by their own power.

Pentheus interrogates the stranger. He learns that he comes from Lydia and is a priest of Dionysus, son of Zeus and Semele, whose mysteries he was taught by the god in person. He refuses to describe the mysteries.

Pentheus cuts the stranger's long curly hair, seizes his thyrsus, and has him taken into the palace stables. A brief choral song is interrupted by the stranger's voice, summoning an earthquake. The ground shakes, pillars collapse, and the stranger emerges. The members of the chorus prostrate themselves in awe. The stranger tells them to arise and describes how effortlessly he escaped Pentheus with Dionysus's help. The god tormented Pentheus with hallucinations. First, he tried to tie up a bull, mistaking the animal for the stranger. Then, Dionysus made it appear that the palace was in flames. Pentheus rushed everywhere shouting for water. Finally, Dionysus cast down pillars and walls.

Now Pentheus storms out of the palace. Seeing the stranger, he demands to know how he escaped. The stranger says that a god helped him. Pentheus is incredulous.

A cowherd arrives from the hills with information for Pentheus. He says that at dawn, he and his companions happened to come with their cattle within sight of the dancing women. They were divided into three companies, led by Autonoe, Agaue, and

Ino, respectively. Their behavior was chaste and decorous. They wore fawn skins and had snakes in their hair. Women who had newborn babies at home nursed gazelles and wolves. One struck her thyrsus against a rock, and produced a fountain of water. Others got milk by scratching the soil.

A herdsman who frequented the city suggested that they could win Pentheus's favor by seizing Agaue. They sneaked up on the women. As they approached, the women started a wild dance. The herdsman telling the story lunged at Agaue. She cried out that they were being hunted. The herdsmen panicked and fled, narrowly escaping the women, who attacked the cattle instead, tearing them to pieces with their bare hands. Then they flew across the fields, pillaging towns, and routing the companies of armed men who tried to stop them.

Pentheus orders an attendant to mobilize the heavy infantry. They will march against the women in the hills.

The stranger tells Pentheus that his forces will be defeated by the women, and volunteers to lead them back to Thebes peaceably. Pentheus tells him to be quiet.

"Wait," says the stranger. "Do you want to *see* the women meeting in the hills?"

"Very much so," Pentheus says. "I would pay a good bit of gold for that."

The stranger tells him that to spy on the women, he will need to wear women's clothing. If the women see that he is a man, they will kill him. This gives Pentheus pause. As much as he wants to spy on the women, he cannot quite agree to wear women's clothing. He enters the palace to think. The stranger tells the chorus that with Dionysus's help, he will now make Pentheus crazy, have him put on women's clothing, and lead him through the streets, so that he will be the laughingstock of Thebes. He will wear women's clothes in Hades, too, after he is slaughtered by this mother.

After a choral song, Pentheus emerges from the palace in women's clothing with the stranger. He is deranged, seeing two suns and a bull instead of the stranger. He is concerned about his appearance. The stranger arranges his hair, straightens the hem of his gown, and tells him how to hold the thyrsus. Pentheus imagines surprising the women, and seeing them "caught like birds in thickets in their dear coils of love." The stranger says that he will lead him there, but that he will be carried back in his mother's arms. They exit in the direction of the mountain.

The chorus sings a song anticipating Pentheus's punishment. At its conclusion, a servant of Pentheus arrives from the mountain with the news that Pentheus is dead and describes what happened. The servant says he followed his master and the stranger to a mountain glen, from which the women were visible in the distance. Pentheus suggested that he could get a better view by climbing a tree. The stranger miraculously bent down a great fir tree, like a bow or the rim of a wheel, seated Pentheus on the top, and allowed it to straighten up slowly. Then he disappeared, and a great voice—apparently that of Dionysus—thundered, "Women, I bring you the man who mocks our mysteries." The women flew toward the tree. They climbed a high rock and threw stones and spears at Pentheus. Failing to hit him, they tried prying the tree up by its roots. Finally, at Agaue's suggestion, they all seized the trunk and just tore the tree down. Pentheus fell on the ground, weeping and screaming. His mother reached him first. He tore off his headband so that she might recognize him, touched her cheeks, and said, "Mother, I am Pentheus, your son! Have mercy, mother! Do not kill me!" But she was dribbling foam, her eyes were spinning. Seizing his left arm by the elbow, she stepped on his chest and pulled it off. Then the rest of the women attacked. His body ended up scattered throughout the woods. His mother put his head on the end of her thyrsus in triumph and is making her way toward the palace.

As the servant leaves, the leader of the chorus announces that Agaue is approaching. Displaying Pentheus's head, Agaue boasts that she has killed a terrible lion. She is anxious to show the head to her father, Cadmus, and to her son, Pentheus, who will nail it high on the palace wall as a trophy.

Cadmus enters with servants carrying a bier. They have been collecting pieces of Pentheus's body. Seeing Cadmus, Agaue shows him her trophy and cannot understand his horrified reaction. Cadmus has her look at the sky, calm down, and collect her thoughts. Then he asks her to look again at the head in her hands. This time she recognizes it, and frantically demands to know who killed her son. Cadmus tells her the story. She remembers nothing but realizes that they have all been punished for denying Dionysus's divinity. She places the head on the bier and rearranges Pentheus's limbs as well as she can.

Dionysus appears above the stage. He declares that Pentheus has suffered justly for trying to imprison him. Agaue and her sisters must leave Thebes to expiate for killing Pentheus. Cadmus and his wife, Harmonia, will be transformed into serpents. In that form, they will accompany a vast, barbarian horde in an ox-drawn wagon as it attacks Greek cities. In the end, however, they will live in the islands of the blessed.

Cadmus and Agaue embrace and bid sad farewells. Agaue says that Dionysus has inflicted terrible suffering on the house of Cadmus. Dionysus responds that he suffered terrible things in Thebes: his name was not honored.

31. The Adventures of Perseus

Source: Apollodorus, *The Library*, 2.4.1 *ff.* (Hellenistic)

Acrisius, king of Argos, consults the oracle about male descendants. He is told that his only child, his daughter Danae, will have a son, but that this boy will kill him. In fear, Acrisius imprisons Danae in a bronze, subterranean chamber. Then, as some say, Acrisius's brother, Proetus, seduces Danae; according to others, Zeus transforms himself into gold and flows through the roof into Danae's lap. One way or the other, Danae gives birth to Perseus. When Acrisius finds out, he does not believe that she was ravished by Zeus. He puts daughter and child into a wooden chest and casts them into the sea. The chest washes ashore on the island of Seriphos. A man named Dictys picks up the child and raises him.

Polydectes, Dictys's brother, is the king of Seriphos. In time, he falls in love with Danae, but is unable to approach her, because Perseus has grown to manhood. He assembles his friends, including Perseus, and says that he is collecting gifts to court Hippodamia, the daughter of King Oenomaus. Perseus declares that he will not refuse to get him anything, even a gorgon's head. Polydectes asks for horses from his other friends, but when he does not receive one from Perseus, he orders him to bring the head of a gorgon, as promised.

Hermes and Athena help Perseus by leading him to the Phorcides (daughters of Phorcys), also known as the Graeae: Enyo, Pemphredo, and Dino, who were elderly from the time of birth. The three of them have only one eye and one tooth, which they take turns using. Perseus seizes them, and refuses to return them unless the Phorcides show him the way to certain nymphs. These nymphs keep the winged sandals; the *kibisis*, which people describe as a satchel or knapsack; and the helmet of Hades, which makes the wearer invisible. The Phorcides tell Perseus the way. Perseus obtains this equipment and an adamantine sickle from Hermes. He flies to Oceanus and finds the gorgons sleeping. They are Stheno, Euryale, and Medusa, the only mortal one.

Serpents are wound round the gorgons' heads. The gorgons have great tusks like boars, bronze hands, and golden wings. Those who see them turn to stone. Perseus stands by them as they sleep, with his head averted. Athena guides his hand. He looks into a bronze shield, in which he sees Medusa's image—and decapitates her. Pegasus, the winged horse, and Chrysaor leap forth. They are offspring of Poseidon, by whom Medusa was pregnant. Perseus puts Medusa's head in the kibisis and flies away. The other gorgons wake up and try to pursue him, but he is invisible.

Arriving in Ethiopia, which King Cepheus rules, Perseus finds the king's daughter, Andromeda, being offered as food to a sea monster. The reason is that Cepheus's wife, Cassiopea, argued with the Nereids over beauty and claimed to be superior to them all. In their fury, the Nereids and Poseidon unleashed a flood and a monster. The oracle promised relief from this disaster if Andromeda was given to the monster to eat. The Ethiopians forced Cepheus to go along, and he tied his daughter to a rock. Seeing her and falling in love, Perseus promises Cepheus to kill the monster in return for his daughter. Oaths are exchanged. Perseus kills the monster and frees Andromeda.

Phineus, the king's brother, was previously engaged to Andromeda and lays plots against Perseus. The plots are discovered, however. Perseus turns Phineus and the other conspirators to stone by showing them Medusa's head.

Perseus returns to Seriphos to find that his mother and Dictys have taken refuge at altars to avoid the violence of King Polydectes. Perseus goes to the palace and turns Polydectes and his friends to stone. He then makes Dictys king. He gives the sandals, kibisis, and helmet to Hermes to return to the nymphs and presents the gorgon's head to Athena. She puts it in the middle of her shield. Some say that Medusa was decapitated because of Athena. In their account, Medusa had boasted that she rivaled Athena in beauty.

Perseus hurries to Argos with Danae and Andromeda in order to see Acrisius, but he flees to northern Greece from fear of the oracle.

Later the King of Larissa in northern Greece holds funeral games in honor of his dead father. Perseus enters. Throwing the discus, he accidentally hits Acrisius on the foot and kills him instantly. Now ashamed to rule Acrisius's former kingdom, Perseus trades cities with the king of neighboring Tiryns. He also fortifies Mycenae. His sons by Andromeda include Perses, the ancestor of the Persian kings, Alcaeus, Sthenelus, and Electryon.[14]

32. The Calydonian Boar Hunt

Source: Ovid, *Metamorphoses*, 8.270–546 (Roman)

Once Calydon, a town on the western coast of Greece, was in deep distress. Oeneus, its king, had offered sacrifices to thank the gods for a prosperous year, but he forgot to include Diana. In anger, the goddess sent a wild boar rampaging through his fields. The boar was big as a bull, with tusks as long as an elephant's. He destroyed fields of ripe grain and vineyards and scattered the flocks. The residents of the countryside crowded inside Calydon's walls.

The situation seemed desperate until Oeneus's son, Meleager, and a select band of youths converged on the scene to win glory. There were the twin sons of Tyndareus, Castor and Pollux; Jason; Theseus, with his friend Pirithous; Telamon; Peleus; Nestor; Laertes; and many others—including Atalanta, the lovely heroine from the Peloponnesian town of Tegea. Her hair was done into a simple bun in back, she carried an ivory quiver on her shoulder and held a bow. Her facial features were girlish for a boy, and vice versa. The moment Meleager saw her, he was on fire. "Happy the man whom she deems worthy!" he sighed, but there was no time to say more.

The hunters entered the heavily wooded fields, released the hounds, and spread nets. They advanced into a marshy area. There the boar suddenly appeared and charged. Jason hurled his spear, but overshot the target. The boar knocked two hunters down and killed a third by slashing his tendons as he fled. The boar would have gotten Nestor, too, but the future Trojan War hero used his spear to vault into a nearby tree. Castor and Pollux arrived on the scene on white horses but were unable to follow the boar into the thickets that he entered next. Telamon pressed after the animal on foot but tripped on some tree roots and fell on his face. As Peleus helped him up, Atalanta bent her bow and struck the boar under his ear. She was no more pleased by her success than Meleager.

---

14   Perseus's grandchildren are central characters in the saga of Heracles. Alcaeus's son, Amphitryon, is Heracles' human foster father; Electryon's daughter, Alcmene, is Heracles' mother; and Sthenelus's son, Eurystheus, gives Heracles his twelve labors.

He was the first to notice the boar bleeding and shouted to Atalanta, "You have won glory!" Hearing this, the others were jealous and ashamed and redoubled their efforts.

A boastful hero named Ancaeus stepped forward to challenge the boar with an ax, "a man's weapon," but the beast was too quick. While Ancaeus rose up on his toes to strike, the boar sunk his tusks into his groin and killed him. Theseus's next throw hit a tree branch; Jason missed the boar and hit an innocent dog instead. Finally, Meleager launched two spears. The first hit the ground, but the second sank into the boar's back. The animal spun around with blood bubbling from his mouth. Meleager stepped forth and sank another spear between the boar's shoulders.

As his friends cheered, Meleager skinned the boar, severed its head, and presented it to Atalanta, saying, "Take the prize that is rightfully mine. My glory was gained with your help."

Atalanta was pleased by the gift and the giver, but others were resentful. Meleager's maternal uncles, Plexippus and Toxeus, were especially angered and seized the head and hide from Atalanta, telling her not to claim masculine honors. Their action infuriated Meleager. Before his uncles knew what was happening, Meleager had killed them both with his sword.

Meleager's mother, Althaea, was on her way to a temple to give thanks for Meleager's victory over the boar when she saw her brothers' corpses being carried back from the hunt. She was overwhelmed with grief. When Althaea learned their killer's identity, however, her feelings changed to thoughts of revenge.

Years before, when Althaea was giving birth to Meleager, the Three Fates appeared in her room and tossed a log into the fire. As they did so, they said: "We give the same amount of time to you, O newborn child, as to this log." As soon as they left, Althaea took the log out of the fire, put out the flames with water, and hid the log away in a storeroom, where it had lain for years, preserving Meleager's life. Now, she retrieved the log and had her servants build a fire. She meant to punish Meleager by burning the log, thus ending his life, but she was overcome for a long time by conflicting emotions. Her love of her son struggled with her devotion to her brothers. She kept putting the log into the fire and taking it out. One moment, tears for her son flooded her eyes; the next, they were dry and cold with anger over her brothers' deaths. At last, the sister in her proved stronger than the mother. She dropped the log into the fire and let it burn.

Far away, Meleager felt a terrible, scorching heat fill his insides. He knew he was dying and even envied Ancaeus, who succumbed to *visible* wounds. As the log in the fire was reduced to ash, he crumpled to the ground, and his soul flitted into the air.

Calydon was overwhelmed with grief. Oeneus lay on the ground, rolling in dirt and cursing his long life. Overwhelmed by remorse, Althaea drove a sword through her chest. Meleager's sisters tended to his funeral, weeping and wailing as they burned his body on a pyre. The sisters gathered his ashes into an urn and buried them under a headstone, where they stayed and wept ceaselessly. At length, Diana's anger was satisfied. She gave the girls wings and beaks and sent them flying through the air,[15] all except two—Gorge and noble Alcmene's daughter-in-law.[16]

33. The Life of Heracles

Source: Apollodorus, *The Library*, 2.4.6--7.7 (Hellenistic)

Electryon became king of Mycenae after the death of Perseus. He was supported by his nephew, Amphitryon, to whom he betrothed his daughter, Alcmene. A rival branch of the family had settled on the Taphian Islands off the west coast of Greece. They raided Electryon's cattle, killing several of his sons in the process. Amphitryon recovered the cattle, but as he was bringing them back into the city, a cow started to run away. Amphitryon threw his club at her. The club bounced off the cow's horns and struck Electryon, killing him. Therefore, Amphitryon and his fiancée, Alcmene, had to go into exile. They settled in Thebes. Another one of Perseus's sons, Sthenelus, took over Mycenae.

In Thebes, Alcmene said that she would not sleep with Amphitryon until he avenged her brothers' deaths. Amphitryon asked Creon, king of Thebes, to let him lead the Theban army against the Taphians. Creon agreed to do so if Amphitryon would first rid Thebes of a monstrous fox, which was fated never to be caught. Amphitryon went to Athens, where he borrowed the king's magical hound, which was fated to catch everything it chased. When the dog set off after the fox, Zeus turned them both to stone.

Now, Amphitryon led the Theban army against the Taphian islanders, conquered them, and hastened back to Thebes and his loving wife. Before he got there, however, Zeus assumed his likeness and lay with Alcmene, making the night three times as long as usual to extend his enjoyment. Amphitryon returned the next day and was surprised to learn that Alcmene thought she had slept with him the night before. The prophet Tiresias then explained what had happened. In due course, Alcmene bore two sons— Heracles, son of Zeus; and Iphicles, who was sired by Amphitryon one night later.

When Heracles was eight months old, Hera sent two huge serpents into his crib. Alcmene called for help from Amphitryon, but baby Heracles strangled the serpents with his bare hands.

As a boy, Heracles was given lyre lessons by Linus, Orpheus's brother. When Linus struck him for misbehaving, Heracles flew into a rage and killed him. He was tried for

---

15   Ovid did not say so, but probably wanted readers to assume that the girls were changed into guinea fowls, which were called *meleagrides* in Greek.

16   Gorge later became queen of Calydon, ruling it with her husband in the absence of male heirs to the throne; Alcmene's daughter-in-law is Deianira, Heracles' second wife. *Cf.* the story of the death of Heracles.

murder and acquitted on a plea of self-defense. For the rest of his childhood, however, Amphitryon had him raised on a cattle farm.

At age 18, Heracles killed a lion that had become a problem for herdsmen in the vicinity of Thebes. During the hunt, he stayed for 50 days with King Thespius of the nearby town of Thespiae. This king had 50 daughters. Wanting grandchildren by Heracles, he had a different one sleep with Heracles each night, though Heracles thought it was the same girl every night. He finally killed the lion and wore its skin and scalp ever after.

Soon afterward, Heracles led the Thebans to a victory over the neighboring Minyans, who had been exacting an annual tribute from Thebes, as a result of an earlier war. As a reward, King Creon had Heracles marry his daughter, Megara, and he soon had three sons. Hera, however, caused him to go mad and kill his children. When he recovered his sanity, he went to Delphi, seeking purification. The priestess told him to migrate to Mycenae, and perform whatever ten services King Eurystheus required. Something like this was fated to happen, because when Heracles was about to be born, Zeus declared that the next one of Perseus's descendants to be born would rule Mycenae. Hera then delayed Heracles' birth, while Eurystheus, a son of Sthenelus—son of Perseus—arrived prematurely.

Eurystheus first ordered Heracles to bring him the skin of the invulnerable lion of Nemea, on the isthmus of Corinth. Heracles chased the lion into a cave, where he choked it to death. Eurystheus was so frightened when Heracles returned with the lion slung over his shoulders that he had a bronze jar made for him to hide in under the earth.

Heracles was next ordered to kill the Hydra of Lerna, a marshy district nearby. The Hydra had a huge body with nine heads, eight of them mortal. Heracles wrestled the Hydra. He smashed its heads with his club—but when he smashed one head, two grew back. Also, a huge crab appeared and bit Heracles' foot. He killed the crab and then enlisted the help of his nephew, Iolaus, Iphicles' son. Iolaus set fire to a piece of wood, and burned the roots of the Hydra's heads as Heracles smashed them. Heracles cut off the immortal head and buried it under a boulder. He slit open the Hydra's body and dipped his arrows in its poison. Eurystheus said that the labor did not count since Iolaus helped Heracles.

The next labor, the third, was to capture the doe of the Cerynites, a river in southern Greece. She had golden antlers and was sacred to Artemis. Heracles chased her for a year and finally brought her down by wounding her with an arrow.

The fourth labor was to capture a boar that lived on Mount Erymanthus in Arcadia. While hunting it, Heracles was entertained by a centaur. Heracles encouraged him to open a jar of wine that belonged to all the centaurs in common. When he did so, a herd of centaurs showed up to protect their wine, and a battle ensued. Heracles chased them to the home of the wise and good centaur, Chiron, famous as a teacher of young heroes. While a group of centaurs cowered around Chiron, Heracles shot an arrow at them. It ended up grazing Chiron in the knee and causing an incurable hurt, much to Heracles' regret. Chiron wished to die, but he could not, for he was immortal. Prometheus offered himself to Zeus to be immortal in his stead, and so Chiron died. The other centaurs scattered. Heracles then tracked down the boar, and brought it to Mycenae.

The fifth labor was to cleanse the stables of Augeas in a single day. Augeas was a king of Elis in the western Peloponnesus and had many herds of cattle. Heracles appeared, and volunteered to clean his stables in return for one tenth of his herds. Augeas agreed. Heracles diverted two rivers, so that they cleaned the stables. Augeas, however, refused to pay up when he learned that the labor had been ordered by Eurystheus. On the other hand, Eurystheus refused to count it among the ten since Heracles had been working for profit.

Heracles' sixth labor was to chase a flock of birds away from Lake Stymphalia in Arcadia. Athena gave Heracles bronze rattles, with which he scared away the birds.

The seventh labor was to capture the Cretan bull. This was either the bull that ferried Europa to Crete for Zeus, or a bull that Poseidon magically produced out of the sea for King Minos. Heracles brought it to Mycenae and then released it to wander around in Greece.

For his eighth labor, Heracles and his comrades had to overcome King Diomedes of Thrace and his forces and capture his man-eating mares. He was successful as usual, killing Diomedes in battle. He released the mares on Mount Olympus, where they were killed by wild beasts.

For Heracles' ninth labor, he and his comrades had to get the belt of Hippolyta, the greatest of the Amazon warriors. Landing in Amazon territory on the shores of the Black Sea, Heracles met Hippolyta, and she agreed to give him her belt. While they talked, however, Hera convinced the other Amazons that Hippolyta was being abducted. They charged Heracles' ship. Seeing them coming, Heracles assumed that Hippolyta was trying to trick him. He killed her, took her belt, and sailed away.

On the return journey, Heracles dropped anchor at Troy. Apollo and Poseidon had recently built the walls of Troy for the Trojans, but their king, Laomedon, refused to pay them the wages that had been promised. Hence, Apollo inflicted a plague on the city, and Poseidon produced a sea monster to attack the Trojans. The monster rode waves onto the shore and snatched Trojans.

An oracle advised King Laomedon that he could rid the city of the monster only by sacrificing his daughter, Hesione. When Heracles arrived, Hesione was fastened to rocks on the shore. Heracles volunteered to kill the sea monster in return for the mares given to Laomedon by Zeus. These mares were compensation to Laomedon for his son, Ganymede, whom Zeus abducted.

Heracles killed the sea monster, but Laomedon refused to hand over the mares. Heracles sailed away, threatening to get revenge.

Heracles' tenth labor took him to the far west, where he had to capture the cattle of Geryon, a giant with three bodies joined at the waist. Geryon was accompanied by a herdsman and a two-headed dog. Heracles traveled west across Libya. When he finally crossed from Libya to Europe, he erected two great pillars. After this, he encountered and killed Geryon and took his cattle. He managed—with some difficulty—to drive the cattle back to Mycenae, where Eurystheus sacrificed them to Hera.

Eurystheus added two more labors since he felt that slaying the Hydra and cleansing the Augean stables should not count. The 11th labor was to go to Hyperborea, the land of the far north, to get the golden apples of the Hesperides (Daughters of the Evening). The apples were guarded by the four Hesperides and by a hundred-headed serpent. En route, Heracles encountered a Libyan king Antaeus, who used to kill strangers in wrestling matches. Antaeus gained strength when he was in contact with the earth because, as some say, he was a son of Gaea. Heracles killed him by holding him up in the air.

In Egypt, the king, Busiris, seized Heracles and tried to sacrifice him. There had been a famine in Egypt. A Cypriot seer prophesied that it would cease if the Egyptians sacrificed a foreigner every year. Busiris first sacrificed the seer and then kept up the custom with foreign travelers. At the altar, Heracles burst out of his bonds, and killed Busiris.

In the Caucasus Mountains, Heracles shot the eagle that was eating Prometheus's liver and released Prometheus. In return for Prometheus, Zeus accepted Chiron, who had agreed to die in his place.

In Hyperborea, acting on Prometheus's advice, Heracles asked Atlas to fetch the golden apples while he, Heracles, held up the sky. Atlas soon returned with the apples, but really did not want to resume holding up the sky. He volunteered to deliver the apples to Eurystheus. Heracles pretended to accept this arrangement, but asked Atlas to hold the sky momentarily while he put a cushion on his head. Atlas set the apples down, and received the sky. Heracles grabbed the apples and left.

The 12th—and final—labor was to bring Hades' dog, Cerberus, out of the underworld. Cerberus had three heads; his body was covered with snakes, and his tail was a serpent. Heracles entered the underworld at Taenarum in Laconia. Outside of Hades' gates, Theseus and his friend, Pirithous, were bound fast where they had been caught trying to abduct Persephone. Heracles freed Theseus, but was forced by an earthquake to abandon Pirithous.

Hades gave Heracles permission to take Cerberus, provided that he did not use any weapons. Heracles forced Cerberus into submission with a headlock, even though the snake in Cerberus's tail bit him.

After his labors, Heracles gave his wife, Megara, to Iolaus and went to Oechalia to seek the hand of Iole, daughter of King Eurytus. The king rejected him for fear that he would kill his children, as he had done in the past. Not long after, Iole's brother sought Heracles' help in looking for some stolen cattle. Heracles received him hospitably, but then went mad and killed him by throwing him off the walls of Tiryns.

After this murder, Heracles was afflicted with a dread disease. He sought help at the oracle of Delphi. When the priestess said that she could not help him, he began to plunder the temple and carry off the sacred tripod.[17] Apollo showed up to fight him, and Zeus threw a thunderbolt between them. Then, Heracles was given an oracle that he could be cured by being sold into slavery for three years.

Heracles' services were purchased by Omphale, queen of Lydia. At the end of three years, Heracles was cured. He then raised an army and sailed against Troy to get even with Laomedon. Telamon, the father of Ajax the Greater, was actually the first warrior in Heracles' army to break into Troy. Seeing this, Heracles was about to kill him so that he would not gain the reputation of being the superior soldier. Understanding the danger, Telamon began collecting stones. When Heracles paused to ask him what he was doing, Telamon said that he was building an altar in honor of "Heracles, the Glorious Victor." Heracles thanked him. He slew Laomedon and his sons, except for one who became known as Priam ("Bought") because Heracles allowed Princess Hesione to ransom him with her veil.

Heracles settled a series of scores on mainland Greece, making war on Augeas, Neleus of Pylos, and the Lacedaemonians. Then in the land of Calydon, he won the hand of the princess Deianira by defeating a rival suitor, the god of the Achelous River, in a wrestling match. The god assumed the shape of a bull during the fight. Heracles broke off one of his horns. Then, during a feast with his new father-in-law, Heracles accidentally killed a lad who was pouring water on his hands. Hence Heracles had to go into exile with his new bride. They planned to settle in Trachis.

En route to Trachis, they came to a river where the centaur, Nessus, ferried passengers across. He claimed that he was given the job by the gods because of his righteousness. Heracles crossed the river by himself but entrusted Deianira to Nessus. While Nessus was carrying her across, he tried to rape her. Hearing her scream, Heracles shot Nessus in the heart as he emerged from the water. Knowing that he was dying from the Hydra's poison on Heracles' arrow, Nessus told Deianira that she could make a love potion by mixing the blood from his wound with the semen that he had spilled on the ground. She collected some of these fluids and kept them with her.

In Trachis, Heracles raised an army to attack Oechalia and punish King Eurytus, Iole's father. He stormed the city, killing the king and his sons, and took Iole captive. Intending to offer sacrifice, he sent his herald, Lichas, home to Trachis to get fine clothing. Deianira learned about Iole from Lichas and smeared Nessus's supposed love charm on the tunic that was being packed for Heracles. As soon as Heracles put it on and warmed it with his body's heat, the poison of the Hydra began to eat into his skin. He lifted Lichas by his feet and threw him into the sea, killing him. When he tried to tear off the tunic, his flesh came with it. He was carried in misery to Trachis. When Deianira learned what happened, she hanged herself.

---

17   In ancient Greece, the term "tripod" referred to a bronze cauldron sitting on three legs. Such tripods were common utensils. For some reason, the tripod also became a symbol of Apollo. A certain sacred tripod was a revered object in Apollo's temple at Delphi.

Heracles ordered his eldest son, Hyllus, to marry Iole when he came of age. He proceeded to Mount Oeta near Trachis, built a pyre, and gave orders to set it on fire. No one would do so except Poeas,[18] a passing shepherd. In gratitude, Heracles gave him his bow and arrows.

While the pyre was burning, thunder sounded, and Heracles floated up to heaven. He was made immortal, reconciled with Hera, and married her daughter, Hebe (Youth).

34. The Death of Heracles

Source: Sophocles, *The Women of Trachis* (Classical Greek tragedy)

The long island of Euboea snakes along the eastern coast of Greece for approximately a hundred miles. Its southern tip lies opposite Athens. Its northern end, Cenaeum, juts toward the famous pass of Thermopylae, where 300 Spartans fought to the death against a million Persians, so it is said. Thermopylae was in the territory of Malis, whose chief city was Trachis, next to Mount Oeta. In myth, Heracles finally died on top of Mount Oeta. At the time, his family was residing in Trachis. The events leading to his death grew out of a war that he was carrying on against a city in southern Euboea, Oechalia, ruled by King Eurytus. The cause of the war was Eurytus's daughter, Iole. At war's end, the victorious Heracles, traveling north toward Trachis, offered sacrifice at Cenaeum, and there fell victim to the deceits of a dead enemy.

Heracles' wife, Deianira, stands outside their house in Trachis, lamenting while her nursemaid listens. As a girl, she was courted by a river god, Achelous, who visited her father in three different shapes: a bull, a serpent, and a man's body with a bull's head. She was terrified that she would have to marry him, but Heracles appeared and won her hand by beating Achelous in a wrestling match. Now Deianira is always worried about Heracles. They have children, whom he rarely sees. He is always away laboring for another man. Since he killed Iphitus, son of Eurytus, they have resided in Trachis. Heracles has been gone for more than a year, and he left a written tablet, implying that he might be in terrible danger.

The nursemaid suggests that Deianira send her eldest son, Hyllus, to look for Heracles. Deianira calls to him and makes that request. Hyllus replies that he already knows his father's whereabouts. For the year past, Heracles was a servant of a Lydian woman. Free now, he is in Euboea, making war on Oechalia. Deianira reveals that the prophecy Heracles left said that he would either die at this time or have a peaceful life. Hyllus says he will hurry to Euboea to learn his father's fate.

---

18   Poeas bequeathed Heracles' weapons to his son, Philoctetes, who used them in the Trojan War.

A group of Trachinian women enter, singing a song to comfort Deianira. She longs for her husband's return, they say, yet he has survived countless adventures in the past. It is wrong for Deianira to despair.

Deianira says that she has never been so worried. In the past, Heracles was always confident. This time, he explained to her how she ought to divide his property after his death. He said that his fate would be settled in a year and three months. At that time, he would either die or live in peace ever after. Now a year and three months have passed, and Deianira is frantic.

A messenger arrives with good news. Heracles, he says, has been victorious in war. Word of his victory was brought to Malis by his herald, Lichas. Lichas himself has been delayed by the people of Malis, who surround him in the meadow where he made his announcement. The messenger says that he hurried ahead with the good news for Deianira, hoping to profit from her gratitude.

Lichas arrives with a group of captive women from Oechalia. He says that Heracles is still in Euboea, arranging a sacrifice to Zeus. Heracles, he adds, spent a year working as a slave for Omphale, a Lydian queen. He had previously visited Eurytus, who insulted him, got drunk, and threw him out of the house. Later, when Eurytus's son, Iphitus, came to Tiryns looking for stray horses, Heracles seized him unawares and threw him off a cliff to his death. This was the reason that Zeus forced Heracles to be a woman's slave for a year. It was Heracles' use of guile that angered Zeus. After a year of servitude, Heracles swore that he would punish the person responsible for his disgrace by enslaving his family. Hence, he has now conquered Oechalia and is sending these captives to be his slaves.

Deianira says she rejoices that Heracles is alive but cannot help feeling sorry for the captive women. She singles out Iole and asks who her parents are, since she seems noble. Lichas says that he has no information about her and that she has not spoken throughout the entire journey. Deianira suggests that they all go inside. She doesn't want the captives to suffer unnecessarily.

As Lichas and the captive women enter the house, the messenger detains Deianira. Lichas, he says, did not tell her the same story that he told the people of Malis. To them, he said that Heracles had fought the whole war in order to obtain the girl that Deianira was asking about. She is the daughter of Eurytus. Heracles had tried to persuade Eurytus to let him have Iole as a secret lover. When Eurytus refused, Heracles fabricated the war against Oechalia. It is not likely, he says, that Iole will actually be a slave in the house, since Heracles is madly in love with her.

When Lichas emerges from the house, Deianira asks him again about Iole. When he denies knowing her, the messenger confronts him with the statements that he made in public. Lichas pretends that the messenger is mad. Deianira urges him to tell the truth. She says that she does not blame her husband or the girl, since "Love rules even the gods as he pleases."

Lichas admits that the messenger told the truth: Heracles conquered Oechalia because he loved Iole, and he never concealed this fact. Lichas took it upon himself to try to hide the truth from her. Deianira says that she will treat Iole kindly, and asks Lichas to return with her to the house, while messages and gifts for Heracles are prepared.

The women sing about the fight between Achelous and Heracles for the hand of Deianira as an example of the power of Aphrodite.

Deianira emerges. She wishes to speak to the women confidentially. She says that she cannot stand the thought of sharing Heracles with Iole, lying "under one sheet waiting for his embrace." She adds that Iole is young, she is just reaching her prime, while Deianira's beauty is fading. Men favor fresh blossoms—and turn away from wilting flowers.

Deianira says, however, that she has a way of dealing with the situation, a gift that she received from Nessus, the centaur. That creature used to ferry people across a river. When Deianira and Heracles were first married, they arrived at its banks, and Nessus carried Deianira across. As he did so, he began to touch her lustfully. Deianira cried out, and Heracles immediately shot Nessus with an arrow. Dying, Nessus told Deianira to collect his blood, especially the portions that were black from the Hydra's poison on Heracles' arrows. He said that it would be a charm to prevent Heracles from loving another woman. Deianira has kept some of this blood in a bronze urn ever since. Now, following Nessus's directions, she has put it on a robe, which she has with her in a wooden box. She tells the women that she will use this charmed robe to win Heracles back from Iole unless they think that the action would be rash. The chorus says that if she thinks it will work, she should try it.

Lichas enters. Deianira gives him the robe as a gift for Heracles. Lichas leaves; Deianira returns to the house.

The women sing. They are looking forward joyfully to Heracles' return.

Deianira enters. Now she is worried about Nessus's charm. She smeared some of his blood onto the robe with a piece of wool and then threw the wool away on the ground. She was shocked later when she saw that the wool had turned to dust in the sunlight, and a purple liquid was oozing out of the ground where it lay. She wonders what motive Nessus could have had to help her. She also recognizes that the Hydra's blood is a deadly poison, which even injured the divine Chiron. She is afraid that she has accidentally killed her husband.

Hyllus enters, cursing his mother. He announces that she has murdered Heracles and describes what happened. Hyllus was joyously reunited with his father in Euboea, where he was preparing a grand sacrifice. Soon, Lichas arrived with Deianira's gift. Heracles put the robe on and began the slaughter of the cattle before the high flames on the altar. He was in a festive mood at first but suddenly began to sweat, overcome by heat and shooting pains that grew ever worse. The robe ate into his flesh. He called to Lichas, demanding to know who was responsible. Lichas told him that the gift came from Deianira alone. In a spasm of pain, Heracles grabbed Lichas by his foot and hurled him through the air. Lichas struck a rock jutting out of the sea, shattering his skull. Heracles was writhing and shrieking, but finally he collapsed on the ground, crying weakly. Seeing Hyllus, he asked him to bring him back to the mainland on a boat.

Hyllus did so, and Heracles will soon be brought to the palace. As for Deianira, Hyllus says, he curses her for "killing the best of all the men on earth." Deianira leaves in silence.

The women sing a song lamenting the situation.

The nursemaid emerges from the house, accompanied by the sound of shrieking and wailing from within. Deianira, she says, has started her final journey. She had secretly watched Hyllus get a mattress for carrying his father home. Then she wandered through the house in tears, handling familiar objects and gazing fondly on her favorite servants. In time, she hurried into the bedroom, spread sheets on the bed that she shared with Heracles, sat on the bed, said farewell to her wedding chamber, and undid her gown, baring her whole left side. At this point, the nurse ran to get Hyllus. When they return, they find that she had cut open her whole side, exposing her liver. Hyllus wails. He learns from the servants that Deianira never intended to kill Heracles and realizes that his angry words drove her to suicide. He throws himself on her, sobbing. The nurse opens the doors, exposing Hyllus with his dead mother in his arms.

Heracles is brought in by a group of servants, led by an old man. Hyllus comes forward. The old man warns him not to wake Heracles up, but it is too late. Heracles cries out in pain and asks why no one will end his suffering by removing his head from his body. The old man asks Hyllus to do so, but Hyllus says that it is beyond his power, or anyone else's, to end Heracles' pain. Heracles then demands that Hyllus bring Deianira to him so that she can be tortured for her crime. He cannot believe that he has been conquered by an unarmed woman.

Hyllus urges Heracles to set his anger aside. He tells him that Deianira has killed herself and had acted in ignorance, trying to save their marriage, using Nessus's blood as a charm. Heracles answers that he now knows for certain that he is dying. Many years ago, Zeus advised him that he would fall at the hands of an enemy who was already dead. Nessus has fulfilled that prophecy.

Heracles asks Hyllus to take him to the top of Mount Oeta, build a funeral pyre of oak and pine, and set him free by lighting it. Hyllus agrees to everything except actually lighting the fire. Heracles relents and says that it will be enough to take him there and build the pyre. He says he has a second, smaller favor. Hyllus agrees and is shocked to learn that Heracles wants him to marry Iole. Heracles says that only Hyllus should have a woman who has lain with him, Heracles. Hyllus tries to refuse since it would horrible for him to sleep with the woman responsible for his mother's death. When Heracles says that it is his command and calls the gods to witness it, Hyllus finally gives in. Heracles asks to be taken to the mountain before his pains return. He is carried away.

Hyllus speaks to the Trachinian women as he watches his father depart: "You see how little compassion the gods have shown in all that has happened. They who are called our fathers, who begot us, can look upon such suffering. What is here now is pitiful for us and shameful for the gods. You have seen a terrible death and many strange agonies, and there is nothing here that is not Zeus."

Source: Euripides, *The Children of Heracles* (Classical Greek tragedy)

Thucydides (2.67.4) reports that in 430 B.C., at the beginning of the war between Athens and Sparta (the approximate date of this play's composition), five Spartan ambassadors were captured by the Athenians en route to Persia, brought to Athens, and immediately executed without a trial.

Heracles' nephew, Iolaus, now old, explains that he has been the protector of Heracles' children for a long time. Eurystheus, king of Mycenae, is resolved to kill Iolaus and the children. They fled Mycenae and have been chased from land to land. Iolaus has now led them to Marathon, hoping that the ruler of Athens will protect them. He has taken refuge at the altar of Zeus with Heracles' younger sons. Alcmene and Heracles' daughters are inside the temple. Hyllus and other older boys are seeking help in other places.

Copreus, Eurystheus's herald, arrives, commands Iolaus to return to Mycenae with his wards, and scuffles with him. A chorus of the elders of Marathon arrives and rebukes Copreus for mistreating old Iolaus. They say that he must consult their ruler, Demophon, son of Theseus. Demophon appears on cue.

Copreus says that Iolaus and the children are citizens of Argos, who have been duly condemned to death. He is claiming them on behalf of King Eurystheus. If they cooperate, they will enjoy the benefits of friendship with Mycenae. Resistance means total war.

Iolaus says that the Argives have no claim on them. Athens is not the sort of city to surrender refugees. Demophon agrees, saying that he will protect the refugees, because they are at an altar and are connected by blood with the Athenians. He also wants to protect his own prestige. Copreus finally goes away, saying that Eurystheus is waiting with a great army and will punish Athens. Demophon leaves to take care of defending the city against the Argive attack.

The chorus sings that Athens will not be intimidated. The Argive king, they say, is acting shamelessly.

Demophon comes back looking glum. He has been consulting the oracles, and all of them agree that a noble maiden must be sacrificed to Persephone to secure a victory. Demophon could not ask an Athenian citizen to make this sacrifice. He does not know what to do.

A maiden, one of Heracles' daughters, Macaria by name, emerges from the temple and asks what is happening. Hearing of the need for a human sacrifice, she instantly volunteers. It would be shameful, she says, if they were unable to save themselves because of their fear of a single death. Iolaus suggests that all the girls draw lots, but Macaria rejects that idea. She feels that it is glorious to die voluntarily, but not to do so because one loses a contest. She says good-bye to her brothers, bidding them to be well, and to care for Iolaus and Alcmene. She says she hopes that there is no afterlife because otherwise there would never be an end to troubles. As she leaves, Iolaus nearly faints from grief.

The chorus sings briefly about the mutability of fate and how Macaria has won renown through her courage.

A servant belonging to Hyllus arrives with news. The servant says that Hyllus has come to Attica with an army. They have joined forces with Demophon's army. Hearing this, Iolaus announces his intention to join in the battle. The servant ridicules the idea, since Iolaus is old and feeble, but Iolaus insists, ordering the servant to get a set of armor from the temple. Alcmene and the chorus try to dissuade him. The servant arrives with the armor, puts it on him, and has to help him walk in the direction of the battle lines.

Time passes, as the chorus sings a song glorifying Athens. Another servant arrives with news of victory by the Athenians and the refugees. He tells how the respective generals harangued their troops, sacrifices were made, the trumpets sounded, and the two sides finally clashed. The Athenians were pushed back for a while but then gained the upper hand. Iolaus begged to be given a chariot, and set his course straight for Eurystheus's chariot. This much the servant saw; the rest is based on second-hand reports. It is said that Iolaus prayed to Zeus and Hebe to get his youth back, just for a day. Then two stars appeared by his chariot, which was enveloped in a dark cloud. When the haze cleared, he was young and muscular. He caught Eurystheus at Sciron's rock, took him prisoner, and is sending him back in chains.

The chorus sings for joy. Guards bring in Eurystheus in chains. Alcmene scolds him for all the misery he caused her family, and says that killing is too good for him. The chorus says that it is against Athenian law to kill a prisoner of war. Alcmene says that she is determined to kill him. Eurystheus speaks up, saying that he will not beg for his life. He says that Hera involved him in the feud with Heracles—and once it began, he just did everything he could to eliminate his enemies. They should have killed him in battle. The person who kills him now will be polluted, but he himself is indifferent to life or death.

Alcmene proposes to kill him and then relinquish his body to the city of Athens for burial. In her view, that will satisfy their religious scruples. Eurystheus says that there is an ancient oracle that he would be buried in Athens and provide protection when they are attacked by the descendants of the children of Heracles.[19] The fact that their descendants will attack Athens shows their true natures, he says.

Alcmene orders the guard to take Eurytheus away to kill him. The chorus goes along, saying, "Take away this man. I want to make sure that our kings are cleared of all responsibility in this."

---

19   Athens' rivals, the Spartans, were supposedly descended from the children of Heracles.

36. The Origin of the Golden Fleece

Source: Apollodorus, *The Library*, I.9.1 (Hellenistic)

Athamas, king of Boeotia, married a goddess, Nephele. They had a son, Phrixus, and a daughter, Helle. Athamas then divorced Nephele and married a mortal woman, Ino, who hated her stepchildren. She caused a famine by persuading the women of Boeotia to roast the seeds. When the crop failed, Athamas consulted the oracle of Delphi. Ino persuaded the messengers to say that the oracle required the sacrifice of Phrixus. The Boeotians forced Athamas to arrange the sacrifice, but Nephele appeared in the nick of time. She arrived with a flying golden ram that carried her son and daughter out of harm's way.

The children flew north. As they approached the Black Sea, Helle slipped off and was drowned. The water where she disappeared was named the Hellespont (sea of Helle) in her honor. Phrixus came to the land of Colchis, where he was hospitably received by the king Aeetes. Phrixus married one of Aeetes' daughters, and they had four sons. He sacrificed the ram to Zeus and gave the fleece to Aeetes, who nailed it to an oak tree in a grove sacred to Ares.

37. The Voyage of the Argo

Source: Apollonius of Rhodes, *The Argonautica* (Hellenistic)

Jason's uncle Pelias has usurped the throne of the kingdom of Iolcus from Jason's father, Aeson. Jason has been raised in the wilderness by Chiron, the centaur. Reaching adulthood, Jason heads for Iolcus, hoping to regain the throne. He loses a sandal crossing a river on the way. Pelias has heard an oracle telling him to beware of the man with one sandal. He decides to get rid of Jason by ordering him to recover the golden fleece, the treasure kept by King Aeetes in the kingdom of Colchis on the shores of the Black Sea.

Jason accepts the assignment. With Athena's help, he builds a ship called the *Argo*, and recruits heroes from all over Greece—notably, Meleager, later famous for organizing the Calydonian boar hunt; Helen's brothers, Polydeuces and Castor; Heracles (accompanied by his boyfriend Hylas); Peleus, the father of Achilles; and Zetes and Calais, wing-footed sons of Boreas, the North Wind.

The *Argo*'s first stop is on the manless island of Lemnos. A year earlier, the men of the island began neglecting their wives in favor of Thracian girls captured in raids. The Lemnian women retaliated by killing them all, husbands and Thracian girlfriends. Only Princess Hypsipyle spared her father, the king, and helped him escape by sea in a wooden chest. Hypsipyle welcomes Jason and the Argonauts, inviting them to settle on the island. Jason refuses, but he and his men participate in a merry revel with the women. Only Heracles remains aloof. The revel continues until Heracles appears, and sarcastically suggests to the drunken Argonauts that they abandon their quest. The embarrassed heroes troop back to the *Argo*.

Next comes the land of the Doliones, where a young, newlywed king greets the Argonauts hospitably. Six-armed giants live in the neighboring hills. They never bother the Doliones, but they do attack the *Argo*. Led by Heracles, the Argonauts slaughter them. They resume their voyage, but contrary winds at night drive them back to the land of the Doliones. They don't know where they are, and in the darkness, the Doliones mistake them for pirates. A battle ensues and the young king is killed. When dawn arrives, everyone involved is full of remorse. The young king's widow hangs herself. The Argonauts delay their journey long enough to attend the funerals.

Back at sea, the Argonauts compete to see who can keep rowing the longest. Eventually, only Heracles is left, moving the whole ship with one oar. Then his oar breaks. The Argonauts land and make camp. While Heracles is off in the woods fashioning a new oar from a pine tree, his boyfriend, Hylas, looks for water. He is seized by a water nymph and dragged under to be her husband. Heracles hears his cries and lurches around the woods looking for him. The other Argonauts happen to rise and set sail early the next morning. They are far out to sea before they notice Heracles' absence. They are about to go back for him when the sea god, Glaucus, appears and tells them that he is not fated to complete the journey.

The next kingdom is ruled by the cruel Amycus, who insists on boxing with—and always killing—travelers who pass through his realm. Polydeuces fights on behalf of the Argonauts, and kills Amycus with a blow to the temple after a long struggle.

Now the Argonauts visit Phineus. He is a prophet being punished by Zeus for revealing too much of the future. Whenever Phineus tries to eat, monstrous bird-women, known as Harpies, snatch most of his food, spraying the remnants with an unbearable odor. This time when the Harpies attack, Zetes and Calais, Boreas's flying sons, drive them away. Only the intervention of Iris, goddess of the rainbow, prevents them from killing the Harpies. They are ordered to leave Phineus alone in the future. The grateful Phineus tells the Argonauts how to deal with the Clashing Rocks and advises them to seek help on the island of Ares.

The Argonauts quickly come to the Clashing Rocks. As Phineus advised, they send a dove flying through them first. He just makes it, losing only a tail feather. This is a good omen, so the *Argo* sails through. Between the rocks, it is buffeted by great waves and is about to be crushed. Athena appears, and pushes the vessel through to safety. The rocks knock off a stern ornament, nothing more.

Next comes a series of brief, strange adventures. The Argonauts are temporarily discouraged when their prophet is killed by a boar, their pilot by illness. They land in a kingdom of hostile Amazons but get away before they are attacked. They visit the Chalybes, legendary iron miners; a second tribe, whose men experience labor pains when their wives give birth; and a third, whose members perform sexual intercourse and other private acts in public, and vice versa. After this they come to the island of Ares. It is infested by birds who drop steely sharp feathers on intruders. Because of

Phineus's advice, they go ashore, making a canopy out of their shields. On the shore, they meet four shipwrecked sons of Phrixus, who had been trying to sail to Greece. (Phrixus was the Greek who brought the golden fleece to Aeetes in the first place.) Grateful for being saved, the four sons become Jason's loyal helpers with knowledge of the situation in Colchis.

Shortly afterward, the *Argo* drops anchor in the Phasis river, hiding among reeds. Colchis lies a few miles upstream.

On Olympus, Hera and Athena, who are well disposed toward Jason, ask Aphrodite to help him, by having Aeetes' daughter, Medea, fall in love with him. Aphrodite makes a deal with Cupid, who is playing dice with Ganymede. For his help, she promises him a toy that once belonged to baby Zeus: a golden ball that leaves a trail of fire in the air, like a comet.

Jason, the sons of Phrixus, and a couple of other Argonauts make their way to Aeetes' palace, where they are given a friendly welcome. Cupid sneaks into the crowd, shoots Medea with an invisible arrow, and flies away.

After dinner, Phrixus's eldest son explains Jason's mission. The request for the golden fleece infuriates Aeetes, but Jason is so politely persistent that Aeetes finally offers him a deal. Jason can have the fleece, if he performs a task that Aeetes himself does on a regular basis. He has a pair of fire-breathing bulls with bronze hooves. He yokes them, plows a large field, and sows dragon's teeth in it. Fierce armed warriors spring up in the field, and Aeetes kills them. He does this all in a single day. If Jason can do the same, he will be deemed worthy of the fleece. Jason is stunned—but finally accepts the offer.

Back on the *Argo*, Jason consults with his comrades. One of Phrixus's sons suggests a meeting between his mother's sister, Medea, and Jason. He explains that Medea is a priestess of Hecate with magical powers, and might be helpful.

When Phrixus's son asks her to meet with Jason, Medea is reluctant, but finally gives in to her romantic feelings. She gets some *prometheum* from her casket. An ointment made from a flower that grew from Prometheus's blood, it makes a person invulnerable for a day. With this, she leaves for the temple of Hecate to meet Jason. Jason sets off in the same direction, magically beautified by Hera. At first, he is accompanied by a seer named Mopsus, but a divinely inspired crow tells him that it would be better if Jason and Medea were alone.

In the temple, Medea gives Jason the prometheum. The pair are attracted to each other, and drag the conversation out with elaborate compliments. The next morning, Jason arrives for his ordeal, protected by the ointment. He manages to yoke the bulls, plow the field, and plant the dragon's teeth. The armed men appear on cue. Jason throws a boulder among them and hides. They start killing each other. Jason rushes into their midst to finish the slaughter, killing some while they are still rooted in the ground. Aeetes returns to his palace, furious.

Terrified at what she has done, Medea runs to the Argonauts' encampment. Jason promises to marry her. They all get onboard the *Argo* and set sail for the grove where the fleece is kept. It is guarded by a giant serpent. Medea puts him to sleep with a song and a potion sprinkled on his eyes. Jason snatches the fleece from the an oak tree.

The *Argo* now flees from Colchian territory, with Aeetes' men in hot pursuit. Remembering that Phineus told them to take a different route home, they head for the mouth of the Danube. There, the *Argo* is overtaken by a part of the Colchian fleet led by Apsyrtus, Medea's brother. He agrees to let Jason keep the fleece, provided that he leave Medea herself in a nearby temple of Artemis until her case is decided by arbiters. Medea is vehemently opposed to this arrangement, but Jason says that the local population supports the Colchians and is reluctant to reject it. At this point, Medea takes charge.

Pretending that she wants to betray Jason, Medea sends word to her brother to meet her alone in the temple of Artemis. When Apsyrtus gets there, Jason is waiting in ambush. He cuts Apsyrtus down, as Medea averts her eyes. In a ritual to avoid punishment for a treacherous murder, Jason cuts off Apsyrtus's arms and legs, licks blood from his wounds three times, and spits it out. Medea raises a torch as a signal to the *Argo*'s crew, which immediately attacks Apsyrtus's ship and kills its entire crew. The *Argo* flees the area under cover of darkness. The local inhabitants are outraged and want to chase the Argonauts, but Hera prevents this with a thunderstorm.

The *Argo* sails west along the Danube. During a storm, the ship's beam speaks. It was made from a sacred oak at the oracle of Zeus in Dodona in northern Greece. Because of the murder of Apsyrtus, it says, the Argonauts have to be purified by the goddess Circe. Further rivers[20] bring the Argo to the Mediterranean west of Italy and Aeaea, the island of Circe. She performs the needed ritual.

The Argonauts next pass the Sirens' island. When their singing starts to distract the crew, Orpheus neutralizes it by playing his lyre. Next comes a triple threat posed by Scylla and Charybdis, who guard either side of a narrow channel—the only alternative, the Wandering Rocks. Hera has enlisted the help of Thetis and her sisters, the Nereids, in protecting the *Argo*. Thetis was married to Peleus and has given birth to Achilles. (Peleus and Thetis are now separated, however. Thetis had hoped to make Achilles immortal by immersing him in fire. Peleus interrupted her while she was performing the ritual, and she stormed out, never to return.) The *Argo* sails toward the Wandering Rocks—and certain disaster. Thetis and her sisters scramble up on the rocks, pick up the ship, and toss it through the air from rock to rock until it plops into open water.

The *Argo* drops anchor at Phaeacia[21] next. Colchian ships arrive at the same time and demand the surrender of Medea from the Phaeacian king, Alcinoos. In bed that night, Alcinoos reveals his decision to his queen, Arete. He will hand Medea over, unless she is married to Jason. Arete has been charmed by Medea. When Alcinoos dozes off, she sends a message to Jason, telling him to get married at once. The next morning, the

---

20   The Argonauts' supposed route is geographically impossible.

21   According to Homer's *Odyssey*, the Phaeacians are the hospitable people who finally enable Odysseus to get home to Ithaca, after ten years of wandering.

wedding ends just as Alcinoos announces his decision. The Colchians are afraid to go back to Aeetes empty-handed. So they settle in Phaeacia.

Back at sea, the *Argo* gets within sight of Greece but is blown off course and ends up in the Syrtes, the dreaded shallows off the coast of northern Africa. Libyan nymphs appear and advise Jason to "pay your mother back for carrying you in her womb." Jason figures out that the *Argo* is his figurative mother and that the Argonauts now have to carry it. Hence, they land and carry the ship across the desert. They finally arrive at the saltwater lake Tritonis, the home of the merman Triton. Searching for fresh water, they come to the garden of Hesperides, goddesses who guard golden apples. In fact, some of their apples have just recently been stolen by Heracles. They direct Jason to a freshwater spring that Heracles created by kicking a rock.

The Argonauts set sail on Tritonis, and are finally guided back into the Mediterranean by Triton. They quickly arrive at Crete, but a giant named Talos prevents their landing by pelting them with boulders. He is the last surviving member of the age of bronze. His only vulnerability is an exposed vein in his ankle. Volunteering to deal with him, Medea stands on the deck singing deadly chants, until Talos grazes his ankle on a sharp rock. His divine blood, or *ichor*, flows out. He collapses and dies.

Off Crete, the *Argo* is shrouded in total darkness. Jason prays to Apollo, who appears and lights a path to a tiny island, which the Argonauts name Anaphe (Revelation). From there, they enjoy smooth sailing back to Iolcus.

38. The Death of Jason's Uncle Pelias

Source: Apollodorus, *The Library*, I.9.27 (Hellenistic)

While Jason and the Argonauts were away, his evil uncle Pelias forced Jason's father, Aeson, to commit suicide by drinking the blood of a sacrificial bull. Jason's mother cursed Pelias and hanged herself. Pelias then murdered her orphaned son, Jason's brother.

When Jason returned, he surrendered the fleece to Pelias. He sailed to the Isthmus of Corinth with the Argonauts and dedicated the *Argo* to Poseidon. He then asked Medea to help him punish Pelias.

Medea went to Iolcus, and demonstrated her magical powers to Pelias's daughters by cutting up an old ram into small pieces, boiling them in a cauldron, and producing a young lamb. With Medea's encouragement, the girls cut up Pelias and boiled the pieces in the same cauldron, but he did not recover. His remains were buried by his son, Acastus, who was also one of the Argonauts. Supported by the citizens of Iolcus, Acastus banished Jason and Medea.

Source: Euripides, *Medea* (Classical Greek tragedy)

Jason and Medea are living in exile in the kingdom of Corinth, which is ruled by a king named Creon.[22] Outside their house, Medea's elderly nurse describes the situation. She says that she wishes Jason had never come to Colchis. He is now planning to divorce Medea, and marry the daughter of King Creon. Medea is furious and may do something desperate.

A pedagogue enters, escorting Medea's two sons, and asks the nurse why she is standing outside talking to herself. She says that she is crazy with grief. They are interrupted by the sound of Medea crying inside.

A chorus of Corinthian women arrives to visit Medea. Medea emerges. She puts her suffering in the broad context of the sorry lot of women. A woman purchases a master in the form of a husband with her dowry. If he is bad, there is no escape since divorce ruins a woman's reputation. When a man is tired of family life, he can seek distractions outside the home. A woman cannot. People say that women have easy lives, since they do not have to go to war, but Medea says that she would rather stand in battle three times than give birth once. Her speech wins over the chorus, which promises not to give away any of her secrets.

King Creon enters, proclaiming that Medea must leave the city immediately—because frankly, he fears her. Medea begs him for just one day to get ready. Creon finally gives in against his better judgment. He says that his lack of a "tyrannical will" has often caused him problems. When he is gone, Medea confides to the chorus that his delay will enable her to kill him, his daughter, and Jason. All she needs now is a safe place to escape to.

Jason arrives to offer Medea money to help her in exile. She refuses, and they quarrel. Jason says that Medea brought the exile on herself by her angry talk. His debt to her, he says, is not as great as she claims. She saved his life in Colchis only because Aphrodite made her love him. He has done a lot for her by bringing her to the civilized land of Greece. The only reason he wants to marry the princess is to provide financial security for their children. Medea is just jealous. Like most women, Jason concludes, she is obsessed with sex.

When Jason storms out, King Aegeus of Athens happens to drop by. He is returning from Delphi with an oracle on how to cure his childlessness: he was told not to "open his wineskin's mouth" until he gets back home. He is taking a detour to Troezen to ask the holy king Pittheus for an interpretation. When Medea tells him about her divorce, he is sympathetic and offers to give her refuge in Athens if she should ever need a place to stay. When he leaves, Medea is jubilant. She now tells the chorus that she will kill the

---

22   Not to be confused with Creon of Thebes, Oedipus's brother-in-law and uncle.

princess and murder her own sons, leaving Jason with nothing. Then she will live in Athens. The chorus begs her to change her mind.

Instead Medea sends for Jason and pretends that she is now sorry for losing her temper. Though she will go into exile, she says, she wonders if the children might be allowed to stay in Corinth. Perhaps Jason could persuade the princess to intercede with the king? To help, she has made a dress and a crown for the children to give to her. Jason agrees and leaves for the palace with the children, their pedagogue, and Medea's gifts.

Soon the pedagogue and children return. The pedagogue reports that the request has been granted. To his bewilderment, this distresses Medea. She dismisses him, keeping her children with her, and delivers a soliloquy in which she wavers on the question of whether she can actually kill them. At one point, she has apparently decided not to. Then the thought of her enemies laughing at her makes her see that killing her sons is the only course open to her. She takes the boys inside the house.

There is a brief choral song on the topic of the worries and sorrows of people with children.

Medea emerges from the house, saying that she is anxiously awaiting news from the palace. A breathless messenger arrives from there. He tells Medea to flee because she has committed an awful crime. Medea demands to learn what happened in detail. The messenger reports that the princess sneered when she first saw the children but was delighted by their gifts, primping in front of a mirror. As she was doing so, she suddenly sickened and sat down on a couch. The color drained from her face, her eyes rolled, her mouth foamed. Then the princess started screaming. Her crown burst into flames, and the dress ate into her flesh. She rose, shaking her head to loosen the crown, but that only fanned the flames. She finally collapsed and died on the floor, scarcely recognizable. Her father arrived, knelt next to her, and kissed her. "*Oimoi*!" he cried. "I wish that I could die with you, my child!"

Then he tried to rise, but found that the gown was sticking to him like ivy to a tree, tearing his flesh. A "horrifying wrestling match" ensued. The old man struggled, but could not free himself. At last, he too gave up and died.

Medea runs into her house. Cries are heard from within. "*Oimoi*! What shall I do to escape Mother's hands?" "I know not, dearest brother. We are being murdered!"

Jason arrives "to protect his sons." Medea appears above the stage in a flying chariot, a gift from her grandfather, Helius. She holds the corpses of her sons. She and Jason trade insults and accusations. Refusing to let Jason touch his sons or have any role in their burial, she flies off toward Athens. As she disappears, the chorus chants, "God finds a way to bring to pass the unexpected."

40. The Early Kings of Athens

Source: Apollodorus's Library, 3.186–190 (Hellenistic).

The earth-born Cecrops was the first king of Athens. He was succeeded by Cranaus, Amphictyon, and Erichthonius. The last was the offspring of Hephaestus and Athena in the following manner. Athena went to Hephaestus to have some weapons made. Being neglected by his wife, Aphrodite, Hephaestus was aroused by the sight of Athena. He chased her, and she ran away. He finally caught up to her with great difficulty since he was lame. In the ensuing struggle, he ended up spilling his semen on her leg. Disgusted, Athena wiped it off with a piece of wool (*erion* in Greek), which she tossed away so that it fell on the earth (*chthon* in Greek). As a result, Erichthonius came into being.

Athena put the infant Erichthonius in a sealed basket, and gave him to the daughters of Cecrops, with strict instructions not to look inside. Opening the basket out of curiosity, they saw a serpent wound around the baby. They were either killed by the serpent or went mad and committed suicide by jumping off the acropolis. Erichthonius was then raised by Athena in her temple.

When Erichthonius grew up, he overthrew Amphictyon to become the fourth king of Athens. Among other things, he established the great quadrennial festival, the Panathenaea, in honor of Athena.

When Erichthonius died, he was succeeded by his son, Pandion.

41. Procne and Philomela

Source: Ovid, *Metamorphoses*, 6.418–678 (Roman)

During Pandion's reign, Athens is besieged by barbarian invaders. The city is saved by the forces of an ally, King Tereus of Thrace. In gratitude, Pandion allows Tereus to marry his daughter, Procne.She leaves Athens to live in Thrace with her husband, and soon she bears him a son, Itys.

After five years of marriage, Procne asks Tereus to bring her beloved sister, Philomela, to Thrace for a visit. Tereus consents and goes to Athens to arrange the visit. When he meets Philomela, he is overcome by lust. Secretly adopting a new plan, he convinces Pandion to send Philomela back to Thrace with him on his ship.

When Tereus and Philomela arrive in Thrace, he drags her into a house in the woods and rapes her. She is outraged and vows to denounce his terrible crime. In fear and anger, Tereus draws his sword and locks Philomela's hands in chains behind her back. Philomela offers him her neck, expecting and even hoping that he will kill her. Instead, he seizes her tongue with a pincers and cuts it off. Then as her tongue writhes and palpates on the floor, Tereus rapes her again and again. He finally leaves her in the house with a guard.

Back in his palace, Tereus tells Procne that her sister died on the journey. A year passes. Philomela finally devises a way to communicate with the outside world. She weaves her story into a tapestry and instructs a serving woman with gestures to take it to the queen.

When Procne sees the tapestry, she understands what has happened. It is the night when Thracian women hold a Bacchic revel outdoors. Procne leads the maenads to the house in the country. They seize Philomela, and bring her back to the palace. There, the sisters are trying to think of appropriate revenge when Procne's young son, Itys—the image of his father—enters the room. Despite her maternal feelings, Procne is overcome with rage. She asks herself, "Why should this boy make pretty speeches while my sister is mute." She and Philomela kill Itys and boil his flesh.

The next day, Procne invites Tereus to a feast. Tereus eats heartily and then calls for Itys. "You are keeping him inside," Procne says. Then Philomela jumps out of a hiding place with Itys's head in her hands. Tereus charges the women to kill them, but they are all transformed into birds. Tereus becomes a hoopoe. The women become birds. Each has some red plumage from the blood she spilled.

Sorrow over this event shortened King Pandion's life. He was succeeded by Erechtheus, who had four sons and four daughters. One of the daughters, Orithyia, was abducted by Boreas, the North Wind.

42. Cephalus and Procris

Source: Ovid, *Metamorphoses*, 7.690–862 (Roman)

Orithyia's sister, Procris, marries Cephalus, a prince of Phocis, the district in which Delphi is located. Cephalus is an avid hunter. One day, Aurora (Dawn) sees him hunting and carries him off to be her lover. Cephalus, however, loves Procris, and never stops thinking about her—or talking about her. Finally, the exasperated Aurora releases him, but she predicts that Cephalus will live to regret his marriage to Procris.

Aurora's warning and her own lustful behavior lead Cephalus to wonder about Procris's fidelity. With the help of Aurora, he disguises himself as a stranger and tests Procris by trying to seduce her with costly gifts. Procris rejects his advances. Cephalus keeps increasing the promised gifts until at last she seems to waver. Then he reveals his true identity—and calls her false. Ashamed and angry, Procris runs off to the woods to live with Diana.

In a short time, Cephalus misses her. He begs for forgiveness and admits that he was wrong and would have failed a similar test. Procris returns, and brings two gifts for Cephalus that she has obtained from Diana: the swiftest of all hunting dogs, and a javelin that never misses its target.

The dog displays its ability when a monstrous fox appears in Theban territory. Cephalus and the dog are recruited to kill the fox. When the fox appears, Cephalus unleashes his dog. He takes off so quickly that he seems to have vanished, leaving only footprints behind. Fox and dog race across the plain until they are suddenly frozen, both changed to marble. Some god has willed that neither should ever be vanquished.

Cephalus's javelin, however, leads to tragedy. Though he loves his wife, he goes hunting every morning. Afterward, he relaxes in cool valleys. He develops the habit of talking to the breeze, *aura* in Latin. "O aura," he says, "come and comfort me. Cool my heat."

One day, somebody overhears Cephalus talking to the breeze, assumes that he has a lover, and tells Procris. Very upset, Procris sneaks through the bushes to spy on Cephalus. Hearing a noise, Cephalus throws his javelin, which pierces her breast. Recognizing her cry, Cephalus runs to her and cradles her in his arms. Knowing that she is dying, she makes a last request. She begs Cephalus not to let "Aura" move into the house that they shared. Realizing what has happened, Cephalus offers his explanations. Procris dies in his arms, gazing lovingly into his eyes.

43. The Origin of the Minotaur

Source: Apollodorus, *The Library,* III.1.3–4 (Hellenistic)

Europa, a Phoenician princess, is carried off to Crete by Zeus in the form of a bull. There, she has three sons by him: Minos, Sarpedon, and Rhadamanthys. She then marries a Cretan ruler named Asterius, who raises her children as his own. When the children grow up, they quarrel and go their separate ways. Only Minos stays in Crete. He marries a Cretan lady named Pasiphae. Upon Asterius's death, Minos wishes to rule Crete, but he has opposition. He claims that the gods wish him to be king, and will grant whatever he prays for. To prove it, he prays to Poseidon to make a bull appear from the sea, adding the promise that he will sacrifice it.

Poseidon produces a very fine bull, and Minos acquires the kingdom. Minos adds the bull to his herds, however, and sacrifices a different one. Angered by this, Poseidon makes Pasiphae fall in love with the bull. Uncertain how to consummate her love, Pasiphae seeks help from the inventor Daedalus. He lives in Crete in exile from Athens, where he committed murder. He killed his young nephew, when the boy made him jealous by inventing the saw.

Daedalus makes a hollow wooden cow on wheels, covers it with a cow's hide, puts Pasiphae inside, and wheels it into the meadow where the bull grazes. The bull mounts it, and in due time, Pasiphae bears a monstrous child named Asterius, but better known as the Minotaur (Minos-bull). He has the face of a bull, but the rest is human.

Complying with oracles, Minos confines the Minotaur in the Labyrinth, a great maze.

Source: Apollodorus's *Library*, 3.15–Epitome 1.21 (Hellenistic)

King Pandion of Athens was driven into exile by a rival family, but his four sons, led by Aegeus, regained control of the city. Aegeus had no children and feared competition from his brothers. Therefore, he consulted the priestess of Apollo at Delphi about offspring. She answered: "Don't open the bulging wineskin's mouth until you reach the heights of Athens." Aegeus did not understand the oracle. He returned to Athens by way of the small town of Troezen, where he stayed with King Pittheus. The latter understood the oracle and caused Aegeus to lie with his daughter, Aethra. In the same night, Poseidon also lay with Aethra.

Aegeus told Aethra that if she had a male child as a result of their union, she should raise him without telling him who his father was. He left a sword and sandals under a boulder, saying that when the boy could roll away the boulder and pick them up, she should send him to Athens.

Back in Athens, Aegeus celebrated the Panathenaic games. Androgeus, son of King Minos of Crete, won all the contests. Then Aegeus sent him against the bull of Marathon, and he was killed. Others say that Androgeus was murdered by jealous rivals en route to new games in Thebes. Enraged, Minos made war on Athens. Unable to capture the city, he prayed to Zeus for vengeance. As a result, the city was laid low by plague and famine. When the Athenians asked the oracle what to do, they were told to give Minos anything he demanded. Minos, in turn, ordered them to send seven youths and seven maidens to Crete every year, as food for the Minotaur.

In Troezen, Aethra had given birth to Theseus. When he was grown, he pushed away the boulder, took up the sword and sandals, and hurried on foot to Athens. En route, he cleared the road of evildoers. He slew Periphetes, called the "Clubman," because of the iron club he carried. Theseus wrested it from him and kept it. He killed Sinis, the "Pine-Bender." Sinis made passers-by bend pine trees until they became too weak to do so, were tossed in the air, and died miserably. Theseus killed Sinis in the same way.

He slew a giant sow named "Phaea," after its breeder, an old lady. Then came Sciron, who lived on the cliffs of Megara. Sciron forced travelers to wash his feet. As they did so, he kicked them into the sea, where they were eaten by a giant turtle. Theseus threw him into the sea by his feet.

In Eleusis, Theseus killed Cercyon, who forced travelers to wrestle, and invariably killed them. Theseus lifted him up high and dashed him to the ground.

Damastes lived beside the road and kept two beds, one small and the other big. Inviting passers-by to spend the night, he laid short men on the big bed and hammered them until they fit it. He laid tall men on the little bed and sawed off the parts of their bodies that projected beyond it.

Having cleared the road, Theseus arrived in Athens. At that time, Medea was married to Aegeus, and persuaded him that Theseus was a traitor. Not realizing that Theseus was actually his son, Aegeus sent him against the bull of Marathon, which Theseus killed. Thereafter, following Medea's advice, Aegeus gave Theseus a cup of poisoned wine. When he was about to drink it, Theseus showed Aegeus his sword. Aegeus struck the cup from Theseus's hands. Medea was sent into exile.

Theseus was then chosen to be among those sent to the Minotaur. Some say that he volunteered. The ship he sailed on had a black sail because of the sad nature of its journey. Aegeus told Theseus to raise white sails on his way back—if he managed to come back alive.

When Theseus arrived in Crete, Minos's daughter, Ariadne, fell in love with him and offered to help him if he would carry her off to Athens to be his wife. Theseus agreed. She asked Daedalus how Theseus might escape the Labyrinth. At his suggestion, she gave Theseus a ball of yarn. Theseus fastened it to the door and drew it after him as he entered the Labyrinth.

Theseus found the Minotaur in the last part of the Labyrinth. He killed him with his fists and found his way out by following the yarn.

That night he arrived with Ariadne on the island of Naxos. There, Dionysus fell in love with Ariadne and carried her off to Lemnos, where she bore four of his children.

In his grief over Ariadne, Theseus forgot to raise a white sail. Seeing the ship with a black sail and thinking that Theseus was dead, Aegeus threw himself off the Athenian acropolis and died.

Learning about Theseus's escape, Minos imprisoned Daedalus and his son, Icarus, inside the Labyrinth. Daedalus constructed wings for himself and his son, and warned his son not to fly too high, lest the glue should melt in the sun, nor to fly near the sea, lest the feathers get too damp. Icarus foolishly disregarded this advice, soared ever higher until the glue melted, fell into the sea, and perished. Daedalus made his way safely to Sicily.

Theseus joined Heracles in his expedition against the Amazons, and carried off Antiope, whom some call Hippolyta. The Amazons marched against Athens but were defeated by Theseus's forces.

Although Theseus had a son named Hippolytus by Antiope, he later divorced her and married Phaedra, the daughter of Minos. Antiope was slain when she appeared in arms at the wedding of Theseus and Phaedra.

After Phaedra had born two children to Theseus, she fell in love with Hippolytus and asked him to lie with her. He fled from her approaches because he hated all women. Fearing what he would say, Phaedra broke down her bedroom doors, tore her own clothes, and falsely charged Hippolytus with rape. Theseus believed her, and prayed to Poseidon that Hippolytus might perish. So when Hippolytus was riding in his chariot and driving beside the sea, Poseidon sent up a bull from the sea. The horses were frightened, the chariot dashed to pieces, and Hippolytus became entangled in the reins and was dragged to death. When the story was made public, Phaedra hanged herself.

Meanwhile, in heaven, a man named Ixion attempted to seduce Hera. To make sure that he was guilty, Zeus made a cloud in the likeness of Hera and laid it beside Ixion.

When Ixion boasted that he had lain with Hera, Zeus attached him to the wheel on which he is forever whirled by the winds through the air. That is his penalty. The cloud, made pregnant by Ixion, gave birth to the Centaurs, creatures with human heads and torsos and horses' legs and bodies.

Ixion was a leader of the tribe known as Lapiths. He had a son named Pirithous by a mortal woman. When Pirithous was courting his wife, he feasted the Centaurs because they were his half brothers. The Centaurs, however, got drunk, and when the bride entered, they tried to rape her. Theseus, who was also at the wedding, helped Pirithous subdue the Centaurs, killing many of them.

Later, Theseus and Pirithous agreed that they should marry daughters of Zeus. With Pirithous's help, Theseus carried off the 12-year-old Helen from Sparta. They then went down to Hades, to try to abduct Persephone as a bride for Pirithous.

While they were in the underworld, Helen's brothers, Castor and Pollux, recaptured Helen, and took Theseus's mother, Aethra, prisoner. They placed a man named Menestheus on the throne of Athens.

In the underworld, feigning friendliness, Hades told Theseus and Pirithous to be seated on the Chair of Forgetfulness. When they did, they grew into it, and were held fast by coils of serpents. Pirithous remained in it forever. Heracles rescued Theseus, and sent him back to Athens. He was driven out by Menestheus, however, and took refuge with Lycomedes on the island of Scyros. Lycomedes, however, killed him by throwing him into a deep hole.

45. The Death of Hippolytus

Source: Euripides, *Hippolytus* (Classical Greek tragedy)

Aphrodite appears outside the palace of Troezen to explain the situation. She says that Hippolytus is the illegitimate son of Theseus and the Amazon, Hippolyta, now deceased, and the ward of Pittheus, king of Troezen. He honors Artemis, spending his time hunting with her, but he spurns Aphrodite and calls her vile. Aphrodite is preparing revenge. She made Theseus's new wife, the Cretan princess Phaedra, fall in love with Hippolytus when he visited Athens some time ago. Now, Theseus has been exiled from Athens to Troezen for a year because he killed some kinsmen in a feud. Phaedra has also come to Troezen, and is mad with desire for her stepson, but has not revealed this secret to anyone. Instead, she has fallen gravely ill, and no one knows why. Aphrodite says that she will make the truth come out in such a way that Theseus will invoke Poseidon's help to cause Hippolytus's death. Poseidon, she says, has granted Theseus the fulfillment of any three wishes.

When Hippolytus returns to the palace from the hunt, Aphrodite exits saying, "He does not know that Hades' gates are open, and that this is the last time he will ever see daylight."

Hippolytus offers a prayer and a garland to a statue of Artemis that stands outside the palace. An elderly servant tells him that he should honor the mighty Aphrodite, whose statue is also present. Hippolytus rejects the suggestion, saying that no deity who works in the dark interests him, and leaves.

A chorus of women enters to learn more about Phaedra's illness. They have heard that she has not eaten for three days, and wonder whether she has offended some deity—or learned that her husband has a mistress, or that a loved one in Crete has died.

Phaedra is carried out of the palace by servants, including her old nurse. The latter tells Phaedra that she has now been brought into the bright sunshine, as she had requested. She asks Phaedra what her illness is, but Phaedra responds with seemingly incoherent wishes to go hunting. The nurse explains to the chorus that she has been unable to learn the cause of Phaedra's distress. Theseus cannot help, since he is out of town consulting an oracle.

The nurse questions Phaedra even more insistently and takes her hand in a gesture of supplication. Phaedra finally relents, admitting that love is the problem and then that the man involved is—"the son of the Amazon." The nurse and the chorus are shocked and dismayed.

Phaedra explains that she had hoped that her madness would eventually subside, but she now sees that it will not and that she must die to preserve her honor. Now the nurse plays down the seriousness of the situation, saying that everybody succumbs to love. When Phaedra refuses to consider the idea of acting on her desires, the nurse volunteers to obtain a charm for Phaedra that will cure her. She refuses to tell Phaedra anything about the charm, except that she must obtain a lock of Hippolytus's hair or a bit of his clothing to make it work. Phaedra begs her not to reveal her secret, whatever she does. The nurse tells her not to worry and leaves.

The chorus sings of the power of Aphrodite and Eros. Their singing stops when Phaedra overhears shouting within the house. It quickly becomes clear that the nurse has told her secret to Hippolytus and that he is angrily denouncing her as a traitor and pimp. Phaedra exits, saying that she must now die at once.

Hippolytus and the nurse emerge from the palace. The nurse evidently obtained a vow of secrecy from Hippolytus before she told him about Phaedra's love. Hippolytus says this is the only thing that prevents him from telling Theseus the whole story. He denounces the nurse, Phaedra, and women in general. He says that Zeus should let people purchase children from his temples rather than propagating through women. He adds that since women use servants to advance their evil schemes, they should be attended only by dumb animals. He says that he will never get his fill of hating women.

Phaedra curses the nurse for her interference and sends her away, refusing to listen to a further suggestion that she wants to make. Phaedra has the chorus swear that it will never reveal any of her secrets. She says that she will now die, but do so in such a way as to preserve her family's honor for her children's sake and get some revenge. She enters the palace.

The chorus's song, wishing for a carefree existence, ends with the cries of the nurse from within the palace: Phaedra has hanged herself.

Theseus returns from his oracle with garlands on his head, showing that he received a favorable message. Hearing the wailing, he asks who has died and is crushed to learn that it is his young wife. After a long passage of lyrical lamentation, he notices a tablet on Phaedra's wrist. When he reads it, his grief intensifies. According to the message that she has left, Phaedra killed herself because Hippolytus raped her.

Theseus prays to Poseidon to grant one of his three prayers by killing Hippolytus on that very day. The chorus begs him to take back his prayer, but Theseus refuses. He adds a decree of banishment to his curse. Either Poseidon will kill Hippolytus or Hippolytus will spend his life as a homeless wanderer.

Hippolytus enters because he has heard Theseus's wailing. Theseus expresses the wish that there were some sign by which one could tell honest people from liars and denounces Hippolytus as a hypocrite. Hippolytus, he says, claimed to be the holiest of men, refraining from meat, conducting rituals invented by Orpheus, and reading sacred books, but his true character has been revealed by Phaedra's death. Hippolytus swears that he is innocent. He says that he is a virgin, ignorant of sex except for what he has heard in talk or seen in pictures, and he doesn't even like to look at those. Furthermore, he has no desire to replace Theseus as a ruler. In an aside, Hippolytus considers breaking his oath to tell Theseus what really happened, but he realizes that Theseus would not believe him anyway. Theseus orders him to go into exile. Hippolytus departs with a group of companions.

After a choral song, a servant enters with the news that Hippolytus is dying. He left Troezen in a chariot with many friends escorting him on his way along the seashore. When he reached the borders of the state, a huge wave rolled onto the beach and disgorged a giant bull. Hippolytus's horses panicked. Hippolytus struggled with them, but they galloped out of control, chased by the bull into a rocky area. There, the chariot crashed, and Hippolytus was fatally injured. The servant adds that he himself would not believe that Hippolytus was guilty of rape even if every woman in the world hanged herself. Theseus gives the servant permission to bring Hippolytus back to the palace. He wants Hippolytus to acknowledge his guilt in light of his divine punishment.

As Theseus waits for Hippolytus, Artemis appears from above and tells Theseus that Hippolytus was innocent. She explains that Phaedra falsely accused him in fear that otherwise the truth of her own illicit passion might come out. She adds that Theseus was a fool to use one of his three wishes to kill his son. He should not have acted so quickly. Theseus says that he wants to die.

The dying Hippolytus enters, supported by servants. Artemis reveals that it was Aphrodite who has caused all the problems. Theseus says that he has no more joy in life, and that he was deceived by the gods. Hippolytus wishes that human beings could crush gods the same way that gods crush humans. Artemis tells him that she will get even by killing Aphrodite's favorite mortal follower. Also, in years to come, brides in

Troezen will dedicate a lock of hair to Hippolytus's ghost. She leaves then, saying that it is not proper for gods to pollute their eyes with the sight of a person dying.

Hippolytus is dying in his father's arms. He formally releases Theseus from guilt for his death, calling upon Artemis to witness his declaration. Theseus says that he weeps for Hippolytus's nobility and virtue. Hippolytus tells him to pray that his legitimate sons are equally virtuous and asks Theseus to cover his face as he dies. Theseus says that he will often think of the evils caused by Aphrodite.

46 The Foundation of Thebes by Cadmus

Source: Ovid, *Metamorphoses*, 2.836–3.130 (Roman)

Jove summons Mercury. Without revealing that one of his love affairs is the reason, he tells him to go to the Phoenician city of Sidon, find the royal cattle, and bring them to the seashore. Soon the cattle are heading towards the indicated spot, which is just where the king's daughter, Europa, customarily plays with other maidens. The father and ruler of the gods assumes the appearance of a bull and joins the herd, mooing and grazing. He is white as fresh snow. His horns are twisted and bright as jewels. His face is serene and friendly.

Europa marvels at the beautiful bull and offers him flowers to eat. He kisses her hands, frolics in the grass, lies on the sand, and lets her pet his chest and put wreathes on his horns. The royal maiden even dares to sit on his back. Little by little, the bull wades into the water, edging away from the shore. Before Europa knows what is happening, he has her in deep water. She trembles, looks back at the shore, and holds on to his horns. Finally, the god casts off his disguise, reveals his true identity, and lands on the island of Crete.[23]

Europa's father, Agenor, orders his son, Cadmus, to find out what happened to his missing sister and adds the punishment of exile for failure. Having searched the world in vain, Cadmus consults the oracle of Apollo about a new home. The oracle says that Cadmus will meet a heifer (Latin *bos*) in a deserted field. He should follow the heifer until she lies down in the grass. At that spot, he should build a city and name the land Boeotia.

Cadmus soon encounters the heifer. When she finally lies down in the grass, he decides to sacrifice her to the gods. He sends his men into the nearby woods to find water. They find a stream emerging from a cave. A huge serpent sacred to Mars lives inside the cave. When the men dip their jars in the water, the serpent sticks his head out. He raises himself high into the sky, above the trees, and attacks the men, killing some with his fangs or venomous breath and crushing others in his coils.

---

23 Europa's child by Jove or Zeus is Minos, king of Cnossus, the capital of Crete.

When his men do not return, Cadmus goes to investigate and battles the serpent. After a furious struggle, he finally backs the monster into an oak tree and nails him to it with a spear through the throat.

Minerva glides down from the sky and orders Cadmus to plant the serpent's teeth in the ground. When he does, the tips of spears burst through the ground, then helmets with waving crests, then the soldiers' chests, their arms, and the rest of their bodies, just as when a curtain is lowered in front of the stage at the beginning of a play.

The warriors fight fiercely among themselves, until only five are left. Minerva tells them to make peace with each other. They join Cadmus in establishing his new city. Soon the city is complete, and Cadmus marries Harmonia, the child of Venus and Mars.

47. Cadmus: The Final Chapter

Source: Ovid, *Metamorphoses*, 4.563–603 (Roman)

Many, many years later, in despair over the countless misfortunes that have befallen his children and grandchildren, Cadmus and Harmonia leave Thebes. After long wandering, they come to Illyria. Here Cadmus says, "Was that a *sacred* serpent I speared when I first came from Sidon? If this is the sin that the gods have been punishing, may I become a serpent!" No sooner has he spoken than he feels scales growing on his hardened skin. He falls on his stomach. His legs merge and arms shrink. With what remains of them, he reaches out to his wife. Tears flow down his still-human face. "Take my hand," he says, "while I still have one." He wants to say more, but his tongue is suddenly split in two. "O gods," cries his wife, "why do you not change me too?" Cadmus licks his wife's face and winds around her bosom and neck. Though the onlookers are terrified, she just strokes his shiny neck. Suddenly, there are two snakes coiled around each other. Soon they hide in the shadows of the nearby woods. To this day, they are peaceful serpents, fleeing men but never wounding them since they remember what they used to be.

48. Amphion and Zethus, Kings of Thebes

Source: Apollodorus, *The Library*, 3.5.5–6 (Hellenistic)

After Cadmus, Thebes was ruled next by his son, Polydorus, and then by Polydorus's son, Labdacus, who died opposing the worship of Dionysus, just like Pentheus. Since Labdacus's son, Laius, was still an infant at this time, royal power was seized by Lycus, a granduncle of Labdacus on his mother's side.

Lycus's brother, Nycteus, had a daughter named Antiope, whom Zeus seduced. When her pregnancy was discovered, she fled in disgrace to the neighboring city of

Sicyon, where she married the king. Her father, Nycteus, committed suicide. Dying, he asked Lycus to punish his daughter and her new husband.

Lycus stormed Sicyon, killed Antiope's husband, and took her prisoner. As she was being marched back to Thebes, she gave birth to twin boys. They were left in the wilderness to die. A herdsman, however, found them and raised them as his own. They were named Amphion and Zethus. Growing up, Amphion was given a lyre by Hermes, he and became a great musician. Zethus became a herdsman, like his foster father.

Back in Thebes, Lycus and his wife, Dirce, imprisoned Antiope in the palace and treated her spitefully. One day, after many years, her bonds came loose by themselves. Fleeing, she came to her sons' cottage. Hearing her story and figuring out that she was their mother, the boys killed Lycus and Dirce. They disposed of the latter by tying her to a bull and then flinging her dead body into a fountain, which is now called "Dirce" after her.

Taking over the city, Amphion and Zethus built its walls. The stones obeyed Amphion's lyre. Zethus married a local goddess named Thebe and named the city after her. Amphion married Niobe, who bore seven sons and seven daughters. Niobe boasted that she was more blessed in children than Leto. Insulted, Leto roused her children, Artemis and Apollo. Artemis shot down Niobe's female children in the house; Apollo killed all the males as they were hunting. Niobe left Thebes and went home to her father Tantalus, who lived on Mount Sipylus in Asia Minor. There, having prayed to Zeus, she was changed into a stone, from which tears flow night and day. In Thebes, when Amphion died, Laius ascended the throne.

49. King Oedipus Learns His True Identity

Source: Sophocles, *Oedipus Rex* (Classical Greek tragedy)

Oedipus's parents were King Laius and Queen Jocasta of Thebes. Learning from an oracle that he would die at his son's hands, Laius ordered the baby Oedipus to be exposed on a mountain and a spike driven through his ankles. The servant entrusted with disposing of the baby was known only as Laius's man, a herdsman. Out of pity, he disregarded his orders and gave the baby to a Corinthian herdsman to pass on to foster parents. The Corinthian gave the baby to Corinth's childless royal couple, Polybus and Merope, who raised him as their own and named him Oedipus ("Swollen Foot") because of the spike's effects.

Years later, a drunken comrade in Corinth accused Oedipus, now a young man, of being illegitimate. This upset Oedipus, who went to the oracle of Delphi to ask who his real parents were. Instead of answering the question, the oracle told Oedipus that he was destined to lie with his mother, "producing unholy offspring," and to slay his father. Oedipus immediately resolved to avoid that fate by never returning to Corinth and fled from the oracle.

Coming to a crossroads, he turned toward Thebes. Here, he encountered an elderly man with a group of servants. They quarreled over the right of way. When the old man swatted him with a goad, Oedipus threw him out of his chariot and killed him and all of his servants—or so he thought. In fact, there was one survivor: Laius's man. He ran back to Thebes with the story that a band of robbers had slaughtered King Laius and the rest of his attendants.

The citizens could not investigate the murder because a monster, the Sphinx, appeared in the countryside, asking people a riddle and killing them when they failed to answer it correctly. At this juncture, Oedipus arrived in the city. Seeing him, Laius's man asked Jocasta for work in the countryside, far from town, and got his wish, because he had always been a good servant. Oedipus confronted the Sphinx and answered her riddle, and the Sphinx killed herself. The grateful citizens of Thebes made Oedipus their new king. He married the newly widowed queen, Jocasta.

Sophocles' play begins years later. Oedipus and Jocasta are the parents of grown children, two sons and two daughters. A plague is decimating the city. Oedipus's brother-in-law, Creon, goes to Delphi to learn why the gods are angry and is told that Laius's murderer must be punished.

Oedipus agrees to investigate the crime. He questions the old blind seer, Tiresias, who suddenly remembers the truth, which he has been repressing. He says, "I knew this well, but blotted it out. Otherwise, I would not have come." Tiresias tries to refuse to talk. When Oedipus starts to badger him, Tiresias blurts out that Oedipus himself is the criminal whom he seeks. Oedipus's temper flares. He accuses Tiresias and Creon of using a fake oracle to overthrow him. Later, Creon appears to defend himself, but Oedipus treats him scornfully too.

Jocasta emerges from the palace to soothe Oedipus. Learning that the quarrel concerns oracles, she belittles them, telling Oedipus that an oracle once predicted that her former husband would be killed by his son. Instead, she says, he was slain by a band of robbers—at a crossroads. Her reference to a crossroads disturbs Oedipus. He tells her about the journey that brought him from Corinth to a crossroads, where he killed an old man, who fit Laius's description. He sends for Laius's man, hoping that he will confirm his old story about a band of robbers.

While they wait for Laius's man, a Corinthian enters with news for Oedipus. His "father," Polybus, has died of old age, and the citizens of Corinth want to make Oedipus their king. Jocasta and Oedipus are relieved to hear of Polybus's death because of the oracle apparently predicting that Oedipus would kill him. Oedipus tells the Corinthian that he cannot return because of the other part of the oracle—that he would marry his mother. Thinking that this information will come as a relief, the Corinthian informs Oedipus that Polybus and Merope were not his real parents. The Corinthian knows that Oedipus was adopted, because he is none other than the former shepherd who gave baby Oedipus to Polybus. He is, however, unable to tell Oedipus who his real parents were. Only a servant called "Laius's man" would know that. During these revelations, Jocasta leaves the stage.

Laius's man finally arrives. Oedipus demands to know who his parents were and threatens him with violence if he refuses to talk. Laius's man reluctantly tells Oedipus that he is the son of Laius and Jocasta. Hearing that, Oedipus rushes into the palace, crying that everything is clear. The chorus sings of the uncertainty of human happiness. One moment, Oedipus seemed to be the happiest of men. Now he is the most wretched!

A servant emerges from inside the palace to describe recent events there. First, Jocasta had rushed into her bedroom, weeping and wailing. The servants were worried, but they were distracted by Oedipus, who rushed into the palace, calling for a sword and demanding to see the queen. As if guided by an invisible power, he burst through the doors into Jocasta's bedroom. There, he found that she had hanged herself. He laid her down, removed brooches from her gown, and jabbed his eyes out with them, striking so often and so forcibly that he created not just a sprinkling of blood but a "hurricane of gore."

The blind Oedipus then makes a final appearance on stage. Addressing the horrified chorus, he asks to be sent into exile as quickly as possible. Creon appears. In view of Oedipus's downfall, he has assumed royal power. He tells Oedipus that he wishes to ask the oracle what to do. For the time being, he wants Oedipus to return to the palace and stay out of public view. As a bit of consolation, he has brought Oedipus's two daughters with him to comfort their father. The girls emerge from the palace. Oedipus laments the sufferings that he has caused them and is finally coaxed back into the palace by Creon. As he departs, the chorus chants:

> "Native resident of Thebes, consider Oedipus,
> One who solved the famous riddle, mightiest of men.
> Everyone who looked on him was jealous of his fate.
> What a tide of grim misfortune overwhelms him now!
> Thus we learn how necessary seeing the final day
> Is for judging mortals blest. Otherwise, refrain.
> Happiness means ending life without being crushed by pain."

50. The Death of Oedipus

Source: Sophocles, *Oedipus at Colonus* (Classical Greek tragedy)

Homeless wanderers, the blind Oedipus and his daughter Antigone arrive in Athenian territory. Oedipus sits on a rock. A local Athenian asks him to leave since he is in an area that is sacred to the Furies. Oedipus says that he must stay there. Then learning that the king of the land is Theseus, he asks the Athenian to summon him. The Athenian says that he will summon other citizens to consider the request.

When the Athenian leaves, Oedipus tells Antigone about a prophecy. According to this, he must end his life in an area sacred to the Furies. He will be a blessing to those who receive him, a curse to those who drive him away.

A chorus of local Athenians arrives and convinces Oedipus to leave the sacred spot temporarily. They then pressure him into revealing his name. Since they have heard his story, they are horrified when he reveals his name and want him to leave the region entirely. When Oedipus and Antigone beg for compassion, however, they agree to wait for Theseus and abide by his decision.

Oedipus's other daughter, Ismene, arrives on horseback. While Antigone has accompanied Oedipus on his wanderings, Ismene has brought them news from the city. Now she informs him that his sons, who originally planned to let Creon rule, are feuding over royal power. The younger, Eteocles, has seized power by winning popular favor. Driven into exile, the elder, Polynices, has married and made alliances in the region of Mycenae, and hopes to conquer Thebes. Meanwhile, oracles speak of the importance of Oedipus in the imminent conflict. For this reason, Creon is on his way to ask Oedipus to come back and live just across the Theban border—in order to honor the oracles without incurring pollution.

Oedipus recalls that when he first discovered the secret of his identity, he wanted to die. Then when he had calmed down and wished to live normally, he was driven out of the city, and his sons did nothing to help him, nor have they done anything for him subsequently. Only his daughters, he says, have acted like men. Oedipus is determined not to help either of his sons.

Members of the chorus say that libations must be poured to the Furies to placate them for Oedipus's violation of the grove. Ismene volunteers for the task. She is directed to the far side of the grove for water.

Theseus arrives, and asks Oedipus what favor he seeks. It is to be buried in Athens. Oedipus says that this will benefit Athens. His spirit will lead Athens to victory over Thebes if those cities ever go to war. He warns him, however, that Creon and his sons may try to seize him to prevent his burial in Athens. Theseus assures him that he will not allow that to happen.

After a choral interlude, in which the site of the action is identified as Colonus (a suburb of Athens), Antigone announces that Creon is coming. Arriving, he declares that all the Theban people want Oedipus to return and that it is a shame for Antigone to lead such a wretched life. Oedipus refuses to return, emphasizing again that he was driven into exile when he wanted to stay in Thebes. Creon then reveals that his men have seized Ismene. Worse, he orders the seizure of Antigone. She is dragged off the stage amid screams and wails.

Theseus arrives. He sends orders for the Athenian army to assemble to save the girls and scolds Creon for his illegal behavior. Creon says that he acted only because he did not think that Athens wanted to protect a man guilty of patricide and incest. This draws a furious rebuttal from Oedipus. He demands to know how he can be held responsible for crimes that were prophesied before he was even conceived. Laius, he says, was trying to kill him at the crossroads. If someone were trying to kill you, he asks Creon, would you defend yourself or would you ask him first whether he was your father? Theseus interrupts the diatribe to take action. He leaves with Creon to catch the Thebans, who have the girls.

The chorus predicts that Theseus and his men will save the girls. As their song ends, Theseus delivers them back into Oedipus's arms. After they embrace, Theseus tells Oedipus that a man from the south has assumed a suppliant position at an altar of Poseidon and seeks to speak with him. Oedipus realizes that it is his son, Polynices. He does not want to listen to him, but Theseus and Antigone persuade him to do so.

Polynices arrives bewailing his own misfortunes and those of Oedipus. He explains that Eteocles gained power in Thebes by winning over the people. In Argos, he has raised an army consisting of seven leaders including himself. Oracles indicate that victory will belong to the side that Oedipus favors. If Polynices wins, he will restore Oedipus to Thebes. All he wants is Oedipus's forgiveness.

Oedipus replies that he is willing to talk to Polynices, but only as a favor to Theseus. Polynices and Eteocles are responsible for Oedipus's sorry condition. He curses them both, predicting that they will kill each other in battle.

Polynices' hopes are crushed. He asks Antigone to see that he is properly buried—if Oedipus's curse is fulfilled, and she happens to be back in Thebes at the time. Antigone begs him to give up his attack on Thebes. Polynices says he could not do anything so cowardly. Antigone wants to know who will follow him after people hear about Oedipus's curse. He says that as a good general he will conceal the truth. They part in tears.

Thunder sounds. Oedipus says that it signals his death and that it is very important to get Theseus. Theseus hears people calling and returns. Oedipus says that he will lead Theseus alone to the secret place where he, Oedipus, will die. Knowledge of this location and other secrets that Oedipus will tell him will keep Athens always safe from attack from Thebes. Though blind, Oedipus leads Theseus and his daughters into the sacred grove.

After a brief choral interlude, a messenger returns with the news that Oedipus is gone. He says that Oedipus led the group that went with him to a basin. There he bathed, and said farewell to his daughters. "Everything that was me, has perished," he said. "You will no longer have the trouble of caring for me. I know how difficult it was, children, but one word alone dissolves all those troubles: love. The man does not exist who loved you more." After a tearful farewell, he sent them away.

When the group looked back from a distance, the messenger adds, Oedipus was gone, and Theseus stood shielding his eyes, as though from some dreadful sight. "Either it was a messenger sent by the gods, or a power from below split the earth. He passed away without pain or disease, a marvelous end if ever a mortal's was."

The girls lament. Antigone asks Theseus to show her Oedipus's grave, but he refuses. The girls decide to return to Thebes to try to prevent their brothers from killing each other.

Source: Sophocles, *Antigone* (Classical Greek tragedy)

Antigone confers with her sister, Ismene, outside the walls of Thebes. She asks whether Ismene has heard about the latest misfortune to befall their wretched family. Ismene says she only knows that their brothers have killed each other in battle and that the invading Argive army has fled. Antigone informs her that King Creon has issued a decree forbidding the burial of their brother, Polynices, because he was a rebel. The penalty for burying him is death by stoning. Antigone wants to know if Ismene will share in the work of burying Polynices. Ismene says that she cannot defy the law of the city. Antigone despises this attitude, saying that she would not accept her help now even if she changed her mind and offered it.

Summoned by Creon, a chorus of leading citizens enters, singing of the glorious victory of Thebes. Creon arrives and repeats his proclamation forbidding the burial of Polynices. The chorus says that they will support it.

A soldier enters with news for Creon. He explains at great length that he is extremely reluctant to say what he has to say. He finally discloses that some dust appeared on Polynices' body. He was the unlucky soldier, selected by lot, to break the news to Creon. The chorus wonders whether the gods could have been responsible. Creon ridicules the idea since Polynices intended to pillage the temples of the gods. He thinks the guilty parties are people opposing him for financial reasons. Creon sends the guard back, with stern orders to find out who sprinkled the dust. The guard is relieved to be getting away with his life. "There is no way," he tells Creon, "that you will see me coming here again."

The chorus sings an ode praising the human race for its inventiveness: "There are many amazing things, but nothing more amazing than man. He crosses the gray sea on the stormy blast," etc. The one problem for which man has found no solution is death.

The soldier from the previous episode appears onstage again, escorting Antigone. He gleefully reveals that he himself caught her burying Polynices. He explains that he and his fellow soldiers had removed the dirt from the corpse and were guarding it carefully, sitting on the windward side to avoid the smell. At noon, there was a dust storm. When the sky cleared, Antigone stood over the body, wailing and pouring dust on it. She did not deny her guilt.

Creon asks Antigone if she knew about his decree. She replies that she did, but she did not feel that his proclamation "enabled any mortal to violate the secure, unwritten laws of the gods; for they are not just for now and yesterday, but they live forever, and no one knows their source."

This infuriates Creon. He says that he would not be a man if Antigone overruled him in this matter. He decides that Ismene must have collaborated, and orders her arrest. When Ismene is brought to him, she says that she was guilty, but Antigone insists that she was not and continues to treat her contemptuously. She says that Ismene has no right to share in her death.

Ismene reminds Creon that his son, Haemon, is engaged to marry Antigone, hoping that this will make him repent, but he is unmoved. "Other people," he says, "have fields fit to plow."

After a choral interlude, Haemon arrives. He begins very politely by saying how much he respects Creon's judgment. Creon justifies his condemnation of Antigone with the argument that nothing is more important than obedience to authority. "It is necessary to protect authority," he says, "and never to be defeated by a woman. If one must fall, it is better to be beaten by a man. We would not wish to be called inferior to women."

Haemon respectfully suggests that Creon should consider the consensus in the city that it is unjust to execute Antigone. Creon replies that the people do not rule the city, he does, and he accuses Haemon of having been enslaved by a woman. Haemon becomes angry in turn. He says that if Antigone dies, she will destroy another. Creon interprets this as a threat against his own life. He orders Antigone to be brought to him so that she can be executed before Haemon's very eyes. Haemon says that *that* will never happen, and storms out.

Creon orders the girls to be brought out for execution. The chorus asks whether he really intends to kill them both. He instantly changes his mind and says that only Antigone must die. He will imprison her alive in a rocky cavern with just enough food to avoid guilt for murder.

Antigone is led to her prison, exchanging lamentations with the chorus. Creon repeats that it will be her choice whether to live or die in the cave. Antigone pauses to explain her devotion to her brother. She says that a husband or a child could be replaced, but since her parents are dead, she will never have another brother.

After a short choral interlude, Tiresias enters. He says that the behavior of the birds and the appearance of sacrificial meats show that the gods are very angry, evidently over the treatment of Polynices' corpse and the punishment of Antigone. Creon should reconsider.

At first, Creon dismisses Tiresias, accusing the whole class of seers of being interested only in making money. Tiresias then makes a terrible prophecy. Creon will pay for the corpse that he denied to Hades with a corpse from his own family, and cities will rise up against him.

Tiresias leaves Creon shaken. After a brief exchange with the chorus, Creon changes his mind and heads out of town with servants to bury Polynices and free Antigone.

The chorus sings a song in honor of Dionysus, the Theban-born deity. At its conclusion, a messenger arrives with the news that Haemon is dead. The commotion draws the attention of Eurydice, Creon's wife and Haemon's mother, out of the palace. She emerges from the palace to ask what has happened.

The messenger says that there is no reason to spare her feelings. He was, he explains, one of the servants following Creon. They first stopped to burn what remained of Polynices' corpse, then they hurried to Antigone's cave. As they approached, they heard miserable groans, which Creon recognized as coming from his son, Haemon. Inside the cave, they found that Antigone had hanged herself . Haemon was embracing her waist. Creon asked him to come out. Haemon glared at him with wild eyes, spat in his face, and lunged at him with his sword but missed. Then he plunged the sword into his own chest and fell on the girl, splattering her white cheek with his red blood.

At the end of the speech, members of the chorus notice that the queen has departed. The messenger goes inside to find out why.

Creon arrives carrying Haemon's corpse, cursing his previous blindness.

A messenger from the palace announces that Queen Eurydice has killed herself. The palace doors open to reveal her corpse. The messenger says that she stabbed herself in the stomach in front of an altar after cursing Creon for Haemon's death.

Creon asks to be led away, "as a foolish man who killed his son and wife without intending to." The chorus has no words of comfort. All they can say is that wisdom is the most important ingredient of happiness.

52. The Beginning of the Trojan War

Source: Byzantine summary of *The Cypria*, by Stasinus (Archaic Greek)

Zeus plans with Themis to start the Trojan War to ease the earth's burden of over-population. Eris ("Strife") arrives while the gods are feasting at the marriage of Peleus and Thetis and starts a fight between Hera, Athena, and Aphrodite over which one is fairest. They are led by Hermes at Zeus's command to Paris on Mount Ida, overlooking Troy. Lured by the promise of marriage with Helen, Paris decides in favor of Aphrodite.

Then Paris builds ships at Aphrodite's suggestion. He lands in Lacedaemon and is entertained by Menelaus in Sparta. He gives gifts to Helen. Later, Menelaus sets sail for Crete, ordering Helen to take care of their guest. At this point, Aphrodite joins Helen and Paris. After they make love, they load up most of Helen's possessions and sail away at night. Hera sends a storm after them. Dropping anchor at Sidon, Paris seizes the city. Having sailed to Troy, he marries Helen.

Iris tells Menelaus what has happened. Back in Greece, he and his brother, Agamemnon, plan an expedition against Troy. They travel all over Greece, recruiting leaders.

All the leaders gather at Aulis. They set sail, reach a city in Asia Minor named Teuthrania, and sack it—thinking that it is Troy. Discovering their error, they reassemble at Aulis. Agamemnon shoots a stag and boasts that he surpasses Artemis in hunting. The goddess sends storm winds that prevent the fleet from sailing. Calchas, the Greeks' priest, tells them that they must sacrifice Iphigenia, Agamemnon's daughter, to Artemis. Iphigenia is summoned as though she is going to marry Achilles and is led to sacrifice instead. At the last second, Artemis snatches her away to the land of the Tauri on the Black Sea, makes her immortal, and puts a stag in her place on the altar.

Just before the fleet arrives at Troy, the Greek warrior Philoctetes is bitten by a snake. Because of the stench from his wound, he is left on the island of Lemnos.

The Greeks try to land at Troy. At first the Trojans prevent them. Protesilaos, the first Greek to reach the shore, is killed by Hector. Then Achilles kills Cycnus, the son of Poseidon, and drives the Trojans back. The Greeks take up their dead and send envoys to the Trojans demanding the surrender of Helen and her treasure. The Trojans refuse. The Greeks assault the city and then lay waste to the countryside and nearby towns.

Most of the Greeks want to go home, but they are restrained by Achilles. He drives off the cattle of Aeneas, sacks Lyrnessus and other neighboring cities, and kills Troilus. Out of the spoils from these victories, Achilles receives a girl named Briseis as a prize. Agamemnon gets a certain Chryseis.

53. The Judgment of Paris

Source: Lucian, *Dialogues of the Gods*, 20 (Greek, 2nd century A.D.)

Aphrodite, Athena, and Hera are arguing over an apple bearing the inscription, "Let the fairest have me." Zeus instructs Hermes to lead them to Paris on Mount Ida for a judgment. Paris is of royal blood, related to Ganymede, and an unspoiled country boy. The goddesses agree. En route, Aphrodite asks Hermes whether Paris is married and learns that he is living with a country woman but is not married to her.

Having flown to Ida, the deities approach Paris on foot so that they will not startle him. Hera remarks that Aphrodite knows the way because of her previous visit to Anchises. Hermes says that it was in the same area that he helped Zeus, disguised as an eagle, kidnap Ganymede, who was piping to his flock at the time. Zeus took the terrified boy in his talons and soared toward heaven. Hermes picked up the shepherd's pipes that the boy dropped.

Paris greets the deities. Learning the situation, he says that he is utterly enthralled by the beauty of each goddess and unable to decide among them. Hermes points out that Zeus's commands cannot be ignored. Paris asks whether he is supposed to view the goddesses naked. Hermes says that it is up to Paris to decide. Paris has the goddesses take off their clothes and then interviews each one separately.

Hera promises to make Paris the king of all "Asia" (i.e., Asia Minor) if he selects her. Paris says his judgment will not be influenced by gifts. Athena's bribe is that Paris will never be defeated in battle. Paris says that he is not interested in warfare since his father's realm is at peace.

Aphrodite encourages Paris to examine her very carefully and tells him that he himself is the most handsome youth in his father's kingdom. His good looks, she says, are wasted in the countryside. He should marry someone like Helen of Sparta. She is the daughter of Leda and Zeus in the form of a swan. She is as white as a swan, as delicate as one would expect a girl raised in an egg to be, and fond of gymnastics and wrestling.

She was the cause of war when Theseus of Athens abducted her as a child. Later, the noblest of the Greeks courted her, and she was given to Menelaus. Aphrodite says that she can arrange a marriage between her and Paris.

Paris does not see how it would be possible to win the love of a married woman. Aphrodite says that she will get the help of Desire, Love, and the Three Graces. Paris is convinced and awards the apple to Aphrodite when she promises to give him Helen.

54. Peleus and Thetis

Source: Apollodorus, *The Library*, 3.13.5–7 (Hellenistic)

Peleus fled his homeland, the island of Aegina, because he had killed a brother out of jealousy. He became the ruler of Phthia in Thessaly. There he married Thetis, daughter of Nereus. She had been courted by Zeus and Poseidon, but Themis prophesied that her son would be mightier than his father, and they withdrew. Others say that, because she had been raised by Hera, Thetis would have nothing to do with Zeus.

Chiron, the wise centaur, told Peleus how to win Thetis. He had to seize her and hold her fast, despite her shape-shifting. He waited for his chance and carried her off—even though she turned to fire, water, and a beast.

He married her on Mount Pelion. The gods celebrated the marriage with music and feasting. Chiron gave Peleus an ashen spear. Poseidon gave him immortal horses.

When Thetis had a child by Peleus, she wanted to make him immortal. Unknown to Peleus, she used to hide their baby in the fire by night in order to destroy the mortal element, but by day she anointed him with ambrosia.[24] But Peleus spied on her, and , seeing the child writhing on the fire, he cried out. Thus prevented from accomplishing her purpose, Thetis forsook her infant son and rejoined the Nereids. Peleus brought the child to Chiron, who received him and fed him on the innards of lions and wild swine and the marrow of bears. He named him Achilles because he had not put his lips to breasts; before then his name was Ligyron.[25]

---

24   In the *Achilleid* (story 48), Statius alludes in passing to the story that Thetis dipped Achilles in the river Styx to make him invulnerable. The first one to mention Achilles' heel explicitly as his only vulnerable spot is Fulgentius (400s A.D.).

25   The prefix *a-* in Greek is equivalent to non- in English; *cheilē* means lips. Apollodorus thinks Achilles meant roughly "no-lips." Ligyron means "shrill or high-pitched."

Source: Statius, *The Achilleid* (Roman)

Statius invokes the help of the Muse and Apollo to tell the entire story of Achilles from his hiding on the island of Scyros to his death at Troy.[26]

Thetis sees Paris returning to Troy with Helen. Knowing the danger that this poses to her son, Thetis tries—and fails—to persuade Neptune to sink Paris's ship. Then she goes to Achilles' teacher, Chiron the centaur, in the wilds of Thessaly. She claims that she needs to take Achilles with her to perform a magical rite of purification. Achilles arrives from the hunt with his friend, Patroclus, embraces his mother, and falls asleep hugging Chiron. Thetis decides to take him to the island of Scyros, where the daughters of the king of Lycomedes are being raised. It is less warlike than other possible hiding places. Thetis summons her dolphin-drawn chariot, picks up Achilles in his sleep, and rides with him over the waves.

When Achilles wakes, Thetis explains that she wants him to put on girls' clothing, and hide from the Greeks among the island's princesses. These girls happen to be playing near the seashore. Achilles sees Deidamia, who is by far the loveliest, and is set aflame with desire for the first time. For this reason, he goes along with his mother's plan. She instructs him on how to look feminine and takes him to King Lycomedes. She introduces Achilles as "Achilles' sister," and asks Lycomedes to take over "her" upbringing, since she herself is kept busy with her son, Achilles. Lycomedes is happy to do so.

Meanwhile war fever has gripped all of Greece because of Paris's crime. The Greek warriors gather at Aulis. They are distressed because Achilles is not present. Even as Chiron's young pupil, Achilles has become famous. They consult their seer, Calchas, on Achilles' whereabouts. He has a vision of the truth, that Achilles is hiding on Scyros, disguised as a girl. Diomedes and Ulysses volunteer to get him.

Back on Scyros, Deidamia has begun to suspect Achilles' secret. He constantly gazes at her, seeks her company, playfully pelts her with flowers, and pokes her with his thyrsus. He gives her lessons on the lyre, and works at weaving under her direction. The truth comes out when he and Lycomedes' daughters observe a festival of Bacchus in a secret grove in the woods. No men are allowed. In the still of the night, Achilles takes advantage of the darkness and solitude to rape Deidamia. Her screams wake her sisters, but they interpret the noise as a signal to dance in Bacchus's honor and do so. Achilles persuades Deidamia not to reveal what has happened. Only her nurse is told the truth, and she helps Deidamia conceal her pregnancy and the birth of a child.

Ulysses and Diomedes arrive on Scyros. They claim to be studying the approaches to Troy in preparation for the Greek invasion. Lycomedes gives them a banquet. Deidamia can barely keep Achilles from revealing himself, while Ulysses speaks of the glorious

---

26   Statius was prevented by his own death in 96 A.D. from completing the poem, which ends abruptly after Achilles' departure from Scyros.

warfare that is about to start. The next day, Achilles and Lycomedes' daughters dance for the entertainment of the visiting Greeks and then enter the palace, where Diomedes has gifts spread out for them. Most are articles designed to appeal to girls—thyrsi, cymbals, decorated furs, and turbans, but a sword and shield are also present and attract the disguised Achilles. As he looks over the weapons, Ulysses whispers to him that it is time for him to act like a man. Then, as Ulysses has arranged, a war trumpet sounds. Lycomedes' daughters scatter in panic, but Achilles picks up the sword and shield as his gown slides off his shoulders.

Hearing Deidamia weep, Achilles—naked but holding his sword and shield—addresses King Lycomedes. He asks for permission to marry his daughter, adding that he has already possessed her. As proof, he orders their child to be placed at Lycomedes' feet. When Ulysses and Diomedes add their appeals, Lycomedes is finally won over.

After one night of married bliss, Achilles bids a tearful farewell to Deidamia and sets sail with Ulysses and Diomedes. Ulysses tells him the story of the judgment of Paris. Achilles tells Ulysses about his youth under Chiron's care. He spent most of his time hunting fierce wild animals—lions, tigers, wolves, bears—and lived on their flesh.

56. The Sacrifice of Iphigenia

Source: Euripides, *Iphigenia at Aulis* (Classical Greek tragedy)

Late at night in the Greek camp at Aulis, Agamemnon has been working on a letter by lamplight. He summons an old servant and explains his predicament. The Greeks have gathered to make war on Troy because Paris ran off with Menelaus's wife, Helen. The priest Calchas announced to the Greek leaders that the expedition would never get to Troy unless Agamemnon sacrificed his daughter, Iphigenia, to Artemis. Agamemnon wanted to dismiss the army, but Menelaus vehemently urged him to sacrifice his daughter. Agamemnon eventually gave in and sent a message to his wife, Clytemnestra, telling her to bring Iphigenia to Troy to marry Achilles. Now, Agamemnon has changed his mind. He has written a second message to his wife, telling her *not* to come because the wedding must be postponed.

Agamemnon seals his new message and gives it to the servant, urging him to get it to Clytemnestra as soon as possible and to be very careful not to miss her carriage since she may already be on her way to Aulis.

A chorus of local girls enters, describing the sights in the Greek camp. They were particularly impressed by seeing the fleet-footed Achilles racing a four-horse chariot—and staying even.

Menelaus enters, dragging the elderly servant. He was watching for the arrival of Iphigenia, saw the old man, seized him, and read his message. Menelaus has come to denounce Agamemnon. He points out that Agamemnon sent for Iphigenia voluntarily. Now he has changed his mind and in so doing reveals that he is an unworthy leader.

Agamemnon shoots back that the whole war is irrational. It is being fought just because of Menelaus's desire to recover an adulterous wife. He says that he will not kill his child. If he did, he would regret it every day of his life.

A messenger enters with the news that Clytemnestra and Iphigenia have arrived in Aulis and are resting in a meadow. The army is aware of their arrival, and is buzzing with rumors. Agamemnon is dumbfounded. He asks what he can say to his wife.

Menelaus has a sudden change of heart. He says that he is overwhelmed by pity for Iphigenia. He was crazy to think that he should sacrifice the love of an excellent brother to win back an evil wife. He tells Agamemnon to dismiss the army.

Agamemnon foresees difficulties. He is afraid that Calchas will reveal his prophecy to the soldiers and that they will turn against Agamemnon. Menelaus says that it would be a simple matter to murder Calchas. Agamemnon agrees that he and all prophets should be killed, but he thinks of a worse problem: Odysseus knows the whole story. He will rouse the army to kill Agamemnon and Menelaus and then Iphigenia. Agamemnon sees no way to avoid the sacrifice.

The chorus sings the praise of moderate love, in contrast to the mad passion of Paris and Helen, which has caused so many problems.

Clytemnestra enters on a chariot with Iphigenia. The maiden is thrilled to see her father and runs to embrace him. Clytemnestra lets her go, saying that out of all her children, Iphigenia is the most devoted to Agamemnon. Iphigenia hugs and kisses Agamemnon but notices his sad demeanor. He pretends to be distracted by routine worries and the prospect of his separation from Iphigenia. Not only will he sail to Troy, he says, but she must go on a long journey too. Beginning to weep, he sends her inside his shelter with a kiss.

Agamemnon apologizes to Clytemnestra, saying that it is always hard for a father to give his daughter away. He answers Clytemnestra's questions about Achilles' ancestry and upbringing. He says that the wedding will occur during the next full moon and suggests that Clytemnestra return to Mycenae to look after their other children. Clytemnestra flatly refuses to leave. Agamemnon is helpless to change her mind. He exits in a mood of despair to make arrangements with Calchas for the sacrifice.

The chorus sings about the sad fate of the maidens of Troy, who are destined to fall into the hands of the conquering Greeks because of Helen.

Achilles enters, demanding to talk to Agamemnon about the delay in the fleet's departure. He is surprised when Clytemnestra emerges from the shelter. He starts to withdraw out of modesty after complimenting her. She urges him to stay since they are soon to be related by marriage. Achilles is bewildered by this statement. Further conversation makes it obvious that Agamemnon has brought Clytemnestra and Iphigenia to Aulis under false pretenses. The elderly servant who tried to deliver Agamemnon's message at the beginning of the play has been eavesdropping and enters to explain the whole story.

Clytemnestra is grief-stricken, and Achilles is angry. He resents the fact that Agamemnon used his name, without his permission, to lure Iphigenia, and he swears that he will not permit the sacrifice to occur. Clytemnestra asks whether he would like to meet Iphigenia, but he declines, afraid that such a meeting would start rumors. Though he is ready to act, Achilles asks Clytemnestra to try to convince Agamemnon to cancel the sacrifice voluntarily first.

The chorus sings of the wedding of Peleus and Thetis and of the imminent sacrifice of Iphigenia, so strange a fate for one raised to marry a king.

Clytemnestra comes out of the shelter to look for Agamemnon. She says that Iphigenia has learned the truth and is weeping copiously inside the shelter.

Agamemnon returns from Calchas. He says that he has come to take Iphigenia to a pre-wedding sacrifice. Clytemnestra has her come outside. Agamemnon asks why she is crying. Instead of explaining, Clytemnestra asks whether he would answer just one question. Agamemnon says that he would be happy to do so. Clytemnestra's question is, "Do you intend to kill our child?" Agamemnon cannot bring himself to respond directly, saying that it is an unreasonable question, and cursing his fate in asides.

Clytemnestra pleads with him to change his mind. She recalls that he killed her first husband and their infant, and was nearly killed, in turn, by Clytemnestra's brothers, Castor and Pollux. Clytemnestra's father, Tyndareus, intervened, however, and brought about their marriage. Since then , Clytemnestra says, she has been a good wife but cannot be expected to continue to be one if Agamemnon kills their daughter. Nor can Agamemnon expect to have the love of his other children if he kills their sister.

Iphigenia also begs for her life. She says that she was Agamemnon's first child and remembers sitting on his lap and talking of how she would be happily married someday and taking care of Agamemnon in his old age. Also, she loves life. Light, she says, is a most pleasant thing to see. Living badly is better than dying well.

Agamemnon leaves, saying that he is forced to act by the Greek army, which will come to Argos and slaughter the entire family if he refuses. Iphigenia continues to lament her fate, wishing that Paris had not been raised by a herdsman when exposed as an infant on Mount Ida and that the Greeks had never landed at Aulis.

Achilles enters with the news that the Greek army is demanding the sacrifice of Iphigenia. He says that he spoke out against the idea and was nearly stoned to death by his own troops among others. Still, he calls for his armor and is prepared to fight to the death to save Iphigenia.

Iphigenia breaks her silence to say that she has reconsidered. She has decided that she is willing—even anxious—to die for Greece. By her sacrifice, she will insure that barbarians no longer drag Greek women out of their homes. Thousands of men will die for Greece in this war. It would not be just for her to refuse to give up her one life. Indeed, the life of one man is worth thousands of women. And finally, if Artemis demands the sacrifice, it is wrong for Iphigenia to oppose her divine will.

Iphigenia's nobility makes a powerful impression on Achilles. He says that the courage she is showing now makes him love her passionately. It may be that she will come to regret her decision. He will be standing by with his armor ready to save her the moment she asks, even if the blade is already touching her throat.

Achilles leaves, and Iphigenia bids Clytemnestra farewell. She prohibits mourning. Clytemnestra asks if there is anything that she can do for her. Iphigenia asks her not to hate Agamemnon. Instead of agreeing, Clytemnestra exclaims that he has been treacherous and unworthy.

Iphigenia asks for an attendant to lead her to the sacrifice. She will not allow Clytemnestra to come along. She departs, singing in honor of Artemis and praying for victory for Greece. The chorus echoes her sentiments. They pray that Artemis produce a glorious victory from Iphigenia's death and wreathe Agamemnon's head with eternal glory.

A messenger returns from the sacrifice. He describes it to Clytemnestra. Agamemnon was weeping with his robe drawn over his eyes. Calchas wreathed Iphigenia's head, while Achilles sprinkled water and barley around the altar and prayed that the girl's sacrifice would bring victory. Calchas took the knife, studying Iphigenia's neck. Then everyone heard the knife strike, but in some way that no one saw the girl disappeared. In her place, a great deer lay panting on the altar, pouring blood. Calchas announced that the goddess had substituted the animal for the maiden and would now bless the Greek expedition. The messenger says that Agamemnon sent him as an eye-witness to the fact that their child did not die but was swept away to heaven and that Clytemnestra's grief and anger should end.

"O child," cries Clytemnestra, "what god has stolen you? How can I speak to you. How can I not conclude that these are just empty words designed to end my bitter pain?"

Agamemnon arrives, saying that they should rejoice because their daughter has joined the gods. Clytemnestra must now go back home. The fleet is ready to sail. It will be a long time before he returns from Troy. He hopes that all will be well with her.

57. The Anger of Achilles

Source: Homer, *The Iliad* (Archaic Greek)

The Greek army is assembled on the shore of Troy, where it has been waging war for ten years. An elderly man with a cart full of treasure approaches. He holds a golden staff festooned with ribbons. He is Chryses, priest of Apollo. The Greeks took his daughter, Chryseis, captive when they raided his city. She is now the slave of Agamemnon, king of Mycenae and the Greeks' supreme commander. Chryses wishes the Greeks well and asks them to exchange his daughter for the gifts he has brought. The other Greeks shout approval, but Agamemnon rejects the offer, saying that Chryseis will grow old in his service, weaving and keeping him company in bed. If he sees Chryses in camp again, his sacred staff will not protect him.

Terrified, Chryses goes back along the shore, praying to Apollo to punish the Greeks. Apollo hears the prayer and rushes toward the Greek camp with his quiver clanging.

Kneeling nearby, he unleashes his arrows, which cause a deadly plague. First mules and dogs die, then soldiers, and the camp is filled with funeral pyres.

After nine days, Achilles calls an assembly. He wants to ask some holy man why Apollo has sent a plague. The Greeks' priest, Calchas, says that he is willing to speak but asks Achilles for a promise of protection since his words may anger a great king. Achilles promises.

Calchas says that the Greeks have to free Chryses' daughter without a ransom to end the plague. This irks Agamemnon, who says that Calchas's prophesies are never beneficial for him. He wanted to keep Chryseis, because he prefers her to his own wife, Clytemnestra. He will give her up to save the army, but he demands to be compensated with a new prize.

Achilles objects, calling Agamemnon the greediest of men. He points out that the Greeks have no spare prizes. They have distributed all the booty that they have won. After they conquer Troy, he says, they will repay Agamemnon for the loss of Chyrseis.

Agamemnon rejects that suggestion. He says that he will not go without a prize. Either the Greeks will give him one, or he will just take one—from anyone he chooses, including Achilles.

This outrages Achilles. He has no personal grievance against the Trojans, he says. He fights only as a favor to Agamemnon and his brother Menelaus. He does more than his share of the work while Agamemnon gets the biggest gifts. He is going home.

Agamemnon tells him to go. Meanwhile, however, he will take Achilles' prize, the slave girl Briseis, as compensation for Chryseis. Hearing this, Achilles reaches for his sword. He is on the verge of killing Agamemnon, but before he does it, Athena appears to him alone. She grabs the hair on the back of his head and tells him to put back his sword. He will be repaid for this insult in the future.

Achilles obeys. Calling Agamemnon a "wineskin with the eyes of a dog and the heart of a deer," he swears a formal oath that Greeks will look for him in vain someday, when they are being slaughtered by the Trojan Hector.

After the elderly King Nestor fails to reconcile Agamemnon and Achilles, the assembly breaks up. Odysseus escorts Chryseis back to her father. Agamemnon sends heralds to Achilles' tent to take Briseis. Achilles receives them courteously and has his comrade, Patroclus, bring the girl to them.

Achilles goes to a lonely spot on the beach, weeps, and calls to his mother, the sea goddess Thetis. When she arrives, Achilles describes what has happened. He reminds her that she claims to have influence with Zeus. Supposedly, Thetis once saved him from a rebellion by Hera, Poseidon, and Athena by bringing him a hundred-armed giant to be a bodyguard. Would she now ask Zeus to punish the Greeks in battle, to teach Agamemnon a lesson? Thetis agrees to do so—in 12 days, when Zeus returns from Ethiopia, where he is attending a feast.

Twelve days later, Thetis flies to Olympus, finds Zeus alone on the mountain's highest peak, and explains what she wants. Zeus lets her know that her favor is not easy since his wife Hera already complains that he helps the Trojans too much. Nevertheless, he assents. Olympus shakes when he nods his head.

During the night, Zeus sends a deceptive dream to Agamemnon, promising him that Troy will fall if he leads the army into battle that morning. Agamemnon rises, shares his dream with the other generals, and assembles the entire host, though Achilles and his men stay in their tents.

At the assembly, Agamemnon tests his troops' morale by pretending to be discouraged, suggesting that they all go home. At once, the assembly breaks up, and the soldiers run for the ships. All that prevents the war from ending at this point is that Hera sends Athena to the scene. She goes to Odysseus and tells him to talk the men into coming back. Odysseus chases down the retreating soldiers, reasoning with kings and abusing common men. The army flows back into the assembly.

Now, a man named Thersites addresses the soldiers. Bow-legged and lame, he is the ugliest man in the army, has round shoulders, a hollow chest, and a bald, pointed head, and loves to criticize his leaders. He urges the Greeks to give up and go home. Agamemnon, he says, is too greedy and has now offended the army's best warrior. Odysseus rises to silence Thersites. He says that the has no right to criticize superior warriors, and if he ever speaks again, Odysseus will strip him naked and flog him. Then, to the cheers of the other soldiers, Odysseus hits Thersites across the back with the scepter that he holds, driving him away in tears.

Odysseus next reminds the army of a sign that they saw when leaving for Troy. A snake climbed a tree, devoured a mother sparrow and eight chicks, and was then changed to stone by the gods. At that time, Calchas predicted that Troy would hold out for nine years and fall in the tenth. And this is the tenth year.

The Greeks disperse for breakfast, then assemble in battle formation, representing the various tribes of Greece. Ajax the Lesser leads the Locrians. He is small and dresses in linen but is a good spearman. Ajax the Greater leads a small fleet from the island of Salamis. Diomedes leads a great fleet from Argos and Tiryns. Agamemnon, the greatest king of all, leads the largest fleet from Mycenae. His brother, Menelaus, leads the men of Sparta. He is eager to avenge the loss of Helen. The elderly Nestor leads the men of Pylos. Odysseus leads a small fleet from Ithaca and other nearby islands. Idomeneus leads the men of Crete. Achilles leads the men of Phthia and nearby regions. They are known as the Myrmidons. They stay in their tents because of Achilles' anger. The others march into the plain.

In Troy, old king Priam is holding an assembly, when the goddess Iris, disguised as a young Trojan lookout, announces that the Greeks are marching toward the city. The Trojans march out to meet them. They are led by Priam's son, Hector. Other Trojan leaders are Aeneas, son of Aphrodite and Anchises, and the archer Pandaros. Foreign allies swell the Trojan army. These include Sarpedon of Lycia and his comrade Glaucus.

As the armies approach each other, Hector's brother Paris sees Menelaus and shrinks back behind the front lines. Hector scolds him for stealing Menelaus's wife but not being man enough to stand up to him in battle—where good looks don't help. Paris acknowledges the justice of Hector's words and volunteers to fight Menelaus in a single combat to end the war. Hector strides between the armies and gets everybody on both sides to sit down so that arrangements can be made for a truce and the single combat. Soldiers on both sides are very happy.

Soon, the fight is underway. After the warriors exchange spear casts, Menelaus charges Paris with a drawn sword, which he shatters on Paris' helmet. Frustrated, he grabs the helmet by hand, spins Paris around, and drags him toward the Greek lines—and certain death. Aphrodite, however, breaks the helmet's chin strap so that it comes off in Menelaus's hand. As Menelaus turns back, Aphrodite wraps Paris in a dark mist, picks him up, and sets him down in his bedroom. Then, disguised as an old seamstress, she finds Helen and tells her to visit Paris in their bedroom. She says that he looks like he has just come from a dance, not a battle. Helen recognizes Aphrodite through her disguise and refuses to go, because of what the Trojan women will say. This draws an angry rebuke from Aphrodite, who threatens to abandon Helen to the hatred of Greeks and Trojans alike. Helen is frightened and obeys.

In the bedroom, Helen scolds Paris for having boasted that he was a better warrior than Menelaus. Paris says that Menelaus just happened to have the gods on his side. They will fight again in the future. For the present, they should go to bed together. He has never desired her more, not even when they made love the first time on the island of Cranae as they were sailing away from Sparta. Helen gives in.

Outside the city walls, Menelaus is storming up and down, looking for Paris. Agamemnon announces that his brother won and that the war should end on the Greeks' terms. Zeus, however, sends Athena to the battlefield to restart the war. She crosses the sky in the form of a comet and then appears on the plain disguised as a young Trojan noble. She sidles up to Pandaros, the archer, and tells him to take a shot at Menelaus. Paris, she says, will give him a huge reward for killing him. Persuaded, Pandaros shoots but only grazes Menelaus's waist. Seeing the blood flow down his leg—like red dye on ivory—Agamemnon fears the worst and summons physicians, who quickly mend the wound. Meanwhile, the two sides put their armor back on and resume their march toward each other. The Greeks advance in silence; the Trojans bleating like sheep. Soon the battle rages, with countless deaths on both sides.

The Greek Diomedes is wounded in the foot by Pandaros. Then, revived by Athena, he goes on a rampage. One of the first to fall to him is Pandaros himself. Diomedes' spear enters Pandaros's face beside the eye, severs his tongue, and comes out the bottom of his jaw. When Aphrodite carries the wounded Aeneas out of harm's way, Diomedes even wounds her in the wrist. Later, with Athena's help, he strikes Ares himself in the belly and forces him to withdraw from battle.

Diomedes finally slows down when he is about to fight the Trojan ally, Glaucus. He asks Glaucus whether he is a god or a mortal man, since he does not want to do battle against the gods. Glaucus responds,

"High-spirited son of Tydeus, why ask about my origins.
Generations of men are like generations of leaves.
Some leaves are flung down to the earth by the breeze, while others
Burst to life in the woods when the season of spring arrives.
Just so a generation of men is born; another passes."

Glaucus goes on to explain that he is the grandson of a great hero, Bellerophon. Hearing this, Diomedes exclaims that his own grandfather, Oeneus, was a friend to Bellerophon. Hence, he and Glaucus have an ancient connection. Instead of fighting, therefore, the two heroes exchange gifts and agree to avoid each other in battle. Glaucus loses out in the exchange of gifts, giving Diomedes golden armor in return for bronze.

Since the Trojans are losing, Hector goes into the city to ask the Trojan women to say special prayers to Athena for help. Before he returns to battle, Hector stops by Paris's bedroom. Paris says that he is just getting ready to fight.

Hector also seeks out his wife, Andromache. She has gone to the city walls with their infant son to watch the battle. Seeing Hector, she tells him that it is cruel of him to risk his life. She was born in a nearby town that was stormed by the Greeks. Achilles killed her father and seven brothers in one day. Her mother then died of an illness. Hector is all she has left. Instead of fighting in the plain, he should adopt a defensive strategy by strengthening the weak spots in the wall.

Hector replies that his pride will not let him act like a coward. He knows that Troy will fall. The worst part is that Andromache will be taken into slavery by the Greeks. Hector says he wants to be dead before that happens.

Hector extends his arms to pick up his baby son. The child cries, frightened by his father's war helmet. Hector and Andromache laugh. Hector takes off his helmet, picks up the boy, and prays that he grow up to be a mighty warrior and bring home bloody spoil to delight his mother's heart.

Turning to Andromache, Hector tells her not to grieve. He will not die before his fated time. She should go back to her work at the loom. War, he says, is the business of men, especially him. As Hector runs back into the battlefield, he is joined by an enthusiastic Paris, who is heading in the same direction.

After more fighting, the gods inspire a Trojan prophet to suggest a single combat to bring the battle to an end for the day. He passes the suggestion on to Hector, who separates the armies, and challenges any Greek to fight him one on one. After a long silence, Menelaus reluctantly volunteers, but he is immediately overridden by Agamemnon, who tells him that he would have no chance against Hector. Nestor then criticizes the Greeks for their fear of Hector and wishes he was young again like the time he killed a giant in single combat. Stung by his words, all the Greeks volunteer—except Menelaus. One is chosen by lot. It turns out to be their best warrior, Ajax the Greater. He and Hector fight. Ajax is dominant, but darkness falls and heralds part them. They exchange gifts, and the two armies retire for the night. There is a truce, during which both sides bury their dead and the Greeks build a defensive wall and trench in front of their camp.

On the next day of battle, the Trojans, aided by Zeus and Achilles' absence, gain the upper hand, driving the Greeks back within their wall. When night falls, the jubilant Trojans pitch camp on the plain.

Meeting with the other kings, Agamemnon is despondent, and regrets offending Achilles. He sends three ambassadors—Odysseus, Ajax the Greater, and Phoenix, Achilles' elderly tutor—to ask him to return to battle. If Achilles agrees, Agamemnon promises to give him seven tripods, ten talents of gold, 20 bronze cauldrons, 12 horses, and seven slave girls from Lesbos, and to return Briseis untouched. After the war, Achilles can have 20 Trojan women of his choice, any one of Agamemnon's three daughters in marriage, and seven of Agamemnon's cities. The ambassadors report Agamemnon's offer in long speeches, but Achilles rejects it. He is considering going home. His mother has told him, he says, that he will die if he stays in Troy, although he will win everlasting glory. If he goes home, he will have a long life but lose his glory. In any event, Agamemnon's gifts mean nothing to him. He cannot forgive his insults.

Later that same night, Diomedes and Odysseus sneak into the Trojan camp, kill a Thracian king who has just arrived to help Troy, and steal his magnificent, snowy white horses.

A new battle begins. The Greeks are being worn down. Agamemnon, Diomedes, and Odysseus are wounded and withdraw from battle. Then the Greek physician himself, Machaon, is wounded and taken back to the camp by Nestor. Watching the battle from the prow of his ship, Achilles notices this, and sends Patroclus to ask Nestor if the wounded soldier is indeed Machaon. Nestor confirms the fact and detains Patroclus, telling him how desperate the Greeks; situation is. He suggests that Patroclus borrow Achilles' armor -- to frighten the Trojans—and lead the Myrmidons into battle, just to keep the Trojans from destroying the Greek fleet. Patroclus leaves to ask Achilles about this, but he must stop on the way to bandage the wounds of a comrade.

Sarpedon and Hector lead an attack against the Greek wall. Finally, Hector breaks through the gate with a huge boulder, and the Trojans pour inside the Greek camp, where the Greeks rally and the battle rages. The best Greek warriors still fighting are the two Ajaxes, Idomeneus of Crete, Menelaus, and Nestor's young son, Antilochus.

The Greeks are given some encouragement by Poseidon, but he does not help them openly, because Zeus has forbidden the gods to interfere in battle and is watching the scene from the top of Mount Ida, south of Troy. Understanding this, Hera decides to put Zeus to sleep. Bathing and dressing, she asks Aphrodite to lend her loveliness and desirability. Hera claims that she is on her way to patch up a quarrel between their parents, Oceanus and Tethys. Aphrodite removes a richly embroidered undergarment, and tells Hera to place it in her bosom. She is sure to get her wish.

Hera next visits the god of Sleep, to ask him to descend on Zeus after she has lain with him. At first, Sleep refuses from fear of Zeus, but Hera wins him over by offering to let him marry Pasithea, one of the younger Graces, whom he has always loved.

While Sleep watches in the form of a bird on the branch of a pine, Hera walks by Zeus. She again claims to be on her way to Oceanus and Tethys. Zeus asks her to lie with him instead. He declares that he has never desired any woman or goddess more—not when he fathered Pirithous on Ixion's wife, Perseus on Danae, Minos on Europa, Dionysus on Semele, or Heracles on Alcmene, not when he made love to Demeter or to Leto—or to Hera herself. Hera objects that somebody might see them if they make love outdoors. Zeus takes care of that by enclosing them in a golden cloud. As they lie down, grass, clover, and hyacinth and crocus blossoms instantly grow out of the ground to cushion them. Soon, Zeus is unconscious.

Sleep rushes to the plain to tell Poseidon to help the Greeks as openly as he wants. Poseidon rouses the two Ajaxes to lead a great rally. Soon, the Trojans are running out of the camp. Ajax knocks Hector out with a boulder. Then, Zeus wakes up and figures out what is going on. He sends Iris to order Poseidon out of the battle and Apollo to revive Hector. Roused by Apollo, Hector leads the Trojans back into the Greek camp, all the way to the ships.

As Ajax the Greater leads a desperate defense of the ships, barely preventing Hector from setting them on fire, Patroclus comes to Achilles in tears, asking him to let him save the ships. Achilles ridicules him, saying that he looks like a baby girl running to her mother, but agrees to his request. The Myrmidons prepare for battle. As they do, Hector finally drives Ajax back and sets fire to the first ship.

Patroclus and the Myrmidons rush into battle. The tide turns. Soon, the Trojans are retreating over the plain. Despite Achilles' command and his own promise, Patroclus does not turn back. He continues his rampage, hoping that Troy will fall that very day. Among the soldiers he kills is Sarpedon, Zeus's son and the best of Troy's allies. Zeus considers saving Sarpedon from his fate but is talked out of it by Hera. When Sarpedon falls, Zeus cries tears of blood and sends Sleep and Death to convey Sarpedon's body back to his homeland of Lycia.

Patroclus reaches the walls of Troy. Troy is not fated to fall at this point, however. To save it, Apollo sneaks up behind Patroclus and slaps him on the back, knocking off his armor, splintering his spear, and dazing him. A Trojan named Euphorbas sticks him in the back with his javelin and runs away. Finally, Hector steps up and drives his sword into his belly, killing him.

Hector recovers the armor of Achilles, which Patroclus had been wearing, but a great battle ensues over the corpse of Patroclus. Antilochus is sent to the camp to tell Achilles that Patroclus is dead. Achilles rolls in the dirt, weeping. His mother hears and arrives with a group of sea goddesses to comfort him. He says that he must avenge Patroclus's death by killing Hector. She points out that he is fated to die soon after Hector does, but that does not shake his resolution. He would like to enter the battle immediately. She tells him to wait until she brings him new armor made by Hephaestus.

Meanwhile, the two Ajaxes and Menelaus are laboring to bring Patroclus's body off the battlefield, barely fending off Hector. Unarmed, Achilles goes to the ditch. Thanks to Athena, a great flame shoots from his head. He lets out a battle cry that panics the Trojans. They retreat in such disorder that 12 of them are killed by their own chariots and spears. The Greeks easily bring Patroclus the rest of the way into the camp.

Thetis arrives at Hephaestus's home, and asks him to make new armor for Achilles. He is happy to comply. The most spectacular piece is a huge shield, in which numerous scenes of war and peace, farming, and herding are depicted in gold, silver, and bronze. The figures on the shield move. The earth turns black beneath the farmers' plows in one scene, while a battle rages in another; a marriage is celebrated in a third scene.

The next morning, Thetis delivers the armor, which is so beautiful that it terrifies the Myrmidons. Agamemnon arrives. He and Achilles announce the end of their quarrel. Achilles says that it was foolish to let a girl cause so much suffering and wishes that Briseis had died on the day she was captured. Agamemnon attributes his behavior to a goddess, Atē (Blindness), a daughter of Zeus. He delivers the gifts he promised, including Briseis, and swears that he never slept with her. Achilles would like to go into battle immediately, but Odysseus convinces him that the other soldiers need to eat first. As Achilles prepares for battle, he bitterly tells the horses that pull his chariot to take better care of him than they did of Patroclus. The lead horse, Xanthos (Goldie), is given the power of speech by Hera. He says that it was not their fault that Patroclus died; he was killed by Apollo, and there was nothing they could have done to save him. They will bring Achilles back today, but he is fated to die soon anyway, and they cannot prevent that either.

Achilles leads the Greeks into battle and slaughters the Trojans. Many flee into a river, the Scamander, which is clogged with the corpses of Trojans killed by Achilles. The river itself comes to life and asks Achilles to stop polluting his waters. When Achilles refuses, the river attacks him, pummeling him with waves. Achilles gets extra strength from Poseidon and Athena, but the Scamander is also reinforced by his tributaries. Finally, Hera has Hephaestus ignite fire all around the river, so that the water starts boiling. The river meekly settles down, begging for mercy.

To enable the Trojans to escape Achilles' attack, Apollo disguises himself as a Trojan and draws Achilles away from the city by taunting him and running away. By the time Apollo reveals himself, they are some distance away, and most of the Trojans are safely within the city gates. Hector, however, stays outside.

On the walls of Troy, Hector's father and mother beg Hector to preserve his own life and Troy's chances of survival by coming inside. Otherwise, Priam foresees that he will be slain by the Greeks, and his own dogs will eat his corpse, mutilating his gray head and beard and private parts. Hector's mother, Hecuba, bares her breasts and holds one out in her hand, asking Hector to have pity on her if she nursed him when he was a baby.

Despite their pleas, Hector stays. He converses with his own spirit. It would be shameful to retreat now, he thinks. Perhaps he should take off his armor and negotiate with Achilles. He could promise to give back Helen and her treasure and let the Greeks have all of Troy's wealth. And yet Achilles might kill him like a woman if he approached him unarmed. He decides that there is no way to avoid fighting him.

As Achilles approaches, however, Hector suddenly panics and flees. Achilles chases him around the walls of Troy three times. Each time, they pass the two springs, one hot and one cold, where the Trojan women wash clothes in times of peace. As they approach the springs the fourth time, Athena draws alongside Hector. She is disguised as his brother, Deiphobos, and volunteers to help him fight Achilles.

Hector turns to face his enemy with the help of "Deiphobos." They exchange spear casts, but neither draws blood. Hector asks the fake Deiphobos for another spear, but no one is there. He realizes what is happening and speaks to his own spirit again. "That was not Deiphobos," he says, "but Athena tricking me. The gods are summoning me to death. That must have been Zeus's plan all along. I will, however, not die without a glorious struggle." With this, Hector draws his sword and charges. Achilles sees a vulnerable spot in Hector's armor at the base of his neck and drives his spear into it. He wounds him fatally but does not sever Hector's windpipe. With his dying breath, Hector asks Achilles to let his parents have his corpse for burial. Achilles says that he would not return Hector's corpse for its weight in gold. He makes holes by the tendons between Hector's heels and his ankles. Inserting leather straps, he ties Hector to his chariot, and drags him around Troy.

On the wall, the Trojans lament. Andromache has been preparing a warm bath for Hector. She hears the cries, runs to the walls, and sees Hector being dragged. At first, she faints. Then she recovers and joins in the lamentation. Now that Hector's son is fatherless, she says, his playmates will treat him with contempt, hitting him and throwing him out of their banquets.

Achilles returns to camp with Hector's body, which he drags in front of Patroclus's bier, then leaves it, exposed for dogs to mangle. Apollo and Aphrodite, however, protect the body from damage. That night, the ghost of Patroclus appears to Achilles in a dream and asks that his body be cremated, since he will not be permitted to cross the river to Hades' house until that happens. The next day, Patroclus is cremated on a great pyre, a hundred feet square. Cattle and sheep are sacrificed. Achilles cuts the throats of four horses, two dogs, and 12 young Trojan prisoners, and burns them on the pyre, too. Then he organizes funeral games with lavish prizes to honor Patroclus. Diomedes wins the chariot race when the favorite crashes. Odysseus upsets Ajax the Lesser in the footrace, when the latter slips and falls face-first in dung left behind by sacrificial oxen.

After the funeral, Achilles is still sad about Patroclus. He spends time crying. Occasionally, he drags Hector's body with his chariot. The gods are angered by this behavior. Thetis goes to Achilles at Zeus's command, and tells him that Zeus wants him to accept ransom for the body. Achilles consents. Meanwhile, Iris appears to Priam, who is in deep mourning, and tells him that he can ransom Hector's body from Achilles. Hermes will escort him safely to the Greek camp.

Priam loads a donkey cart with treasures, and sets out across the plain at dusk. He is met by Hermes disguised as a young Myrmidon. With Hermes' help, Priam comes to Achilles' shelter and bursts in on him just as he finishes eating dinner. He asks Achilles for mercy. He once had 50 sons, he says, 19 by one mother. Now, most of them are dead, including the best one, and he has done something unheard of: kissed the hands of the man who killed his children.

The appeal moves Achilles to tears as he thinks of his own father. He tells Priam that Zeus has two urns beside his throne, one with blessings, the other with evils, and he scatters them indiscriminately. Then when Priam asks if he may have Hector's body immediately, Achilles flares up at him. He says that he will give up the body because his mother brought him a message from Zeus telling him to. He is also aware that Priam must have had divine help getting into his shelter. Achilles then leaves to have servants unload Priam's ransom, wash and anoint Hector's body, and load it on the wagon. Afterward, he and Priam share a meal, and Priam is given a place to sleep. In the middle of the night, Hermes wakes Priam, and tells him to leave before he is discovered by the other Greeks. As the sun rises, Priam's daughter, Cassandra, standing atop the Trojan citadel, sees him returning to the city, and summons the people of Troy. Andromache, Hecuba, and Helen mourn for Hector. Helen has the last word, saying that Hector never let the other Trojans speak harshly to her. Priam announces that Achilles has granted a 12-day truce to the Trojans. During this time, they bury Hector, tamer of horses.

58. The Death of Achilles

Source: Byzantine summary of *The Aethiopid*, by Arctinus of Miletus (Archaic Greek)

The Amazon Penthesilea arrives to fight for the Trojans. She is the Thracian daughter of Ares. Achilles kills her while she is fighting valiantly. The Trojans bury her. Achilles kills the cowardly Greek, Thersites, for accusing him of having fallen in love with Penthesilea.

Memnon, the son of Eos (Dawn) and Tithonus, appears to help the Trojans. He wears armor made by Hephaestus. In the next battle, Nestor's son, Antilochus, is killed by Memnon. Then, Achilles kills Memnon. Obtaining permission from Zeus, Eos gives Memnon immortality. Achilles routs the Trojans. Rushing into the city, he is killed by Paris and Apollo.[27] There is a mighty battle over his body. Ajax carries it to the ships, while Odysseus fights off the Trojans. The Greeks bury Antilochus, and lay Achilles' body in state. Thetis arrives with her sisters and the Muses to mourn for her son. Afterward, she snatches her son's body from the pyre and transports it to White Island. The Greeks build a burial mound and hold a contest, in which Achilles' armor is the prize. Odysseus and Ajax quarrel over it.

---

27   There is no detailed account of Achilles' death among early authors. The statement that Achilles died of an arrow to the ankle first appears in the *Fabulae* of Hyginus, brief synopses of myths that seem to have been written in the 2nd century A.D.

59. The Death of Ajax

Source: Sophocles, *Ajax* (Classical Greek tragedy)

Odysseus is prowling around the beach at Troy, near the shelter of Ajax the Greater. Appearing in the sky, Athena asks him what he is doing. He says that he has come to spy on his enemy. There is a report that Ajax attacked the Greeks' herds in the night. Athena tells him what actually happened. In his anger over not winning the contest for Achilles' armor, Ajax resolved to murder Agamemnon, Menelaus, and Odysseus. Athena watched as Ajax snuck through the night to Agamemnon's doors. Then she drove him crazy so that he attacked the herds instead, thinking that they were men. He even dragged some animals back to his tent and is now torturing them.

To show off her power, Athena calls Ajax out of his tent, over the objections of a terrified Odysseus. Ajax cannot see Odysseus, however. He tells Athena that one of his "prisoners" is Odysseus, and he intends to flog him and kill him. When Ajax returns to his tent, Odysseus says that he feels sorry for him even though he is his enemy.

As Odysseus exits, a chorus of sailors enters. They are followers of Ajax from his native island of Salamis. They have heard terrible stories about Ajax's violence—spread by Odysseus—and hope that he will discredit them. Tecmessa emerges from the tent. She is Ajax's beloved Phrygian captive, the mother of his young son, Eurysaces. She describes how Ajax left the shelter in the middle of the night with his sword drawn. When Tecmessa asked what he was doing, he answered her with a brief proverb: "Silence becomes women." He soon returned to the shelter driving bulls, dogs, and sheep. Inside, he decapitated some and beat and abused others as though they were human beings. He tied a ram to a pillar and whipped it. Then his sanity slowly returned. When he was fully aware of what he had done, he sat down among the slaughtered carcasses, clutching his head in silence. Then he began crying, wailing terribly in a manner that he would have called womanly in the past.

Tecmessa opens the door of the shelter so that the sailors can try to comfort their leader. Ajax denounces Agamemnon and Menelaus for awarding Achilles' armor to Odysseus. He then says that he has decided to kill himself. He feels that he cannot return home in disgrace. He is obviously hated by the gods and by the Greeks and Trojans alike. He could seek death in battle, but by doing so he would please the Greek commanders, whom he detests.

Tecmessa begs Ajax to change his mind. She says that ever since he destroyed her city, taking her captive, she has had an enviable life. Now both she and their little boy would be helpless without him. Also, Ajax's father and mother long to see him safe at home.

Without responding, Ajax has his son brought out of the shelter. He prays that his son will be more fortunate than his father, but similar in other ways. If so, he says, he will not be a bad man. He gives his great shield to his son and asks his crew to see that he is cared for by his half brother, Teucer, who is absent on a raiding party. Fearing the worst, Tecmessa again begs Ajax to relent. He tells her that she has spoken too much already and returns to the shelter.

After a choral interlude, Ajax emerges from the shelter, apparently in an altered state of mind. He says that everything changes in the course of time and that he himself has changed from steely resolution to womanly tenderness under the influence of his wife. He says that he intends to go a seaside meadow to bathe and pray that Athena release him from madness. He will also bury his sword. It was a gift from his enemy, Hector, given to him after they fought in single combat; it has brought Ajax nothing but bad luck. In the future, he will be more flexible, bowing to necessity, just as snow melts in summer and night yields dawn.

After the chorus sings a song expressing their relief, a messenger enters. He has been sent by Teucer, who just returned from his raid. His message is not to let Ajax leave his shelter on this day. This request is based on advice just given to Teucer by the Greek priest Calchas. According to him, Athena is temporarily angry at Ajax because he once boasted that he would win glory at Troy without the help of the gods. Any weakling, he declared, could triumph with divine assistance.

Hearing this, Tecmessa and the chorus exit to look for Ajax, leaving the stage empty. When Ajax enters, the scene is assumed to have become a meadow by seashore. He carefully plants his sword in the ground and prays to Zeus that Teucer, rather than some enemy, will recover his body. He bids farewell to the sunlight, to Salamis and Athens, his comrades and kinsmen at Troy—and falls on his sword and dies, rolling into the bushes out of sight.

The chorus enters the dancing area as Tecmessa appears on stage. Soon she begins wailing terribly because she sees Ajax's body. Teucer arrives and is equally grief-stricken.

Menelaus and Agamemon enter. They try to enforce a decree denying Ajax a proper burial. Teucer is determined to defy it. Before violence erupts, Odysseus intervenes. He says that even though Ajax was his enemy, he was obviously courageous and noble. Besides, a victory over a corpse brings no honor. Heeding his words, Agememnon and Menelaus permit the funeral to proceed.

60. Philoctetes

Source: Sophocles, *Philoctetes* (Classical Greek Tragedy)

After the death of Achilles and the arrival of his son Neoptolemus, the Greeks at Troy learned from the prophet Helenus that they had to have Heracles' bow and arrows to win the war. These belonged to a Greek warrior named Philoctetes. On the way to Troy, however, Philoctetes was bitten by a poisonous snake, and the resulting wound was so foul smelling, and Philoctetes' moans so disturbing, that the Greek leaders abandoned him on the deserted island of Lemnos. He has languished there ever since.

Odysseus and Neoptolemus appear outside Philoctetes' cave on Lemnos. They have come to retrieve Heracles' weapons. As they inspect the cave, Odysseus explains their need for caution.He says that after what happened ten years before, Philoctetes will undoubtedly want to kill Odysseus the moment he sees him. He will never willingly help the Greeks now. They will need to use deception to achieve their goal. Odysseus says that Neoptolemus must seek out Philoctetes, feigning ignorance of his identity, and introduce himself as the son of Achilles. He must say that after his arrival in Troy, he was enraged at the awarding of his father's arms to Odysseus. Hence, he left Troy and is on his way home. In this way, he will win Philoctetes' trust.It will then be easy to acquire the bow and arrows. Neoptolemus does not like to lie, but Odysseus assures him that it is necessary and exits.

The chorus of Neoptolemus's crewmen enters and asks what they must do. Neoptolemus tells them to be ready to play their part when he gives them the sign. They express pity for Philoctetes. Cries of pain are heard, and Philoctetes himself enters limping. He asks Neoptolemus and his sailors who they are and why they have come. Neoptolemus identifies himself and listens to Philoctetes' story. He responds with the false version of events at Troy that Odysseus concocted. Philoctetes asks how Ajax could have allowed such a thing to happen, and he is informed of Ajax's suicide and the deaths of many others about whom he inquires. Philoctetes says that all the good men are dead, while the bad ones live on.Neoptolemus says that he is ready to leave for Greece.Philoctetes begs to be taken along so he can end his exile. The chorus plays its part by pleading with Neoptolemus on Philoctetes' behalf. Neoptolemus consents.

A Greek sailor sent by Odysseus arrives. He is disguised as a merchant and says that he has come to give Neoptolemus a warning: Greeks are coming from Troy to take him back. As for Philoctetes, Odysseus is on his way to seize him. Convinced of danger, Philoctetes is now desperate to leave. First, however, he wants to retrieve a pain-killing herb that he keeps in the cave. Neoptolemus asks him if the bow he is carrying is the famous one of Heracles; hearing that it is, he asks if he will be allowed to touch it. Philoctetes says that he will be allowed to touch the bow, and the two enter the cave.

The chorus sings of the past misery of Philoctetes and the likelihood that he will now see his home once again. Neoptolemus and Philoctetes return. Philoctetes' wound flares up, leaving him in excruciating pain. In his pain, he hands his bow to Neoptolemus, warning him not to let anyone else touch it. As his pain subsides, he falls asleep from exhaustion. The crewmen urge Neoptolemus to leave with the bow, but he cannot bring himself to do so.

Philoctetes wakes up, feeling better, and thanks Neoptolemus and the chorus for standing by him. Neoptolemus cannot keep up the charade any longer. He tells Philoctetes that he must return to Troy. Philoctetes is shocked and enraged and demands his bow back.

At this point, Odysseus bursts in. Far from being willing to return to Troy, Philoctetes curses and denounces him at length. Odysseus says that it is enough that they have Philoctetes' bow. He orders Neoptolemus to come along with him, bringing the bow. Neoptolemus tells the crewmen to wait with Philoctetes until they depart in case he changes his mind. Then he leaves, taking the bow, as Odysseus commanded.

Philoctetes sings of his unending misery, while the chorus sings to encourage him to consider the advantages of going to Troy.

Suddenly, Odysseus and Neoptolemus return, arguing. Seeing them, Philoctetes retreats into his cave. In fact, Neoptolemus has come to give the bow and arrows back to Philoctetes. Odysseus threatens him with the fury of the entire Greek army if he does so, but Neoptolemus is determined, and Odysseus exits in disgust.

Neoptolemus summons Philoctetes. He is astonished and gladly accepts the bow back. Odysseus comes back again, still insisting that Philoctetes must go to Troy with him. Philoctetes aims an arrow at Odysseus, but Neoptolemus prevents him from shooting. Odysseus retreats in safety.

Neoptolemus tries to persuade Philoctetes to forgive the Greeks. It is fate, he says, for the war to end soon with the help of his bow. Philoctetes, however, is convinced that nothing good will happen to him at Troy and reminds Neoptolemus that he had promised to take him home—not to Troy. Neoptolemus says that he will keep his promise, and the two prepare to depart for Greece.

The ghost of Heracles appears over the cave. Having earned immortality after his death, Heracles has come now to proclaim the will of Zeus. Philoctetes, he says, must go to Troy, where his wound will be healed by Asclepius. Using his bow, Philoctetes will kill Paris. He will then return home with glory and riches after the sack of Troy. An awestruck Neoptolemus and Philoctetes swear to abide by this divine command, and the chorus invokes the aid of the sea-nymphs for their journey, as everyone exits.

61. The Fall of Troy

Source: Byzantine summaries of *The Little Iliad*, by Lesches of Mitylene, and *The Sack of Ilium*, by Arctinus of Miletus (Archaic Greek)

The awarding of Achilles' armor takes place and Odysseus wins, thanks to Athena's scheming. Ajax goes mad, attacks the Greeks' herd, and kills himself.

Odysseus captures the Trojan prophet ,Helenus. Because of his prophecies about the fall of Troy, Diomedes brings Philoctetes from Lemnos. Philoctetes is cured by the Greek physician and kills Paris in single combat. Paris's corpse is mutilated by Menelaus, but the Trojans recover it for burial.

Paris's brother, Deiphobus, marries Helen. Odysseus brings Neoptolemus, Achilles' son, from Scyros and gives him his father's armor.

Following Athena's instructions, a Greek named Epeus builds a wooden horse. Then, after putting their best men in it and burning their huts, the Greeks sail to the island of Tenedos.

The Trojans are suspicious of the horse and stand around debating what they should do with it. Some want to hurl it to destruction and others to burn it, but still others say that it should be dedicated to Athena in her temple. Finally, this last opinion prevails, and the Trojans celebrate the end of the war. They destroy a part of their city wall to get the wooden horse inside and feast as though they had conquered the Greeks.

The fall of the city follows. Menelaus kills Deiphobus, but he spares Helen when he sees her bare-breasted. Ajax the Lesser seizes Cassandra in the temple of Athena, toppling the sacred statue of Athena as he does so. Angered at this, the Greeks wish to stone him, but he takes refuge at the altar of Athena. Achilles' son, Neoptolemus, kills Priam, who has taken refuge at the temple of Zeus, and he claims Hector's wife, Andromache, as part of his booty. He or Odysseus snatches her infant son, Astyanax, and throws him to his death from the Trojan citadel.

The Greeks burn the city and sacrifice Priam's daughter, Polyxena, at the tomb of Achilles.

62. Priam's Family in Captivity

Source: Euripides, *Trojan Women* (Classical Greek Drama)

Poseidon appears on the shore near Troy. He says that he has come to bid farewell to the city, which he has loved since he and Apollo built its walls. Priam is dead, and the Greeks are loading the treasures of Troy on their ships. Some female captives have been set aside to be the slaves of the Greek kings. They are waiting in a nearby tent with Helen. Queen Hecuba, however, lies on the ground outside. She does not yet know that her daughter, Polyxena, has been sacrificed on Achilles' grave.

Athena enters, saying that she wants to ask Poseidon for a favor. She is angry, because Ajax the Lesser dragged Cassandra from her temple, and the Greeks did nothing to punish him. She wants storms to wreck their fleet. Zeus has promised thunder. She needs Poseidon to churn up great waves. He agrees to do so.

Hecuba wakes up and sings a song of lamentation, placing blame on Helen. A chorus of Trojan women enter, joining her song. They fear that the Greeks are getting ready to take them away.

The Greek herald, Talthybius, enters to announce how the women are to be distributed. Cassandra has been given to Agamemnon to be his secret lover. Hecuba's daughter, Polyxena, is "a servant of Achilles' tomb." Hecuba asks whether Polyxena "still sees the light." Talthybius replies that "fate" has her. She has been freed from her troubles. Instead of seeking clarification, Hecuba asks about Andromache, Hector's wife, and learns that she has been given to Neoptolemus, Achilles' son. Finally, Hecuba learns that she herself now belongs to Odysseus. She is outraged, calling him foul and dishonest.

Talthybius says that he has to take Cassandra with him and will return for the others. Then he notices fire inside the women's shelter and wonders what is happening. Hecuba assures him that it is just her "maenad daughter, Casssandra."

Cassandra enters, holding burning torches and singing a mock-marriage hymn. "Blest is the groom! Happy am I to be married in a royal bed in Argos! While you keep weeping and moaning for Troy, I'm lighting the torches for my wedding."

Hecuba takes the torches away. Cassandra tells her to be happy since Agamemnon is going to die and her wedding will be involved. Compared to Agamemnon's home, she says, Troy is a happy place.

Talthybius tells Cassandra to follow him to Agamemon's ship. In an aside, he says that he would not marry such a deranged girl. He adds that since she is insane, he will ignore her threats to Agamemnon.

Cassandra predicts that it will take Odysseus ten more years to reach home, and he will find new sorrows there. As for Agamemnon, he will be buried evilly by night. Cassandra's own naked corpse will lie by his tomb for beasts to feed on. Saying that, she removes garlands and ornaments signifying that she is a priestess of Apollo and tells Talthybius to lead her away.

Hecuba collapses on the ground and laments her sufferings. The chorus joins in, singing a song that recalls the celebration when the Trojans took the wooden horse into the city. Everyone thought that peace had returned. In the midst of the celebration, war descended on the city, men were murdered, and brides violated.

Hector's wife, Andromache, enters on a wagon. She holds her baby son, Astyanax, in her arms. Hector's armor is arranged at her feet. She is being taken to Neoptolemus. She, too, laments her fate.

When Hecuba mentions Cassandra's fate, Andromache says that there is something she does not know: Polyxena is dead! Now Hecuba realizes what Talthybius meant. She cries out that she pities Polyxena, but Andromache says that her own fate is even worse. Death is like never having been born. The dead feel nothing. People who go from good fortune to bad miss their former happiness.

Andromache says that she did everything right. She avoided appearing in public and witty speech. She kept quiet in her husband's presence but imposed her will when necessary. Now she must choose between betraying Hector and being hated by her new master. She says that it usually takes just a single night of love to win over a woman's heart, but she despises women who accept a new man.

Hecuba tells Andromache to forget her marriage to Hector and win her new master's love. That way, her son will grow to manhood. Someday, he or his children might rebuild Troy.

Talthybius arrives and says that he wishes that he did not have to bring his horrible news. At the urging of Odysseus, the Greeks have decreed that the infant Astyanax must be thrown off the city's walls. Talthybius tells Andromache to give up the baby without cursing the Greeks. If she does so, the baby will have a decent funeral. Andromache hands him over, crying. She curses Helen, saying that she is not the child of Zeus but of Vengeance, Envy, Slaughter, Death, and all the earth's evils. As for herself, she tells the Greeks to throw her in the ship. She's going to her "lovely wedding" after having killed her child.

The chorus sings of Ganymede and Tithonus, loved by Zeus and the goddess Eos (Dawn), respectively. The gods, they say, used to love Troy, but now they have forgotten it.

Menelaus arrives to claim Helen, who is among the captive women. He says that the war was not fought to regain her but to punish Paris. He intends to take Helen back to Greece and have her stoned to death.

Helen is brought out and asks to be given a chance to plead for her life. Hecuba asks Menelaus to grant her request, but to let Hecuba herself refute her. Menelaus consents.

Helen says that the ultimate blame for the war lies with Hecuba, because she allowed the infant Paris to live despite a warning: Helen dreamed that she bore a burning torch that destroyed the city. She adds that her own fate was sealed when Paris gave his judgment among the goddesses. If he had chosen Athena or Hera, his reward would be royal power or prowess in warfare. Either way, he would have defeated the Greeks. Hence, Helen saved Greece from an Asiatic ruler. After Paris died in battle, Helen tried repeatedly to escape but was caught by Trojan guards again and again as she lowered a rope down the walls. Finally, Deiphobus married her by force.

Hecuba replies that the story of the judgment of Paris is unbelievable. Hera and Athena would not be so vain and childish. Aphrodite did not travel to Greece with Paris. As a goddess, she could have simply transported Helen to Troy if she had wanted to. Helen saw Paris's good looks and wealthy clothing and was overcome by desire. Her mind became "Aphrodite." In fact, Aphrodite just means folly. Her name even starts the same way as "intemperance" (*aphrosyne*). Helen must have left of her own free will. Otherwise, her brothers, Castor and Pollux, would have heard her screams and saved her. In Troy, if she dropped ropes down the walls, she never fashioned a noose or sharpened a dagger to kill herself, as any decent wife would have done. Hecuba urges Menelaus to kill Helen to show that the price of adultery is death.

Menelaus says that he agrees. He will have her stoned in Greece. Helen pleads for mercy on her knees, but Menelaus orders his servants to take her away. Hecuba begs him not to travel on the same ship with Helen. Menelaus says that he won't.

The chorus calls on Zeus, praying that Helen's boat is destroyed by Zeus's lightning.

Talthybius brings the corpse of Asytanax on Hector's shield. He says that Neoptolemus had to depart because of news that his grandfather, Peleus, was fighting an invader. He took Andromache with him. She asked that Hecuba tend to the baby's funeral, using Hector's shield in place of a coffin. Talthybius says that he will dig a grave for the boy while Hecuba prepares his body for burial.

Hecuba weeps over Astyanax's bloodied corpse. She recalls that he once promised to provide *her* a splendid funeral. She thinks that his epitaph should be: "The Greeks killed this baby because they feared him."

Captive women bring robes and ornaments for the corpse. Hecuba arranges them but soon asks the soldiers to take the body away to its humble grave. "I think it makes little difference to the dead," she says, "if they have a rich funeral. That is the empty ostentation of the living."

Talthybius arrives a final time. He gives the order to Greek soldiers to burn Troy and tells the women that they must now leave for the ships. As the women are led off, they see flames engulfing the city and hear the crash of its collapsing buildings.

63. The Death of Agamemnon

Source: Aeschylus, *Agamemnon* (Classical Greek tragedy)

Agamemnon's father, Atreus, gained royal power in Mycenae after a vicious struggle with his brother, Thyestes. Among their reciprocal atrocities, Atreus murdered Thyestes' young sons, and tricked him into eating their flesh. Thyestes survived long enough to sire another son, Aegisthus. While Agamemnon was away at Troy, Aegisthus and Clytemnestra joined forces. Both had reasons to hate Agamemnon.

A slave is standing on the roof of Agamemnon's palace. He is there to watch for a signal fire announcing the capture of Troy by the Greeks. He complains about the hardships that he has endured, sleeping on the roof. And then he sees the signal that he has been waiting for and shouts to Queen Clytemnestra to wake up. He says he hopes that Agamemnon gets home safely. As for the rest, he says, "a great ox has stepped on my tongue."

A chorus of old men comes to the palace to ask why Clytemnestra is offering joyous sacrifices. Did she get some news? As they enter, they sing about the Greeks' departure to Troy, with special emphasis on the sacrifice of Agamemnon's daughter, Iphigenia:

Winds from the Strymon were causing
inertia, famine, and madness,
inferior anchorage ruining cables
and ships. The endless waiting
withered the flower of Argives. And when the seer howled
a different and heavier
cure for the bitter
storm at the chiefs, invoked

the will of Artemis, made the Atreids strike the ground with their scepters and weep.

The elderly monarch spoke:
"Heavy the doom for defiance and heavy for killing my lovely child,
for polluting paternal hands
with innocent blood at the altar. Which way is free of evils?
Deserting the ships?
Failing my allies?
Their frantic, passionate
thirst to slaughter the maiden and stop the wind is just. Let us hope for the best."

When he buckled Necessity's strap,
a changing wind, unholy,
polluted, swirled through his mind.
He resolved that nothing would stop him.
Delusion's counsel initiates
woe by making mortals reckless. He dared
to kill his daughter to shore up a war avenging a woman
and bless his ships.
Hungry for battle, her judges
ignored her prayers, her innocent
age, her appeals to her father.
She sank to the ground as he prayed,
wrapping her robe around her.
He enjoined his attendants to lift her above the altar
at once like a yearling goat and restrain her beautiful mouth
from uttering curses

with the taciturn force of a gag.
Shedding her saffron gown,
demure as a work of art, she pierced her slayers in turn
with piteous darts of the eyes and longed
to call their names
because she had often honored
her father's manly feasts with a loving
hymn in her innocent voice when he poured the third libation.

I saw and tell no more.
Calchas's arts are effective.
Justice allocates knowledge to those who have suffered. The future

is known when it happens. Be glad until then.
Why grieve prematurely?
At dawn the light will glare.

Clytemnestra enters and tells the chorus that Troy has fallen. The chorus is skeptical, even though she describes her signal fires. It was prearranged that when Troy fell, a fire would be lit on Mount Ida. This would be the signal to slaves stationed on Lemnos to light a similar fire, and so on, to the promontory of Athos and down the coast of Greece to Mount Cithaeron, and across the Saronic gulf to Argos.

The chorus sings of the fall of Troy, brought low by Paris's sin, who "chased a bird, like a child and brought unbearable disgrace to his city." They also refer to the hardships of the war from the point of view of the Greeks. Ares is the "money changer of bodies, sending jars of tightly packed dust in return for men." The people's grief is mixed with resentment against the sons of Atreus.

The chorus doubts that Clytemnestra's signals are really trustworthy. They see a herald approaching and are anxious to learn the truth. He confirms that the Greeks are victorious and that Agamemnon will soon arrive. The herald describes some of the sufferings that the army endured at Troy but says that it can all be forgotten now, since the end was good.

Clytemnestra appears to say that she already knew the herald's news. The herald should report back to Agamemnon that she is as faithful to him as the day he left. She has not known pleasure from a man, any more than she has been dipping molten bronze in cold water.

Before the herald leaves, he informs the chorus that Menelaus's ship was separated from Agamemnon's in a bad storm on the way home. It is not known what became of him.

The chorus sings about Helen, whose beauty and charm spelled destruction for Troy. They compare Troy's fate to a man raising a playful lion cub as a pet. In time, it reveals its parental character, slaughtering the herds, and the house runs with blood.

Agamemnon arrives in a chariot with Cassandra beside him. He greets the gods of Argos and gives them thanks for victory over Troy. Soon he will hold an assembly to set the state in order, using medicine, burning, and amputation to correct whatever problems have arisen.

Clytemnestra bids Agamemnon welcome. She says that she constantly heard rumors of his death. If Agamemnon had actually been wounded every time she was told that he had been, he would have been as full of holes as a fishing net. She explains that she sent her son, Orestes, to a friend, Strophius of Phocis, for safekeeping, since she was worried about revolution in Agamemnon's absence. Finally, she suggests that Agamemnon enter the palace walking on a fine purple tapestry, which her serving women spread before him.

Agamemnon says that Clytemnestra's speech was appropriate for his absence: it lasted a long time. He does not, however, wish to ruin the expensive tapestry. Clytemnestra insists, saying that Troy's king Priam would not have been afraid to do so—and that it would be gracious of him to yield on this one matter. Agamemnon reluctantly gives in. As he enters, he tells his servants to bring Cassandra into the palace and to treat her well. She is a gift from the Greek army, the choice flower of his booty.

There is a choral interlude. The chorus is anxious but cannot say why. "Why does this fear steadily flutter before my prophetic heart?" they ask.

Clytemnestra appears and tells Cassandra to come inside the palace, but she does not respond—either to the queen or to the chorus, which encourages her to obey. Clytemnestra tells her either to do something or if she does not understand what is being said, to give a signal with her hand. When nothing happens, Clytemnestra returns to the palace, exasperated.

Now Cassandra starts moaning, accusing Apollo of having destroyed her. She speaks obscurely of the cursed palace, "babies bewailing slaughter and roasted flesh eaten by a father," and a new atrocity brewing inside. Finally, she says that her prophecy will no longer "glance shyly from behind a veil like a young bride." In answer to the chorus's question, she says that Apollo gave her prophetic powers because he loved her.

"Did you two come together for the production of children?"

"I promised Apollo, but I lied."

"How then did you escape harm from Apollo's anger?"

"I could never persuade anyone of anything."

Cassandra prophesies that Agamemnon will be killed by a hated bitch, a female killer of the male, a Scylla, a viper. Impressed , the chorus asks what *man* will commit this horrible crime. Before Cassandra can clarify, she is overcome by pain. She angrily removes garlands that she wears as a sign of her sacred status and enters the palace where, she says, she is doomed to die.

The chorus's ensuing song is interrupted by the cries of Agamemnon. "*Oimoi!* I have been struck a fine blow within! *Oimoi!* I have been struck again, a second blow."

The chorus is not sure what is happening, or whether they should try to do something. Before they can decide, the palace doors open, and Clytemnestra appears—standing over the corpses of Agamemnon and Cassandra. She openly acknowledges that she has been lying out of necessity, but she maintains that Agamemnon deserved to die and that she is happy about what she has done. Dying, she says, Agamemnon sprinkled her with drops of blood, and she rejoiced like a field when its flowers bloom. Agamemnon's murder was justified, she says, by his murder of Iphigenia. She feels safe because she has the protection of her faithful friend, Aegisthus. As for Cassandra, since she shared Agamemnon's bed, it is not unfitting that she share his death. And Cassandra's death adds extra pleasure to Clytemnestra's own enjoyment in bed.

Aegisthus appears with guards. He announces that he participated in the murder of Agamemnon because Atreus, Agamemnon's father, usurped the throne of Argos from Thyestes, the father of Aegisthus, and tricked him into eating his children's flesh. At last, this crime has been avenged. The chorus says that the Argives will never let him get away with the murder and calls him a coward. They also hope that Orestes will come home and exact revenge for his father's death. Aegisthus's guard is on the verge of attacking when Clytemnestra intervenes, urging everybody to calm down. She tells Aegisthus to ignore the empty words of the chorus. Together, they will bring order to their household.

64. The Deaths of Clytemnestra and Aegisthus

Aeschylus, *The Libation Bearers* (Classical Greek tragedy)

Orestes arrives with his friend, Pylades, at the tomb of Agamemnon outside the palace. He deposits a lock of hair as an offering. Women with urns approach, evidently to pour libations at the grave. Orestes recognizes his sister, Electra, among them. He and Pylades hide.

The chorus of slave women reveals that they have been sent to the grave to make offerings because of ill-omened dreams. Despite being slaves, they mourn for Agamemnon. Electra asks them what kind of prayers she can say. At their suggestion, she prays for Orestes' welfare and for an avenger to come.

Electra is startled to find on the tomb a lock of hair that looks just like her own. She thinks it must belong to Orestes but is reluctant to believe that he has actually returned. Then as further evidence, she finds footprints that match her own exactly.

Orestes emerges from hiding and identifies himself, proving his identity by matching his hair with the lock on the tomb and showing Electra his cloak, which she herself wove. He has returned because Apollo's oracle commanded him to kill his father's killers. Apollo spoke of horrible punishments if Orestes neglected his orders: "diseases attacking flesh with wild jaws, cankers eating normal tissues, white fur growing on diseased skin." Electra and Orestes pray to the ghost of Agamemnon to help them.

Orestes asks why Clytemnestra has suddenly ordered that offerings be made at Agamemnon's tomb. The chorus explains that she was motivated by a dream. "She dreamed that she gave birth to a serpent."

"In what way did the dream end?" Orestes asks.

"She wrapped it in swaddling clothes like a child."

"What sort of food did the baby snake require?"

"In the dream, she offered it her breast."

"How was her nipple not injured?"

"In fact, it drew a clot of blood with his milk."

Orestes interprets the dream as prefiguring his killing of his mother. He tells Electra to return to the house. He and Pylades will attempt to get in, disguised as travelers from Phocis.

After a choral interlude, Orestes knocks at the palace door. He is greeted politely by Clytemnestra, who offers him food and lodging. He says that a man named Strophius asked him to deliver the news that a certain Orestes had died. Clytemnestra acts sad, saying that the curse against the house has struck again. Nevertheless, she brings Orestes and Pylades inside the palace. The fact that they bring bad news, she says, will not lessen her hospitality.

Outside, just as the chorus wonders if it can help Orestes, his old nursemaid, Cilissa, emerges from the palace. She has been sent to tell Aegisthus to come to hear about Orestes' death. She says that Clytemnestra only pretended to be saddened by the news, and that Aegisthus will be overjoyed. She herself is crushed by it. She raised Orestes from infancy and remembers how hard it was. "A child in swaddling clothes," she says, "does not say whether he is hungry or thirsty or has to make water. A baby's young stomach is a law unto itself. I tried to prophesy its needs but often erred and became a washerwoman."

The chorus asks whether Clytemnestra wanted Aegisthus to bring his bodyguard. Cilissa says that she did. The chorus tells her to alter the message then, telling Aegisthus to come at once *alone*. Cilissa does not understand why but is happy to comply.

The chorus prays to the gods to help Orestes. Aegisthus arrives and asks how he can find out about Orestes' death. The chorus directs him inside the palace. In a few moments, there is a cry from inside. A frantic slave emerges from the palace, shouting that Aegisthus is dead. The slave is looking for Clytemnestra since "her neck is nearly on the chopping block." Clytemnestra appears, and asks what the noise is all about.

"The man is alive and killing the dead!" the slave exclaims.

"I understand the riddle," says Clytemnestra. "We shall die by deceit, just as we killed. Somebody give me an ax, quickly!"

Orestes appears, addressing Clytemnestra. "I am looking for you too," he says. Clytemnestra cries out that "dearest Aegisthus" must be dead.

"Do you love him?" asks Orestes. "You will lie in the same tomb then. If you die, you will never be unfaithful to him."

Clytemnestra bares her breast and asks Orestes to have pity, remembering that she nursed him. Orestes asks Pylades if he should be ashamed to kill his mother.

"What then becomes of Apollo's oracle?" he asks. "Make all men your enemies rather than the gods."

Orestes says that Pylades is right. Clytemnestra tries to argue some more, but in vain. She tells him to beware a mother's curse, but he says that he could not escape his father's curse if he does not kill her. Clytemnestra says that she feels like one who cries over a tomb in vain. Orestes escorts her inside the palace. His final words are, "You killed one whom it was not lawful to kill. Now suffer that which is not lawful."

After a choral interlude, the palace doors open to reveal Orestes standing above the corpses of Aegisthus and Clytemnestra. He displays the robe that they used to entangle Agamemnon when they killed him. He acknowledges that his victory is polluted. His mind, he says, seems to be veering out of control. He wishes to state that he acted in accordance with Apollo's command and will now take refuge in his sanctuary. Suddenly, he sees hideous creatures coming toward him, like Gorgons with robes of black and tangles of snakes for hair. There are not visions, he says, but the rabid dogs of his mother.

The chorus says that only Apollo can liberate him from these evils and wishes Orestes good luck as he flees.

65. The Trial of Orestes

Aeschylus, *The Eumenides*[28] (Classical Greek tragedy)

The Pythia, the priestess of Apollo at Delphi, prays outside the temple to the deities who have prophesied in this place: Gaea and her daughters, Themis and Phoebe. Phoebe, she says, gave the shrine as a birthday present to Apollo, who thus acquired the title "Phoebus." The Pythia invokes the blessings of other gods, then enters the shrine to prophesy.

Immediately, the Pythia comes back out of the temple, terrified. Inside, a man has taken refuge at the *omphalos* ("navel"), a sacred stone representing the center of the earth. The man's hands and sword are dripping with blood. He carries an olive branch with wool ribbons, a sign of supplication. Sleeping around him in chairs are monstrous women, looking like Gorgons or Harpies. They are dark and disgusting. They snore with unendurable exhalations and drip foul liquid from their eyes. Their clothes are not fit for human society. She says that Apollo himself must deal with them and leaves.

The doors of the temple open, revealing Orestes surrounded by sleeping Furies. Apollo and Hermes stand beside him. Apollo tells Orestes that he has put his pursuers to sleep. Now Orestes must run to Athens. It is there that judges for his case are to be found. Orestes obeys, with Hermes leading the way.

Clytemnestra's ghost enters the temple and wakes up the Furies. She is indignant that they are letting their prey get away. Her death must not go unpunished. The Furies wake up. They are full of resentment at the way the "younger gods" like Apollo are mistreating them. They are determined that Orestes will not escape.

Apollo enters and orders the Furies out of his temple. They argue about the case. The Furies say that Clytemnestra's crime was not so bad because she did not shed kindred blood. Apollo maintains that the bond between man and wife is very sacred.

The scene shifts to Athens. Orestes appears outside Athena's temple, asking the goddess for help. The chorus of Furies arrives, tracking him. They sing about their inexorable power to punish violence against gods, guests, or parents.

Athena appears from the plains of Troy, where Greek leaders were honoring her. She asks what has brought this crowd to her temple. The Furies say that Orestes is a matricide. Orestes lays out the details. He emphasizes the fact that he slew Clytemnestra at

---

28   The chorus consists of the punitive goddesses known to English speakers as the "Furies." Their Greek name is the "*Erinyes*." The Greeks, however, often used a euphemistic designation for them, the "*Eumenides*" (the kindly ones). In the play, the *Erinyes* are transformed into *Eumenides* in fact. In the text of the play, they are not named directly at all.

Apollo's insistence. Athena says that the case is too hard for any mortal to decide, and that it is not even right for her to give judgment in cases of wrathful murder. She will choose judges from worthy citizens of her city, thus establishing an institution for all time.

The chorus sings of the importance of the fear that they inspire. If they are overthrown, murder will run rampant.

Athena opens the trial. The Furies question Orestes, who admits killing his mother. They declare that they are right to pursue him because he spilled kindred blood, whereas Clytemnestra did not.

Apollo argues that killing a father and king is especially grave. The Furies cite the example of Zeus overthrowing his father, Cronus. Apollo replies that it was within Zeus's power to *undo* the injuries he inflicted on Cronus, but Agamemnon's death was permanent. Apollo's concluding argument is that there is no connection by blood between sons and mothers. The parent is the father. The mother just nourishes the seed. In fact, there can be a father with no mother. The proof is Athena, who was not born from a maternal womb, but from Zeus.[29]

As Apollo and the Furies continue to bicker, the voting proceeds. Athena announces that she votes for Orestes. Hence if the other ballots are tied, he will be acquitted. She says that she votes for him because she herself had no mother and therefore favors the father. When the ballots are taken out of the urn and counted, they are even. Orestes is acquitted.

Orestes swears that never in all time to come will any leader of Argos ever take hostile action against Athens. His spirit will always help Argos, so long as Argos remains the faithful ally of Athens.

The Furies indignantly threaten Athens with plague and famine. Athena says that they have not been treated with contempt. The ballots were tied. Orestes was freed only on the strength of the testimony of Apollo, who speaks for Zeus. Athena adds that if the Furies take up residence on the Athenian acropolis, they will receive rich honors from Athenian men and women. Athena's persistence finally gets the Furies' attention. They ask what powers they will have in Athens. Athena tells them that no household will prosper without their consent. Now the Furies say that their anger is gone and volunteer to bless the land. They pray that Athens might be free of drought, plague, famine, and civil war. They exit in a stately procession, singing.

---

29 According to Hesiod, *Theogony* (886–900, 924–926), Athena was born from Zeus's forehead because he swallowed her mother, Metis (Wisdom), when she was pregnant with Athena. He did so, because of the prophecy that Metis would subsequently bear a son greater than Zeus.

Source: Euripides, *Helen* (Classical Greek Tragedy)

Helen appears in front of an Egyptian tomb belonging to the late king Proteus. There is a royal palace in the background. In a soliloquy, she explains her presence in Egypt. Angered by the judgment of Paris, Hera saved her from actually going to Troy. Instead, she made a phantom Helen out of air to accompany Paris. The real Helen was concealed in a mist by Hermes and whisked away to Egypt. Hermes assured her that her husband Menelaus would eventually learn the truth and come for her. That was long ago. Now her situation is dire. Proteus, the kindly king who welcomed her to Egypt, is dead. His son, Theoclymenus, is determined to marry her. She has come to the tomb of Proteus, seeking sanctuary.

A Greek warrior, Teucer, arrives on the scene. He is shocked to see a woman who looks so much like Helen but assumes that she could not be her. Helen questions him. She learns that he has been banished from his home, Salamis, by his father, Telamon, because he didn't die with his brother, Ajax, at Troy. Later, Apollo instructed him to found a new Salamis on the island of Cyprus, and he has come to Egypt seeking further advice from the prophetess Theonoe, sister of Theoclymenus. Teucer adds that the Trojan War has been over for seven years. He says that Menelaus was seen at the end, dragging Helen away by the hair but never made it back to Greece; he is presumed dead. Helen warns Teucer that Theoclymenus kills all the Greeks he finds in his land. Teucer exits hastily.

Helen is crushed by Teucer's news, especially the fact that Menelaus is presumed dead. She laments and is joined by servant women who have been washing clothes nearby. They suggest that she consult with the prophetess Theonoe since the Greek man may have been wrong about Menelaus's death. Helen agrees, and all head into the palace.

Menelaus now enters in a bedraggled state, uncertain of where he is. He has been trying to get home from Troy for seven years and most recently has suffered a shipwreck. Only Helen herself and a few crew members survived by clinging to wreckage. They are now in a nearby cave. He has set out to look for food and clothing.

He approaches the palace, loudly demanding assistance. A servant woman warns him to be quiet. She tells him that he will be put to death if the king learns of his presence. She adds that he is in Egypt and that the former king, Proteus, is dead. Furthermore, Helen of Sparta has been living there since before the war even started. Menelaus does not know what to make of this information but decides to wait for Theoclymenus to return, in order to ask him for assistance.

Helen and the chorus emerge after meeting with Theonoe, who has assured them that Menelaus is still alive. Heading back to Proteus's tomb, Helen notices the shabby stranger lurking nearby. Fearing that he is one of Theoclymenus's men, she rushes to the tomb. He approaches, astonished at seeing a woman who looks identical to his wife. She is equally astounded at his looks—and quickly realizes that he is Menelaus.

Helen tells Menelaus about the phantom that was sent to Troy. He cannot quite believe the story until a breathless crew member arrives from the cave and tells him that the Helen in the cave suddenly announced that she was just a phantom and vanished into thin air.

Thus reunited, Menelaus and the real Helen turn their minds to planning their escape. Theonoe emerges from the palace with a procession of sulfur-burning attendants. She agrees not to reveal Menelaus's identity to her brother, Theoclymenus, since Proteus would not have wished her to.

After rejecting Menelaus's suggestions for escaping—e.g. by stealing a chariot—Helen suggests an elaborate plan. Menelaus will disguise himself as a shipwrecked sailor and will pretend to bring news that Menelaus has died at sea. When Helen hears this, she will ask Theoclymenus to let her perform a ritual burial at sea in memory of her husband. Menelaus and his men will seize control of the ship provided for that purpose and head for home. With all of that agreed upon, Helen goes into the palace to cut her hair, a sign of mourning, and put on black clothes.

Theoclymenus now arrives with his retinue. He has heard that a Greek has been seen nearby and wants him found and killed. Helen emerges with her shorn hair, dressed in black and weeping. She tells Theoclymenus that the ragged stranger near the tomb has brought the news of Menelaus's death. Now she must honor him in the way of her people. Menelaus adds that the dead man's possessions must be tossed overboard, well away from the shore, so they do not wash up again. The three of them enter the palace to see to the preparations.

The chorus sings about Demeter's grief at the loss of Persephone and how her sad music was changed to glad when her daughter was restored.

Helen emerges and tells the chorus that Theonoe kept her promise by not exposing their plans to her brother. Theoclymenus enters, directing the servants to carry the offerings to the ship he has provided. He asks Helen to stay behind, fearing she might throw herself overboard out of grief. She scoffs at this, saying that she has no such intention, and that it is essential she be present for the ritual. Theoclymenus then instructs the stranger (Menelaus) to go along as an escort, to make sure Helen returns safely. They leave. The chorus passes time by praying to Helen's brothers, the Dioscuri, to aid her journey home.

A breathless messenger arrives with the news that the ship was seized by Menelaus and his men once they were well out to sea, and they have escaped with Helen. Theoclymenus is enraged, and blames Theonoe for betraying him. He grabs a spear, and is only prevented from killing her by being held back by a servant. Then, the Dioscuri appear and restrain Theoclymenus, telling him that he must not work against the gods' will. Helen was fated to go home. Theoclymenus acquiesces.

Source: Euripides, *Iphigenia among the Taurians* (Classical Greek Tragedy)

It was commonly believed that Agamemnon sacrificed his daughter, Iphigenia, to Artemis at the beginning of the Trojan War. In some accounts, however, Iphigenia was rescued at the last moment and spirited away to a distant temple of Artemis to be her priestess. Euripides expands on that version. The action unfolds in front of a temple on the far northern shore of the Black Sea (modern-day Crimea), a place inhabited by a barbarous race, the Taurians.

Iphigenia emerges from the temple of the Taurian Artemis and talks to the air about her life. Her father, Agamemnon of Mycenae, once vowed to Artemis to sacrifice the most beautiful thing found on his lands that year. That was the year that Iphigenia was born, although no one realized the connection at the time. Later, however, at the gathering of the Greek army at Aulis, Calchas informed Agamemnon that Iphigenia had to be sacrificed to Artemis in fulfillment of his old vow. So Iphigenia was brought to Aulis on the pretext of being married to Achilles, but she was actually sacrificed to Artemis—or so people thought. In fact, Artemis substituted a deer in Iphigenia's place at the last moment and brought Iphigenia herself to this faraway land to serve the Taurians as their high priestess. Here, she oversees the sacrifice of all foreigners who are caught by barbarous inhabitants of the land.

But just now she has had a disturbing dream. She saw her family home in Mycenae collapse until only one pillar was left standing. This pillar then seemed to grow a head of hair and speak in a male voice. She touched its forehead as she touches victims about to be sacrificed. The pillar must, she thinks, symbolize her brother Orestes, the last of their line, and the dream symbolizes his death. She goes back inside the palace to pray and pour libations.

Orestes and his friend, Pylades, enter the scene. Orestes is seeking absolution for his mother's death and has traveled to the Taurians on the orders of Apollo, who has instructed him to bring back the local cult-statue of Artemis, a wooden image that fell from heaven. Only in this way can Orestes be cleansed of pollution for killing his mother. He and Pylades stealthily examine the layout of the temple, planning to make their attempt after dark, and they exit.

Iphigenia reappears with a chorus of maidens to perform the libation and mourn. The chorus consists of Greek slave girls provided by the Taurian king to assist Iphigenia.

A local herdsman enters with news. A Greek ship was seen approaching the coast. Two young men waded ashore from it. They have now been captured, and the king has ordered Iphigenia to prepare for the customary sacrifice. The chorus wonders who they could be, and if by some chance, they may have news of home. Still upset by Orestes' supposed death, Iphigenia is determined to show the latest victims no mercy.

Orestes and Pylades are brought before Iphigenia. Orestes refuses to divulge his name. He does, however, admit to being from Mycenae. The reference to home rekindles Iphigenia's desire to send a message to her family.

She has a letter composed and gives it to Orestes, telling him that he will not be killed if he agrees to deliver it. Orestes refuses if it means his friend Pylades must remain behind to die. Iphigenia then makes the same offer to Pylades. He, too, refuses at first, but Orestes begs him to save himself. Otherwise, he says, people will despise him for allowing his faithful friend to die in a search undertaken for his sake. Pylades finally gives in and takes the letter. He has one concern: What if something unforeseen occurs, and the letter is lost or destroyed?

In response, Iphigenia say that she will read the letter aloud so that Pylades will be able to repeat it from memory, if necessary. It is to be delivered, she begins, to her brother Orestes. When his name is spoken, Orestes is amazed—and reveals his identity. Iphigenia is skeptical at first, but Orestes persuades her of his identity with his detailed knowledge of their childhood home. He remembers a tapestry that she made, showing Helius turning his chariot around.

Orestes reveals the reason for coming. Iphigenia is ready to help, but she must do so without the Taurians knowing. She proposes the following scheme. She will say that, since Orestes is a matricide, he and his accomplice, Pylades, must be cleansed in the sea before they can be sacrificed. She will add that their presence has polluted the sacred statue of Artemis, which must also be cleansed. Having made their way to the shore in ritual isolation, they will escape on Orestes' ship.

After another choral song, King Thoas enters, to see whether the captives have been sacrificed. He meets Iphigenia just as she emerges from the temple, carrying the statue. She tells him that the victims' pollution necessitates cleaning them and the statue in the Oceanus. Thoas assigns some of his men to follow her as escorts, but at Iphigenia's urging, he orders them and all his citizens to keep their distance—and not even to look at the polluted victims and the statue.

After a choral song in honor of Apollo, an excited soldier arrives, desperate to inform Thoas of events. The chorus tries to dissuade him, but the soldier is insistent. He tells Thoas that after Iphigenia dismissed her escorts, the sounds of chanting were heard coming from the shore. After some time, concerns about her safety led them to investigate. They found Orestes, Pylades, and Iphigenia boarding a ship to escape. A skirmish ensued, but the local guards were too few to stop the Greek ship's departure. When the ship reached the harbor's mouth, however, great waves drove them back toward the shore. Hence, there was still time to catch them.

Thoas orders his cavalry to rush to the shore and others to man ships. All the Greeks must be captured and tortured to death! At this point, however, Athena appears above the temple. She informs Thoas that it is the will of the gods for Orestes and Iphigenia to go back home and that he must not attempt to prevent it. In fact, Poseidon has already smoothed the sea to ease their voyage. Thoas says that he knows enough not to resist the will of the gods. He wishes Iphigenia and Orestes well. They are welcome to the statue. In fact, he will even free the Greek slave girls, and send them home.

68. The Return of Odysseus

Source: Homer, *The Odyssey* (Archaic Greek)

The Trojan War is over. All the survivors have made their way home, except for Odysseus. He has been captured on an island by the goddess Calypso. She wants to marry Odysseus.

In his palace, Zeus complains that mortal men blame the gods unfairly for suffering beyond their lot, but they cause their own problems by their foolishness. For example, the gods warned Aegisthus not to kill Agamemnon and court his wife. Aegisthus ignored the advice. Now Agamemnon's son, Orestes, has killed him.

Athena asks why the gods are punishing Odysseus. Zeus explains that Poseidon is angry at Odysseus for blinding his son Polyphemus, but that it is time to arrange for Odysseus's homecoming. Athena suggests that Hermes go tell Calypso to release Odysseus. She herself will go to Ithaca and inspire Odysseus's son, Telemachus, to denounce his mother's suitors, who are slaughtering his sheep and cattle, and to look for his father in mainland Greece.

Athena goes to Ithaca, disguised as a foreign friend of Odysseus. She finds Telemachus brooding in the midst of Penelope's suitors, who are gambling, listening to music, drinking wine, and getting ready for a feast. Athena tells him to hold an assembly to denounce the suitors and then to sail to the mainland looking for news of Odysseus. Then she disappears into the air like a bird. Telemachus suspects that he has been visited by a god.

The next day, Telemachus holds an assembly to denounce the suitors and request a ship. He breaks down crying as he describes his plight. Antinous, the leading suitor, says that the problem is Penelope's indecisiveness. She sends encouraging notes to individual suitors. A few years ago, she announced that she would select a new husband when she finished weaving a burial sheet for her father-in-law, Laertes, Odysseus's father. She wove during the day but undid her weaving in secret at night. In the fourth year, the women servants revealed the trick to the suitors, and Penelope had to finish the job—but still she delays.

The assembly does nothing to help Telemachus with the suitors, since opinions are angrily divided on that issue, but friends will help him sail to the mainland. Telemachus sails to Pylos, keeping his journey a secret from Penelope. King Nestor receives him hospitably and describes the Greeks' departure from Troy. Athena was angry at the army. In a drunken assembly, opinion was divided on whether to stay and make a sacrifice to her or to sail home at once. Half the army stayed at Troy with Agamemnon. Nestor, Odysseus, and Diomedes joined Menelaus in sailing at once, but Odysseus soon changed his mind and went back. Nestor and Diomedes had smooth sailing all the way home. Menelaus was delayed by the death of his pilot and then blown off course to Egypt. He returned seven years later, on the same day that Orestes killed Aegisthus.

Nestor recommends that Telemachus visit Menelaus himself to see if he knows anything about Odysseus. He provides a chariot and his young son, Pisistratus, as a traveling companion. Menelaus receives the boy's hospitably a day later. He invites them to join an ongoing feast even before he learns their identities. Telemachus, however, gives himself away by crying when Menelaus mentions how much he misses his wartime comrades, especially Odysseus. Helen joins the conversation. To prevent it from being too maudlin, she slips some nepenthe into the wine. This is a potion that she acquired in Egypt. It is so powerful that a person who takes it would not be saddened by seeing his parents, brother, or child put to the sword.

Early the next morning, Menelaus tells Telemachus what he knows about his father. Menelaus was stuck with no winds on the island of Pharos, off the Egyptian shore. Walking along the shore, he met a goddess named Eidothea, who told him that her father could help him. He was Proteus, the old man of the sea. If Menelaus caught him while he napped on the sand with his herd of seals—and held onto him while he changed his shape—Proteus would eventually resume his original form and answer all questions. With Eidothea's help, Menelaus and selected crew members ambushed Proteus by hiding under seal skins. In Menelaus's grasp, Proteus changed into a lion, a serpent, a panther, a boar, water, and a tree. Then, as an old man again, he told Menelaus that he had to return to Egypt and offer sacrifice to Zeus to get home safely. In addition, Proteus revealed that Ajax the Lesser had been lost at sea going home, that Agamemnon had been murdered, and that Odysseus was a prisoner on Calypso's island. Proteus's final piece of information was that Menelaus would not die but be sent by the gods to the Elysian plain because he was the son-in-law of Zeus.

Meanwhile, back in Ithaca, the suitors learn about Telemachus's journey. Antinous dispatches a ship with 20 crewmen to ambush Telemachus on his way back.

Hermes makes the long flight to Calypso's island. She welcomes him into her cave but is resentful when she learns that she has to let Odysseus go. She says that the gods are always jealous when goddesses take mortal men as lovers. Nevertheless, she will obey. Odysseus has been spending his days weeping on the shore his nights sleeping with Calypso against his will. She finds him on the shore, and tells him that she will help him make a raft and head for home. Odysseus makes her swear that she is not playing a trick on him. Back in the cave, Calypso asks Odysseus over dinner if he is sure that he prefers a long, difficult journey to staying with her and being immortal. He says that Penelope cannot be compared to a goddess, but his only desire is to go home. That night, they make love inside the cave. The next morning, Odysseus starts to work on a raft. Five days later, he puts out to sea.

After 18 days without sleep, Odysseus spies the island of Phaeacia. Poseidon happens to be in the area, returning from an Ethiopian festival, notices Odysseus, and unleashes a violent storm. Odysseus's raft is demolished. He ends up swimming for three days and then nearly being killed by the surf on Phaeacia's rocky coast before he gains the shore at the mouth of a river and falls asleep naked in a pile of leaves.

That night, Athena appears to the Phaeacian princess Nausicaa in a dream, and suggests she wash her family's laundry at the river when she wakes up. Nausicaa has many suitors, she says, and will soon need clean clothes for her wedding day. In the morning, Nausicaa and some girl servants load clothes in a mule wagon and make their way to the mouth of the river at the seashore. While the clothes are drying, the girls play with a ball. Nausicaa is the tallest and loveliest. When they are ready to leave, she throws the ball too hard, and it goes in the river. The girls scream, waking up Odysseus. He emerges from the bushes, breaking off a branch to cover his genitals. The girls all scatter except Nausicaa. Keeping his distance, Odysseus asks if she is a goddess or a mortal girl. If a goddess, he says, she must be Artemis. He goes on to ask for a rag to wear and directions into town. Nausicaa provides clothing and directions to the palace. After Odysseus is bathed, dressed, and magically beautified by Athena, Nausicaa confides to the serving girls that he is just the kind of man she would like to marry.

Nausicaa's parents are King Alcinoos and Queen Arete. They live in a palace made of bronze, gold, and silver, and are surrounded by a garden whose trees bear fruit all year round. The Phaeacian men excel all others in sailing, the women in weaving.

Odysseus enters the palace at the end of a feast, calls down blessings on the Phaeacians, and says that he seeks a convoy to his native land. He then assumes the position of a suppliant in the hearth. The eldest Phaeacian noble suggests that they give the stranger some food. Alcinoos agrees and announces that tomorrow they will invite more nobles to the palace, welcome the stranger properly with a new feast, and arrange a convoy.

At an assembly the next morning, Alcinoos commands that a ship with a crew of 52 be prepared to take the stranger home. Meanwhile, he decrees, they will entertain him. All the kings of Phaeacia must come to Alcinoos's palace. When they assemble, a blind bard named Demodocus sings about a quarrel between Odysseus and Achilles. Odysseus weeps quietly. Only Alcinoos notices.

Alcinoos suggests that they go outside for the athletic contests. After several competitions, Alcinoos's son invites Odysseus to compete. When Odysseus declines, a young Phaeacian says that he looks more like a merchant than an athlete. Enraged, Odysseus takes one of the weights that the Phaeacians are throwing and tosses it well past the farthest marks. Alcinoos apologizes for the youngster's insult and has Demodocus sing the story of the love of Ares and Aphrodite.

Demodocus tells how Hephaestus's wife, Aphrodite, was making love secretly to Ares, using her own marriage bed when Hephaestus was not at home. Helius saw this and told Hephaestus. Hephaestus spread subtle metal bonds above the bed, like a spiderweb, and pretended to go to the island of Lemnos. Ares saw him leave, went to the house immediately, and took Aphrodite into the bed. As they slept, the bonds fell on them so that they could not get away. Hephaestus doubled back, opened his door, and shouted for Zeus and the other gods to come and see how Aphrodite was dishonoring him. Though the goddesses avoided the scene, the male gods came and laughed uncontrollably. Apollo asked Hermes how he would like to be in Ares' position. Hermes said that he would be glad to lie next to golden Aphrodite, even with three times as many bonds and all the gods and goddesses watching.

After the song, all return to the palace for another meal. Odysseus happens to see Nausicaa standing beside a pillar. She says she hopes that he will remember her when he gets home. Odysseus says that he will pray to her as to a goddess for the rest of his days, since she saved his life.

At dinner, Odysseus asks Demodocus to sing about the Trojan horse. When he begins, Odysseus weeps. Alcinoos stops the music and asks that Odysseus state his name and explain why he weeps whenever he hears about the Trojan War. Odysseus identifies himself and volunteers to tell the assembly about his difficult journey homeward from Troy.

This is the story that Odysseus tells:

Soon after leaving Troy, he sacked the city of the Cicones, killing the men and capturing their wives and many possessions. He ordered his men to flee at once, but they refused and stayed on the shore, feasting. The Cicones and their neighbors launched a counterattack the next morning. Odysseus lost six men from each of his ships.

The fleet then survived a storm but was driven off course rounding the southern tip of Greece. Ten days later, it washed ashore in the land of the Lotus Eaters. Odysseus's scouts mingled with the Lotus Eaters. They were harmless, but the men who ate the sweet lotus blossoms lost all desire to return home. Odysseus had to force them back to the ship.

Next, the fleet landed on a goat-infested island, opposite the harbor of the lawless Cyclopes. Odysseus took one ship and 12 crewmen to the mainland. He also brought some very potent wine. This was a gift from Maron, a priest of Apollo, whose household the Greeks spared when they attacked the Cicones.

Odysseus and his companions entered a cave belonging to a giant shepherd, who was out tending his flocks. The cave was full of lambs and kids. Odysseus's companions wanted to steal them and leave, but Odysseus insisted on staying to ask for gifts from the cave's owner.

The owner, a Cyclops, returned. He shut the doorway with a boulder so large that 22 wagons could not have budged it. Fixing a meal and tending to his chores, he noticed Odysseus and his companions and asked where they came from. Odysseus said that they were Greeks from Troy and asked for a gift in the name of Zeus. The Cyclops said that he had no respect for Zeus. He leapt up, seized two of Odysseus's men, dashed their brains out on the ground, and ate them. He then drank some milk, lay down, and slept. Odysseus would have killed him with his sword, but he and his men all would have died in the cave with no one to move the boulder.

The next morning, the Cyclops rose, built a fire, ate two more men, let his flock out to graze, replaced the boulder, and walked away whistling. In the cave, Odysseus found a stick the size of a ship's mast. He sharpened its point, hid it under manure, and chose four companions by lot to help him use it. The Cyclops returned, took care of his chores, seized two men, and ate them. Odysseus then offered him some wine. Trying it, the Cyclops was pleased, took some more, and asked Odysseus to tell him his name so that he could give him a gift. Odysseus replied that his name was Noman. The Cyclops said that his gift would be that he would eat Noman last. He then fell asleep, belching up wine and pieces of flesh. Odysseus and his companions retrieved the sharpened stick and heated it in the fire until it glowed. Then they plunged it into the eye of the Cyclops, and twisted it like a drill. His eye sizzled and popped. He let out a great roar. Other Cyclopes gathered around outside the cave, and calling him by his name, Polyphemus, asked what the trouble was. Polyphemus replied that "Noman" was murdering him. They replied that if no man was hurting him, his pain must come from Zeus, and left.

Odysseus tied his companions underneath some sheep. He himself clung to the belly of the lead ram. In the morning, Polyphemus sat by the door of the cave, examining the sheep as they went out to graze but not feeling the men underneath them. The ram came out last. Polyphemus stopped him and asked why he was lagging behind, since he was usually the first to leave. He then decided that the ram must be grieving for his eye and let him pass, with Odysseus hanging on below.

When Odysseus and his companions reached their ship, Odysseus shouted to Polyphemus that Zeus had punished him. Polyphemus broke off part of a mountain peak and threw it at the ship. It landed in front and drove the ship back to mainland. Odysseus's crew tried to silence him, but he shouted again. "If anyone asks the name of the man who blinded you," he screamed, "it is Odysseus of Ithaca!" Hearing this, Polyphemus prayed to his father, Poseidon, that Odysseus of Ithaca would never get home—or at least that he would get home late, with no companions, and face further troubles when he did. He then hurled another boulder that drove the ship forward across the harbor to the island where the rest of the fleet was anchored.

The fleet made its way to the kingdom of Aeolus. King Aeolus lived in a wealthy palace with six sons and six daughters, who were married to each other. After entertaining Odysseus for a month, he gave him a leather bag with a silver cord, containing all the unfavorable winds, since Zeus had placed him in charge of the winds. Wafted by a west wind, Odysseus's fleet drew within sight of Ithaca in ten days. At this point, Odysseus fell asleep. His companions thought that the bag contained gold or silver from Aeolus. They opened it. Instantly, the bad winds blew the ships back into the midst of the sea. The fleet headed back to Aeolus's kingdom. Odysseus asked him for more help, but Aeolus refused. He said that it would be unlawful to help a man who was evidently hated by the gods.

Another week of sailing brought the fleet to the land of the Laestrygonians. This contained a sheltered harbor with calm water, where the other ships came to rest. Odysseus himself dropped anchor on the rocky coast outside the harbor. Three of his men went ashore to investigate. They met the king's daughter at a spring and followed her into a palace. There they saw her mother, a disgusting giantess. She, in turn, summoned her husband. Also a giant, he immediately snatched one of the men and ate him.

Then he raised a shout, and thousands of Laestrygonians poured out of their houses. They attacked the fleet in the harbor, crushing the ships with boulders and spearing the men like fish. Odysseus ran to his ship, cut his anchor line with his sword, and got away.

Reduced to one ship, Odysseus landed on Aeaea, the home of the goddess Circe. Hunting for food, Odysseus saw smoke rising in the middle of the island. He divided the crew into two groups of 23, one led by him, the other by the crewman Eurylochus. By lot, Eurylochus's group was chosen to investigate the smoke.

Outside Circe's house, wolves and lions fawned on Eurylochus and the others like friendly dogs. Circe was heard singing inside. She invited them in. All except Eurylochus entered. She served them a mixture of cheese, barley, honey, wine, and magic drugs. Then by striking them with a wand, she changed their bodies into those of pigs, although their minds were unaltered. She drove them into her pig sties and tossed them some acorns.

Outside, Eurylochus panicked, even though he did not know what was happening in Circe's house, and ran back to Odysseus, begging him to leave the island. Odysseus, however, went to investigate. On his way, he met Hermes, who told him all about Circe, and said he would give him a drug to ward off her magic. When her magic fails, he said, she will suggest that they go to bed together. Before agreeing, Odysseus should have her swear not to make him unmanly when he is naked. He then gave Odysseus a plant, moly, that was an antidote to Circe's drugs.

Odysseus entered Circe's house and events fell out as foretold. When Circe swore not to make Odysseus unmanly, they went to bed together. Afterward, Circe prepared a meal, but Odysseus would not eat until his companions were restored to human form. The men looked better than ever, but they wept loudly over their ordeal. Circe became a hospitable hostess, entertaining Odysseus and his men for a full year. Then his men suggested that it was time to leave. That night Odysseus brought up the subject in bed with Circe. She told him that to get home safely, he would have to consult the seer, Tiresias, in Hades' kingdom, and she provided directions. Odysseus's ships would be blown by the North Wind to the shores of Oceanus. There, Odysseus should dig a trench and fill it with honey, wine, water, and barley. Then he should slay a ram and a black sheep, letting the blood spill into the trench. This would attract the ghosts. When they drank the blood, they would talk to him. Odysseus should hold the others back and speak with Tiresias first.

At dawn, Odysseus set sail. In departing, he lost a young crewman without realizing it. Young Elpenor had slept on Circe's roof for coolness after drinking a lot of wine. When the sounds of departure woke him up, he forget where he was, slipped, fell, and broke his neck.

Circe provided a fair wind that brought Odysseus's ship to a land always covered by mist on the shores of Oceanus. Odysseus followed Circe's instructions, and soon ghosts gathered around him and the trench. First came Elpenor. Odysseus asked him how he had gotten to the land of the dead so quickly. Elpenor described his accident and begged Odysseus to find his body and bury it when he returned to Aeaea.

Odysseus then recognized the ghost of his mother, Anticleia. He wept since he had left her alive in Ithaca. But he did not let her spirit approach the trench before he talked to Tiresias. The prophet appeared next and told Odysseus his future. Odysseus would encounter the herds of the Sun, grazing on the island of Thrinacria. If he did not hurt them, he might get home. If he did hurt them, he might still get home, but late and without companions—and he would find trouble waiting for him. Once at home, he had to travel inland, carrying a ship's oar. When another traveler referred to the oar as a "winnowing fan," he should fix it in the earth and offer sacrifice to Poseidon. Death would come to him gently from the sea in old age.

Next, Anticleia's ghost drank the dark blood and spoke, asking why Odysseus had come, and describing the situation at Ithaca. Penelope longed for Odysseus's return, Telemachus was treated respectfully in the neighborhood, Odysseus's father, Laertes, was deeply depressed because of Odysseus's long absence, and Anticleia herself had died from longing to see him. Odysseus tried to embrace her three times, but she vanished in his arms. She explained that once mortals die, they no longer have bones or flesh. Anticleia's spirit was followed by those of a number of famous ladies: Oedipus's mother, Epicaste; Nestor's mother, Chloris; Leda; and others.

Odysseus interrupts his own tale at this point to say that it is time to go to bed. Alcinoos and the others ask him to continue. Alcinoos wants to know if he saw any comrades from Troy in the underworld. Odysseus says that the next soul he saw was Agamemnon's.

Agamemnon drank the blood, and wept at seeing Odysseus. He was lamenting his own murder by Aegisthus and Clytemnestra. They ambushed him at a feast. The last thing he heard was Cassandra's piteous cries. Clytemnestra did not even bother to close his eyes and mouth for him when he died. Agamemnon advised Odysseus to return home secretly to avoid a similar fate.

Achilles approached in a group of great warriors. Odysseus said that the Greeks honored Achilles more than anyone when he was alive and that he was very powerful among the dead. Therefore, he should not lament his death. Achilles replied:

> Do not make light of my death, noble Odysseus.
> I'd rather dwell on earth and serve another,
> a landless man who is barely getting by,
> than be the lord of all the withered dead.

Achilles also asked about his father and son. Odysseus had no news of Peleus, but described Neoptolemus as an outstanding young warrior. Cheered, Achilles walked across the fields of asphodel with lengthened strides.

The soul of Ajax the Greater did not speak to Odysseus. He was still grieving over the judgment by which Achilles' armor was awarded to Odysseus. Odysseus felt that he could have gotten him to talk eventually, but he wished to see other spirits. He watched Minos making judgments among the dead, Orion hunting, and Tityos, Tantalus, and

Sisyphus being punished for their sins. Finally, he saw a phantom of Heracles. (Heracles himself lived with the gods.) The phantom greeted Odysseus as a fellow long-suffering hero. Finally, Odysseus grew afraid of all the ghosts and returned to his ship.

Back on Circe's island, Elpenor was buried. The men feasted on food provided by Circe. At night she lay with Odysseus, telling him about forthcoming dangers. He would come to the Sirens, who fatally enchanted men with their song. They lived in a meadow surrounded by corpses. If Odysseus wanted to hear them, he should tie himself to the ship's mast and put wax in his men's ears. After that, one way led to the Wandering Rocks, which nothing could pass through—although Hera did enable Jason and the Argonauts to do so. The other way led between two crags. Scylla, a six-headed monster, lived in one. She devoured six sailors from every ship that passed. On the other side, Charybdis sucked the water down three times a day and spat it out. It would be better, Circe said, to sacrifice six sailors to Scylla than risk the whole ship by sailing over Charybdis. Odysseus would then come to Thrinacria, where the sheep and cattle of the Sun grazed. If he hurt these, his ship and companions would be lost, and his own return delayed.

The next day, the ship approached the island of the Sirens in a dead calm. Odysseus had himself tied to the mast and put wax in his men's ears. When Odysseus heard the Sirens claiming to know all about Troy and everything else, he wanted to be freed to listen and signaled to his men with his eyebrows, but they ignored him.

The straits were now near. Odysseus directed the crew to row quickly past Scylla's crag. On the other side of the channel, Charybdis sucked the water down. When Odysseus tore his eyes away from that spectacle, he saw six of his crew being hoisted through the air toward Scylla's mouths. The men shrieked and stretched their hands to him for help as she ate them.

Soon, the ship was passing Thrinacria. Odysseus urged the crew to keep going, but Eurylochus argued that it was dangerous to sail at night. Odysseus gave in, urging the men not to harm the herds on the island. As they slept, Zeus sent a great storm, which made it impossible to leave the island. The storm winds blew steadily for a month. Supplies ran out. They had to live by fishing and killing birds. Hunger became a problem. One day, Odysseus went off by himself to pray; he fell asleep. While he was gone, Eurylochus persuaded the rest of the crew to slaughter some of the cattle. They could appease Helius later by building a temple in Ithaca. Besides, he argued, any form of death was preferable to starvation. As soon as they slaughtered the cattle, one of the goddesses guarding them reported the fact to Helius. He instantly went to Zeus to demand revenge. Otherwise, he said, he would go shine in Hades. Zeus promised to blast the crew's ship. (Odysseus learned about this from Calypso, who heard it from Hermes.) Back on the island, Odysseus was horrified, but the deed was done. The crew feasted for six days on the cattle, whose hides crawled and flesh mooed. On the seventh day, the storm winds stopped blowing. Odysseus and his men set sail. As soon as they were out of sight of land, Zeus destroyed the ship in a sudden thunderstorm. All members of the crew drowned. As the ship disintegrated, Odysseus strapped the mast and keel together and rode out the storm. By dawn the following day, he found himself back at the straits of Scylla and Charybdis. As he drifted over Charybdis, she sucked the water down. Stretching, Odysseus caught the branch of an overhanging fig tree and clung to it like a bat until Charybdis vomited up the mast and keel many hours later. Odysseus plopped down beside them and rode them for nine days. On the tenth, he landed on Ogygia, Calypso's island.

Here Odysseus ends his tale, since he has already told Alcinoos about Calypso. Alcinoos decrees that more gifts should be given to Odysseus, and all retire for the night. The next day is taken up with another feast at the palace. When the sun finally sets, Odysseus is given a royal escort to the ship. He falls into a sound sleep on the deck. The ship races over the waves, arriving at Ithaca as the morning star appears in the sky. The Phaeacian crew lays the sleeping Odysseus on the shore and piles his gifts under a nearby olive tree. Learning of Odysseus's safe return, Poseidon is annoyed. When the Phaeacian ship comes back within sight of its home port, Poseidon turns it to stone. Seeing this, Alcinoos remembers an ancient prophecy that Poseidon would eventually petrify one of their ships and then hide the Phaeacian city with a mountain. The Phaeacians pray and offer sacrifice to Poseidon to prevent the rest of the prophecy from coming true.

When Odysseus wakes up, he does not know where he is because Athena has covered the land in mist. When she approaches disguised as a shepherd, Odysseus asks the name of the land. Though inwardly delighted to hear her say Ithaca, he tells an elaborate lie, claiming to be a Cretan veteran of Troy trying to get to Pylos. Amused, Athena identifies herself and assures Odysseus that he really is home. They hide his gifts in a cave. Athena says that they must plan an attack on the suitors who have taken over Odysseus's palace for the last three years. She tells him to go first, disguised as a beggar, to the hut of his swineherd. Meanwhile, she will see to it that Telemachus returns from Sparta. She strikes Odysseus with a wand, transforming him into a pathetic beggar in appearance.

Eumaeus, the swineherd, receives the "beggar" with outstanding hospitality. After they dine on young porkers, a stormy night descends. The "beggar" sleeps snug in an extra blanket that he wheedles from Eumaeus, but the swineherd spends the night outdoors, keeping watch over his pigs.

On the same night, Athena appears to Telemachus in a dream, telling him that it is time to go home. She warns him about the suitors' ambush and tells him to stop first at Eumaeus's shelter when he gets back to Ithaca.

Back in Eumaeus's shelter, the beggar is eager to go to the palace to beg and observe the suitors, but Eumaeus persuades him to wait for Telemachus there in the shelter.

Telemachus arrives at Eumaeus's hut as he and the beggar prepare breakfast. Telemachus sends Eumaeus to the palace to tell Penelope that he is safe. When he is gone, Athena appears outside the door of the shelter, making herself visible just to Odysseus, and signals to him with her eyebrows to come outside. When he does, she tells him to reveal his identity to his son and transforms him back to his regal, robust appearance.

Telemachus is startled by the transformation. At first he thinks that some god is tricking him, but when Odysseus insists that he is telling the truth, they embrace and weep noisily, like grief-stricken vultures. Then they discuss the suitors. Telemachus does not see how it will be possible to attack them, since there are a hundred and eight of them, but Odysseus says that they will be helped by Athena and Zeus. He gives Telemachus the job of putting the suitors' weapons away in a storeroom at an appropriate time.

In Ithaca, Eumaeus arrives at the palace at the same time as a sailor from Telemachus's ship. Both have the job of reporting Telemachus's safe return to Penelope and do so. Antinous, the leading suitor, is upset that Telemachus has eluded the ambush, and wants to lay another plan to kill him. Another suitor named Amphinomus objects, saying that it is dreadful to kill a member of a royal family. He would approve only if they had clear signs of divine favor from Zeus. The other suitors go along with this point of view. Eumaeus returns to his shelter. Just before he enters, Athena transforms Odysseus into the beggar again.

At dawn, Telemachus leaves for the palace. He is followed somewhat later by Eumaeus and the beggar. En route, they meet Melanthius, a goatherd who has befriended the suitors. He insults the beggar and kicks him in the thigh. Inwardly, Odysseus considers killing Melanthius but decides to restrain himself. Outside the palace, Odysseus sees his former hunting dog, Argus, who is now suffering from old age and neglect. Lying on a pile of manure, infested by fleas, the dog recognizes Odysseus, lifts his head, wags his tail, and dies.

Inside the palace, the beggar asks the feasting suitors for food. All give him something, except for their leader, Antinous, who refuses—and ends up hitting the beggar with a footstool to get rid of him. The other suitors disapprove of this action, saying that the beggar might be a god in disguise. Penelope is also offended by Antinous's action and says that she would like to talk to the beggar to see if he has any news of Odysseus. At the beggar's suggestion, however, the interview is postponed until the end of the evening.

A real beggar arrives at the palace. He is an oversized glutton whom the suitors call Irus because he carries messages for them.[30] Antinous insists that the two beggars have a boxing match. The prize is a grilled goat's stomach full of fat and blood and the exclusive right to beg at the palace. Inwardly, Odysseus decides just to knock Irus out, not kill him. He strikes him in the neck, below the ear, crushing several bones, and drags him outside, unconscious. When Odysseus returns, Antinous gives him his goat's stomach, and Amphinomus brings him bread. The beggar tells Amphinomus that disaster often catches human beings by surprise and that he should leave the palace while he still can. Amphinomus knows that he is right, but just walks away, shaking his head, since he has been doomed by Athena to be killed by Telemachus.

---

30   Iris was the lovely goddess of the rainbow, and one of the gods' messengers. *Irus* is the masculine form of the name. The name, "Rainbow," was a comical one for this character.

Beautified by Athena, Penelope appears to the suitors. She says that the time for her to select a husband is drawing near, but complains that rival suitors in the past brought gifts. The suitors dispatch heralds, who quickly return with a large number of valuable gifts, mostly jewelry.

Of the maids who are sleeping with the suitors, the prettiest is Melantho. Her lover is Eurymachos, the most influential suitor after Antinous. Later in the evening, the beggar starts a quarrel with Melantho by volunteering to take care of the torches so that the maids can go to bed early. Eurymachos gets involved and ends up throwing a footstool at the beggar. Amphinomus, however, restores order, and persuades everyone to retire for the night.

Now the beggar joins Penelope. He claims to be a Cretan and to have met Odysseus when he was on his way to Troy. He says that he is sure that Odysseus is on his way home. Penelope is skeptical, but has the oldest, most loyal of the maids, Euryclea, bring a basin to wash the beggar's feet. As she begins to do so, the disguised Odysseus is suddenly panic-stricken. He has a scar on his knee that Euryclea will certainly recognize. He got it as a youth on a boar hunt when he visited his maternal grandfather, Autolycus, a famous trickster. (Autolycus gave Odysseus his name as a way of commemorating the fact that he [Autolycus] had often been "angered" [*odyssamenos*]. So that is how Odysseus came to have that name.) Euryclea recognizes the scar, drops Odysseus's foot so that it knocks over the basin, and starts to cry out to Penelope, but Penelope is momentarily distracted by Athena. Odysseus grabs Euryclea by the throat and tells her to keep his secret. Euryclea is happy to cooperate.

When they resume their talk, Penelope asks the beggar to evaluate a dream. She has 20 pet geese. In her dream, they were all killed by an eagle, and she was grief-stricken. The eagle then perched on a rafter and announced that the dream was a vision of the future. The geese, he continued, represented the suitors and he, the eagle, was really Odysseus. The beggar says that the dream is a sure sign of the suitors' forthcoming destruction. Penelope, however, argues that some dreams come from the underworld through a gateway of horn and are true, but others come through a gateway of ivory and are deceptive. In any event, she plans to have a contest the following day. She will marry the suitor who can string Odysseus's old bow and shoot an arrow through 12 axes. The beggar encourages her to hold the contest. Odysseus will be back, he says, before any of them can string his bow.

In the morning, the household prepares for another feast. Eumaeus arrives with three pigs, Melanthius with goats, and a certain Philoetius, a loyal cowherd, with a heifer. Outside, the suitors discuss making another attempt on Telemachus's life, but an eagle clutching a dove appears on their left. Amphinomus announces that their plot would not succeed. They agree, and turn toward the palace. Inside, Athena inspires the suitors to act badly in order to anger Odysseus. One of them throws an ox's foot at the beggar as a "gift." Telemachus rebukes him sternly, and Athena stirs hysterical laughing in the suitors. A wandering prophet, who has joined the feasting, rises amid the laughter to leave the palace, saying that he sees darkness enveloping the suitors, blood on the walls, and ghosts in the courtyard. This makes the suitors laugh even harder.

Penelope fetches the bow from a storeroom, enters the dining hall with it, and announces the contest. Telemachus quickly sets up the target of 12 axes. He laughs as he does so and apologizes, saying that he has no reason to laugh on such an occasion. When the target is ready, he tests the bow himself. He is about to string it when the beggar catches his eye and shakes his head.

When the first suitor fails to string the bow, Antinous has the goatherd, Melanthius, heat the bow and grease it. When others fail to string it, Antinous says that they cannot succeed because it is a feast day of the archer Apollo. They will try again tomorrow. The beggar asks if he can try. Antinous and Eurymachos oppose the idea, but they are overruled by Penelope and Telemachus. Eumaeus gives the beggar the bow. He strings it effortlessly, like a musician with a lyre. Thunder sounds. He shoots an arrow through the axes. Then he tells Telemachus that the time has come for a banquet with music and dancing.

Throwing off his rags, the beggar leaps onto the steps leading to the main doorway. "Now," he says, "I will hit another target that no man has ever hit." With this, he shoots Antinous in the throat with an arrow, just as the suitor is about to take a drink of wine from a golden goblet. His wine and his blood mix on the floor as he falls.

The other suitors assume that this is an accident and warn the beggar of the dire consequences, but then he reveals his identity, saying, "Dogs! You thought that I would never return."

The suitors are terrified. Eurymachos says that Antinous was responsible for the suitors' crimes and offers to pay Odysseus back for all damages. Odysseus rejects the offer. Eurymachos then urges the suitors to charge Odysseus in a mass. Odysseus shoots Eurymachos down with an arrow that strikes his chest beside a nipple and lodges in his liver. Amphinomus draws his sword and tries to push his way past Odysseus, but Telemachus spears him in the back.

Odysseus continues to drop suitors with arrows, while Telemachus brings armor and weapons out of the storeroom. Noticing this, the suitors send Melanthius to the storeroom to get weapons for themselves. After three trips, he is caught in the act by Telemachus and Eumaeus. They tie him up and hang him to a rafter.

The battle rages. Though outnumbered, Odysseus and friends are aided by the gods. Their spears never miss; the suitors' always do. Soon, all the suitors lie in the dining hall like dead fish. Odysseus has Telemachus and the herdsmen take the corpses outside, while the 12 disloyal maids are made to clean up the blood. When they are finished, Odysseus tells Telemachus to take them outside and strike them down with swords "until they forget Aphrodite." Telemachus takes them outside, but decides against killing them with a "pure" death. Instead, he hangs them all in nooses attached to a single cable. They struggle briefly with their dangling feet. Melanthius is then brought into the courtyard where his nose, ears, genitals, hands, and feet are cut off and fed to the dogs.

An elderly maid wakes Penelope out of a sound sleep to tell her the news. When Penelope comes down stairs, she refuses to believe in Odysseus's identity. They sit on separate sides of the dining hall for some time, eyeing each other. Finally, Penelope asks a maid to move the bed that Odysseus made for them into the corridor. Odysseus immediately flares up. He says that it is not possible to move the bed, since he carved it out of a giant olive tree still rooted in the ground. This knowledge is the proof that Penelope was hoping for. Now they embrace. She feels like a sailor who barely reaches land after nearly drowning at sea. Odysseus and Penelope go to bed, make love, and exchange stories. Athena delays sunrise so that they have plenty of time.

Hermes leads the souls of the suitors into the land of the dead, where the ghosts of Agamemnon and Achilles are conversing. Agamemnon recalls Achilles' funeral. Achilles' body was recovered from the Trojans after a huge battle. He was mourned for 18 days by Thetis and the other goddesses of the sea. The nine Muses sang a dirge. His bones were placed in a golden urn with the bones of Patroclus and buried in a mound that is visible for miles around. Funeral games were held, for which Thetis provided divinely manufactured prizes. In contrast, Agamemnon says, he himself had no funeral after being murdered by his wife.

Seeing the suitors' souls, Agamemnon asks what caused the death of so many youths. One suitor summarizes the whole story, emphasizing Penelope's claim that she had to weave a burial sheet for Laertes. He also assumes that the archery contest was Odysseus's idea. Agamemnon praises Penelope as being the opposite in character from his wife, whose treachery has given all women a bad name.

In the morning, Odysseus and his comrades go to a farmhouse that is part of the royal estate. Odysseus finds his father, Laertes, pulling up weeds in the vineyard. He is dressed in a dirty, patched tunic, with leather gloves and leggings for protection against thorns. Odysseus pretends to think that he is a slave and jokes that he takes better care of the vineyard than his masters do of him. Odysseus claims to be Eperitus from Alybas ("Man of Strife from Wanderville") and to be looking for Odysseus, who visited him five years ago. He says that they parted in friendship and were looking forward to seeing each other again. At this, Laertes breaks down crying. Odysseus then reveals his true identity, proving it with his scar and detailed knowledge of the trees in the vineyard.

After a joyous reunion, father and son return to the farmhouse to deal with the threat posed by the relatives of the suitors, who will probably be looking for revenge. In town, Antinous's father, Eupeithes, urges an assembly to attack Odysseus, who is responsible for the loss of the entire fleet, as well as the murders that he has just committed. Others speak in Odysseus's defense, but over half follow Eupeithes. Odysseus and friends arm and march forth to meet them. They are joined by Athena, disguised as Mentor. Odysseus urges Telemachus not to be a disgrace to his family's name in battle. Telemachus says that he certainly will not be. "Dear gods, what a day!" exclaims Laertes. "My son and my grandson competing over courage!"

"Mentor" tells Laertes to say a prayer to Athena and hurl his spear. Laertes is filled with power, hurls his weapon, and hits Eupeithes in the face, killing him. The two sides clash. Athena lets out a great shout that causes panic among the Ithacans, who retreat headlong. Then Zeus stops the battle with a thunderbolt. Disguised as Mentor, Athena administers oaths to both sides, establishing peace.

69. The Death of Odysseus

Source: Byzantine summary of *The Telegony*, by Eugammon of Cyrene (Archaic Greek)

Odysseus goes to Thesprotia, where he marries the queen, Callidice. A war breaks out between the Thesprotians, led by Odysseus, and a neighboring tribe. Ares routs Odysseus's army until Athena intervenes. The two gods fight until Apollo separates them.

After the death of Callidice, her son by Odysseus inherits the throne. Odysseus returns to Ithaca. In the meantime, Telegonus, Circe's son by Odysseus, is traveling in search of his father. He lands on Ithaca and ravages the island. Odysseus comes out to defend his country, but is killed by his son—unwittingly. On learning his victim's identity, Telegonus transports his father's body, together with Penelope and Telemachus, to his mother's island, Aeaea. There, Circe makes them immortal. Telegonus marries Penelope; Telemachus marries Circe.

70. Episodes from the Earlier Lives of Scylla, Polyphemus, and Circe

Source: Ovid, *Metamorphoses*, 13.734–14.73 (Roman)

Scylla is a beautiful maiden who likes to hide from her many suitors with the nymphs of the sea. When she complains about her suitors, the lovely Nereid, Galatea, says that Scylla is lucky to be pursued by normal men, whom she can reject. She says that she once loved a downy-cheeked, 16-year-old boy named Acis, the son of Faunus. While she pursued him, however, the horrible Cyclops, Polyphemus, pursued her. Trying to impress her, he combed his hair with a rake, trimmed his beard with a sickle, and practiced making winsome faces, using a pool of water for a mirror. At night, after he brought his sheep home, he would serenade Galatea. "O Galatea," he would sing,

> Whiter than snowy privet leaves,
> more blossoming than meadows, loftier than an alder,
> brighter than glass, more playful than a kid,
> more delicate than conch shells, polished by the sea,
> better than winter sun or summer shade,
> grander than apples, statelier than a plane tree,

shinier than ice, sweeter than ripened grapes,
softer than goose's down or cottage cheese

... etc., etc. He offered to share his cave with her and to provide her with apples, grapes, strawberries, cherries, plums, chestnuts, milk, and cheese from his herds, and deer, rabbits, and goats—even a pair of bear cubs as pets. He added that when he thought about Galatea preferring Acis to him, he felt as though Mount Aetna were erupting in his chest.

Galatea was not won over. Polyphemus rose like a bull in rut to look for Galatea and saw her with Acis. Galatea dove into the sea and got away. Polyphemus, however, tore off a piece of a mountain, hurled it at Acis, and struck him, wounding him fatally. As Acis's blood gushed out, it turned into a stream of water. The stream split the earth, and created a river. Then a new Acis appeared in its midst. He had become a river god.

When Galatea finishes her story, Scylla goes for a walk and is chased by the merman, Glaucus. He tells her that he was once a normal human fisherman, but he ate some magical grass and was transformed into a fishy god. Scylla runs away from him anyway. Hence, Glaucus goes to the sorceress, Circe, hoping to get help in winning Scylla's love. Circe, however, falls in love with Glaucus. When he rejects her because he is still in love with Scylla, Circe is inflamed by jealousy and puts a magic potion in Scylla's bathing place. As a result, the next time Scylla wades into this pool, she notices that her lower body is surrounded by monstrous heads. At first, she cannot comprehend that they are part of her and tries to run away from them. In the end, she remains a lovely maiden above the waist, but she has become a many-headed dog beneath. She makes her home in a cliff overlooking the sea. From there she attacks Odysseus's ship—because he has been Circe's lover.

71. Aeneas Leads Trojan Survivors to the Promised Land

Source: Vergil, *Aeneid* (Roman)

Aeneas, the son of Venus and the Trojan noble Anchises, is one of the few Trojan warriors to escape from the sack of Troy. With his father, his son, Ascanius, and a handful of refugees, he wanders the Mediterranean looking for a new homeland. Juno still holds a grudge against the Trojans. As they are sailing along the coast of northern Africa, she bribes Aeolus, king of the winds, to unleash his storm winds and sink the fleet. The bribe is a beautiful sea nymph for a wife. Aeolus complies. By the time Neptune restores order, the fleet is wrecked on the shore.

In heaven, Venus asks Jove to have mercy on her son. Jove comforts her by revealing Aeneas's fate. He will eventually make a home for his people in Italy. He will establish a city named Lavinium. His son, Ascanius, will build a new city named Alba Longa. Three hundred years later, his descendants, Romulus and Remus, will found a third city,

Rome. Under a ruler named Caesar, Rome will bring permanent peace and prosperity to the world. (Caesar's family name, Iulius, will recall Aeneas's son, Ascanius. In Troy, also known as Ilium, Ascanius was also called Ilus. People now call him Iulus.)

The Trojans washed ashore near the new city of Carthage, which was being built by a Phoenician lady named Dido. She was the sister of the evil king of Tyre, Pygmalion, and the wife of a wealthy merchant, Sychaeus. Hoping to get his wealth, Pygmalion murdered Sychaeus. In a dream, Sychaeus's ghost told Dido what happened, urged her to flee the evil kingdom, and directed her to his hidden treasure. She gathered a group of friends and made her way to the site of the future Carthage.

Given directions by his mother (disguised as a young huntress), Aeneas makes his way to Carthage. Dido receives him and his companions hospitably. To make certain that Dido treats Aeneas well, Venus sends Cupid to Troy, disguised as Ascanius. At a feast welcoming the Trojans, Cupid works his magic on Dido. As she falls deeper into his power, she asks Aeneas to tell the full story of the fall of Troy and his later wanderings.

Aeneas begins on the day the Trojans were stunned to find that the Greeks had apparently sailed home, leaving a huge wooden horse behind. They toured the Greek camp, and gaped at the horse. Laocoon, a priest of Neptune, ran out of the city, shouting, "Whatever it is, I fear the Greeks, even bearing gifts," and he threw a spear at the horse.

Next, a ragged Greek named Sinon was hauled before Priam. Sinon had been "captured" by shepherds, but he was actually planted by the Greeks. He claimed that just before the Greeks departed, his personal enemy, Ulysses, bribed the priests to demand that he be sacrificed, but he managed to escape at the last moment. The Trojans pitied him and asked about the horse. He said that Minerva was angry because the Greeks had stolen her sacred statue, known as the Palladium, from Troy and sent it home to Greece. To appease her anger, they had to return to Greece, get the statue, and start the war all over again. The horse was a gift to Minerva to placate her in the interim. According to the Greek priest, if the Trojans harmed the horse, they would suffer horrible retribution, but if they took it into their city, they would end up invading Greece, instead of vice versa. Hence, the Greeks deliberately made the horse too big to get through the gate.

Meanwhile, Laocoon was sacrificing on the shore. Two giant serpents appeared in the waves. They attacked Laocoon and his two sons, devouring them all. Then they slithered into the temple of Minerva in the city, and disappeared beneath her statue. The Trojans interpreted this as a sign that they should honor the horse. Amid music and cheering, they dragged it into the city.

That night, while the Trojans slept, the Greeks inside the horse slipped out, and the rest of their fleet, which had hidden behind an island, returned. Aeneas was awakened by Hector's ghost in time to arm and put up some resistance. While fighting near Priam's palace, he happened to see the king's death. Achilles' son, Pyrrhus, chased Priam's young son, Polites, into the courtyard and killed him as his parents watched. Priam rose and feebly cast a javelin at Pyrrhus, saying that his father was a nobler man. Pyrrhus sneered that he could soon complain to Achilles in person, dragged him slipping in Polites' blood to the altar, and killed him like a sacrificial victim.

Aeneas also saw Helen hiding in a temple and was about to kill her when his mother, Venus, appeared and told him not to. She said that the fall of Troy was really the work of the gods and revealed many divine figures moving around in the darkness.

Back in his own house, Aeneas wanted to lead his family to safety. At first, his father refused to leave, but then a flame appeared over young Ascanius's head. Anchises saw this as a favorable omen and prayed for confirmation. Thunder sounded, and a shooting star streaked across the sky. Satisfied, Anchises packed up the Penates, small statues of the family's ancestors. He was so feeble, that Aeneas had to carry him—piggyback—out of the city, taking Ascanius by the hand. Aeneas's wife, Creusa, brought up the rear. Outside the city, Aeneas found that Creusa was missing. He ran back to find her, defying death at every turn. Finally, her ghost appeared to him, saying that he had to go on without her.

Aeneas sailed with a small fleet in search of a new homeland, guided by the prophecies and portents that came their way. Told at Delos to seek their ancient homeland, they tried to settle in Crete, but were thwarted by disease and barren fields. The Penates then appeared to Aeneas in a dream and told him that Italy was the ancient homeland in question. Trojans had ancestors from both places.

On the west coast of Greece, Aeneas met Hector's widow, Andromache, who fainted when she first saw him. She had been the slave of Pyrrhus, Achilles' son, but was eventually freed by him and was allowed to marry a fellow Trojan, Helenus. He was a prophet who had earned Pyrrhus's trust. He took over the kingdom when Pyrrhus died. Helenus told Aeneas that the sign of his new homeland would be a giant white sow nursing forty piglets.

Next, Aeneas's fleet landed by Mount Aetna, Sicily, at night. At dawn, a ragged Greek rushed into the Trojan camp, asking for protection. He had been in Odysseus's fleet, but was left behind by mistake, and had spent three hellish months on the island hiding from its giant, one-eyed cannibals. At this point, he would be grateful, he said, to be killed by a normal human being. As he spoke, Polyphemus appeared, wading into the surf to wash his pustulating eye socket. The Trojans put the Greek onboard and sailed away. Polyphemus heard them and waded after them but was unable to catch up.

The last stop before Carthage was at Drepanum, also in Sicily. Here, old Anchises finally died and was buried. A few days later, the Trojan fleet was wrecked in the storm.

By the time Aeneas stops talking, Dido has fallen in love with him. This creates a conflict for her: When Sychaeus died, she swore that she would never remarry. She describes her feelings to her sister Anna, who convinces her taht her self-denial does not benefit her dead husband. Marriage to Aeneas would be good for her and for her kingdom.

In heaven, Juno talks Venus into promoting a marriage between Dido and Aeneas. Juno just wants to prevent Aeneas from founding a new city, a second Troy. As a goddess of peace and love, Venus goes along, but she doubts that Jove will let the union last.

The next day, as fate would have it, the Trojans and the Carthaginians decide to go hunting in the countryside together. Far from the city, they are overtaken (thanks to Juno) by a sudden thunderstorm. All scatter. Dido and Aeneas find themselves alone together in a cave. Nature takes its course, as mountain nymphs wail in the wind and rain outside. In Dido's mind, they are now married.

After the hunt, Dido and Aeneas are inseparable. An African king, who was courting Dido himself, hears rumors of the affair and complains to Jove in his prayers. Jove is angry because Aeneas is neglecting his fated mission. He sends Mercury to Aeneas to tell him that it is time to ship out. Aeneas is duly impressed and gives secret orders to his men to finish repairing the fleet. Before he can find the right time to tell Dido, she figures out what is going on, denounces him angrily— yet begs him to stay just a little longer. Aeneas remains inflexible, even when Anna comes to him with a last desperate plea to postpone his departure.

Meanwhile, Dido has built a pyre in her courtyard with Anna's help. A sword that Aeneas gave to Dido and the bed that they shared are piled on top of it. Dido pretends that all this is part of a magical ceremony that will either bring Aeneas back or enable her to forget him entirely.

In the middle of the night after Anna's visit, Mercury wakes Aeneas and tells him to set sail before Dido resorts to force to keep him. At dawn, Dido ascends a tower and sees the Trojan fleet scurrying over the waves. She curses Aeneas and prays for eternal hostility between her people and his. She then sends her nursemaid off to get Anna to "participate in a sacrifice." Alone, she climbs on top of the pyre in the courtyard, flings herself on the marriage bed, and falls on Aeneas's sword. Anna bursts in hysterically, mounts the pyre, and cradles Dido in her arms. Trapped between life and death, Dido tries and fails to lift her head to look at her sister. At last, Juno takes pity on her and sends Iris, goddess of the rainbow, to end Dido's misery. Since Dido was dying by suicide, before her fated time, the Fates had not snipped the golden hair on her head to dedicate her to Orcus, god of the dead. Iris descends in her beautiful, multicolored robe, and snips the hair. Dido's soul flies off to the underworld. Aboard their ships, Aeneas and the Trojans see the smoke from Dido's funeral pyre rising over Troy and wonder what it means.

When the weather turns bad, they land at the friendly Sicilian town of Drepanum. It happens to be a year since Anchises' death. Aeneas holds games in his honor. The celebration is marred by Juno. She inspires the Trojan women, who are tired of wandering, to set fire to the ships. Answering Aeneas's prayer, Jove puts out the fire with a rainstorm.

That night, Anchises' ghost tells Aeneas to let the Trojans who so desire stay in Sicily and found their own city. Aeneas himself must visit Anchises in the underworld and then establish himself in Italy. The Sibyl, priestess of Apollo at Cumae, will guide him to the land of the dead. Aeneas follows this advice, and makes his way to Cumae on the Bay of Naples. There, Aeneas finds the Sibyl. As they meet, Apollo takes possession of her. She becomes frenzied, bucking and reeling around the temple as the god's words issue from her mouth. She prophesies a terrible war for Aeneas. When she calms down, Aeneas asks her to take him to the land of the dead. She agrees to do so if he can produce a golden bough from the woods nearby. Also, she says, one of his crewmen has died, and must be buried.

A search turns up the corpse of Aeneas's trumpeter, Misenus. He was foolish enough to challenge the gods to a trumpeting contest. Offended, the trumpeter Triton, Neptune's son, held him under the water until he died. While Aeneas looks for wood for Misenus's pyre, a pair of doves—his mother's birds—guide him to the golden bough, which he picks. After Misenus's funeral, he goes to the Sibyl, bough in hand. She leads him down into the depths of a dark cave. They are surrounded by horrible apparitions (Diseases, Old Age, Malicious Joys). Aeneas reaches for his sword, but the Sibyl tells him just to ignore them because they are harmless.

At the bottom of the descent, souls of the dead line up to be ferried across the River Styx by the vigorous old boatman, Charon. Some souls must wait a hundred years because they have not been properly buried. Charon ferries Aeneas and Sibyl across the Styx when he sees the golden bough. On the far side, Sibyl puts Cerberus, Pluto's three-headed dog, to sleep with a piece of drugged cake and leads Aeneas into the Fields of Mourning, the resting place of souls who died for love. Here, Aeneas barely makes out the figure of Dido, like a crescent moon with clouds drifting by. "So the rumor was true!" he exclaims awkwardly. He swears that he did not think she would be so upset by his leaving and asks her to talk with him for a while. Dido turns away in silence and rejoins the ghost of her husband, Sychaeus.

The next sector is filled with dead soldiers. Here Aeneas meets his cousin Deiphobos, who was married to Helen briefly, between Paris's death and the fall of Troy. Deiphobos's ears are missing and his nose is mutilated. He explains that this happened during the sack of Troy. His "excellent wife," Helen, let Menelaus and Ulysses into their bedroom after hiding Deiphobos's weapons.

This brings Aeneas and the Sibyl to a crossroads. To the left lies the triple-walled dungeon of Tartarus, where sinners are punished by the Furies. Encircled by a river of fire, it cannot be approached without pollution. The Sibyl describes some its inmates. They include the most famous sinners, Tityos, Tantalus, Pirithous, etc., and anonymous evildoers, men who betray their countries for money, fathers who sleep with their daughters, etc.

Aeneas and the Sibyl turn away from Tartarus, place the golden bough at the gates of the palace of Pluto and Proserpina, and head for the Elysian fields. This is a beautiful park, where good souls pass their time in wrestling matches, chariot races, choral dancing, and other pleasant activities. Aeneas and Anchises meet and greet each other tearfully. Aeneas asks about a crowd of spirits on a nearby river bank. Anchises explains that one divine spirit pervades the entire universe. An individual's soul is a fragment of the divine soul, but it acquires impurities from being combined with a body. After death, the souls of the good are purified and linger in Elysium for an age but are then summoned to drink from the River Lethe (Forgetfulness) and be reborn. The souls that Aeneas asked about include his future descendants—e.g., Romulus, the founder of Rome; Augustus, who will extend Rome's power to the ends of the earth; the generals who will subjugate Greece; and others.[31]

Aeneas and the Sibyl return to the land of the living by the Gate of Ivory, from which false dreams emerge, rather than the Gate of Horn, which is associated with true ones.

The Trojans sail north to the mouth of the Tiber. Here, Aeneas befriends Latinus, king of the local tribe, the Latins. Influenced by an oracle, he agrees to unify their two peoples and betroths his daughter, Lavinia, to Aeneas. The only problem is that the Latin queen, Amata, wants Lavinia to marry Turnus, the king of the neighboring Rutulians. A Fury, sent by Juno, stirs uncontrollable resentment in the hearts of Amata and Turnus. The Fury also incites a brawl between the Trojans and the Italians. Ascanius happens to be hunting. The Fury arranges that he flush and shoot a sacred deer, the special pet of the Latins' royal gamekeeper. The Latins clamor for war. Unable to calm them down, Latinus resigns. The Latins prepare to attack the Trojan camp.

Meanwhile, the god of the Tiber appears to Aeneas in a dream, and tells him to get help from Pallanteum, which lies upstream—on the future site of Rome. On his way, Aeneas encounters a giant white sow with 40 piglets, and sacrifices her to the gods. At Pallanteum, he befriends the king, Evander, a Greek immigrant. An old enemy of the Latins, he turns his army over to Aeneas, together with his young son Pallas. In parting, he prays to die rather than ever hear the dreaded news that his son has died in battle.

In Aeneas's absence, the Latins surround the Trojan fort and try to burn the fleet. This fleet, however, was made out of pines sacred to Jove's mother, Rhea. The boats are fated to become sea goddesses when their sailing is done. As the Latins approach, the boats dive into the water beak first, like dolphins, and then the heads of the same number of goddesses appear swimming out to sea.

The next day, the battle is joined outside the Trojan camp. Turnus manages to get inside the Trojan fort, but the defenders close the gate behind him. Turnus is a great warrior, and wreaks havoc inside the camp by himself, but he neglects to open the gate to let his comrades in. If he had, Vergil says, the Trojans would have lost the war. Instead, he fights on alone until he is exhausted, then escapes by leaping into the Tiber, which skirts the Trojan camp.

About this time, Aeneas arrives with reinforcements. Pallas attracts the attention of Turnus by leading a charge. They fight, and Turnus's spear pierces Pallas's chest. Turnus takes an ornate belt from the dying boy as a trophy. Hearing of Pallas's death, Aeneas charges toward Turnus, slaughtering everyone in the way. To prolong Turnus's life, Juno

---

31 The last spirit mentioned is that of Augustus's nephew, Marcellus, who died at the age of 20 to the great sorrow of his mother, Octavia, Augustus's sister. Anchises describes the grief that the boy's death will bring to Rome. There is a legend that when Vergil recited these lines to the imperial family, Octavia fainted.

makes an image of Aeneas out of a cloud and uses it to lure Turnus onto a boat. Once aboard, a gale blows the boat all the way back to his hometown of Ardea.

Aeneas escorts Pallas's body back to Pallanteum. His grief-stricken father asks only one thing of Aeneas: the death of Turnus.

There is a truce, in order to bury the dead. At its conclusion, Turnus sends the Italian cavalry against the Trojans. It is led by a great female warrior, Camilla. She grew up in the wilderness with her father, an exiled tyrant whom no city would admit. She fights with one breast exposed, in the style of the Amazons, and dominates the battle all day. She is finally killed by a cowardly Trojan ally, who hits her in the breast with a spear thrown from a distance.

During the night, the Latins vote for peace. The dispute is to be settled by single combat between Turnus and Aeneas. The next morning, however, Juno inspires a Latin warrior to break the truce by shooting down a Trojan, and soon a battle rages. Aeneas is wounded in the leg by an arrow and has to withdraw.

Turnus goes on a rampage. Venus miraculously heals Aeneas, who returns to battle. Turnus's sister, Juturna, now enters the story. She was transformed into the goddess of a local fountain by Jove, who raped her when she was a virgin. Now she disguises herself as Turnus's charioteer and drives him from one engagement to another, carefully avoiding Aeneas. This tactic finally fails, however, when Aeneas charges the Latins' city, and Turnus leaves the chariot to stop him.

In their first clash, Turnus's sword beaks. He realizes that he must have picked up the wrong sword by mistake since his sword was made by Vulcan, and would never break. He flees Aeneas, shouting for someone to bring him his *good* sword. Aeneas cannot catch him because of his leg wound.

Juturna finally shows up with the good sword. In heaven, however, Juno agrees to let Turnus die, provided that after the Trojan-Latin merger, the Latin name and language— not the Trojan—will prevail. Jove sends a fear-inspiring Fury to hover over Turnus. Juturna abandons him. Turnus spots a boulder, so big that 12 modern men could not budge it. He lifts it and throws it at Aeneas, but he is unsteady and the boulder falls short. Aeneas hits Turnus in the thigh with his spear. Lying on the ground defenseless, Turnus asks to be spared or at least given a proper burial. Aeneas is about to spare him. Then he notices Pallas's belt, and strikes him dead.

72. Romulus and Remus

Source: Livy, *The History of Rome from the Foundation of the City*, I.3–6 (Roman)

The descendants of Aeneas ruled in Alba Longa for 12 generations. The thirteenth king should have been Numitor, but his younger brother, Amulius, forcibly seized the throne instead. He killed Numitor's sons and forced his only daughter, Rhea Silva, to become a Vestal virgin so that she would not bear any rival claimants to the throne. Mars, however, raped Rhea Silva. When her pregnancy was discovered, she was consigned to prison. There she gave birth to twin boys. At Amulius's orders, they were put in a basket and set afloat on the Tiber to drown.

On that day, the Tiber had overflowed its banks. Rather than being washed out to sea, the basket with the boys in it was deposited on the bank by receding waters. A mother wolf happened along and adopted the boys, suckling them and licking them affectionately. A herdsman found them being nursed by the wolf and took them home to raise as his own. Others say that this story arose, because the wife of the herdsman who raised the boys was a prostitute. In Latin slang, a prostitute is called a wolf.

The boys were named Romulus and Remus, and were raised as herdsmen. They had such strength and energy that they became the leaders of their fellow herdsmen, and led raids on local robbers. Eventually, the robbers ambushed them, captured Remus, and took him to Amulius, saying that he had been robbing Numitor's herds. During the course of the hearing, all parties began to suspect the true identity of Remus and his twin brother. Realizing that time was short, Romulus organized a surprise attack on the king's house with the help of his fellow herdsmen. Overpowering the guards, they assassinated Amulius. Numitor assembled the people, laid out the facts, and was made king by unanimous consent.

Because of overcrowding in Alba and their own ambitious natures, Romulus and Remus decided to build a city at the spot on the Tiber where they had been nursed by the wolf. To decide which one would be the king, they stationed themselves on high spots to look for favorable signs in the flight of birds. Remus stood on the Aventine Hill, Romulus on the Palatine. Soon, six vultures appeared to Remus in a favorable location. Then 12 vultures appeared to Romulus. This caused a quarrel between the brothers and their respective followers. It turned violent, and Remus was killed.

Others say that Romulus had started to build a wall for the new city, when Remus jumped over it as a joke. Romulus killed him in a rage, saying "So perish all who over-leap my fortifications!"

73. The Rape of the Sabine Women

Source: Livy, *The History of Rome from the Foundation of the City* (Roman)

The city of Rome was growing. Romulus increased its population in a standard way, by opening it to the poor and fugitives of other communities. These flocked to the city, looking for a new start. Romulus created a hundred senators to govern the city.

The only problem was a shortage of women. It was made worse by the fact that neighboring communities would not recognize marriages with Romans. Romulus tried to win them over with diplomacy, but failed.

Concealing his resentment, Romulus prepared to celebrate a great festival of Neptune called the *Consualia*. The new citizens of Rome lavished all of their modest wealth on preparations for spectacular entertainments, and the citizens of surrounding communities were all invited to attend. Many came out of curiosity to see the new city. Among these were the neighboring Sabines, who came with their wives and children. All the visitors were hospitably entertained by the Romans. Just when the games were supposed to begin, a signal was given, and the Roman men charged the crowd, each seizing the young woman of his choice.

A few conspicuously beautiful girls had been designated for leading senators. One of these was seized by men working for a senator named Thalassius. As they were taking her to him, they prevented others from seizing her by shouting *Thalassio!* ("For Thalassius!") To this day, well-wishers at Roman weddings shout "*Thalassio!*"

The festival broke up in a panic. The girls' parents escaped to their homes. The girls themselves were angry and frightened. Romulus visited them individually, saying that their parents were really to blame and that their new husbands would treat them with respect and affection. In time, the girls lost their resentment.

Relatives of three smaller communities which had lost girls to the Romans launched ill-conceived attacks against Rome and were easily defeated by Romulus; but the Sabines posed a greater threat. They were led by a famous king named Titus Tatius. He gained access to the Roman citadel by bribing a Roman girl named Tarpeia, whose father was the officer in charge of the citadel. Once inside, the Sabines crushed Tarpeia beneath their shields. Some say that they merely wanted it to appear that they had captured the fort by force. Others say it was because Tarpeia had demanded as part of her payment what Sabines "wore on their left arms."(At this time, the Sabines wore golden bracelets on their left arms—but they also carried their shields on them.)

A fierce battle occurred in the Roman forum between Romans and Sabines. At its height, the Sabine girls pushed themselves between the opposing armies. They said that they were now mothers. The fathers of their babies were fighting on one side; the grandfathers on the other. "If you have to kill somebody," they said, "kill us. We would rather die than live as widows or orphans."

Immediately, all the soldiers stopped fighting and fell into a deep silence. Not only did the Romans and Sabines make peace, but they united their two communities—with Rome as the center of government.

74. The Death of Romulus

Source: Livy, *History of Rome*, I.18 (Roman)

Throughout his career, Romulus was loved by the common people and the soldiers, but he was less popular with the Senate. One day, he was reviewing the troops on the Campus Martius, surrounded by senators. There was a sudden thunderstorm. He was enveloped in a cloud and never seen again. The senators declared that he had been carried into heaven by a whirlwind. The army went along with the story, but soon rumors spread that the senators had killed him.

A man named Julius Proculus, who was famous for his wisdom, then took a timely action. He summoned an assembly of all citizens and declared that Romulus's spirit had appeared to him. He had descended at dawn from heaven and given Proculus a message for the Roman people. "By heaven's will," he supposedly declared, "Rome shall be the capital of the world. No power on earth can stand against Roman arms."

Proculus's story ended the grief and suspicion that the army and the poor felt after the disappearance of Romulus.

75. The Birth of the Roman Republic

Source: Livy, *History of Rome*, 1.49–60 (Roman)

After Romulus, Rome was ruled by other kings, his successors, for over 200 years. The seventh and last king of Rome, Lucius Tarquinius Superbus (the Proud) gained the throne in violent coup d'état. His predecessor, Servius Tullius, was Tarquinius's own father-in-law, and Tarquinius had him assassinated with the help of his wife, the king's wicked daughter, Tullia. It is said that when Tullia was returning to her house from the forum on the day of the assassination, she encountered her father's dead body in the road and drove her carriage over it. Thereafter, the roadway in which this occurred was called the *Vicus Sceleratus*, Street of Crime.

Tarquinius ruled by terror, condemning citizens to death if he suspected them of treason—or simply disliked them or desired their wealth. He forced the common people to labor at public works, especially Rome's great sewer.

Once, a giant snake appeared in his palace. Considering this to be a terrible portent, Tarquinius sent an embassy to the oracle of Delphi to interpret it. The ambassadors were two of his sons and his nephew, Lucius Junius Brutus.[32] Brutus secretly longed for freedom and justice in Rome, but he was afraid of drawing attention to himself. Hence, he pretended to be stupid and indolent, even accepting the nickname Brutus, which means stupid. When he went to Delphi, he dedicated a hollow wooden staff that was filled with gold as a gift to Apollo. This was a symbol of his character.

The oracle of Delphi predicted the next one of the ambassadors to kiss his mother would rule in Rome. Tarquinius's two sons decided to conceal the oracle from their brother, Sextus, who was not present, and to cast lots to decide who would kiss their mother first. Brutus, however, interpreted the oracle differently. As he left the temple, he deliberately stumbled, fell to the ground, and secretly kissed mother earth.

---

32   The ancestor of the later L. Junius Brutus involved in the assassination of Julius Caesar in 44 B.C.

Later, Tarquinius declared war on the town of Ardea, simply because he envied its wealth. After an attempt to storm its walls failed, the Roman army laid siege to it. The men conducting the siege, especially the officers, had many idle hours. By chance, Sextus Tarquinius, the king's son, was drinking with a group of other officers, when the subject of wives came up. Each man boasted that his own wife was the best. One of the officers, Collatinus, was especially proud of his wife, Lucretia. He suggested that they ride back to Rome and see how their wives were acting when their husbands came home unexpectedly. All agreed.

The other wives were discovered wasting time with their friends in banquets and other luxurious activities. Though it was late at night, Lucretia was working at her loom and supervising the work of her maids. She received her husband and his friends graciously.

Lucretia won the contest. Sextus Tarquinius, however, was overcome by a wicked desire. A few days later, he returned secretly to Lucretia's house. She welcomed him as an honored guest, giving him a meal and a place to sleep. In the still of the night, he entered Lucretia's bedroom with a drawn sword. Holding her down with his left hand on her breast, he said: "Be still, Lucretia. I am Sextus Tarquinius. I have a sword. You will die if you say a word." Sextus then declared his love, begged her to submit, mixed threats with his prayers, and said anything to win her over. When he saw that she was still unwilling, he said that he would not just kill her; he would kill a slave and place his naked body beside hers. People would believe that she had died because she was caught committing adultery. This threat made Lucretia submit. Some time later, Sextus departed, exulting in his victory.

Lucretia sent messages to her father and husband, asking them to come at once with trusted friends. Collatinus brought Brutus. They found Lucretia sitting sadly in her chamber and asked her whether she was well. She said: "Not at all. What is well for a woman whose honor has been lost? Collatinus, the imprint of another man is in your bed. Only my body was violated. My soul is innocent, and death will be my witness. Promise me that the adulterer will not get away with his crime. He is Sextus Tarquinius. He came here last night, an enemy disguised as a friend, and took his pleasure, a fatal one for me and for him too, if you are men."

The men promised to punish Sextus and tried to comfort Lucretia, saying that she was not guilty of anything. She said, "You will consider what to do about Sextus. As for me, I absolve myself from guilt, but not from punishment. Never in the future shall a shameless woman live because of the precedent set by Lucretia." She then removed a knife that she had concealed in her clothing, plunged it into her heart, and fell to the ground, dead.

While the others were weeping, Brutus removed the bloody knife from the wound, raised it high, and said, "By this woman's blood, most pure 'til wronged by royalty, I swear that I shall pursue Lucius Tarquinius Superbus, his evil wife, and their entire brood with steel, fire, and all the other resources at my command and that I will never allow any of them—or anyone else—to be a king in Rome!"

The Romans rallied around Brutus. The king and his family were driven out of Rome. Sextus tried to take refuge in the town of Gabii, but he was murdered by enemies settling an old score. In the year in which Tarquinius was exiled (traditionally 510 B.C.), the Romans outlawed monarchy. They began electing two consuls annually to direct the Senate. The first two elected were Brutus and Collatinus.

Appendix I: Some Myths of Other Nations

1: The Hittite Cronus (1400/1200 B.C.)

Source: A broken tablet with cuneiform inscriptions dating between 1400 and 1200 B.C., recovered from the ruins of the royal archives of Hattusa, the Hittite capital in modern Turkey. See Hans G. Gueterbock, "The Hittite Version of the Hurrian Kumarbi Myths: Oriental Forerunners of Hesiod," American Journal of Archaeology 52 (1948) 123–34. Except for minor word changes, e.g., "you" for "thou," Gueterbock's translation of the preserved portion of the text is given in its entirety below.

Formerly, in former years, Alalu was king in heaven. Alalu is sitting on the throne, and the mighty Anu, the first of the gods, is standing in front of him. He bows down to his feet and puts the drinking cups in his hand.

For nine full years, Alalu was king in heaven. In the ninth year, Anu fought against Alalu. He overcame Alalu, so that he fled from him and went down to the dark earth. He went down to the dark earth, while Anu sat on his throne. Anu is sitting on the throne, and the mighty Kumarbi is giving him drink. He bows down to his feet and puts the drinking cups into his hands.

Nine full years, Anu was king in heaven. In the ninth year, Anu fought against Kumarbi. Anu could not withstand Kumarbi's eyes any more. He escaped from Kumarbi's hand and fled. Anu flew like a bird toward heaven. Kumarbi rushed after him. He took Anu by the feet and pulled him down from heaven.

Kumarbi bit off Anu's testicles so that his manhood was absorbed into Kumarbi's interior. When Kumarbi had swallowed Anu's manhood, he rejoiced and laughed. Anu turned back to him and spoke: "You feel joy in your interior because you have swallowed my manhood. Do not feel joy in your interior! I have planted a seed in your interior because you swallowed my manhood. I have impregnated you with the great storm god, and secondly with the river Aranzah (Tigris), and thirdly with the great god Tasmisus. I have planted the seed of three fearful gods in your interior. In the end you will strike the rocks of the mountains with your head!"

2. Enuma Elish, The Babylonian Creation Myth

This story is inscribed on numerous Babylonian tablets, the earliest from the first millennium B.C. The following is an extremely condensed version based on Stephanie Dalley, Myths from Mesopotamia: Creation, the Flood, Gilgamesh, and Others. *Oxford, 2000, 233—60. The traditional title, "Enuma Elish," is how the account begins in Babylonian. The phrase means, "When the up-high did not yet exist."*

When heaven and earth did not yet exist, there were two gods, Apsu and Tiamat. Apsu, the male, was god of fresh water, while the female, Tiamat, was goddess of the salt sea. They mingled their waters and bore Lahmu and Lahamu, a pair of serpents, who then produced Anshar and Kishar. These gods had three mighty children, Anu, Enlil and Ea, and many others.

The uproar of her children caused distress in the belly of Tiamat, and she and Apsu debated how to deal with this commotion. Apsu recommended eliminating them, as they were preventing him from sleeping, but Tiamat was more indulgent. Ea learned of Apsu's plan and came upon him stealthily and slew his father. Having done so, he sired a magnificent son, Marduk.

Tiamat was furious and created an army of monsters, creatures, and beasts to put down the rebellious youngsters. Ea was not powerful enough to fight Tiamat, so he turned to Marduk. He agreed to battle Tiamat in exchange for being acknowledged as the supreme god and gaining ownership of the Tablets of Destiny.

Marduk rode out in his tempest-chariot to confront Tiamat. Marduk was armed with his bow, his thunderbolts, storms, and a special net. He trapped Tiamat with this net, and when she opened her mouth to swallow him, he cast his thundering tempest into her mouth. Having stunned her, he finished her off with an arrow to the belly. Her followers tried to flee, but Marduk caught them and tied them up.

He sliced the body of Tiamat in two like a fish. From one half he made the dome of the sky, and from the other he created the earth. He established the gods' dwellings, and ordained the cycles of the sun, moon, and heavens. Marduk took the blood of Tiamat's supreme general, Qingu, and made humanity from it. He then made rivers, plants, and animals, and thus was the universe completed.

3. The Saga of Gilgamesh

Gilgamesh was a king of the Mesopotamian city-state of Uruk, sometime between 2700 and 2500 B.C. Different versions of his legend were recorded throughout the Near East in Sumerian, Hittite, and Akkadian (the language of Assyria and Babylonia). The synopsis below is based on John Gardner and John Maier, Gilgamesh Translated from the Sin-leqi-unninni version, *Knopf, 1984. The Gardner-Maier translation is based, in turn, on an Akkadian version found on clay tablets in ancient Nineveh, in the library of the Assyrian king, Ashurbanipal (668–627 B.C.). It was composed in Akkadian between 1600 and 1000 B.C. The text survives on 12 clay tablets. A number of these are incomplete. Parts of the story below that lack detail—e.g., the slaying of Humbaba—are those where large parts of the original text are missing. At the end of the story, the dead Enkidu abruptly reappears, alive, and then dies again. The explanation of this anomaly is not known.*

This is the story of Gilgamesh who looked into the abyss. He learned all things, even what happened before the flood, and he built the walls of Uruk.

Gilgamesh is so mighty that he runs wild in Uruk, disrupting everyone's lives and sleeping with brides before their grooms do. The gods hear the people's complaints. Anu, god of the sky, tells a mother goddess named Aruru to create a rival for Gilgamesh, so that the people of Uruk will be left in peace. Aruru creates Enkidu, a great fighter. He lives in the wilderness with the animals and drinks with them at the water hole. He destroys traps set for the animals and otherwise helps them escape a hunter known as the "Stalker."

At his father's suggestion, the Stalker goes to Uruk and asks Gilgamesh for help with Enkidu. Gilgamesh gives him a temple prostitute to take to the water hole. He explains that she will show herself naked to Enkidu. This will turn the animals against him.

When Enkidu arrives at the water hole, the Stalker tells the prostitute to "open her legs and show him her beauty." She does so. Enkidu spends six days and seven nights copulating with her. Afterward, the animals run away from him. He returns to the prostitute and kneels before her. She tells him that he has become wise, like a god, and that she will take him to Uruk and introduce him to Gilgamesh. Longing for a friend, Enkidu agrees.

When Enkidu and the prostitute arrive in the city, they learn that Gilgamesh is causing trouble by sleeping with other men's brides. Enkidu challenges Gilgamesh to a fight outside a bride's house. After a long struggle, Gilgamesh emerges victorious, but he praises Enkidu's strength and valor. Enkidu weeps at his words. He and Gilgamesh embrace.

Now that they are friends, Enkidu tells Gilgamesh about a monster named Humbaba, who guards the cedar forest. Gilgamesh urges Enkidu to join him in killing Humbaba. Enkidu is reluctant at first, but Gilgamesh wins him over. Before they leave, Ninsun, Gilgamesh's mother, adopts Enkidu, making him Gilgamesh's brother.

Gilgamesh and Enkidu enter the cedar forest, overpower Humbaba, and cut off his head. After that, Gilgamesh bathes and changes clothes. The goddess Ishtar appears to him and offers to become his lover. Gilgamesh rejects her haughtily, saying that he cannot trust her. She is, he says, "a cooking fire that goes out in the cold, a water skin that soaks the one who lifts it." He then lists Ishtar's previous lovers, all of whom have suffered bad fates. They are: Tammuz, a shepherd who is now mourned annually; a bird; the lion; the stallion; a shepherd who was turned into a wolf; and her father's gardener, who ended up as a frog.

Ishtar goes to her father and mother, Anu and Antum, to complain about Gilgamesh. She demands that they give her the bull of heaven so that it can kill Gilgamesh. Anu and Antum reluctantly agree.

When the bull arrives in Uruk, he snorts ferociously. With each snort, he opens a hole in the earth that swallows hundreds of the men of Uruk. Enkidu jumps on the bull and fights him. The bull spits, and Enkidu throws his excrement at him. Finally, Gilgamesh stabs the bull in the back of the neck, killing him.

Ishtar comes to the walls of Uruk, mourning the bull. Enkidu throws one of the bull's bloody thighbones at her. Later, he and Gilgamesh bathe and march through the city in triumph. Then they lie down to sleep.

Enkidu wakes up and reports a disturbing dream. In it, Enlil, the storm god, wants Enkidu to die in compensation for the deaths of Humbaba and the bull of heaven. Shamash, the god of justice, objects, but he is overruled.

As the dream foretold, Enkidu becomes gravely ill. He is bedridden for 12 days and dies. Gilgamesh is sorely grieved. He builds a precious statue of Enkidu. He himself wears a dog's skin. His grief only deepens. He realizes that he, too, will die, just like Enkidu. Finally, he decides to visit the wise man, Utnapishtim, the survivor of the great flood.

At the beginning of this journey, Gilgamesh comes to the twin peaks of Mount Mashu, home of Shamash. His way leads through a long tunnel in the mountain. The entrance is guarded by scorpion men. Their spokesman warns Gilgamesh that he must travel through 12 double hours of thick darkness. Gilgamesh plunges ahead. After enduring 12 double hours, he sees light.

In the region of light, he meets Siduri, the barmaid. He explains his quest to Siduri. He dwells on his sadness at Enkidus's death. "Six days and seven nights I wept over him until a worm fell out of his nose. Then I was afraid. In fear of death I roam the wilderness." Siduri tells him that he must cross the sea that includes the waters of death and that no one except Shamash, the god of justice, has ever made the crossing. There is, however, a boatman named Urshanabi, who might ferry him across.

Gilgamesh finds Urshanabi and explains his mission to him, repeating what he said to Siduri. Urshanabi tells him to go to the forest and cut down poles 60 cubits in length and to bring them back. Gilgamesh does so. Using these, they set sail and cover the distance of a month and a half in three days. At this point, they pass the waters of death, which Gilgamesh must be careful not to touch. Afterward, Gilgamesh's poles wear out, but he has Urshanabi use his shirt like a sail on the final leg of the journey.

Gilgamesh explains his quest to Utnapishtim, giving the same speech for the third time. Utnapishtim replies that mortal lives are not meant to be permanent. Gilgamesh notes, however, that he and Utnapishtim look alike. He wants to know how Utnapishtim earned the favor of the gods.

Utnapishtim tells his story. He lived in Surippak when the gods decided to cause the flood. The god Ea warned Utnapishtim to build an ark, loading it with the seed of every living thing. Ea also suggested an explanation to give to the other people of Surippak. Utnapishtim told them that he himself was fleeing the anger of Enlil, the storm god, but Enlil was going to rain favors down on the rest of the city.

Utnapishtim built a huge ark with an acre of floor space and six decks. The rains came in such a violent storm that even the gods were terrified. After this, Utnapishtim floated free for 12 days. Finally, his ark ran aground on Mount Nisir.

To learn whether dry land had reappeared, Utnapishtim released a dove, a swallow, and a crow. The first two returned. When the crow did not, he knew that the waters had receded.

Utnapishtim offered a sacrifice, and the gods gathered around. They regretted the flood, blaming it on Enlil. Ea said that only evildoers should be punished. To diminish the number of people on earth, there were lions, wolves, famine, and plague. Enlil took Utnapishtim by the hand and declared that he and his wife were to be like gods and live at the source of all rivers.

Utnaphistim asks Gilgamesh, rhetorically, who will assemble the gods on his behalf. He says, however, that he can test his worthiness for immortality by staying awake for six days and seven nights. No sooner has he spoken than Gilgamesh falls asleep. Utnapishtim tells his wife to mark the days that Gilgamesh sleeps by baking bread. Gilgamesh sleeps for seven days. When he awakes, he thinks that he has been asleep for only a moment, but Utnapishtim points out the seven stale loaves of bread at his side.

Gilgamesh is despondent. "Wherever I set my feet," he says, "there Death is." Utnapishtim tells Urshanabi to bathe and shave Gilgamesh and provide him with fresh clothes.

Refreshed, Gilgamesh boards the boat for his return journey. Utnapishtim's wife objects that her husband has not given him anything in return for his efforts. Utnapishtim brings Gilgamesh's boat back to the shore and tells him that there is a thorn plant that will give him everlasting life. Hearing this, Gilgamesh knows what to do. He ties stones to his feet and sinks to the bottom of the sea. There he plucks the plant, cuts the stones loose from his feet, and reemerges with the plant in hand. He tells Urshanabi that he will take it to the elders of Uruk and share it with him. It will restore his youth.

Gilgamesh travels back to Uruk with Urshanabi. On his way, he sees a pool of cool water and bathes in it, leaving the plant on the shore. As he bathes, a serpent smells it and carries it away. As it does, it sheds its old skin. Gilgamesh weeps when he discovers his loss. He returns to Uruk and recovers his spirits just enough to show off the walls that he built to Urshanabi.

Gilgamesh converses with Enkidu. He wishes he left his drum in the carpenter's house. Instead, he let it fall into the underworld. Enkidu volunteers to get it for him. Gilgamesh gives him advice on how to visit the underworld safely. He must not, for example, wear clean clothes, which will identify him as an outsider. He should not throw his throwing stick there. That will arouse the ghosts.

Enkidu descends to the underworld. He disregards all of Gilgamesh's instructions and is seized. Learning this, Gilgamesh complains to the gods. Neither Enlil nor Sin, god of the moon, responds to his complaints, but Ea tells the warrior god, Nergal, to open a hole in the underworld so that the ghost of Enkidu can explain the ways of death to Gilgamesh.

Enkidu comes through the hole like a dream. He and Gilgamesh try to embrace and kiss and exchange words.

Enkidu tells Gilgamesh that his body is being eaten by vermin and is filled with dirt. Of the men in the underworld, the one with one son is weeping, those with more sons are proportionately more fortunate. The man with seven sons is close to the gods. The victim of sudden death sleeps on a couch. The man who died in battle is comforted by his father, and his wife tends to his corpse. The one thrown into the field wanders restlessly. The one who left no one alive to love him eats scraps thrown into a gutter, unfit for dogs.

4. The Egyptian Tale of Two Brothers (c. 1200 B.C.)

Source: A papyrus ["Papyrus d'Orbiney," British Museum Papyrus 10183] writ-ten by a scribe named Enna, who lived at the end of the Nineteenth Dynasty, i.e., around 1200 B.C. The synopsis below is based on James B. Pritchard (ed.), Ancient Near Eastern Texts Relating to the Old Testament, *Princeton, 1969, 13–15.*

Anubis had a house and a wife. His younger brother, Bata, lived with them as a son. Bata worked in the fields, doing the plowing and reaping and all the chores. He spent his nights in the stables with the cattle. In the morning, he drove the cattle into the fields. The cattle talked to him, telling him where the best pastures were.

One afternoon during the planting season, Bata and Anubis were working in the fields. When they ran out of seeds, Bata returned to the house to get some more. There, he filled a large container with seeds and hoisted it over his shoulders. Anubis's wife saw him. Lusting after him, she said, "You have great strength. I have been watching you at work. Let us go to bed together. I will make you some fine clothes."

Bata was angry. He said, "You are like a mother to me. Your husband, my brother, is like a father to me. Don't ever say such a thing again." He picked up the seeds and went back to the field.

That evening, Anubis's wife was afraid that Bata would tell her husband. When her husband came home, she lay in the dark, vomiting. Her husband asked her what was wrong. She said that Bata had propositioned her and had beaten her to keep her from talking. She said that she would kill herself if Anubis did not kill Bata.

Anubis was angry. He sharpened his spear and waited inside the stable to kill his brother when he brought the cows back from the fields. As the first two cows entered the stable, however, they saw what was going to happen and warned Bata. He fled with his brother chasing him.

As Bata fled, he prayed to Re-Herakhty, a god of justice. Re heard his prayers and separated the brothers with a river full of crocodiles.

Standing on the far side of the river, Bata declared what had really happened. He then cut off his penis and threw it into the water, where it was eaten by a catfish. Anubis wept for him but could not join him because of the crocodiles in the river.

Bata told Anubis that he would now go to the Valley of the Pines but would eventually need Anubis's help. Bata said that he was going to remove his own heart and place it in a blossom in a pine tree. When and if the pine tree is cut down, Anubis must come and find Bata's heart and put it in a bowl of cool water, so that Bata can revive and punish his attacker. The sign that Bata needs Anubis's help will be that a cup of beer that Anubis is drinking will start foaming spontaneously.

Bata left for the Valley of the Pine. Anubis returned to his house, killed his wife, and threw her body to the dogs.

In the Valley of the Pine, Bata built a house and filled it with good things. The gods felt sorry for him and created a woman as his mate. She was more beautiful than any other woman and had a portion of every god in her. Bata loved her greatly, asked her never to leave, and told her all his secrets.

One day, while the woman was walking outside, the sea attempted to seize her. Although she escaped, a pine tree obtained a lock of her hair and gave it to the sea, which carried it to the place where the pharaoh's workers did his laundry. The scent of her perfume thus got into the pharaoh's clothing and led to an investigation. At the suggestion of the pharaoh's wise men, expeditions were sent to the Valley of the Pine to seize the maiden. The maiden was taken to the pharaoh and became his chief wife. She told the pharaoh how Bata had hidden his heart in a pine tree. At her suggestion, he sent soldiers to cut down the tree.

The next day, Anubis's beer produced foam. He traveled to the Valley of the Pine and found Bata lying dead in his bed. After four years of searching, he found Bata's heart and placed it in cool water, bringing Bata back to life.

To get revenge on his wife, Bata transformed himself into a beautiful, multicolored bull and went to the pharaoh's palace with Anubis on his back. Seeing the bull, the pharaoh was delighted, and rewarded Anubis for bringing it to him, along with the bull's weight in silver and gold, and many other gifts.

Several days later, inside the palace, the bull approached the pharaoh's new wife. "Behold!" he said, "I am still alive! I am Bata. I know you had the pine tree chopped down to end my life. Yet I live, as a bull!"

The woman was afraid. She prepared drinks for the pharaoh, putting him into a festive mood, and won a promise from him to grant her any wish. Then she said, "I want to eat the liver of that worthless bull!" The king was chagrined, but he fulfilled his promise. As the body of the bull was being carted off, two drops of blood fell in the entranceway of the palace. These grew into two great Persea trees during a single night. People marveled and rejoiced at the miraculous trees.

A few days later, the pharaoh's wife was sitting under one of the Persea trees when Bata spoke to her. "False one," he said, "I am Bata! I am still alive. I know that you had me killed when I was a bull."

Once more, the pharaoh's wife extorted a favor from her husband. She demanded that he cut down the Persea trees and make them into furniture. As the pharaoh's carpenters were performing this task, the pharaoh's wife watched. A splinter flew up and went into her mouth. She swallowed it and instantly became pregnant.

In due time, she bore a son. The pharaoh was pleased, and made the child the prince of the entire land. Many years later, the pharaoh ascended to heaven. The child became pharaoh. He had the woman brought to him. She was judged by palace officials, and her fate was agreed upon. The new pharaoh made his elder brother a prince. The new pharaoh ruled for 30 years. He passed away and his elder brother succeeded him on the throne.

5. Isis and Osiris

Source: Plutarch, *Concerning Isis and Osiris,* **approx. 120 A.D.**

This is the only known narrative version of the history of Isis and Osiris, deities of fundamental importance to ancient Egyptian religion. It is, however, written in Greek by a Greek author, Plutarch, who substitutes Greek names for Egyptian equivalents. Plutarch apparently was influenced by Greek myths in reconstructing the story.

When the Sun learned of the mating of Rhea (Egyptian *Nut*) and Cronus (Egyptian *Geb*), he forbade Rhea from giving birth in any month of the year. To help Rhea, however, Hermes (Egyptian *Thoth*) challenged the moon to a game of senet.[33] Each time he won, he took a little time away from the moon's cycle. At the end, Hermes had won a total of five days, which were added to the end of the year, so that it consisted of 12 months of 30 days each and five intercalary days belonging to no month.

On the first of those days, then, Osiris was born; on the second, the elder Horus, known to the Greeks as Apollo. On the third day, Typhon (Seth) burst violently from the womb. Thereafter, this day was considered one of bad luck by the Egyptians. No business was transacted, and no one was permitted to wash until after sunset. On the fourth day, Isis was born, and on the fifth day, Nephthys, whom some call Aphrodite, and some Nike (Victory). Nephthys clung to Typhon, whereas Isis and Osiris had already become lovers while still in their mother's womb. Some say elder Horus was actually their child.

After inheriting the earth from his father, Osiris improved the life of the Egyptians by teaching them cultivation, instituting laws, and establishing religion. Once he had brought these benefits to Egypt, he wandered the world to spread this knowledge to others, bringing civilization through speech, music, and his persuasive charm.

Typhon coveted Osiris's kingship and formed a conspiracy to usurp him. He could not operate openly because of Isis's vigilance. Upon Osiris's return from foreign lands, Typhon carried out a treacherous plan. Having secretly measured Osiris's body, he constructed a lavish chest exactly matching these measurements. He then presented the chest at a feast of the gods, where it was admired as a work of supreme craftsmanship. Typhon offered to give the marvelous chest to whoever fit inside it perfectly. After several tried and failed to fit inside the chest, Osiris proved to be a perfect fit. Typhon slammed the lid shut, sealed it with molten lead, and cast it into the river.

The chest drifted out to sea and came to rest at Byblos in Phoenicia. Here, a huge tree instantly grew up, enclosing the chest, and when the king of Byblos learned of this tree he had it made into a pillar for his palace, unaware of what was concealed inside.

Meanwhile, Isis had begun a worldwide search for the body of Osiris. She eventually found her way to Byblos. Here, she sat in human form by a well, speaking to no one, dejected and weeping. When the queen learned about this strange woman, she summoned her to the palace and employed her as a nursemaid for her newborn son.

Isis loved the child, nursing him with her finger instead of her breast. Each night, she secretly left him in the hearth to burn away his mortal parts, while she herself circled the pillar concealing Osiris's body in the form of a swallow. One night, the queen burst in on these activities. The spell was ruined, and Isis's identity was revealed. She then had the pillar taken down and opened to reveal the body within the hidden chest. Upon seeing Osiris's remains, Isis's grief was so intense it caused the king's youngest son to

---

33   An ancient Egyptian board game, in which game pieces are moved around a grid of 30 squares.

drop dead. His elder son died in a similar way when he accompanied Isis back to Egypt with the chest.

In Egypt, Isis concealed the chest in a secret spot in the Delta. Typhon discovered it there by chance while out hunting by moonlight. Recognizing it as the body of Osiris, he cut it into 14 pieces and scattered them throughout Egypt. When Isis returned and found what had happened, she searched for each of the pieces. Although some say she had each one entombed separately, most assert that her goal was to reassemble the pieces—and thus ensure Osiris's afterlife. On this account, she successfully gathered all the pieces except one, his phallus. That had been eaten by an oxyrhynchus fish. She created a new phallus for him and consecrated it, an action commemorated in a great Egyptian festival.

Horus would grow up to take his place on his father's throne by defeating Typhon. Osiris once visited his son from the afterworld to help train him for the coming conflict. He asked him what animal would be most useful to someone going into battle. Horus replied, "A horse." Osiris asked him why had he not picked something like a lion instead. Horus explained, "A lion might be useful to a man who needs help in fighting, but a horse is superior in its ability to help pursue one's enemy, prevent their escape, and destroy them." Hearing this answer, Osiris knew his son was ready to confront Typhon.

The battle lasted many days, but Horus eventually prevailed. Typhon was delivered to Isis in shackles, but she released him and allowed him to go free. In his anger over this, Horus tore the crown from his mother's head, but Hermes gave her a new crown in the form of a cow's head.

Typhon accused Horus of being illegitimate, but with Hermes' help, this was proven to be false. Horus and Typhon fought two more times, and Typhon was defeated both times. Osiris and Isis mated after Osiris's death. Thus, Isis became the mother of Harpocrates, who was born prematurely and with defective legs.

6. The Death of the Daughter of the Sun (1900 A.D.)

This is a slightly condensed version of a story collected from an eastern band Cherokee storyteller by a U.S. government anthropologist. It originally appeared in James Mooney, Myths of the Cherokee, *Government Printing Office, 1900.* Myths of the Cherokee *was reprinted in 1970 by the Johnson Reprint Corporation.*

The Sun lived on the far side of the sky, but her daughter lived in the middle, and every day the Sun stopped at her daughter's house for a meal.

The Sun hated the people on the earth because they never looked at her without squinting. She said to her brother, the Moon, "My grandchildren are ugly. They make faces whenever they look at me." But the Moon said, "I think they are very handsome." People always smiled pleasantly when they looked at him.

The Sun decided to kill the people. She sent down such hot rays that they died of fever by the hundreds. The people sought the help of their advisers, the little men from the stars.

The little men transformed two of their number into snakes, the Spreading Adder and the Copperhead, and sent them to the door of the house of the daughter of the Sun in order to bite the Sun when she arrived the next day. They hid, but when the Sun arrived, the Spreading Adder was blinded by her light and could only spit out yellow slime. He does this to the present day whenever he tries to bite. The Sun called him a nasty thing and went into the house. The Copperhead crawled off without doing anything.

One of the little men was now transformed into a rattlesnake. He quickly went to the house and coiled up by the door. When the Sun's daughter opened the door to look for her mother, he sprang and bit her. She fell dead. Since then, we pray to the rattlesnake and do not kill him because he is kind and never tries to bite if we do not disturb him.

When the Sun found her daughter dead, she went into the house and grieved. Now the world was dark all the time because the Sun would not come out. The people went again to the little men. The little men told the people that if they wanted the Sun to come out again, they must bring her daughter back from the ghost country in the dark land in the west. The little men chose seven men to go and gave each a wooden rod. They told them to take a box with them. When they got to the ghost country, they would find all the ghosts at a dance. They were to stand outside the circle, and when the young woman passed in the dance, they were to strike her with their rods. She would eventually fall to the ground. Then they were to put her into the box and bring her back to her mother. They were not to open the box, even a little way, until they were all the way home.

The men took the rods and the box and traveled for seven days to the west until they came to the dark land. The ghosts were having a dance. The young woman was in the outside circle, and as she whirled around to where the seven men were standing, one struck her with his rod. She turned her head and saw him but kept dancing. When she came around a second time, another touched her with his rod and then another and another until the seventh round when she fell to the ground. They put her into the box and closed the lid.

They picked up the box and started home. In a little while, the girl woke up and begged to be let out of the box, but the men made no answer. Soon, she called again and said that she was hungry, but still the men made no answer and went on. A little while later, she asked for a drink and pleaded so much that it was hard to listen to her, but the men who carried the box said nothing and still went on. When they were very nearly home, she called again and begged them to raise the lid just a little because she was smothering. The men were afraid that she was really dying, so they lifted the lid just enough to give her some air, but as they did so there was a fluttering sound inside and something flew past them into the thicket. Then they heard a red bird crying, "Kwish!

Kwish! Kwish!" in the bushes. They shut the lid and went on again, but when they got home and opened the box, it was empty.

This is how we know that the red bird is the daughter of the Sun, and if the men had kept the box closed, they would have brought her home safely, and we could bring back our other friends from the ghost country—but now when people die, we can never bring them back.

The Sun had been glad when the men started toward the ghost country, but when they came back without her daughter, she grieved and cried until her tears caused a flood, and the people were afraid that the world would be drowned. So they sent their best-looking young men and women to amuse the Sun so that she would stop crying. The young men and women danced and sang their best songs, but the Sun kept her face covered and paid no attention. At last, the drummer suddenly changed his rhythm. The Sun lifted up her face and was so pleased at the sight that she forgot her grief and smiled.

7. Geriguiaguiatugo's Revenge (1942)

This is a slightly condensed version of one of many stories told to Portuguese missionaries by Ukeiwaguuo, a chief of the Bororo Indians of central Brazil. It was first published in 1942. For a Bororo narrative, it is unusually long and coherent. The complete English translation and other information is found in Wilber and Simoneau, editors, Folk Literature of the Bororo Indians, *UCLA Latin American Center Publications, 1983.*

Long ago, the ancestors were preparing penis sheaths for an initiation ceremony. One of the women looking for suitable palm leaves in the forest was Korogo. While she searched, she was seduced by her son, Geriguiaguiatugo. When she returned, her husband, Bokwadorireu, noticed that feathers of the kind that young men wear for decoration were sticking to her belt. Suspicious, Bokwadorireu commanded the boys of the tribe to do a dance in which they wore their ornamental feathers. Bokwadorireu was distressed to see that only his son's feathers matched those on his wife's belt.

In anger, Bokwadorireu ordered Geriguiaguiatugo to steal a rattle from the lake of dead souls. Geriguiaguiatugo asked his grandmother for advice. She told him that his life would be in danger, and that he should get help from the hummingbird. Geriguiaguiatugo did so. The hummingbird snipped the string securing the rattle. The souls said, "Um! Um! Um!"[34] and gave chase, but the hummingbird got away and delivered the rattle to Geriguiaguiatugo, who gave it to his father.

---

34   The missionaries who recorded the story describe this as a guttural and nasal sound made with the mouth closed.

Bokwadorireu sent Geriguiaguiatugo back to the lake of dead souls for rattles two more times. The second rattle is described as smaller than the first, and the third is said to have been made out of strings. A blue dove recovered the second rattle for Geriguiaguiatugo, and a locust recovered the third. Although the blue dove got away unharmed, the dead souls managed to injure the relatively slow locust.

Next, Bokwadorireu asked Geriguiaguiatugo to come with him to hunt red and yellow macaws, whose nests were high on a steep cliff. Before departing, Geriguiaguiatugo's grandmother warned him of danger and gave him a walking stick.

Bokwadorireu had Geriguiaguiatugo climb up a tall tree trunk to the macaws' nests on the cliff. He then let the tree trunk fall. Geriguiaguiatugo saved himself by sticking his grandmother's walking stick into the cliff. He then clambered to the top of the cliff by means of an overhanging branch. There, he killed a large number of lizards for food. He ate some, and tied others to his belt and arm bands. They began to decay, and smelled so bad that Geriguiaguiatugo fainted. In this state, vultures swarmed over him, eating the lizards and Geriguiaguiatugo's buttocks. He recovered briefly and fought off the birds, but they returned later and finished the job, leaving him with no buttocks at all. Then, they grabbed him by his belt and arm and leg bands and carried him down to the ground.

When Geriguiaguiatugo woke up, he was hungry, but whatever he ate fell right out of him. Fortunately, he remembered a story that his grandmother had told him about a man who remedied the same problem by molding the missing parts of his body out of a potato. This is what Geriguiaguiatugo did, and it solved his problem.

Geriguiaguiatugo now went looking for his grandmother. Although her old village had been deserted, he was able to track her to her new one, where she was living with Geriguiaguiatugo's younger brother. After he rejoined them, a great rainstorm put out all the fires in the forest. Everybody came to Geriguiaguiatugo's grandmother to get new fire. Among the people who came was Kiareware, another wife of Bokwadorireu. She was stunned to see Geriguiaguiatugo and reported back to Bokwadorireu that his son was still alive. Taking his ceremonial rattle, Bokwadorireu went to welcome his son back with a traditional song of greeting—as though nothing had happened—but Geriguiaguiatugo could not forget the wrong that his father had done to him.

One day, he searched the woods and finally found a forked branch that looked like deer antlers when he put it on his head. He then sent a request to his father through his brother to institute a deer hunt. His father did so. When the Indians were spread out in the forest, Geriguiaguiatugo asked his brother to ascertain their father's location. His brother transformed himself into an agouti[35] and was soon able to report Bokwadorireu's position. Geriguiaguiatugo then transformed himself into a stag and charged his father. He picked him up in the air on his antlers and threw him into a nearby lake. The piranhas fell upon him, and in a short time there was nothing left of him but bones picked clean. Only his lungs floated to the surface, and they were

---

35   A burrowing rodent that resembles a chipmunk.

changed to a herb whose leaves, similar to a lung, grow on the surface of the water to this day. Geriguiaguiatugo returned to the village and punished his father's two wives.

Appendix 2: Three of Plato's Philosophical Myths

Plato's philosophical writings, known collectively as his dialogues, contain many passages in which Socrates and Plato's other characters use stories with some of the attributes of myth to make philosophical points. This appendix contains three of his most famous myths.

1. The Origin of Love According to Aristophanes (4th century B.C.)

Source: Plato's Symposium. The Symposium *is Plato's recreation of conversation that supposedly occurred in 416 B.C. at a banquet celebrating a victory by a young tragic poet, Agathon. The guests, including Socrates, decided not to get drunk, as usual, but to give speeches in praise of Eros [Love] instead. Of the speeches, this one, attributed to the comic poet Aristophanes, is the most memorable. It contrasts with Socrates' speech, in which love is defined as the quest for the everlasting possession of the good, not devotion to an individual person.*

In the past, human beings were different from what they are now. There were three sexes: male, female, and mixed. Original human beings were round. Each had four hands and four feet, one head with two faces, looking opposite ways, four ears, and two sets of genitals. These creatures could walk as we do but could also roll over and over at a great rate, supported by four hands and feet, like acrobats going over and over with their legs in the air.

Of the three original sexes, the male was originally a child of the sun; the female, a child of the earth; and the male-female, or androgyne, a child of the moon. They were all round and moved in circles like their parents.

Like the giants Otus and Ephialtes, these original human beings were proud and attacked heaven. Zeus thought about annihilating them with his thunderbolts, but he did not want to end the sacrifice and worship that they provided to the gods. Hence, he decided to humble them by slicing them in half. This would also increase their number and their offerings to the gods. If they continued to be proud, Zeus said that he would slice them in half again, so that they would hop around on one leg.

Zeus began cutting the people in half. As he did so, he had Apollo give their faces a twist so that they could see what they had suffered and learn humility. Apollo was also instructed to heal their wounds. He pulled skin over the belly, as we call it, and made a mouth in the middle, which he tied in a knot. This is called the navel. He smoothed out most of the wrinkles but left a few in the region of the belly and navel, as a reminder.

After the division, the isolated parts started coming together, throwing their arms about one another. They would all have perished from hunger because they did not like to do anything as separate halves. In pity, Zeus came up with a solution. He moved their genitals to the front of their new bodies. Previously, they had sown their seeds in the ground, like grasshoppers. After this change, the male sowed his seed in the female so that they could breed by mutual embrace, or if a male came to a male, they might be satisfied and go about the business of life.

Hence, an ancient desire has been implanted in us to regain our original natures, making one out of two. Men who descend from the original male-female, or androgynous, creatures are lascivious. Adulterers come from this group, as do promiscuous women. Women who descend from the original females have female companions and lovers. Men who descend from the original males hang around other men and embrace them. They are the best of boys and youths because they are the most manly. When they grow up, they are our statesmen. They are lovers of youths and not inclined to marry or beget children, although they may do so in obedience to the law.

When anyone finds his or her missing half, the pair are overwhelmed with love, friendship, and intimacy, and will not willingly leave each other's sight. Their desire goes beyond intercourse. If Hephaestus came to them with his tools and asked them what they wanted, they would be unable to say. But if he then asked them if they wanted him to meld them together into one being so that they would always be together, all lovers would have to acknowledge that this action alone would fulfill their ancient need.

If we are not obedient to the gods, there is a danger that we will be split again and go around like sculptures carved in relief or like heads on coins. If we are pious, however, we may find our true loves and return to our original natures. This alone is what heals us and makes us happy and blessed. Eros, the god of love, is the source of this gift. All should praise him.

2: The Allegories of the Line and the Cave (4th century B.C.)

Source: *Plato's Republic*, **6.507–7.517**

During the course of the famous conversation, in which Socrates and his friends describe an ideal state ruled by a philosopher king, a young man named Glaucon, Plato's brother, asks Socrates to describe the nature of goodness in itself. Socrates says that he can only describe the "child of the good." He says that there are many good and beautiful things, and there are also the *ideas* of goodness and beauty. The many good and beautiful things are visible but cannot be understood. The ideas of goodness and beauty can be known, but not seen. Things are located in the visible world; ideas are located in the world of the intelligible.

Visible things are seen by the power of vision, but vision requires something else—namely, light—in order to work. The sun is the source of light, and therefore, lord of vision. The sun is not sight, but it is the author of sight. The sun enables sight to work. The sun is the child of the good. Its operation in the visible world is like that of the good in the intelligible world.

The soul is like the eye. It recognizes truth, but it needs assistance to do so. What enables it to recognize truth is the idea of the good.

The nature of the visible and intelligible worlds can be understood by imagining a line that is divided in half and then subdivided so that it has a total of four sections. The first half represents the visible world. Its lower end represents the world of images, such as shadows and reflections in pools. The higher end represents individual creatures: animals, men, plants, and so forth.

The same kind of subdivision exists in the intelligible world. In the lower end, the soul borrows figures from the visible world to formulate theories. In the upper end, it passes out of theories and reaches principles that do not depend on images.

Glaucon says that he does not understand Socrates perfectly. Socrates offers an image to clarify his meaning.

Human beings, he says, are like prisoners living in an underground cave that has a mouth opening toward daylight. These prisoners have been in the cave since infancy. They are facing the back wall of the cave. Their legs and necks are chained so that they cannot move and see only what is in front of them. Above and behind them, there is a fire. Between the fire and the prisoners, there is a wall or a screen. People pass back and forth behind the wall, holding up statues and figures of wood. These articles cast shadows on the back wall where the prisoners can see them.

Naturally, the prisoners are absolutely certain that the shadows are the only things that are real.

If a prisoner happens to be freed from his chains and is led into the daylight, he does not have an easy time with his changed circumstances. At first, because of the glare, he is unable to see real things clearly, and he remains convinced for a long time that the shadows of his former life are truer. When he is finally able to see all the sights of the upper world, he concludes that the sun is the true source of the seasons and the lord of visible world. He pities his former fellow prisoners and is glad to be in the upper world. Yet when he returns to the cave, he has trouble getting around in the darkness and looks ridiculous. Despite what he says, the prisoners conclude that he has been blinded by entering the upper world and that his talk of it is madness. If somebody else tries to lead another prisoner into the upper light, they arrest him and kill him.

3. The Myth of Er (4th century B.C.)

Source: Plato's The Republic, *10.614–621. Though it is best known for its description of an ideal state, the fundamental question addressed in Plato's* Republic *is whether or not virtue is the key to happiness. After arguing extensively in favor of virtue on rational grounds, Plato's spokesman, Socrates, concludes the massive dialogue with this fanciful account of what happens when we die.*

Er, the son of Armenius, a Pamphylian, was slain in battle, but his body did not decompose. Twelve days later, he returned to life as he was lying on his funeral pyre, and said that he had been sent as a messenger from the afterlife.

He reported that, upon dying he found himself with a great throng in a mysterious place. There were judges and two holes apiece in the sky and ground, respectively. When souls approached the judges, sinners were sent into the ground with their crimes attached to their backs; good people were sent into the sky wearing their good deeds on their chest. Er was told to stay in the area and report his observations back on earth.

Er listened to the accounts of people returning from the earth and the sky. Souls from the sky told of indescribably beautiful sights and sounds; those from the earth, of miserable torments. Sojourns in either place lasted a thousand years. Each sin was punished, each good deed rewarded—ten times over. The most terrible thing was what happened to Ardiaeus the tyrant and several companions, all hopelessly evil. When they were about to emerge from the earth, the hole gave a great bellow, and fiery demons carried them back to eternal torment, binding them, whipping them, and dragging them over thorns.

After reminiscing for a week in a meadow, the souls proceeded to the Spindle of Necessity. This is a great shaft of many-colored light and steel that supports the eight spheres of heaven, which rotate at different speeds. A Siren perches on each of the spheres, singing a single note. The shaft is held between the knees of the goddess Necessity. Lachesis (the Measurer), Clotho (the Spinner), and Atropos (the Irreversible)—the three Fates of the past, present, and future, respectively—stand around, keeping the spheres rotating.

Assembling the souls before the spindle, a spokesman announced that they would now choose new lives. They were given a free choice of many lives in the form of samples laid in front them. Numbered lots were cast in the crowd. Each person, except Er, was instructed to choose a new life, according to the number that had fallen to him. The spokesman stressed that everyone was free to honor virtue as much as he chose. The responsibility lay with the chooser, not God.

The first chooser had gone to heaven after his previous life, mostly because he had lived in a well-governed state, which made it easy to be virtuous. He carelessly chose the life of a tyrant. Then he regretted his choice when he discovered that was destined to devour his own children. Heroes bitter over their sufferings chose to return as animals: Orpheus as a swan; Ajax as a lion; Agamemnon as an eagle. Atalanta chose to be a male athlete. Epeus, who designed the Trojan horse, became a craftswoman; Thersites, a monkey. Odysseus chose last but found the life that he wanted most of all and would have taken if he had gone first, that of a carefree private man.

After making their choices, the souls walked around the spindle, where the three Fates confirmed their destinies. A guardian spirit was attached to each one. From there, they marched in scorching heat to the plain of Forgetfulness and camped on the banks of the river Lethe (Oblivion). All except Er were required to drink a certain amount. Those who were unwise drank more than was necessary. Once they drank, they forgot everything that had happened. During the night, there was an earthquake and a thunderstorm. The souls flew upward like shooting stars. The next thing Er knew, he was waking up on his pyre.

Appendix 3: Pronouncing Glossary

Guide to the Pronunciation of Names and Places

The sign **ə** is called a schwa. It stands for the vowel sound with which the word "America" begins and ends. That sound is very frequent in unstressed syllables. It occurs, for example, in final –er(e.g., dinner = di´ -nər) and in final –us (e.g., Columbus = kə-lum´-bəs).

a stands for the vowel sound in bad, ban, bare.

ä for the vowel sound in father, often represented in English words by "o," e.g., bother, odd, optical, car, calm, con.

ā for the vowel sound in bay, day, sail, same.

e for the vowel sound in bet, egg, self.

ē for the vowel sound in be, seem, eel.

i for the vowel sound in tin, hit, kill, beer.

ī for the vowel sound in eye, bite, rise.

ō for the vowel sound in go, home, rose, pour.

ö for the vowel sound in law, ought, orb.

u for the vowel sound in foot, pull, look.

ū for the vowel sound in loot, moon, room, Zeus.

au for the vowel sound in out, loud, our, owl.

oi stands for the vowel sound in boy, rejoice, avoid.

I. Personal Names

Acastus (ə-ka´ stəs) Son of Pelias, he banished Jason.

Achaeus (ə-kē´ -əs) Son of Xuthus, eponymous ancestor of the Achaean Greeks.

Achelous (a´kə-lō´-əs) A river in western Greece, personified as a god who wrestled Heracles for the privilege of marrying Deianira.

Acheron (aʹkə-rän) River in the Underworld.

Achilles (ə-kilʹ-lēz) Son of Peleus and Thetis, the Greeks' greatest warrior at Troy.

Acis (aʹ-sis) Son of Faunus, loved by Galatea.

Acrisius (ə-krēʹ-sē-əs) King of Argos, Perseus's grandfather.

Actaeon (ak-tēʹ-än) Grandson of Cadmus, slain by Artemis.

Adonis (ə-däʹ-nəs) Handsome son of Cinyras and Myrrha, loved by Aphrodite.

Aeetes (ē-ēʹ-tēz) King of Colchis, possessor of the golden fleece.

Aegeus (ēʹ-jē-əs) King of Athens, Theseus's father.

Aegisthus (ē-jisʹ-thəs) Son of Thyestes, Clytemnestra's illicit lover.

Aeneas (ə-nēʹ-əs) Son of Aphrodite, prince of Troy; led survivors to Italy.

Aethra (ēʹ-thrə) Daughter of King Pittheus of Troezen, mother of Theseus.

Aeolus (ēʹ-ə-ləs) King of the winds.

Aeson (ēʹ-sən) Jason's father.

Aether (ē-thər) The bright upper air.

Aethlius (ēthʹ-lē-əs) Endymion's father.

Agaue (ə-gäʹ-vē) Daughter of Cadmus, Pentheus's mother.

Agamedes (a-gə-mēʹ-dēz) An architect of Apollo's temple at Delphi.

Agamemnon (aʹ-gə-memʹ-nän) King of Mycenae; leader of the Greek army at Troy.

Agenor (aʹ-gə-nōr) Phoenician king; father of Cadmus and Europa.

Aglaea (ə-glēʹ-ə) The youngest of the three Graces; married Hephaestus.

Ajax (āʹ-jax) **the Lesser** A mean-spirited Greek warrior at Troy; son of Oileus; raped Cassandra.

Ajax (āʹ-jax) **the Greater** The second-best Greek warrior at Troy after Achilles; son of Telamon.

Alcaeus (al-sēʹ-əs) Perseus's son; father of Amphitryon.

Alcinous (al-sinʹ-ō-əs) King of Phaeacia.

Alcyoneus (al-sēʹ-ə-nūs) One of the giants vanquished by Zeus.

Alcmene (alk-mēʹ-nē). Heracles' mother.

Althaea (al-thēʹ-ə) Meleager's mother.

Amata (ə-mäʹ-tə) Latinus's wife; queen of Latium.

Amazons (aʹ-mə-zäns) A tribe of women warriors whose homeland is usually located on the northern shore of the Black Sea.

Amphictyon (am fikʹ –tē-ən) Third king of Athens.

Amphinomus (am-finʹ-ə-məs) The most virtuous of Penelope's suitors.

Amphion (am-fīʹ-än) Antiope's son; ruled Thebes with his brother Zethus for a generation.

Amphitrite (am-fə-trēʹ-tē) Sea goddess; wife of Poseidon.

Amphitryon (am-fiʹ-trē-ən) Alcmene's husband; Heracles' foster father.

Amulius (ə-mūʹ-lē-əs) Usurped the Roman throne from his brother Numitor.

Amycus (aʹ-mə-kəs) Boxer beaten by Polydeuces.

Ancaeus (an-sēʹ-əs) Warrior killed in Calydonian boar hunt.

Anchises (an-kīʹ-sēs) Trojan noble; Aphrodite's lover; father of Aeneas.

Andromeda (an-dräʹ-mə-də) Royal maiden saved by, and married to, Perseus.

Antaeus (an-tē´-əs). Fierce Libyan king slain by Heracles.

Anticleia (an-tə-klī´-ə) Odysseus's mother.

Androgeus (an-drō´ –jē-əs) Minos's son, killed in Greece.

Andromache (an-drä´–mə-kē) Hector's wife.

Anna (an´nə) Dido's sister.

Antaeus (an´ –tē -əs) Giant slain by Heracles.

Antigone (an-tig´-ə-nē) Oedipus's daughter; punished for burying her brother.

Antilochus (an-til´-ə-kəs) Nestor's son; the youngest of the great Greek warriors at Troy.

Antinous (an-tin´-ō-əs) The leader of Penelope's suitors.

Antiope (an-tī´-ə-pē) 1. Theban princess visited by Zeus in the form of a satyr; the mother of Amphion and Zethus. 2. In some sources, the name of Hippolytus's mother, an Amazon.

Aphrodite (a-frə-dī´-tē) Goddess of love, identified with the Roman Venus.

Apsyrtus (ap-sər´ -təs) Medea's brother.

Arachne (ə-rak´-nē) Young woman famous for weaving. Her name means spider in Greek.

Arete (ar´-ə-tā) Queen of Phaeacia.

Ariadne (ar´ -ē-ad´ -nē) Minos's daughter; helped Theseus escape the labyrinth. Argo (är´-gō) The ship that carried Jason and the Argonauts.

Argonauts (är´-gə-nöts) The heroes who joined Jason's quest for the Golden Fleece.

Argus (är´-gəs).1. The hundred-eyed giant appointed by Hera to guard Io. 2. Odysseus's dog. 3. The builder of the *Argo*.

Artemis (är´-tə-məs) Goddess of hunting; Apollo's sister, identified with the Roman Diana.

Ascanius (a-skā´-nē-əs) Aeneas's son.

Asclepius (as-klə´ –pē -əs) A healer, son of Apollo; described variously as a god or hero.

Asterius (a-ster´-ē-əs) Europa's Cretan husband.

Astyanax (a-stī´-ə-naks) Hector's infant son.

Atalanta (a´-tə-lan´-tə) Fleet-footed maiden finally caught by Hippomenes with the help of golden apples.

Ate (ä´ -tā) Delusion or intellectual blindness, personified as a goddess who causes tragic mistakes.

Athamas (ä´-thə-məs) Ino's husband.

Athena (ə-thē´-nə) Goddess of wisdom; also called Pallas, identified with the Roman Minerva.

Atlas (at´-ləs) Brother of Prometheus; punished by Zeus for fighting on the side of the Titans by being made to hold up the dome of the sky.

Atreids (ā´-trē-ids) Sons of Atreus, Agamemnon and Menelaus.

Atreus (ā´-trē-əs) King of Mycenae; father of Agamemnon and Menelaus.

Atropos (a´-trə-pəs) "The Inflexible One," one of the three Fates.

Augeas (ö-jē´-əs) King of Elis. Heracles cleaned his stables.

Augustus (ö-gəs´-təs) Also called Octavian, Julius Caesar's nephew and adopted son, the first Roman emperor.

Aurora (ö-rōr´-ə) Dawn; Roman name for the Greek Eos.

Autolycus (ö-tä´-lə-kəs) Odysseus's maternal grandfather, a trickster.

Autonoe (ö-tä´-nō-ē) Daughter of Cadmus; mother of Actaeon.

Bacchus (bä´-kəs) Alternative Greek name for Dionysus, often used by Roman sources.

Bellerophon (bə-lər´-ə-fän) Legendary hero, slew the Chimera, grandfather of Glaucus and Sarpedon.

Boreas (bōr´-ē-əs) The North Wind personified as a god.

Briareus (brī-ar´-ē-əs) One of the three hundred-armed giants born to Uranus and Gaea.

Briseis (brī-sē´-əs) Slave girl prized by Achilles.

Brutus, Lucius Junius (brū´-təs, lū´-shəs jū´-nē-əs) Rome's liberator and first consul.

Busiris (bū –sir´ -əs) Egyptian king slain by Heracles.

Cadmus (kad´-məs, Greek **Kadmos**) Phoenician by birth; the founder and first king of Thebes.

Calais (kə-lā´ –is). Son of Boreas, the North Wind.

Calchas (kal´-kəs) Priest and seer for the Greek army at Troy.

Callidice (kal-ə-dī´-sē) Queen of Thesprotia; married Odysseus.

Calyce (kal´-ə-kē Endymion's mother.

Calypso (kə-lip´-sō) The lonely goddess who kept Odysseus on her island for years, hoping to marry him.

Camilla (kə-mil´-ə) Woman warrior who stood with the Italians against the Trojans.

Cassandra (kə-sän´-drə) Trojan priestess of Apollo with knowledge of the future; slain by Clytemnestra.

Cassiopea (ka´-sē-ə-pē´-ə) Queen of Ethiopia; mother of Andromeda.

Castor (ka´-stər) Castor and Pollux are the two male offspring of Leda and Zeus in the form of a swan; the brothers of Helen and Clytemnestra, also known as the Dioscuri (Zeus's boys).

Cecrops (sē´-kräps) First king of Athens.

Celeus (sē´-lē-əs) King of Eleusis.

Centaurs (sen´ –tōrs) A race of half-human, half-horse children of Ixion and a cloud.

Cephalus (se´-fä-ləs) Prince of Phocis; married Procris.

Cepheus (se´-fē-əs) King of Ethiopia; father of Andromeda.

Cerberus (sər´-bə-rəs) Hades' three-headed dog.

Cercyon (sər´ –sē-ən) Wrestler killed by Theseus.

Ceres (sir´-ēz)Roman goddess of grain, identified with the Greek Demeter.

Chaos (kā´-äs) The void, emptiness; the first being, according to Hesiod's *Thegony*.

Charites (kär´-ə-tēz) The three Graces; daughters of Zeus, personifying beauty.

Charon (kar´-än) Boatman in the Underworld; ferries souls of the dead across the Acheron or Styx rivers.

Charybdis (kə-rib´-dəs) A whirlpool that nearly swallows Odysseus.

Chalybes (kal´-ə-bēz) People dwelling on the southern shore of the Black Sea, famous for iron mines and forges.

Chiron (kī´-rän) The virtuous centaur, tutor of heroes such as Achilles and Jason.

Chloris (klōr´-is) Nestor's mother.

Chrysaor (krī´-sā-ōr) Offspring of Medusa and Poseidon; brother of Pegasus, not described in extant sources.

Chryseis (krī-sē´-əs) Agamemnon's favorite slave girl, the daughter of Chryses.

Chryses (krī′-sēz) Priest of Apollo; father of Chryseis.

Cicones (sik′-ə-nēz) Thracian people, allies of Troy; attacked by Odysseus during his return.

Cilissa (sə-li′-sə) Orestes' old nursemaid.

Cinyras (sin′-ə-rəs) Pygmalion's grandson; Myrrha's father and lover.

Circe (sər′-sē). Goddess who turns men into pigs; Odysseus's lover.

Clotho (klō′-thō) "Spinner"; one of the three Fates.

Clymene (kli′-mə-nē) Phaethon's mother.

Clytemnestra (klī′-tem-nəs′-trə) Agamemnon's wife and slayer; Helen's sister.

Collatinus (kō-lə-tī′-nəs) Lucretia's husband.

Copreus (cä′-prē-əs) Eurystheus's herald.

Cottus (kät′-təs) One of the three hundred-armed giants born to Uranus and Gaea.

Cranaus (kra-nā′-əs) Second king of Athens.

Creon (krē′-än) 1. Oedipus's brother-in-law and uncle; ruled Thebes after Oedipus. 2. King of Corinth; he betrothed his daughter to Jason.

Creusa (kre-ū′-sə) Aeneas's wife; killed during the fall of Troy.

Cronus (krō′-nəs) King of the Titans; overthrew Uranus, and was overthrown by Zeus; identified with the Roman Saturn.

Cupid (kyū′-pəd) Personification of Love and Desire; identified with the Greek Eros.

Cybele (si′-bə-lē). A powerful Near Eastern mother goddess.

Cyclops (sī′–kläps), **Cyclopes** (sī-klō′-pēz) One-eyed giants, offspring of Gaea and Uranus. Odysseus's adversary, Polyphemus, and his neighbors were unrelated one-eyed giants, also known as Cyclopes.

Cycnus (sik′-nəs) 1. Phaethon's friend; turned into a swan. 2. Son of Poseidon; killed by Achilles.

Daedalus (dē′-də-ləs) Athenian inventor who designed the Cretan Labyrinth.

Damastes (də-mas′-tēz) Evildoer killed by Theseus.

Danae (da′-nə-ē) Princess of Argos; visited by Zeus as a shower of gold; mother of Perseus.

Daphne (daf′-nē) Daughter of the Peneus river god; transformed into a laurel tree.

Deianira (dē′-yə-nī′-rə) Heracles' wife; she accidentally killed him with a poisoned shirt.

Deidamia (dē′-yə-də-mī′-ə) Lycomedes' daughter; married Achilles.

Deiphobus (dē-if′-ə-bəs) Hector's brother; married Helen when Paris was killed.

Delphyne (del-fē′–nē). A snake girl who guarded Zeus's muscles for Typhoeus.

Demeter (di-mē′-tər) Goddess of grain; Zeus's sister.

Demodocus (də-mä′-də-kəs) The bard in the land of the Phaeacians. **Demophon** (də′-mə-fän) 1. Infant son of Celeus and Metanira of Eleusis. 2. Theseus's Son; king of Athens.

Deucalion (dyū-kāl′-yən) Son of Prometheus; survived the great flood.

Diana (dī-a′-nə) Roman goddess of hunting, identified with the Greek Artemis.

Dictys (dik′-tēz) Brother of Polydectes; king of Seriphos; saved Danae and baby Perseus.

Dido (dī′-dō) Phoenician queen; founder of Carthage.

Dike (dē′-kā) Justice personified as a goddess.

Dino (dī′-nō) One of the three Graeae.

Diomedes (dī-ō-mē′-dēz) 1. King of Tiryns; great Greek warrior at Troy. 2. Thracian king with maneating horses; slain by Heracles.

Dioscuri (dī′-əs-kyu′ rī) "Zeus's Boys," Castor and Pollux.

Dirce (dir′ −sē) Lycus's wife.

Doliones (dō-lē-ō′-nēz) Mythical people visited by Jason and the Argonauts.

Dorus (dōr′ −əs) Son of Hellen; eponymous ancestor of the Dorian Greeks.

Eidothea (ī-dō-thē′-a) Daughter of Proteus.

Eileithyia (ī-lī′-thē-ə) Goddess of childbirth.

Eirene (ī-rē′-n′ē) Peace personified as a goddess.

Electra (i-lek′-trə) Orestes' sister.

Electryon (e-lek′-trē-ən) Son of Perseus; father of Heracles' mother Alcmene.

Elpenor (el′-pə-nōr) Odysseus's young companion; died in an accidental fall.

Endymion (en-di′-mē-ən) Founder of Elis; loved by Selene.

Enyo (en′ −ī −ō) One of the three Graeae.

Eos (ē′-äs). Dawn personified as a goddess. The Roman Aurora.

Epeus (ə-pē′ −əs) Greek warrior at Troy, who designed the wooden horse.

Ephialtes (e-fē-al′ −tēz) One of the giants vanquished by Zeus.

Epicaste (e-pə-kas′-tā) Name given by Odysseus for Oedipus's mother, also known as Jocasta.

Epimetheus (ə-pē-mē′-thē-əs) Prometheus's less intelligent brother.

Er (ər′) A soldier who returned from the dead in a story created by Plato.

Erebus (er′-ə-bəs). A dark region between earth and Tartarus.

Erechtheus (er-ək-thē-əs) Sixth king of Athens.

Erginus (er′-gə-nəs) Father of the architects Agamedes and Trophonius.

Erichthonius (ar-ik-thō′-nē-əs) Fourth king of Athens.

Erinyes (i-rin′-ē-ēz) Dreaded underworld goddesses who punish sinners. Also called Eumenides in Greek and identified with the Roman Furies. Singular:

Erinys (i-ri′-nəs).

Eris (er′ −is) Strife or discord personified as a goddess.

Eros (er′-äs) Personification of love and desire, depicted by Hesiod as one of the original deities, by others as Aphrodite's child; identified with the Roman Cupid.

Eteocles (ə-tē′-ə-klēz) Oedipus's son, supported by Creon in war with his brother.

Eumenides (yū-men′-ə-dēz) "Kindly Ones," a euphemistic name for the Erinyes.

Eumaeus (yū-mē′-us) The virtuous pig herder who shelters Odysseus in disguise.

Eunomia (yū-nō′-mē-ə) Lawfulness personified as a goddess.

Eupeithes (yū-pē′-thēz) Antinoos's father, slain by Laertes.

Euphorbas (yū-fōr′ -bəs) Trojan who wounded Patroclus.

Europa (yū-rō′-pə) Phoenician princess abducted by Zeus in the form of a bull; Cadmus's sister; mother of Minos.

Euryale (yər −rī′ ə -lē) One of the three Gorgons; Medusa's sister.

Eurydice (yū-ri′-də-sē) 1. Orpheus's wife. 2. Creon's wife, queen of Thebes.

Euryclea (yūr-ə-klē′-ə) Odysseus's elderly nursemaid.

Eurylochus (yū-ri′-lə-kəs) The leading troublemaker in Odysseus's crew.

Eurymachus (yū-ri´-mə-chəs) The most outspoken of Penelope's suitors.

Eurynome (yū-ri´-nə-ē) Daughter of Oceanus, mother of the three Graces.

Eurysaces (yūr-ə-sā´ –shēz) Son of Ajax the Greater.

Eurytus (yūr´-ə-təs). King of Oechalia, Heracles' enemy.

Eurystheus (yū-ris´-thē-əs) Perseus's grandson; king of Mycenae; Heracles' enemy.

Evander (ē-van´-dər) King of Pallanteum on the later site of Rome; Aeneas's ally.

Faunus (f ö ´-nəs) Roman god often identified with the Greek Pan.

Furies (fyur´-ēz) Roman name for the Erinyes.

Gaea (jē´-ə) Personification of the earth; Uranus's mother and wife.

Galatea (ga-lə-tē´-ə) A Nereid loved by Polyphemus.

Ganymede (ga´-ni-mēd) Handsome Trojan youth kidnapped by Zeus to be his cup bearer.

Geryon (jer´-ē-ən) A giant with three bodies joined at the waist.

Glaucon (glau´-kən) Plato's brother; a speaker in *The Republic*.

Glaucus (glau´-kəs) 1. A sea god loved by Circe. 2. A Greek fighting at Troy; Sarpedon's comrade.

Gorge (gōr´ –gē) Meleager's sister.

Graces (grā´-səz) Three minor goddesses, daughters of Zeus; personifications of grace and charm.

Graeae (grī´-ī) Three goddesses symbolizing old age, they share one eye and one tooth. Names: Enyo, Pemphredo, and Dino.

Gorgons (gor´-gəns) Three hideous sisters, Stheno, Euryale, and Medusa, with snakes for hair. Their look turned men to stone.

Gyges (gī´-jēz).One of the three hundred-armed giants born to Uranus and Gaea.

Hades (hā´-dēz) God of the dead; Zeus's brother, also called Pluto; identified with the Roman Orcus.

Haemon (hē´ -mən) Creon's son; Antigone's fiancé.

Harmonia (har-mō´-nē-ə) Daughter of Ares and Aphrodite; wife of Cadmus.

Harpies (har´-pēz) Monstrous bird women who tormented the blind prophet Phineus.

Hebe (hē´ –bē) Youth personified as a goddess; married Heracles.

Hecate (he´-kə-tē) A goddess of the Underworld associated with magic.

Hector (hek´-tər) King Priam's eldest son and Troy's greatest warrior; Paris's brother.

Hecuba (he´-kyə-bə) Priam's wife; Hector's mother.

Helen (he´-lən) Queen of Sparta; caused the Trojan War by leaving her husband, Menelaus, for Paris, prince of Troy.

Helenus (he´-lə-nəs) Trojan prophet.

Helius (hē´-lē-əs) The sun personified as a great god, usually distinct from Apollo.

Helle (hel´-lē) Sister of Phrixus; she drowned in the "Hellespont."

Hellen (hel´ -lēn) Son of Deucalion and Pyrrha, the eponymous ancestor of the Hellenic (Greek) race.

Hephaestus (hi-fes´-təs) Blacksmith of the gods, identified with the Roman Vulcan.

Hera (hir´-ə) Goddess of marriage; Zeus's sister and wife.

Heracles (har´-ə-klēz) Son of Zeus, a great hero renowned for 12 death-defying labors, among many other exploits; known to Romans as Hercules.

Hercules (hər´-kyə-lēz) The Roman form of the Greek name Heracles.

Hermaphroditus (her-maf-rō-dī´-təs). Son of Hermes and Aphrodite; united with a nymph against his will.

Hermes (hər´-mēz, Greek Hermēs); The gods' messenger; patron of tricksters and Thieves; guide to the underworld.

Hesione (he-sī´-ō-nē) Princess of Troy saved from a sea monster by Heracles.

Hesperides (he-sper´-ə-dēz) Goddesses who guard an orchard where golden apples grow. Their name means "Children of Evening" (*hesperos*).

Hestia (hes´-tē-ə) Goddess of the hearth; Zeus' sister; identified with the Roman Vesta.

Hippodamia (hip-pə-dä-mī´-ə) Daughter of King Oenomaus of Elis.

Hippolyta (hip-pä´-lə-tə) 1. Amazon queen killed by Heracles. 2. Hippolytus's mother, also an Amazon.

Hippolytus (hip-pä´-lə-təs) Son of Theseus and the Amazon Hippolyta.

Hippomenes (hi-pä´-mə-nēz) The youth who won Atalanta's hand in a footrace.

Horae (hōr´-ī) The Seasons personified as three goddesses.

Hyacinthus (hī-ə-sin´-thəs) Spartan youth loved by Apollo.

Hylas (hī´-ləs) Heracles' boyfriend.

Hyllus (hi´-ləs) Heracles' eldest son.

Hypsipyle (hip-sip´-i-lē) Lemnian princess who spared her father.

Iapetus (ī-a´-pə-təs) A Titan; the father of Prometheus.

Iambe (ī-am´-bē) Comedic daughter of Celeus and Metanira.

Icarus (i´-kə-rəs) Daedalus's son.

Idomeneus (i-däm´-ə-nüs) Cretan king; Greek warrior at Troy.

Iduia (i-dwē´-ə) Daughter of Oceanus; mother of Medea.

Inachus (in´-ə-kəs) River in southern Greece, personified as a god; the father of Io.

Ino (i´-nō) Daughter of Cadmus; Dionysus's foster mother.

Io (ī´-ō)Maiden loved by Zeus and transformed into a heifer by Hera.

Iolaus (i-ō-lā´-əs) Heracles' nephew' son of Iolaus.

Iole (i´-ə-lē) Daughter of Eurytus; king of Oechalia; loved by Heracles.

Ion (ī´-än) Son of Xuthus, eponymous ancestor of the Ionian Greeks.

Iphicles (if´-ə-klēz) Son of Alcmene and Amphitryon; Heracles' half-brother; father of Iolaus.

Iphitus (if´-ə-təs) Iole's brother, slain by Heracles. **Iphigenia** (if´-ə-jə-nī´-ə) Agamemnon's daughter, sacrificed to obtain favorable winds.

Iris (ī´-rəs) Goddess of the rainbow; like Hermes, a messenger of the gods.

Isis (ī´-səs) Egyptian goddess; sister and wife of Osiris, usually represented with cow's horns.

Ismene (is-mē´-nē) Oedipus's daughter; Antigone's sister.

Irus (ī´-rəs) Derisive nickname of the beggar in the Odyssey, *cf.* Iris.

Itys (i´-tēz) Son of Tereus and Procne.

Ixion (ik´-sē-ən) King of the Lapiths; fathered the Centaurs when he slept with a cloud resembling Hera.

Jason (jā-sən, Greek Iasōn) Thessalian hero famous for retrieving the Golden Fleece.

Jocasta (jō-kas´-tə) Queen of Thebes; Oedipus's mother and wife.

Jove (jōv) Alternative name for Jupiter, the Roman Zeus; king of the gods.

Junius See **Brutus**.

Juno (jū´-nō) Roman goddess identified with Hera; goddess of marriage.

Juturna (jū-tər´-nə) Turnus's sister.

Jupiter (jū´-pə-tər) Roman god identified with Zeus; king of the gods; also called Jove.

Labdacus (läb-dä´-kəs) Laius's father; third king of Thebes.

Lachesis (la´-kə-səs) The Distributer; one of the three Fates.

Laertes (lā-ər´-tēz) Odysseus's father.

Laestrygonians (lī-strə-gō´-nē-əns) Tribe of giants who slaughtered Odysseus's men in their harbor.

Laius (lā´-əs) Oedipus's father; king of Thebes.

Laocoon (lā-ä´-kə-wän) Trojan priest who wanted to destroy the wooden horse.

Laomedon (lā-ä´-me-dən) Early king of Troy; father of Ganymede.

Lapiths (la´-piths) Tribe of Greeks; fought the Centaurs, led by Pirithous.

Latinus (lə-tī´-nəs) King of Latium; resigned to avoid fighting Aeneas.

Latona (lə-tō´-nə) The Roman Leto.

Lavinia (lə-vi´-nē-ə) Latinus's daughter; engaged to Aeneas.

Learchus (lē-ar´-kəs) Son of Ino and Athamas; slain by the latter.

Leda (lē´-də) Spartan queen visited by Zeus in the form of a swan; mother of Helen, Clytemnestra, and the Dioscuri.

Leto (lē´-tō) A goddess; daughter of the Titans Coeus and Phoebe; mother of Apollo and Artemis; the Roman Latona.

Leucothea (lū-kō´-thē-ə) Ino's name after she became a sea goddess.

Lichas (lī´-kəs) Heracles' herald.

Linus (lī´-nəs) Heracles' lyre teacher.

Lucius See **Brutus** and **Tarquinius**.

Lucretia (lū-krē´-shə) Roman noblewoman raped by Sextus Tarquinius.

Lycaon (lə-kā´-ən) A wicked king turned into a wolf by Zeus.

Lycomedes (li´-kə-mē´-dēz) King of the island of Scyros; killed Theseus. His daughter married Achilles.

Lycus (lī´-kəs) Illegitimate ruler of Thebes; Labdacus's successor.

Lydia (li´-dē-ə) An ancient kingdom in present-day western Turkey.

Macaria (mə-kār´-ē-ə) Daughter of Heracles, who volunteers to be sacrificed.

Machaon (mə-kā´-ən) Physician of the Greek army at Troy.

Maenads (mē´-nads) Literally, mad or raving women; specifically, the followers of Dionysus.

Maia (mī´-yə) Minor goddess; mother of Hermes.

Maron (mar´-ən) Priest of Apollo among the Cicones.

Medea (me-dē´-ə) Sorceress and princess of Colchis; helped Jason seize the Golden Fleece.

Medusa (me-dū´-sə) The Gorgon decapitated by Perseus.

Megara (me´-gə-rə) Daughter of Creon; Heracles' first wife.

Melanthius (me-lan´-thē-əs) A goatherd who befriends Penelope's suitors.

Melantho (me-lan´-thō) One of Penelope's impudent maids, sleeping with Eurymachus.

Meleager (mel-ē-ā´-jər) Hero of the Calydonian boar hunt.

Melicertes (mel-ə-ser´-tēz) Son of Ino and Athamas; deified as Palaemon.

Memnon (mem´ –nän) Son of Eos (Dawn) and Tithonus; killed by Achilles.

Menelaus (me-nə-lā´-əs) Helen's husband; brother of Agamemnon.

Mentor (men´-tör) Elderly Ithacan; loyal to Odysseus.

Menestheus (mə-nes´-thē-əs) Theseus's successor as king of Athens.

Mercury (mər´-kyər-rē) Roman god identified with Hermes.

Merope (mər´-rō-pē) Oedipus's mother by adoption.

Metanira (me-tə-nī´-rə) Queen of Eleusis.

Metis (mā´-təs) Counsel or wisdom personified; Zeus's first wife.

Midas (mī´-dəs) Legendary king of Phrygia.

Minerva (mə-nər´-və) Roman goddess identified with Athena.

Minos (mī´-nōs) King of Crete; son of Zeus and Europa.

Minotaur (mi´-nə-tör) Humanoid monster with a bull's head; the offspring of Queen Pasiphae and a bull.

Minyans (min´-yəns) Greek tribe in the area of Thebes; defeated by Heracles.

Misenus (mī –sē´-nəs) Aeneas's trumpeter; killed by Triton.

Mnemosyne (ni-mä´-sə-nē) Memory personified as a goddess; the mother of the Muses.

Moirae (moi´-rī) The three Fates.

Mopsus (mäp´-səs) A seer who accompanied Jason and the Argonauts.

Muses (mū´-ziz) Nine daughters of Zeus and Mnemosyne (Memory); patrons of the arts.

Mycenae (mī-sē´-nē) With Thebes, the leading city of Bronze-Age Greece.

Myrmidons (mər´-mi-däns) Greek tribe led by Achilles; fierce warriors.

Myrrha (mər´-rə) Cinyras's daughter.

Nausicaa (nö-si´-kə-ə) Princess of Phaeacia; loans Odysseus clothing.

Neleus (nē´-lē-əs) King of Pylos; father of Nestor.

Nemesis (ne´-mə-səs) Vengeance personified as a goddess.

Nephele (ne´ -fə-lē) Goddess whose name means Cloud; mother of Phrixus and Helle.

Neoptolemus (nē-äp-tä´-lə-məs) Achilles' son; the Roman Pyrrhus.

Neptune (nep´-tūn) Roman god identified with Poseidon.

Nereids (nir´-ē-əds) Sea goddesses; the 50 daughters of Nereus, an elderly seagod.

Nereus (nir´-ē-əs) Elderly sea god.

Nessus (ne´-səs) Centaur responsible for Heracles' death.

Nestor (ne´-stər) King of Pylos, eldest Greek warrior at Troy.

Niobe (nī-ō´-bē) Theban queen; daughter of Tantalus; wife of Amphion; mother of 14 children.

Numitor (nū-mi´ -t r̄) Rightful 13th king of Rome; Rhea Silva's father.

Nycteus (nik´ –tē-əs) Lycus's brother; Antiope's father.

Oceanids (ō-shē´-ə-nids) The daughters of Oceanus.

Oceanus (ō-shē'-ə-nəs) Personification of the ocean, envisioned as a river encircling the inhabited portions of the earth.

Odysseus (ō-di'-shəs) Greek warrior at Troy; hero of Homer's *Odyssey*.

Oedipus (e'-də-pəs) King of Thebes who unknowingly killed his father and married his mother.

Oeneus (ē' –nē-əs) Meleager's father; Diomedes' grandfather.

Oenomaus (ē'-nə-maus) King of Elis; to marry his daughter, you had to beat him in a chariot race.

Omphale (ŏm'-fə-lē) Queen of Lydia. Heracles gained purification by serving as her slave.

Orcus (ōr'-kəs) Roman god of the dead.

Orestes (ōr-es'-tēz) Son of Agamemnon and Clytemnestra.

Orion (ə-rī' -ən) A giant hunter slain by Artemis

Orithyia (ōr-ī'-thē-ə) Daughter of Pandion; abducted by Boreas.

Orpheus (ōr'-fē-əs) Mortal son of Apollo; great musician.

Orthys (ōr'-thēz) A mountain near Olympus, occupied by the Titans in their war against Zeus.

Otus (ō'-təs) Giant who attacked Mount Olympus.

Palaemon (pə-lē'-mən) Melicertes' name after he became a sea god.

Pallas (pal'-ləs) 1. Alternative name for Athena. 2. Prince of Pallanteum in the Aeneid; son of Evander; killed by Turnus.

Pan (pan) Great rustic god of shepherds; depicted as humanoid except for goat's hooves, tail, and horns.

Pandaros (pan'-də-rəs) Trojan warrior tricked by Athena into restarting hostilities.

Pandion (pan-dī'-än) Fifth king of Athens; father of Aegeus.

Pandora (pan-dōr'-ə) The woman created by Zeus as a punishment for mankind.

Paris (par'-əs) Prince of Troy who ran off with Helen; son of Priam and brother of Hector.

Pasiphae (pa'-si-fē) Minos's wife; mother of the Minotaur.

Pasithea (pa-si' –thē-ə) One of the Graces; loved by Sleep.

Patroclus (pə-trō'-kləs) Achilles' beloved comrade at Troy.

Pegasus (pe'-gə-səs) Winged horse; the offspring of Medusa.

Peleus (pē'-lē-əs) Thessalian king and father of Achilles.

Pelias (pē'-lē-äs) Jason's evil uncle; unrightful king of Iolcus.

Pelops (pē'-läps) Son of Tantalus.

Pemphredo (pem-frē' –dō) One of the three Graeae.

Penates (pe-nä'-tēz) Roman household gods; guardians of the storeroom (*penus*).

Penthesilea (pən-thə-si-lē' -ə) Amazon warrior; ally of Trojans; killed by Achilles.

Penelope (pə-nel'-ō-pē) Wife of Odysseus.

Peneus (pən-nē'-əs) A river in Thessaly; personified as a god; the father of Daphne.

Pentheus (pen'-thē-əs) Cadmus's grandson, acting as king for his grandfather when Dionysus returns.

Periphetes (per-ə-fē' –tēz) Club-wielding villain killed by Theseus.

Perses (pər' –sēz) Son of Perseus; the Persians' eponymous ancestor.

Perseis (pər-sē´-is) Daughter of Oceanus; mother of Circe and Aeetes.

Perseus (pər´ -sē-əs) Zeus's son by Danae; slew Medusa.

Persephone (pər-se´-fə-nē) Daughter of Zeus and Demeter; married to Hades.

Phaea (fē´ -ə) The name of an old woman and her giant sow, which Theseus killed.

Phaedra (fē´ –drə) Minos's daughter; Ariadne's sister; Theseus's wife; loved her stepson, Hippolytus.

Phaethon (fā´-ə-thon). Son of the god of the Sun, crashed his father's chariot.

Philoctetes (fi´-läk-tē´-tēz) Warrior who inherited Heracles' bow and arrows, and was abandoned en route to Troy because of a snakebite.

Philoetius (fə-lē´-tē-əs) A cowherd loyal to Odysseus.

Philomela (fi-lə-mē´-lə) Procne's sister; assaulted by Tereus.

Phineus (fi´-nē-əs) 1. Andromeda's uncle and fiancé. 2. Blind prophet tormented by the Harpies.

Phrixus (frik´-səs) Son of Athamas and Nephele; saved from being sacrificed by a flying ram with a golden fleece.

Phoebus (fē´-bəs) An alternate name for Apollo, meaning radiant or bright.

Pisistratus (pī-sis´-trə-təs) Nestor's young son in the *Odyssey*.

Phoenix (fē´ –niks) Achilles' elderly tutor.

Phorcides (fōr´ -sə-dēz) Children of Phorcys, the Graeae.

Phorcys (fōr´ –sēz) Son of Gaea; father of the Graeae.

Pirithous (pi-rith´-ō-əs) King of Lapiths; Theseus's friend.

Pittheus (pit´-the-əs) King of Troezen; father of Theseus's mother, Aethra.

Plexippus (plek-si´ pəs) One of Meleager's uncles.

Pluto (plū´-tō) Alternative name for Hades, "the Wealthy."

Poeas (pē´ -əs) Philoctetes' father.

Polites (pä´-lə-tēz) Young son of Priam; slain by Neoptolemus.

Pollux (pä´-ləks) See **Castor**.

Polydectes (pä´-lə-dek´ –tēz) King of Seriphos Island; Danae's unwelcome suitor.

Polydorus (pä´-lə-dō´-rəs) Cadmus's son; second king of Thebes.

Polynices (pä´-lə-nī´-sēz) Oedipus's son; fought against Creon and his brother, Eteocles.

Polyphemus (pä-lə-fē´-məs) A one-eyed, cannibalistic giant; Odysseus's adversary in Homer's Odyssey.

Polyxena (pä-lək´ -sə-nə) Daughter of Priam; sacrificed on Achilles' grave.

Porphyrion (pōr-fir´ –ē-ən) One of the giants vanquished by Zeus.

Poseidon (pō-sī´-dən) God of the sea; Zeus's brother.

Priam (prī´-am) King of Troy during the Trojan War; father of Hector and Paris.

Proculus (prä´-ku-ləs) Roman visited by the spirit of Romulus.

Procne (präk´-nē) Athenian girl married to Tereus.

Procris (prō´-kris) Orithyia's sister; married to Cephalus.

Proetus (prō-ē´-tus) Acrisius's brother.

Prometheus (prō-mē´-the-əs) Son the Titan Iapetus Zeus's adversary on behalf of humankind.

Propoetus (prō-pē´-təs) Man of Cyprus. His daughters were the first prostitutes.

Proserpina (prō-sǝr´-pǝ-nǝ) Roman goddess identified with Persephone.

Protesilaos (prō-tǝ-si-lā´-ǝs) Greek warrior; first casualty of the Trojan War.

Proteus (prō´-tē-ǝs) 1. Shape-shifting sea god in Homer's *Odyssey*. 2. Egyptian king in Euripides' *Helen*.

Protogeneia (prō-tǝ-jǝ-nī´-a) Daughter of Deucalion and Pyrrha.

Pygmalion (pig-mā´-lē-ǝn) 1. Sculptor of Cyprus. His statue was brought to life by Aphrodite. 2. Dido's evil brother; killed her husband, Sychaeus.

Pylades (pī´-lǝ-dēz) Orestes' faithful friend.

Pyrrha (pir´-ǝ) Daughter of Epimetheus; wife of Deucalion.

Pyrrhus (pir´-ǝs) Roman name for Achilles' son, Neoptolemus.

Pythia (pi´-thē-ǝ) The title given to the priestess of Apollo at Delphi.

Pytho (pī-thō). The name given by Apollo to the serpent that he slew near Delphi; aslo a name for Delphi itself.

Remus (rē´-mǝs) Romulus's brother, killed by him.

Rhadamanthys (ra-dä-man´-thēz) Son of Minos.

Rhea (rē´-ǝ) Titan goddess; sister and wife of Uranus.

Rhea Silva (rē´-ǝ sil´-vǝ) Mother of Romulus and Remus.

Romulus (räm´-ǝ-lǝs) Founder of the city of Rome; son of Mars.

Sabaeans (sǝ-bē´-ǝns) Native people of Arabia.

Sabines (sā´-bīns) Italian tribe unified with the Romans after warfare.

Salmacis (sal´-mǝ-sis) The name of a fountain and its resident nymph, who attacked Hermaphroditus.

Sarpedon (sär-pē´-dǝn). 1. Minos's brother; son of Zeus and Europa. 2. Grandson of no. 1, son of Zeus and Laodamia; fought on the side of Troy; killed by Patroclus.

Saturn (sa´-tǝrn) Roman god identified with Cronus.

Satyr (sā´-tǝr) A mythological male follower of Dionysus, usually depicted as humanoid, except for horse's hooves and tail; devoted to wine and sex.

Scamander (skǝ-man´-dǝr) River near Troy; it comes to life to battle Achilles.

Sciron (skī´-rän) Evildoer slain by Theseus; kicked people into the sea to be eaten by a giant turtle!

Scylla (si´-lǝ) Monstrous maiden whose lower body terminates in six heads that devour passing sailors.

Selene (sǝ-lē´-nē) The moon personified as a goddess.

Semele (se´-mǝ-lē) Daughter of Cadmus; loved by Zeus.

Servius Tullius (sǝr´-vē-ǝs tū´-lē-ǝs) Roman king assassinated by his son-in-law, Tarquinius.

Sextus. See **Tarquinius**.

Sibyl (si´-bil). Priestess of Apollo at Cumae; Aeneas's guide to the Underworld.

Silenus (sī-lē´-nǝs) The eldest satyr.

Sinis (si´-nǝs) The pine-bender, a villain killed by Theseus.

Sinon (si´-nän) Greek who persuaded the Trojans to take the wooden horse inside their walls.

Sirens (sī´-rǝns) Goddesses who bewitch sailors with their songs.

Sisyphus (sis´-ǝ-fǝs) Sinner punished in the Underworld for trying to cheat death.

Sthenelus (sthen´ –ə-ləs) Son of Perseus; father of Heracles' enemy, Eurystheus.

Stheno (sthe´ –nō) One of the Gorgons; Medusa's sister.

Strophius (strō´-phē-əs) Friend of Agamemnon. Orestes grew up in his household.

Superbus. See **Tarquinius.**

Sychaeus (si-kē´-əs) Dido's husband; killed by her brother.

Syrinx (sir´-inks) A nymph whose name means pipe, or reed. She fled Pan, and was changed into a clump of reeds.

Talos (ta´-ləs) Bronze-Age giant who guarded Crete; slain by Medea.

Talthybius (tal-thə´ –bē-əs) Herald of the Greeks at Troy.

Tantalus (tan´-təl-əs) Son of Zeus; punished in the Underworld for trying to feed the flesh of his son, Pelops, to the gods.

Tarpeia (tar-pē´-ə) Roman girl who betrayed city.

Tarquinius(tar-quin´-ē-əs) 1. **Sextus** (sex´-təs) **Tarquinius**. Son of **Tarquinius Superbus**; raped Lucretia. 2. **Tarquinius Superbus** (sū-per´-bəs). "Tarquin the Proud," last king of Rome; driven out by Brutus.

Tauri (tau´-rē) Barbarian people living on the shores of the Black Sea.

Tecmessa (tek-mes´-ə) Wife of Ajax the Greater.

Telamon (te´-lə-män) Father of Ajax the Greater.

Telegonus (tə-leg´-ä-nəs) Odysseus's son by Circe.

Telemachus (tə-le´-mə-kəs) Odysseus's son.

Tereus (ter´-ē-əs) Thracian king; married to Procne.

Tethys (te´ thēs) Titan goddess; wife of Oceanus.

Teucer (tū´ –sər) Brother of Ajax the Greater.

Thalassius (thə-la´-sē-əs) Prominent Roman senator at the time of the rape of the Sabine women.

Thebe (thē´ –bē) Zethus's wife, of whom nothing further is known.

Themis (the´-məs) A Titan; the mother by Zeus of the three Fates.

Theoclymenus (thē-ä-kli´-mə-nəs) Egyptian king in Euripides' *Helen*.

Theonoe (thē-ä´-nō-ē) Egyptian priestess in Euripides' *Helen*.

Thersites (thər-sī´-tez) Ugly Greek warrior at Troy, who urged the assembly to abandon the war.

Theseus (thē´-sē-əs) King and hero of Athens; killed the Minotaur.

Thespius (thes´ -pē-əs) King whose 50 daughters slept with Heracles.

Thetis (thē´-tis) A sea goddess; one of the 50 daughters of Nereus and Achilles' mother.

Thoas (thō´ –äs) King of the Tauri in Euripides' *Iphigenia among the Taurians*.

Thyestes (thī-es´-tēz) Atreus's brother and bitter rival, tricked by him into eating his children's flesh.

Tiresias (tī-rē´-sē-əs) Infallible blind prophet of Thebes.

Tithonus (ti-thō´-nəs) Trojan noble loved by Eos (Dawn).

Titans (tī´-təns) The children of Uranus and Gaea, namely Cronus and Rhea and their brothers and sisters. They overthrew Uranus, and were overthrown by Zeus and his brothers and sisters.

Titus Tatius (tī´-təs tā´-shəs)

Tityus (ti´-tē-əs) Giant punished in the Underworld for attempting to rape Leto.

Toxeus (täk´-sūs). One of Meleager's uncles.

Triton (trī´-tən). Son of Poseidon, depicted as a young merman blowing on a conch shell trumpet.

Trophonius (trä-fōn´-ē-əs) One of the architects of Apollo's temple at Delphi.

Tros (trōs) Early king of Troy. The city was named after him, though it was also called Ilium after another early king, Ilus.

Tullia (tū´-lē-ə) Servius Tullius's daughter.

Tullius. See **Servius**.

Turnus (tər´-nəs) King of an Italian tribe, the Rutulians, Aeneas' adversary. Leader of the Italians in the war against the Trojans; killed by Aeneas.

Tydeus (ti´-dē-əs) Father of the great Greek warrior at Troy, Diomedes.

Tyndareus (tin-dār´-ē-əs) King of Sparta; Leda's husband.

Typhaon (ti´-fə-ən) Monster born of Hera alone when she was angry about Athena's birth.

Typhoeus (tī-fō´yūs) Monstrous giant; child of Tartarus and Gaea; buried under Mount Aetna by Zeus after a great battle.

Ulysses (ū-li´-sēz) The Roman name for Odysseus.

Uranus (yūr´-ə-nəs) Personification of the sky; first king of the gods; overthrown by Cronus.

Venus (vē´-nəs) Roman goddess identified with Aphrodite.

Vesta (ves´-tə) Roman goddess identified with Hestia.

Vulcan (vul´-kən) Roman god identified with Hephaestus.

Xanthus (zan´ thəs) "Goldie," Achilles' horse, briefly given the power of speech.

Xuthus (zū´-thəs) Son of Hellen; father of Achaeus and Ion.

Zetes (zē´-tēz) Son of Boreas, the North Wind.

Zethus (zē´-thəs) Amphion's brother; co-ruler of Thebes.

Zeus (zūs) King of the gods; overthrew his father, Cronus, and the other Titans.

II. Places

Achelous (a´kə-lō´-əs) One of the longest rivers in Greece (140 miles), it rises in the mountains of northwestern Greece, and empties into the Ionian sea opposite Ithaca.

Acheron (a´-kə-rän) A mythical river in the Underworld.

Aeaea (ē-ē´-ä) Circe's mythological island.

Aegina (i-jī´-nə) Island in the Saronic Gulf, about 20 miles south of Athens' harbor, Piraeus.

Aetna (et´-nə) Volcanic mountain in Sicily.

Alba Longa (al´-bə l n̄´-gə) Ancient town on the shores of the Alban Lake, 15 miles southeast of Rome. Supposedly founded by Aeneas. Corresponds to modern Castel Gandolfo.

Alpheus (al-fē´-əs) River in the northwest Peloponnesus.

Anaphe (ə-na´-fē) A small Aegean island (16 square miles), the southernmost of the Cyclades group, about 70 miles north of Crete.

Arabia (ə-rā´-bē-ə) The Arabian peninsula, an area corresponding to modern Saudi Arabia with Jordan, Yemen, Oman, and the Gulf States.

Arcadia (är-kā´-dē-ə) Rural area in the middle of the Peloponnesus.

Ardea (är´-dē-ə) Town in Italy, 23 miles south of Rome, close to the Mediterranean coast. The town of Turnus and the Rutulians in legend; now an independent municipality.

Argos (är´-gs̄) Polis in the northeast Peloponnesus, near the Bronze Age citadels of Mycenae and Tiryns. Argos is also used for the whole surrounding region, and sometimes, interchangeably with Mycenae.

Asia Minor (ā´shə mī´-nər) Modern Turkey, home in antiquity to numerous Greek *poleis* on the coast, and the kingdoms of Lydia, Phrygia, Caria, and Lycia.

Athens (a´-thenz).The leading *polis* of the classical Greek world and capital of the modern nation.

Athos (a´-thōs) Promontory in the northern Aegean Sea.

Aulis (ö-ləs). Ancient settlement on the east coast of Boeotia where the mainland comes closest to Euboea, the site of the sacrifice of Iphigenia. Corresponds to the modern municipality of Avlida.

Black Sea (blak sē) The great sea lying north of modern Turkey.

Boeotia (bē -ō´-shə) Region of Greece lying northwest of Athens. Its chief city was Thebes.

Bosporus (bäs´-pər-əs) Narrow strait connecting the Propontis and Hellespont with the Black Sea. See **Hellespont**.

Calydon (ka´-lə-dän) Ancient town in northwestern Greece, site of the Calydonian boar hunt. Parts of a wall and a temple to Artemis remain.

Caria (kar´-ē-ə) A region occupying the southwestern corner of modern Turkey.

Carthage (kär´-thij) Great Phoenician city located in modern Tunis.

Caucasus (kö´-kə-səs) Mountain range east of the Black Sea.

Cenaeum (sə-nē´-əm) The name in antiquity of the promontory on Euboea's northwestern tip.

Cerynites (ser-ə-nē´-təs) River in Arcadia.

Ciconians' (si-kō´–nē-əns) city. Also known as Ismarus, an ancient Thracian town possibly corresponding to the municipality of Maroneia, Greece, in the extreme northeastern extension of Greece toward the Hellespont.

Cilicia (sə-li´-shē-ə) Region in Asia Minor, the southeastern coast of modern Turkey, near Cyprus.

Citheron (si –thē´- n̄)Mountain range about 10 miles southwest of Thebes; maximum elevation 4,623 feet.

Cnossus (nä´-səs) Bronze Age palace complex, capital of ancient Crete, on the outskirts of the modern port city of Heraklion.

Colchis (käl´-kəs) Kingdom on the east coast of the Black Sea corresponding to the modern city of Kutaisi, Georgia, straddling the ancient Phasis River (the modern Rioni), 50 miles inland.

Colonus (kə-lō´-nəs) Deme in ancient Attica, about a mile northwest of Athens, featuring of the Hill of the Horseman Colonus, with a grove sacred to the Eumenides. Today a residential district of Athens.

Corinth (kor´-inth) Major ancient *polis* and modern city at the southwestern end of the isthmus of Greece.

Cos (kōs) Island (111 sq. miles) just off the southwestern corner of the modern Turkish coast.

Cranae (kra´-nə-ē) Uncertain, possibly a tiny island off the coast of the Peloponnesus just 500 feet from shore, 20 miles south of Sparta. Now part of the small port city of Gythio.

Crete (krēt) Major Mediterranean island (3,219 sq. miles) about 165 miles due south of Athens.

Crisa (kri´-sə) Ancient *polis* in the foothills of Mount Parnassus, 2.5 miles southwest of Delphi. Now the village of Chrisso, with a population of 1,000.

Cyllene (si-lē´-nē) Mountain in northeastern Arcadia, west of Corinth, 7,789 feet high.

Cyprus (sī´-prəs) Major island (3,571 sq. miles) in the eastern Mediterranean. About 500 miles southeast of Athens and 100 miles from the coast of Syria.

Cythera (sith´-ər-ə) Island six miles off the coast of the southern Peloponnesus. Area: 180 sq. miles.

Danube (dan´-yūb) The great river forming in Germany and emptying into the western Black Sea. 1771 miles long.

Delos (dē´ - lōs) A tiny island (1 square mile) about 70 miles southeast of the Attic coast, part of the Cyclades chain of islands.

Delphi (del´-fī) Precinct of the temple of Apollo on Mount Parnassus.

Dodona (də-dō´-nə) Ancient shrine to Zeus in northwestern Greece.

Egypt (ē´-jipt) The same as the modern nation.

Eleusis (i-lū´-səs) Ancient kingdom, which became part of Attica, eight miles northwest of Athens. Site of the famous temple of Demeter. Modern Eleusina, an industrial suburb of Athens.

Elis (ē´-lis) Ancient city and region of the northwest Peloponnesus, where the Olympic games originated. The former city is now a tiny village and archaeological site.

Eridanus (er-i-da´-nəs) A mythical river. Also the name of a small stream running through Athens.

Erymanthus (er-i-man´-thəs) Mountain range in northwestern Peloponnesus. Highest peak, 7,297 feet.

Euboea (yū-bē´-ə) The long island that snakes along the eastern coast of Greece for approximately 80 miles from Attica to Thermopylae. Area: 1,423 sq. miles. It comes within 130 feet of the mainland shore at Aulis.

Gabii (ga´-bə-ē) Ancient town 11 miles east of Rome.

Hebrus (hē´-brəs). The modern Maritsa River, which forms in Bulgaria, first flowing east and then south into the Aegean. It forms part of the border between Greece and Bulgaria in the north, and Greece and Turkey in the east. It is approximately 300 miles long.

Hellespont (he´-ləs-pänt) Also known as the Dardanelles, the southernmost part of the waterway between the Aegean and the Black Sea. A narrow channel from one to three miles in width, it flows into the Propontis or Sea of Marmara, which is over 40 miles wide, and then into the Bosporus strait, about a mile wide on average.

Haemus (hē´-mə) Mountain range in Bulgaria, south of Danube. Highest peak 7,795 feet.

Hyperborea (hī-pər-bō´-ē-ə) A mythical region in the far north.

Ida (ī´-də) A mountain southeast of the ruins of Troy, with an elevation of 5,797 feet.

Ilium (i´-lē-əm) Alternative name for Troy.

Illyria (i-lir´-ē-ə) A region corresponding to the former Yugoslavia.

Inachus (in´-ə-kəs) The modern Panitsa River, it flows south through the region of Argos east of the city, and empties into the Argolic gulf near Nauplion.

Iolcus (ī-ōl´-kəs) A Mycenaean city or palace complex in Thessaly. Its remains are thought to have been discovered at Dimini on the outskirts of the modern city of Volos, a port on the gulf of Pagasae.

Ithaca (ith´-ə-kə) Small island (45 square miles) off the coast of western Greece, probably the same as the modern Ithaca, which lies some 50 miles west of the entrance to the Gulf of Corinth.

Lacedaemon (la-sə-dē´-mən) Alternative name for Sparta.

Laconia (lə-kō´-nē-ə) The region in the southeastern Peloponnesus in which Sparta, also known as Lacedaemon, was located.

Larissa (lə-ris´-sə)Major city of Thessaly then and now, about 25 miles southwest of Mount Olympus.

Lemnos (lem´-näs) Island in the northern Aegean about 40 miles from the Turkish coast, opposite ancient Troy. 184 square miles.

Lerna (ler´-nə) Ancient city in the region of Argos, about 7 miles southwest of the city, on the shore.

Lesbos (les´-bōs) Large island (684 sq. miles) in the northern Aegean, south of Troy and Mount Ida, three and a half miles from the Turkish coast.

Lethe (lē-thē) Literally, "Forgetfulness," a mythical river in the Underworld.

Liguria (li-gyər´-ē-ə) Far northwest extension of Italy, adjoining southern France.

Locris (lō´-krəs) Three different regions in central Greece were controlled by people calling themselves Locrians. One occupied part of the northern shore of the Gulf of Corinth; the other two controlled discrete portions of the eastern coast of Greece facing Euboea, north of Attica and Boeotia.

Lycia (li´-shə) Region encompassing the southwestern extremity of the Turkish coast, occupied by the non-Greek, Indo-European Lycians, who were conquered by the Persians in the sixth century A.D.

Lydia (li´-dē-ə) Ancient nation corresponding to western Turkey. Renowned for its wealth until conquered by Persia in the sixth century. Sardis is its capital.

Lyrnessus (ler-nə´-səs) A town in the vicinity of Troy, known only as the supposed birthplace of Briseis.

Malis (mal´-ləs) A district in southern Thessaly, opposite the northwestern tip of Euboea and including the pass of Thermopylae.

Marathon (mar´-ə-thän) Town in Attica about 18 miles northeast of Athens. On the adjoining plain and beach, the Athenians defeated the Persians in 490 B.C. The actual distance that a runner must traverse to go from Marathon to Athens is 21.4 miles.

Mecone (mə-kō´-nē) An earlier name for the *polis* of Sicyon.

Megara (me´-gə-rə) City on the isthmus, about 18 miles west of Athens.

Mycenae (mī-sē´-nē). Bronze Age citadel in the region of Argos, about six miles north of Argos.

Naxos (nak´-säs) Aegean island 90 miles southeast of Attic shore, 166 square miles.

Nemea (ne´-mē-ə) A town in the northwestern Peloponnesus, about 17 miles southwest of Corinth, 13 miles northwest of Argos.

Nile (nīl) The great river of Egypt.

Nysa (nī´-sə) Mythical mountain where the baby Dionysus was raised.

Oechalia (ē-kā´-lē-ə) A city ruled by King Eurytus, located in Sophocles' *Women of Trachis* in Euboea, but in Thessaly in other sources.

Oeta (ē´-tə). Mountain in southern Thessaly, 7,080 feet high. An eastern spur coming close to the shore opposite northern Euboea created the famous Thermopylae Pass.

Olympus (ō-lim´-pəs) The highest mountain in Greece, with numerous peaks, the highest of which is 9,570 feet. It is on the boundary between Thessaly and Macedonia.

Onchestus (än-kəs´-təs) A town in Boeotia about ten miles northwest of Thebes. Scanty remains survive.

Orthys (ōr´-thēz) Mountain in central Greece, southwest of Iolcus, on the coast opposite the northwestern end of Euboea. Elevation: 5,663 feet.

Pactolus (pak-tō´-ləs) A stream forming on Mount Tmolus and flowing past Sardis.

Pallene (pə-lē´-ne) Westernmost of the three large promontories extended from Greece's northeastern coast.

Pallanteum (pə-lan´-tē-əm) Legendary town built by the Greek Evander on the banks of the Tiber, on the site of the future Rome.

Parnassus (pār-na´-səs) On the north shore of the Corinthian Gulf, the 8,000-foot-high mountain is the traditional home of Apollo and the Muses. Delphi is located on its shoulder.

Peloponnesus (pe-le-pə-nē´-səs) The great peninsula that forms the Greek mainland south of the isthmus.

Peneus (pə-nē´-əs) River flowing east through Thessaly and entering the sea south of Mount Olympus.

Persia (per´-shə) Imperial nation corresponding to modern Iran.

Phaeacia (fē-ā´-shə) Mythical kingdom, whose sailors transported Odysseus back to Ithaca.

Pharos (far´-äs) An island (now a peninsula) just off the coast of Alexandria, Egypt, the site of a lighthouse that was one of the Seven Wonders of the World. In the *Odyssey*, Menelaus says that he was stranded on the island of Pharos off the Egyptian coast, but describes it as being a day's sail distant from the shore.

Phasis (fa´-sis) The modern Rioni, a river flowing into the Black Sea from the east. See **Colchis**.

Phocis (fō´-kis) A region of mainland Greece on the north shore of the Corinth Gulf. Delphi is located in Phocis.

Phoenicia (fi-ni´-shə) Ancient nation on the eastern coast of the Mediterranean, corresponding to modern Syria and Lebanon

Phrygia (fri´-jē-ə) Ancient country in central Turkey, absorbed by the Persian empire.

Phthia (fthē-ə) The southernmost portion of Thessaly; around Mount Orthys, it is known as Phthiotis. The ancient capital of the region was referred to as Phthia, Achilles' birthplace, but this city has not been located by archaeologists.

Pieria (pī-ir´-ē-ə) Region of southern Macedonia at the foot of Mount Olympus, said to be the birthplace of the Muses.

Pylos (pī´-läs) King Nestor's Bronze Age kingdom. It is located on the west coast of the Peloponnesus, but sources disagree on its precise location.

Pytho (pī´-thō) Another name for Delphi.

Rome (rōm) The ancient imperial city on the Tiber, capital of Italy.

Salamis (sa´-lə-məs) A small island (36 sq. miles) in the Saronic Gulf just west of Athens. It is separated from the shore by straits less than a mile wide.

Sardis (sär´-dəs) Capital of the ancient kingdom of Lydia in western Turkey, about 5 miles due east of the coastal city of Izmir (ancient Smyrna).

Saronic Gulf (sə-rä´-nik) The gulf south of Athens, containing the islands of Salamis and Aegina. About 30 miles wide at its mouth.

Scyros (skē´-rōs) Aegean island about 25 miles east of central Euboea, 86 square miles.

Scythia (si´-thē-ə) Land of the nomadic Scythian people, north of the Black Sea.

Scamander (skə-man´-dər) River flowing for 60 miles from Mount Ida past Troy into the Hellespont. Now called the Menderes.

Seriphos (sə-rī´-fəs) Small Aegean island, 29 sq. miles, about 70 miles southeast of Athens.

Sicily (si´-sə-lē) The largest Mediterranean island (9,926 sq. miles), southwest of Italy.

Sicyon (si´-kē-ən) Ancient *polis*, now a village and archaeological site, on the southern shore of the Gulf of Corinth, about 25 miles west of Corinth.

Sidon (sī´-dən) City on the coast of modern Lebanon. One of the chief cities of the Phoenicians in antiquity.

Sipylus (si´-pi-ləs) A mountain in Lydia, a few miles from the Turkish coast, north of Izmir (ancient Smyrna). Modern name Spil Dagi, it lies south of the modern town of Manisa. Elevation: 4,964 feet.

Sparta (spär´-tə) The *polis* in the southeastern Peloponnesus, a dominant power in classical Greece, now a small town.

Styx (stiks) Mythical river in the Underworld.

Strymon (strī´-mōn) River in Macedonia, the ancient boundary between it and Thrace. The modern Struma, a sizeable river, about 250 miles in length.

Stymphalia (stim-fä´-lē-ə) A small lake in Arcadia, about 25 miles southwest of Corinth.

Syrtes (sər´-tēz) The gulf of Sidra off the coast of Libya, proverbially dangerous for ancient sailors because of shallows and currents.

Taenarum (tē´-nə-rəm) The southernmost cape or promontory of the Peloponnesus, about 50 miles due south of Sparta.

Taphian Islands (ta´-fē-ən) Also known as Echinades. Several small islands northeast of Ithaca, the largest now known as Meganissi.

Tauria (tö-rē-ə). The peninsula in the northern Black Sea, known also in antiquity as the Chersonese. It is now known as Crimea. Its inhabitants were known as the Tauri (t¯´-rē).

Tegea (te´-jē-ə). Ancient *polis* in Arcadia, about 30 miles due north of Sparta, on the outskirts of the modern town of Tripoli.

Teuthrania (tū-thrä´-nē-ə) Legendary city on the northern Turkish coast, south of Troy.

Thebes (thēbs) A Bronze Age citadel and chief city of Boeotia to the present day. About 30 miles northwest of Athens.

Thermopylae (thir-mä´-pə-lē) Narrow pass in Malis connecting Thessaly with the rest of central Greece, where a spur of Mount Oeta comes close to the coast.

Thespiae (thes´-pi-ē) Town in Boeotia, about nine miles southwest of Thebes.

Thesprotia (thes-prō´-shə) A district in Epirus, the region west of Thessaly, bordering on the Adriatic sea.

Thessaly (the´-sə-lē) The region of Greece north of Euboea, extending from Thermopylae to the region of Mount Olympus and Macedonia.

Tiryns (tir´-inz) Bronze Age citadel in Argolis, about five miles southeast of Argos, on the shore.

Tmolus (tmō´-ləs) Mountain in Lydia, modern Boz Dag, 6,562 feet high. Ancient Sardis lay at its foot on the north.

Trachis (trä´-kis) An ancient *polis* northwest of Thermopylae.

Troezen (trē´-zen) Town on the north coast of Argos, opposite Aegina.

Troy (troi) The Bronze Age city attacked by the Greeks in the Trojan War, located on Turkey's northwestern shore, about five miles southeast of the mouth of the Hellespont.

Tyre (tīr) Town on the southern coast of Lebanon, ancient capital of Phoenicia.